Dave

SNOW COUNTRY TALES

Suzuki Bokushi

Country Tales

Life in the Other Japan

translated by Jeffrey Hunter
with Rose Lesser

introduction by Anne Walthall

New York • WEATHERHILL • *Tokyo*

Publication of this book was assisted by
a grant from the Japan Foundation.

FIRST EDITION, 1986

Published by John Weatherhill, Inc., of New York and Tokyo, with editorial offices at 7-6-13 Roppongi, Minato-ku, Tokyo 106, Japan. Protected by copyright under terms of the International Copyright Union; all rights reserved. Printed in Japan.

Library of Congress Cataloging in Publication Data: Suzuki, Bokushi, 1770–1842. / Snow country tales. / Translation of: Hokuetsu seppu. / 1. Niigata-ken (Japan)—Social life and customs. 2. Snow—Japan—Niigata-ken. 3. Winter—Japan—Niigata-ken. / I. Hunter, Jeffrey. II. Lesser, Rose. III. Title. / DS894.59.N544S9513   1986   952'.1   86-13169 / ISBN 0-8348-0210-4

to J.H.M.
and
the people of Echigo

Contents

Preface • xv
Introduction • xxxi

BOOK ONE

How the Earth's Vapors Become Snow • 3
Shapes of Snowflakes • 5
The Amount of Snowfall • 8
Signs of Snow • 9
Preparations for the Snowfall • 9
The First Snow • 10
The Depth of the Snow • 11
Snow Poles • 12
Clearing the Snow • 13
Foam Snow • 16
Roads in the Snow • 16
Buried Under the Snow • 17
Creeping Through the Snow Womb • 21
Floods in the Snow • 22
Hunting Bears in the Snow • 26
A White Bear • 30
Saved by a Bear • 30

CONTENTS

Snow Insects • 37
Blizzards • 38
Fires in the Snow • 45
Crevice Mountain • 46
Avalanches • 47

BOOK TWO

The Story of an Avalanche Victim • 55
A Temple Avalanche • 60
Gyokuzan's Illustrations of Snow • 61
Echigo Crepe • 62
Varieties of Crepe • 63
Ramie • 64
Spinning Ramie • 64
Twisting the Thread • 65
The Weaver Women • 66
The Mad Weaver Maiden • 67
The Loom Chamber • 68
The Mysterious Power of the Spirit
of the Loom Chamber • 69
Bleaching Crepe • 73
Crepe Markets • 77
Powder Avalanches • 78
The Blossom-Water Celebration
in the Snow • 79
Oddities at Hishiyama • 86
The Ancient Ways of Akiyama • 87
Foxfire • 99
To Catch a Fox • 101
Signs of the Geese's Feeding Grounds • 103
Heaven's Net • 104
When Geese Take Flight • 104
Crossing the Iceplank of Shibumi River • 105

CONTENTS

BOOK THREE

The Butterflies of Shibumi River • *109*
Thoughts on the Chinese Character for "Salmon" • *112*
Salmon Dishes • *114*
Where Salmon Are Found • *115*
The Life Cycle of Salmon • *116*
Weirs and Traps • *119*
Scoop Nets • *122*
A Fisherman Drowns • *122*
So Waterfall • *126*
Methods of Catching Salmon • *127*
The Sandbank Race of the Salmon • *127*
Icicles • *128*
The Icicles of Oikake Rock • *129*
Icicles Round the Waterfall • *131*
Winter Ascetics • *131*
The Merits of Winter Asceticism • *136*
A Ghost in the Snow • *137*
The Hair Mound at Sekiyama Village • *143*
Hunting Deer in the Snow • *145*
The Giant Cat of Tomariyama • *146*
Mountain Talk • *148*
Snow Games • *149*
A Blind Man Snows In • *150*

BOOK FOUR

Castle Towns of Echigo • *159*
Ancient Sites in Old Poems • *160*
New Year in the Snow • *164*
Snowball Contests • *168*
Shuttlecock and Battledore • *169*
A Sale of Roasted Riceballs in a Blizzard • *169*

CONTENTS

Theatricals in the Snow • *174*
Ice Pillars in the House • *179*
Snow Gear • *180*
Sleds • *184*
Hoarfrost • *190*
Early Summer Snow • *191*
Shaved Ice • *192*
Differing Amounts of Snow • *197*
The Hall-pushing at Urasa • *199*

BOOK FIVE

Bagging a Bear in an Avalanche • *207*
Funerals in the Snow • *209*
Dragon Lights • *210*
Poems in Basho's Hand • *212*
Petrifying Valley • *215*
A Petrified Tortoise • *218*
Luminous Stones • *219*
Rice-Cake Blossoms • *228*
Contributions for the Way Gods • *229*
The Festival of the Way Gods • *231*
Explanations of the Origins of Tempura
and Steamed Bean Sweets • *236*
Wolves in the Snow • *239*

BOOK SIX

Bird-chasing Towers • *249*
Snow and Frost • *252*
The Fires of Hell Valley • *253*
Famous People of Echigo • *258*
Jointless Stupas • *259*

CONTENTS

Abbot Hokko • *261*
Congratulatory Poems • *265*
The Strange Thing About Nigoro Village • *266*
The Seven Kettles of Tashiro • *268*

BOOK SEVEN

Strange Beasts • *275*
Asbestos • *280*
The Mummy of Priest Kochi • *282*
The Buried Ship • *284*
The White Raven • *284*
A Two-headed Snake • *285*
Floating Islands • *285*
The Stone-tossing Deity • *286*
A Beauty • *286*
The Bridge Signpost from Mount Omei • *289*
Mount Naeba • *292*
Snows of April and May • *297*
The Crane's Gratitude • *301*

Glossary • *303*

The Setting of *Snow Country Tales*

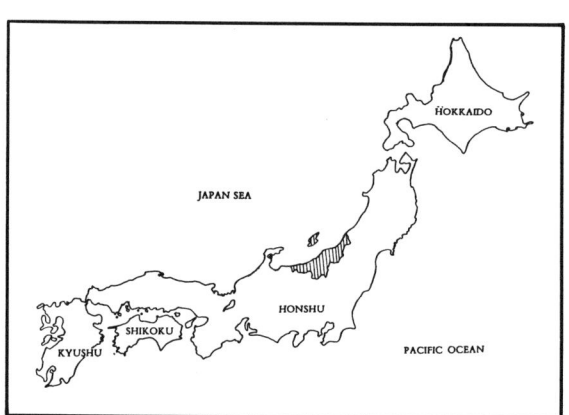

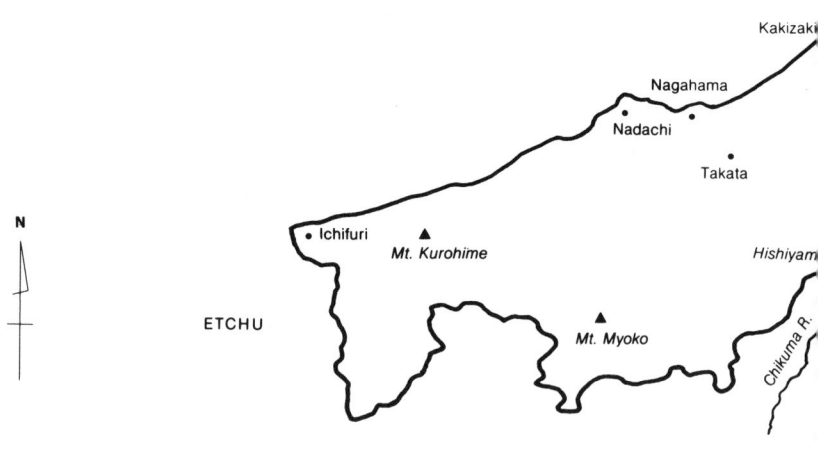

Bokushi's Akiyama Journey

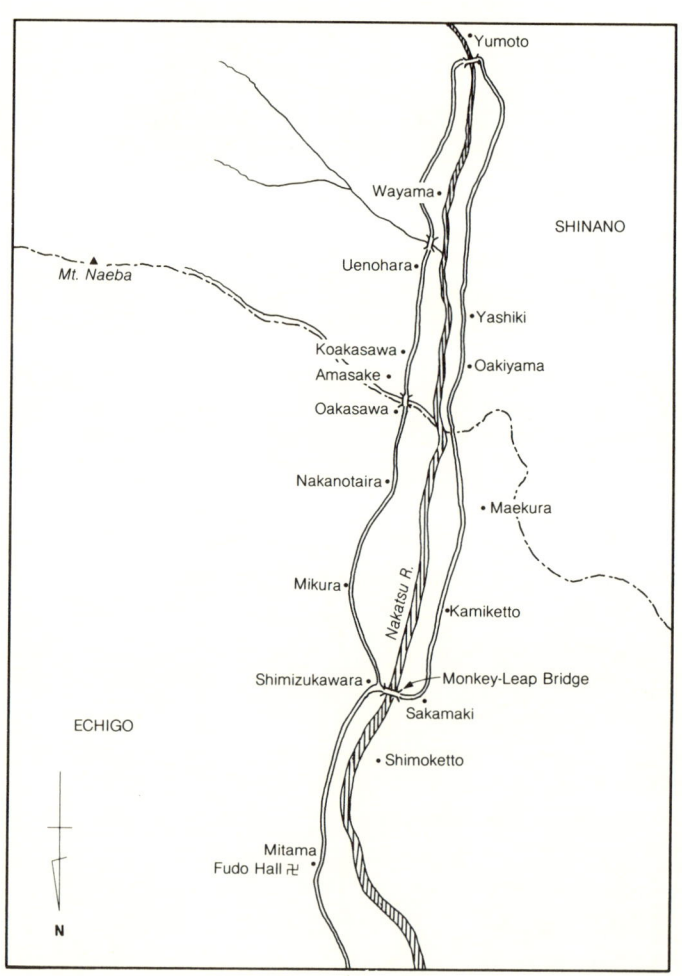

Preface

In September 1932, on the Tsugaru Strait ferry returning from Hokkaido to Japan's main island, Honshu, my husband-to-be, Dr. Kenji Takahashi, crossed my path. As Japan's first geobotanist and a pioneer of mountaineering and skiing, he was at home in even the most isolated mountainous regions. The following New Year he took me to Echigo (modern Niigata Prefecture), his beloved "snow country." I had been in Japan for three years, roving around the back country on all four main islands; I had read most of the literature on Japan; I prided myself on knowing Japan fairly well. Yet nothing had prepared me for this.

From cradle to grave, life here centers around the snow. Streets in winter change to icy, towering snow walls, impassable during a squall. Steep shafts are dug in the snow over house entrances to leave air space for the hermetically snow-sealed dwellings. To prevent being completely cut off from neighbors and the surrounding town or village, people dig long narrow tunnels through the snow for foot traffic. In those early days, the convenience of mechanization had yet to come. Power shovels and bulldozers were unknown. Man-high snow brought overland travel to a halt. If you happened to be rich, you could hire poor farmers to tread down a path for you with their huge wooden snowshoes, if the weather permitted, that is, and lasted. Sleds are of no use in winter; they are only for spring when the snow packs and freezes. With skis one cannot proceed, just as

PREFACE

one cannot reach the far shore in a sinking boat. This I had to learn the hard way through one of my first experiences in the southwest of Echigo, in the "Strange Heights," or Myoko area.

It was in January. I was to guide my younger brother-in-law from the train station up a steep slope to the village of Sugisawamura. Normally it's a two-hour climb, the route leading over a tiny plateau past a number of utility poles before arriving in the village. We arrived at 2 P.M. As I'd been there numerous times in summer, I was sure of the way. But heavy snow had been falling for hours; it fell in huge, featherlike flakes. One could not see a handsbreadth ahead. We pushed ourselves upward through the falling snow, already waist-high, proceeding at a snail's pace. It was dark when we reached the plateau—yet nowhere a sign of our landmark, the electricity poles. If I've missed the way, I thought in despair, we'll both die this night. Just then my young charge shouted, "Help! I'm stuck!" Working my way toward him, I laughed happily with relief: he was sitting on one of the poles, the village was at hand, we were safe!

Niigata is situated in central Honshu. It is one of its most mountainous provinces, bounded on the north by the Sea of Japan, and the Myoko mountain range is its snow-richest territory. From the Asian continent, from Siberia, come strong seasonal winds. As they pick up evaporation from the sea their humidity increases. Approaching the Japan Sea coast (what the Japanese call *ura Nihon*, "the backside of Japan"), clouds form, becoming denser the nearer they come to the land. Obstructed by the high mountains, they cool and change into huge amounts of heavy snow. Once the winds drop their load of snow and pass beyond the mountains, moving in the direction of the Pacific Ocean, the air becomes dry.

Though the houses are built to withstand the heavy burden of snow that falls in winter, there's always the danger of their collapsing, and the villagers must constantly engage in the Tantalean task of shoveling off the roofs. A single night's snowfall, however, and all is as it was the day before. By midwinter the accumulating snow creates a wall as high as the roof. And in spite of all these trials, the people are warmhearted and generous, always ready to welcome the stranger and share what they have.

PREFACE

The hardships, the poverty, the unshakable determination of these undefeatable folks, the grace with which they endeavored, struck me. How did they carry on without despairing, with the knowledge that year after year they would go through this again and again? How did they manage to keep oxen and horses and themselves, living under the same roof and buried under the snow for four or five frustrating winter months until spring (that came in summer), in good health? How did the children fare who had to stay put, unable to play outside? And how were they able, in the few snow-free months, to produce a rice known as the finest in Asia?

People beyond the snow wall—Japanese and foreigners alike—knew nothing about this "other Japan," except that it produced good cloth. This unawareness struck me each time I returned from the snow country. In winter, outsiders shunned the snow-plagued province. Even the tireless wanderer Basho, in all his rich poetry, never mentions the snow of Echigo. Therefore I promised my friends in Echigo to tell the world of their plight, their courage, their life in the snow country.

Where was I to begin? An entirely new world had to be described. Then, in 1936, in Yuzawa (nowadays Tokyo's favorite ski ground and hot-spring resort) a Mr. Hanzaemon Takahashi handed me a book, a Japanese classic from the year 1835: *Hokuetsu Seppu,* or *Snow Country Tales.* Therein the author, Suzuki Bokushi, waiting for spring, had used the long winter night to record all that was knowable about his native place. I felt I had found a way to fulfill my promise, and so I began with a translation.

Translating the archaic Japanese of Suzuki's classic was a slow process. Then, just after my daughter was born, World War II broke out, bringing deprivation and bomb alerts. There were endless military drills at a moment's notice. I had to substitute at these drills for my husband, who was seriously ill. Medicine was scarce and enough money to live on had to come from language lessons held throughout the day. Isolated from any other Westerner, cut off from home contacts for seven years, despair got hold of me and I was tempted to give up.

But there was that little book. I spent an hour each early morning

PREFACE

working on it. Reliving the struggles of the snow country folk for this one hour, I forgot my own. I had experienced the hardships of World War I, yet in time they had come to an end. These people's hardships lasted a whole lifetime, nay, generations. But they carried on, and, knowing this, I too carried on.

A few years after my husband's death in December 1947, I became a language teacher at Hosei University and moved from Kyoto, where we had been living, to the Tokyo-Yokohama area. Twelve years after the war's end, life began to normalize for my daughter and me. I had found decent living quarters and was able to retrieve the books and papers I had had to leave behind in Kyoto. My translation, written with an old typewriter on odd bits of paper I'd managed to get hold of in wartime, was barely readable, but now I could take up the work anew, and—I could go and see my friends in Echigo again!

Life in Niigata has changed drastically since the war. Modern transportation and TV have broken through the thick snow wall. Near train stations, snow plows keep the main roads free in winter. With hot springs situated at the base of the slopes, the snow, once a curse, has become a blessing, bringing floods of skiers from the cities. Telephones, cars, trucks, unheard of at a farmer's home before, are common now. Good roads lead up to even the highest mountain settlement, though they have to be rebuilt after each winter. Wherever the topography permits it, tractors and rice-planting machines have come into use. Modern kitchens with gas or electric ovens and wood stoves are common in many a farmhouse.

Horses and oxen—once the pride of every rice farmer—have disappeared, save for an exceptional one on a lonely mountain farm. So have the old women with their ebony black lacquered teeth, the sign of matrimony. No more can one enjoy the landscape from the open-air bath put up at the roadside before the house. It used to be that you sat in a wooden tub in hot water up to your shoulders, and a friendly passerby might offer to scrub your back! Now if you fall off the treacherous snow-wall street (as I did) and shoot upside down into someone's entrance below like a rocket right into a housewife's steaming washtub, no more will she throw up her arms and cry, "The devil! The devil!" and run off, having never seen a foreigner. These

Emerging from the entrance to his house, an old man sets out to clear the snow dressed in traditional snow gear. (Takeshi Yoneyama)

Shoveling the snow off the roof before it collapses. (Takeshi Yoneyama)

Sawing and carting away blocks of snow to prepare the rice seedling beds. (Takeshi Yoneyama)

The main street of Muikamachi in Minami Uonuma-gun buried in twelve feet of snow, 1961. (Nakamata Masayoshi)

Bleaching crepe on the snow at Shiozawa-machi, Minami Uonuma-gun. (Nakamata Masayoshi)

A snow tunnel (*mabu*) leading from one side of the street to the other. (Takeshi Yoneyama)

PREFACE

days, after a beautiful *kayabuki* (thatched) house has collapsed in a year of extraordinarily heavy snow, many replace them with prefabricated houses; the traditional thatched house is too expensive. So the *kayabuki*—so much cooler in summer, so much warmer in winter—are becoming rare.

And yet, life in Echigo remains very much what it has always been, for topography and climate have refused to become modern. As of old, the snow is ruler, snow dictates life exactly as it did when Bokushi wrote this book. Even in the few weeks between the rice harvest in September or October and the first snowfall, this tyrant grants no respite. If one happens to be there then, one can observe the strange sight of twelve- to fifteen-foot poles being tied teepee fashion around trees in an effort to protect them from the fast approaching heavy winter snows. Twenty to thirty poles in all might be required for just one tree! Around the lower half of weaker conifer trees often a heavy wooden fence is erected. Every tree and shrub people wish to keep unharmed until spring requires such elaborate protection. Not only plants, even stone temple lanterns and tombstones need to be protected. Such energy and expense this devours.

In April the men return from their winter factory work in the cities to help with the farming. Although the ground everywhere is still covered with two or three feet of snow, seedbeds must be prepared, and then the paddies as well. Since the snow left untouched lasts through May, Echigoans hasten the melting by repeatedly sprinkling water or ash on its surface. Those fortunate enough to live on the Echigo Plain use bulldozers. Elsewhere, though, men and women work feverishly with big handsaws, cutting the snow on their fields into huge blocks, carting them off one by one for dumping. The seedbeds present a peculiar sight. Already prepared before the first snowfall, they're constantly filled with water throughout the winter season to keep the amassing snow to a minimum, while all around the snow accumulates, creating steep walls as much as ten feet in height. From afar they look like empty swimming pools: to prepare for sowing the seeds, the farmer must climb in and out of the seedbeds on a long ladder and remove the remaining snow cover block by block!

PREFACE

Finally, how will you pay homage to your beloved deceased ones when the entire graveyard is hidden under fifteen feet of snow? Here again the Echigoan's uncanny ability to adapt: at the spot where the tombstone is thought to be the family erects a likeness sculpted of snow. So, throughout the long snow season (longer than winter, it lasts through spring into early summer), whenever they want to bring flowers and pay their respects, they always have a place to go.

Knowing what unthinkable trials the Echigoan faces in his lifetime, it is no wonder that many of the younger generation wander off, choosing to live the easier life in the city. But Echigo's beauty is unsurpassed. Its sky is the bluest, its air the purest, its water comes down from the mountains like a necklace of crystal pearls. And so some stay who would not trade their native place for any other, however easy life there might be. Even newcomers from large cities, from Tokyo, come and stay.

Moved by the faithfulness of these brave men and women to their beloved Echigo, I could not abandon my promise to one day have published an English translation of *Hokuetsu Seppu*. I actively sought a publisher and was eventually introduced to Weatherhill, where Jeffrey Hunter took an interest in my project. Over the next three years we worked together to produce a new translation. Once more I opened the yellowed pages of that little book, covered with my notes, and line by line, word by word, I studied the translation and Suzuki's original. I found the patience for this effort in the promise that my long-held dream would soon be realized. And with this publication the promise made long ago has finally been met.

I wish to express my deep appreciation to the countless people who through the years encouraged and generously supported this work; it is impossible to name them all here individually, but to each and every one I offer my heartfelt thanks. I would like to give special mention to the Bokushi Kenkyukai; Dr. Michael Cooper; George Farina; Helen Hardacre; the Japan Foundation; Naomi Kanda; the Kyoto Academic Alpine Club; Shigeru Matsui; Dr. Kenichi Murata; Katsuo Shimamura; Shigeyoshi Omi; Hanzaemon Takahashi; Dr. Mitsuru Takahashi; Reiko Yamanouchi; and Takeshi Yoneyama. To the staff of John Weatherhill, too, go my thanks for their dedication

PREFACE

to this project. But most of all I must thank the people of Echigo.

Whenever I take up a bowl of rice, I do so with reverence and gratitude to the people of the snow country for having taught me patience and endurance.

ROSE LESSER

A Note on the Translation

One of the first decisions a translator faces is the audience he should direct the translation to. In Suzuki Bokushi's *Snow Country Tales,* there is much to occupy the specialist, whether historian, anthropologist, or scholar of literature or religion. But the goal of this translation has been to make Bokushi's (I use his literary name, as is the practice with figures in Japanese art and literature) fascinating work accessible, interesting, and enjoyable to the general reader. I believe I borrow the author's mantle here. Though Bokushi the autodidact took delight in showing off the gems of arcane wisdom that he had plucked from the Chinese and Japanese classics, *Snow Country Tales* was an appeal to the readers of urban Japan to turn their gaze for a while to the lives of their fellows over the snow wall, to recognize and understand another Japan within Japan, an unknown realm tucked away in a forgotten corner of their own familiar world. Bokushi succeeded in attracting a wide audience—his book became a bestseller in old Edo—and I have tried to follow his lead in my approach to the translation.

A major step in this direction was the decision to forgo footnotes. They interrupt the flow of the text, often go unread, and encourage the translator to leave the task of carrying the original into English only half-done, while explaining endlessly away in the notes. Instead, all personal and place names and titles of works have been assembled in a glossary. I have tried to provide the necessary context for passages referring to ideas or practices that might otherwise be myste-

PREFACE

rious, but sometimes the iceberg tip that Bokushi touches is attached to a submerged mass of information so large and important to understanding what he's getting at that this hasn't been possible. Those subjects I would like to outline below, to prepare the reader and for later reference.

COSMOLOGY AND PREMODERN SCIENCE Bokushi saw the world through the traditional cosmology of China and Japan. The main idea that surfaces in the *Tales* is the philosophy of yin and yang. Yin is the negative, female, passive, dark, potential cosmic force; its complement (for they are not opposites) is yang, which is positive, male, active, light, and actual. All things, whether animal, vegetable, or mineral, were thought to be a dynamic composition of yin and yang forces. Each maintained its own balance between the two; some creatures, objects, or even abstract concepts were predominantly yin (females, water, even numbers) and others were predominantly yang (males, fire, odd numbers). The yin-yang model served as a way to categorize and explain the universe, and it is not without its proponents even today, in the age of the binary circuit.

Bokushi describes such phenomena as snow, frost, and natural gas in yin-yang terms. Folk festivals such as the Blossom-Water Celebration are also interpreted as an interplay of yin and yang or female and male forces.

Other ancient Chinese cosmological beliefs appear in the *Tales* as well. In "Snow Insects," for example, Bokushi claims that each of the five elements of Chinese physics—earth, water, fire, air, and metal—produces insects. And the idea of lucky and unlucky directions plays an important role in the story of the little blind masseur who, on New Year's Eve, comes tumbling in through a window that faces the lucky direction. Lucky and unlucky directions changed from year to year as part of a calendrical cycle that included twelve zoomorphic signs which were associated with years (in a twelve-year cycle), hours of the day, and points of the compass.

But in addition to this reliance on traditional cosmological explanations, Bokushi and his circle of naturalists were observant amateur scientists bent on understanding natural phenomena and putting them to practical use, as can be seen in the accounts of the discovery of asbestos fiber and natural gas. He speaks often of "those interested in curiosities, wonders, and ancient things," men of education and leisure who were fascinated by everything in the world around them and studied it with amazing diligence. Bokushi's most frequently adopted method of reasoning was to combine observation, either firsthand or reported, with induction from the "established theories" of his cosmology and arguments from authority in the form of references to classic works, a system he shared with all other scholars and "men of science" in his day.

THE CALENDAR AND SEASONS   The calendar of old Japan is a subject of great importance in a work as concerned with weather and the seasons as *Snow Country Tales*. Following Chinese practice, the Japanese used two calendars, an official lunar one and an unofficial solar one. In the lunar calendar, each month began with a new moon and lasted the duration of a full cycle of the moon's phases. Since twelve lunar months, however, total only about 353 days, it was necessary to adjust the lunar calendar with an intercalary month approximately once every thirty months.

The phases of the moon, however, do not necessarily correspond to the movement of the sun or the seasons, so Japanese farmers used an unofficial solar calendar quite close in its reckoning to the natural year. According to this calendar, the year was divided into twelve periods called *setsu* of exactly the same length: approximately 30.44 days. The first *setsu*, called Beginning of Spring (Risshun), marked the New Year, which fell on February 4 or 5 according to the Gregorian calendar. Summer (Rikka) began on May 5 or 6; autumn (Risshu) the 7 or 8 of August; and winter (Ritto) the 7 or 8 of November.

The combination of these two calendars meant that the lunar New Year, which could begin anytime from January 21 through February 19 (depending on how close the lunar year cycle was to being adjusted to the natural year with an intercalary month), was regarded as the start of spring. Even given central Japan's relatively mild climate, from the Western point of view this is a bit early for spring, just as August 7 or 8—the hottest part of the year in Japan—seems too early for autumn. But that was the system. It is this different view of the beginnings of the seasons, in particular, that the Western reader must bear in mind when he reads Bokushi's description of the snows of spring and summer.

The months are known by two sets of names in Japan. One is descriptive, but it is used mostly in poetry and doesn't concern us here. The most widely used system is numerical: the First Month, the Second Month, and so forth. I have given the months their English names, following the very approximate formula of adding one month to the Japanese version, so that the First Month becomes February, the Second Month March, and so on. An immediate and roughly accurate impression of the months and seasons is so important in appreciating much that Bokushi says, and I concluded that the anomaly of New Year in February was less distracting for the reader than being forced to mentally subtract one month at each mention of a date or season.

ERAS Until 1868 the Japanese used the era system of dating. When a new emperor assumed the throne, the age was christened with a new name. Before 1868, a reigning emperor might also change the era name to initiate a new start or to ward off an evil omen. Bokushi was engaged in the composition of *Snow Country Tales* from his late twenties through his sixties, spanning the Kyowa (1801–4), Bunka (1804–18), Bunsei (1818–30), and Tempo (1830–44) eras. He also refers, of course, to earlier eras of Japanese history in the work. Since he doesn't always give the specific year, era names with their inclusive dates are used in the translation.

POLITICAL DIVISIONS AND GEOGRAPHY Edo-period Japan was divided into sixty-seven provinces, of which Echigo was one of the larger in area. The provinces were further subdivided into counties (variously pronounced *gun, kori,* or *gori*). In Echigo there were seven counties: Iwafune, Kambara, Uonuma, Santo, Kariwa, Kubiki, and Koshi. Within each county were settlements of various sizes. The stopping points along the national highway network were called post towns (*eki*). In addition, there were castle towns (*jokamachi*), the capitals of the fiefs into which the province was divided. Bokushi lists Murakami, Shibata, Kurokawa, Mikkaichi, Yoita, Shiiya, Nagaoka, Takata, and Itoikawa as the castle towns of Echigo.

PREFACE

Each was governed by a daimyo with a stipend in rice and, often, a number of armed soldiers. In addition to the castle towns there were market towns, villages, and tiny mountain hamlets. The ancient term *sho* (also *so,* manor) was still in use in Bokushi's day, but it referred to a general area rather than an official administrative unit.

Readers familiar with the Echigo region may note that Bokushi's geographical information is sometimes inaccurate. Though he traveled widely, he didn't visit all the places he wrote about, and when he relied on secondhand reports he sometimes got them wrong. He makes mistakes with names of temples and villages and rivers and puts things in places they never were. I have corrected him in the text when simply orthography is the problem. For example, Bokushi's "Tsumaari" has been corrected to "Tsumari" and his "Myohoji" to "Nyohoji." Where the facts are mistaken, I have let his version stand and noted the correct information in the Glossary. The names of geographical features such as mountains and rivers are not, as a rule, translated, though if their meaning is part of a tale, it is given.

RELIGION   Japan is a land that has nurtured and domesticated several religious traditions. At least five are important in *Snow Country Tales:* Buddhism, Shinto, Confucianism, Taoism, and the amorphous but no less influential practices and beliefs of the native folk tradition.

The school of Buddhism known as the Jodo, or Pure Land, Sect was the most widely followed in Echigo. This was partly because Shinran (1173–1262), the founder of one of the major Pure Land subsects, spent many years proselytizing in the region after he was banished to Echigo in 1207. The main teaching of the Pure Land Sect was that anyone, no matter how lowly, could attain salvation by calling on the name of Amida Buddha, who ruled over the Pure Land of the West. The practice of reciting the Buddha's name, or nembutsu (literally, "thinking of the Buddha"), is referred to frequently in the *Tales,* where it is revealed as a charm against evil and a call for divine protection as well as a more strictly Buddhist practice, both private and public.

Buddhism is strongly associated in Japan with the rites of death, and it was the custom to grant posthumous Buddhist names to the

PREFACE

deceased to insure the success of their quest for enlightenment. Without proper burial services, a spirit wandered the world restlessly, like Kiku's ghost in "A Ghost in the Snow." Only when Kiku has had her hair cut off in a ceremonial tonsure, symbolizing entrance to the Buddhist order, does she find eternal rest.

Pilgrimage was an established form of Buddhist practice in Bokushi's day, and remains so to a lesser degree even today. To fulfill a religious vow the practitioner took up a wandering life for a prescribed period of time, visiting and making offerings at a particular temple or circuit of temples. Bokushi records the visit of two pilgrims in "Congratulatory Poems," and relates how father and daughter embark on a pilgrimage at the tragic ending of "Wolves in the Snow." Visits to Shinto shrines were also popular.

Though the organized religious hierarchy of Bokushi's day was predominantly Buddhist, the native Japanese religion Shinto, together with related folk beliefs and practices, figures largely in *Snow Country Tales,* particularly in the descriptions of festivals, such as the Blossom-Water Celebration, the Hall-pushing at Urasa, soliciting contributions for the Way Gods, and the Sagicho Festival, and in the stories and descriptions of purification rites ("The Mysterious Power of the Spirit of the Loom Chamber") or ascetic practices ("The Merits of Winter Asceticism").

The subject is a vast and complex one, and most of Bokushi's anecdotes can be appreciated in their context, without further explanation. What may be most important to know is that Shinto deities, or *kami,* were thought to dwell in a wide variety of forms, including waterfalls, rocks, rivers, mountains, animals, men and women, the weaver's loom, and straw sandals. They are propitiated by ceremonial offerings and "pure" behavior, for Shinto is greatly occupied with ritual purification and defilement. Salt, water, and the sacred *shimenawa* straw rope were regarded as purifying things, while sexual activity, menstruation, death, and disease were thought to cause contamination. Fertility rites such as the activities that accompanied soliciting contributions for the Way Gods and the Blossom-Water Celebration were also associated with Shinto and folk religious practices, as was the belief in the supernatural power of the fox—vividly documented by Bokushi—who was enshrined as the deity Inari Daimyojin.

The relationship between Shinto and Buddhism was amicable and syncretic, for the most part. Many of the elements of the hall-pushing festival, though it was held in a Buddhist temple, are non-Buddhist in origin; the asceticism of the winter nembutsu practice combines elements of the two religions; and in "Ancient Sites in Old Poems," a Buddhist deity is said to have manifested itself as the Shinto god of Mount Iyahiko, an example of the popular belief that many Shinto gods were provisional forms of a Buddhist deity (*honji suijaku*).

In addition to Shinto and Buddhism, Confucian and Taoist influences are frequently encountered in the *Tales*. The yin-yang cosmology, the idea of holy sages dwelling in the mountains (like the white-haired old man who rides down the slopes of Mount Hishiyama to predict an avalanche), and the prescriptions of traditional Chinese medicine (the healing effects of the gall bladders of bears, for example) were all closely linked with Taoism in China and Japan. Mention is made of a Koshin Mound in "Luminous Stones." This mound served as the site for a folk festival deriving partly from Taoist sources. The Festival of the Way Gods is also colored by Taoism.

Confucianism is represented in *Snow Country Tales* mostly by references to filial piety, one of the prime Confucian virtues. Devotion to one's parents, sometimes carried to an extreme that seems unnatural to a Westerner, was an ideal of behavior in China and Japan that is regularly invoked in the *Tales,* for example in "Bagging a Bear in an Avalanche" or "To Catch a Fox." Bokushi's general tone is strongly moral in a Confucian fashion. He includes many stories of filial piety and virtue rewarded, and cannot resist drawing morals from the things he describes. Animals, especially, become Confucian models in his hands, whether it be the virtuous character of the bear, the example of matrimonial bliss set by salmon, the teamwork and discipline of wild geese, or, in his last tale, "The Crane's Gratitude."

THE LITERATI Bokushi earnestly sought membership in the class of educated and artistically inclined men who might be called Japan's literati. They were mostly located in the three major cities, Edo,

PREFACE

Kyoto, and Osaka. Bokushi corresponded with the most illustrious men of letters of his day and sought the companionship of poets, painters, and antiquarians and naturalists—men interested in curiosities, natural or man-made, and ancient things and ways. In addition to his correspondents from the capitals, he enjoyed the company of a small circle of like-minded men in his provincial setting. He frequently refers to his "fellow poets," and seems to have exchanged verses with them regularly. It was the practice for these men to don literary names with poetic associations. As "Bokushi" was Suzuki's literary name, "Kyozan" was the pen name of Iwase Momoki, Suzuki's editor and a contributor to the work, whose additions are often prefaced with "Momoki says" or "Momoki adds."

Bokushi took great pains to demonstrate his familiarity with the range of classical Chinese and Japanese learning, and he sprinkles his writing with references to both well-known and obscure works. Many of these he probably knew only from anthologies or snippets quoted in more popular writings. English translations of the titles are often eccentric at best (*The Deep Blue Memory Jewel of All Things*, for example), but at least they provide a hint of the work's content, and I have, with only a few exceptions, used the translated titles in the text. The original titles and other pertinent information are provided in the Glossary.

With this small dose of background, I hope Bokushi's tales will stand on their own. Aside from the few adaptations mentioned above, I have tried to preserve the spirit and letter of the text. Occasionally I have deleted the ubiquitous "In the first book I . . . " or "Later I will explain . . . " variety of cross-references. In very rare instances I have omitted a phrase or sentence that would thoroughly derail a complicated passage in English. Bokushi's own parenthetical notes have been inserted in the running text whenever possible. Except for two uninspired biographies unrelated to the snow country (one of Sugawara Michizane, the other of Basho), two brief, repetitive entries (one on avalanches, the other on the New Year), forewords to the original publication, and several interpolative passages by Kyozan, Bokushi's manuscript is here in its entirety.

Some of the illustrations that accompany the work are by Kyozan's son Kyosui and others are by Bokushi himself, who was an amateur painter (he has left beautiful renditions of the scenery of Akiyama in ink and colors to illustrate his separate booklet recording that journey). In addition, many of Kyosui's paintings were based on Bokushi's preliminary drawings. They are invaluable in visualizing some of the less familiar aspects of life in the snow country, and one could only wish for more.

A final word about literary style is necessary. Bokushi's original manuscript was heavily edited by Kyozan, who was responsible for seeing that the "Old Man's" (as he called Bokushi) book was brought into print. Kyozan manipulated the text throughout and added to it with increasing frequency as the work progressed, finally being forced to identify his extended comments by name. A few episodes, such as "Explanations of the Origins of Tempura and Steamed Bean Sweets," "A Beauty," and "The Fires of Hell Valley" are entirely the products of his brush. Bokushi also composed several pieces at Kyozan's urging. A definite lack of enthusiasm for his subject can be detected in these entries. "A Two-headed Snake" and "Floating Islands," both toward the end of the work, are examples.

Kyozan's style is quite different from Bokushi's. The difference is that between an earnest, moralizing, old-fashioned rustic struggling to express himself with the conventional similes of literary jargon and a jaded, slightly supercilious, glibly literate, fashionable sophisticate whose writing is so clever that it occasionally twists back upon itself. Each has his own weaknesses. Bokushi cannot forgo a moral; Momoki cannot resist a pun. Yet each grows eloquent when enthusiasm for his subject lifts him out of the realm of the ordinary, and each has contributed his share of passages of power and beauty.

Rose Lesser brought *Hokuetsu Seppu* to my attention, as she has to the attention of hundreds of others over the years. Her determination to see the work, which means so much to her, published in English was the catalyst that set me to begin to translate it and pushed me on toward its eventual conclusion. But that I did it strikes me as not at all strange or coincidental, for I was born and raised in the snow country of the United States, in Wisconsin. Of course there can be no comparison between the awful weight of the snow burden

PREFACE

borne by the people of Echigo 150 years ago and modern American life, no matter how wintry. But some things are similar if not the same, alike enough to strike a resonant note of broader human experience. As a child, I remember my father cutting tunnels through drifts of snow that reached to the roof so that we could get out of our front door (in the days before snowblowers). And I walked my own high snow pathways along the streets to school, tumbling five or six feet into the road below if I took a false step. Most of all, I remember feeling what Bokushi felt, buried in snow for so many months of the year. While the winter winds whipping over the western prairies battled with the arctic damp looming over Lake Michigan, we all waited in the half-light, longing for sun and warmth and spring, for forsythia and robins, and for the year to begin again.

JEFFREY HUNTER

Introduction:
The Life and Times of Suzuki Bokushi

Anyone who has ever studied Japanese literature has read Yasunari Kawabata's *Snow Country* and savored his depiction of the land and its people. Few readers know, however, that his source for local customs was *Hokuetsu Seppu* by Suzuki Bokushi (1770–1842).[1] Unlike Kawabata, Bokushi spent practically his entire life in the snow country, then known as Echigo Province. He evoked the sights of his homeland not to create a backdrop to an urban dilettante's love affair but to communicate what it was really like to inhabit a region dominated by snow.

Until the creation of ski resorts in modern times, the few visitors to the Japan Sea coast planned their trips to coincide with summer. To mention Echigo or Sado, the large, not-far-distant island, was to bring a shudder. These were places of exile for men who had committed heinous crimes against the state. Isolated and feared, Echigo was terra incognita, a place of strange customs and stranger creatures. Even Matsuo Basho (1644–94), who traveled through the area on his famous journey to the back country depicted in *Oku no Hosomichi* (The Narrow Road of Oku), saw no reason to linger.[2] The experience of living buried under snow was not one that appealed to outsiders.

It did not necessarily appeal to the peasants, hunters, woodcutters, fishermen, weavers, and merchants who lived in Echigo, but they made the best of it. In the towns and villages that dotted the region, they developed special tools suited to their occupations, placated their local gods with festivals, repeated the myths of the region

INTRODUCTION

along with gossip of more recent happenings, and paid taxes. Bokushi described what they did, drew pictures of their utensils, and recorded their stories. He little discussed tax bills, perhaps because taxes are a feature of every society and hence not unique to Echigo, or perhaps because the rulers of his time insisted that everything pertaining to themselves and their administration be censored.

The peasants where Bokushi lived paid taxes to the *bakufu,* the house government of the shogun. At that time, the shogun was the hereditary office of the Tokugawa family. Possessed of one fourth of Japan's agrarian resources, the *bakufu* controlled nationwide the trade routes, the currency, and the standards for handwriting. To administer its lands, it dispatched intendants called *daikan* drawn from the ranks of the shogun's vassals, the samurai. When one of these men visited his office in the province, maybe once or twice a year, he would have the local notables like Bokushi call on him. Sometimes he even held a banquet for them. In his merchant persona, Bokushi paid no regular taxes since the ruling authorities had not figured out how to tax mercantile profits, but he was expected to be generous in loaning the government money. For these gifts he was rewarded with letters of commendation, often in the intendant's own handwriting.

The nearest town of any size was Nagaoka, a castle town under the rule of the Makino family located south of present-day Niigata City. West of Nagaoka was Takata, a larger town as befitted the large domain ruled by the Sakakibara family. These rulers, the daimyo, always spent half their time in Edo to prove their loyalty to the shogun, and their retainers lived exclusively in the castle town. Except for patrols through outlying areas, the sight of a samurai was rare in the countryside. As long as they outwardly obeyed the regulations and restrictions of their rulers, rural inhabitants were left in peace to manage their own affairs.

The samurai thought themselves superior to the peasants, artisans, and merchants they ruled, an assumption shared to some extent by their subjects, and they claimed a position as role models for the rest of society. The elaborate ceremonies for their weddings were aped by wealthy peasants. It was a great honor when a mere commoner was given permission to carry two swords or use a surname, marks of distinction reserved by shogunal decree for the ruling class. Even

INTRODUCTION

peasant children were known to imitate the manners of the samurai in their games. Yet samurai were admired more in the abstract than in the flesh. Bokushi recounted how one samurai was punished by the gods for his arrogance. In their everyday life, he and the people he knew followed their own customs. Peasant widows, for example, were more likely to marry again and again than to dedicate their lives to their husband's memory like samurai women did. The respect paid to samurai as a class did not always extend to each individual member of it, and the samurai code of behavior was imitated only when it was convenient.

In the social order carefully devised by the early Tokugawa shoguns, every person's occupation was fixed for all generations, and no one was supposed to mingle with people outside one's own status. If one's ancestors were peasants, then oneself was a peasant. Merchants and artisans were supposed to live in castle towns under the watchful eye of their superiors, the samurai, and travel to the countryside only to trade and buy supplies. By the early nineteenth century, the reality was quite different. Bokushi's grandfather left the land to open a pawnshop and deal in *chijimi* crepe. Although Bokushi practiced the business management skills of the merchant, his mother and many of his wives were from peasant households.

Bokushi belonged to that class of families known as *gono*—peasant entrepreneurs. Although his family still had ties to the land, its wealth and status far exceeded that of a rich peasant. Like his counterparts all over Japan, Bokushi had capital to market the local surplus, an education in keeping accounts, and a wide circle of acquaintances outside the village based on business relations, kinship ties, and a common addiction to the writing of haiku to serve as commercial contacts. He had advantages over merchants from outside as well, for he knew intimately local markets, products, and workers. The samurai feared the peasant entrepreneurs who monopolized the wealth of the countryside and increasingly its political offices as well, who invaded the fields of scholarship and speculative thought previously the special province of the warrior, and who even set their sons to learning the martial arts. In their pursuit of profit and edification, peasant entrepreneurs freely crossed status barriers to mingle with urban intellectuals and merchants. The people men like Bokushi associated with were defined less by their status than by their wealth and erudition.

By the early nineteenth century, post towns and villages often contained men skilled in Nativism, Noh, and Confucian studies, and the arts of painting, tea ceremony, and flower arranging. The circulation of poetry, books, and ideas paralleled and was based on the economic flow of goods and services. Bokushi belonged to a local cultural circle approximately five to eight miles in radius that met on a monthly basis. Each local circle was integrated into regional circles and through them connected to the national urban centers of Edo, Kyoto, and Osaka.[3] At his sixty-first birthday, Bokushi drew on these circles to collect art and writings dedicated to himself from all over Japan.

The central activity of local cultural circles was the writing of poetry. Basho's technique of emphasizing the details of the ordinary world had a powerful impact on literate peasants. Through writing poetry, they could make the immediacy of their daily experience into art and validate their lives. As Bokushi said, "To live a long life without making the most of it is incompatible with the original purpose of being human. . . . If one takes pleasure in elegant accomplishments, then there is nothing common about one's work."[4] The writing of poetry was an exercise open to priests, merchants, and peasants alike. It reinforced the bonds forged by commerce and opened up new avenues of communication in areas beyond the purview of the ruling class.

Poetry writing was only for the wealthy and educated. Under the Tokugawa status system, peasants were tied to the land and were expected to devote their energies to growing crops, preferably rice. To survive the long harsh winters, those in Echigo had to perform other tasks as well. Then as now, men would leave their families and travel to Edo in search of work during the long winter months. For hours, days, weeks, and months, their daughters wove the crepe that made Echigo cloth famous. Some families took up fishing, others specialized in woodcutting. Peasants were given a place of honor in the ideology of the ruling class, but, as Bokushi depicted it in *Hokuetsu Seppu,* their miserable day-to-day existence was precarious indeed.

It was not, however, an insular existence. Bokushi's hometown,

INTRODUCTION

Shiozawa, was a post town on the road beween Edo and the Japan Sea. Established and maintained by the *bakufu,* post towns lined the national roads that linked Edo with the provinces. Even today, railways and highways follow the approximate route of these ancient tracks. Some post towns have developed into thriving industrial or tourist towns; others have been swallowed by their neighbors. Located about three to six miles apart, they provided inns for daimyo and their retinue on their way to serve in Edo plus porters and packhorses to carry their baggage. *Bakufu* couriers either on foot or in palanquins stopped for rest and refreshment. In good weather they could cover the distance between Edo and Shiozawa in four days. Communications between private individuals took considerably longer. By relying on merchant friends who had business in Edo, Bokushi could send a letter to the capital and expect a reply in about two months.

The post towns were built to serve the needs of the ruling class, but with the spread of commerce and cottage industries like crepe weaving, they began to provide services for commoners as well. Packhorse trains paraded by loaded with goods for the city. Pilgrims on their way to and from the shrines of Ise and points west walked through town. The sick hoping for a cure at nearby hot springs, crepe buyers, beggars, and thieves thronged the road. Every spring the cloth market brought merchants from the great urban centers. Occasionally a troupe of traveling players would stop to give a performance of the most popular spectacles on the Edo stage. All of these different groups brought news of different places and customs, events and disasters to entertain and edify the local population.

The inhabitants of Echigo varied the monotony of their lifelong routine with travel and the search for entertainment. Even the poorest peasant might go several villages away to watch an open-air performance of *The Forty-Seven Loyal Retainers.* In their poetry-writing circles, Bokushi and his friends held contests to select the best poem or the best four thousand poems and then presented them engraved on plaques to local temples. They traveled together to local hot springs for their health and made pleasure excursions to famous baths farther away. On his business trips to Edo, Bokushi did not neglect to visit the beautiful beaches at Enoshima and the temples of Kama-

INTRODUCTION

kura. His daughter, too, traveled widely, making a pilgrimage with three friends to Ise and Kompira, then going to the theater and sightseeing in Osaka. Years later she visited Edo and Enoshima. For an Edo-period provincial, there were few greater pleasures than to go places and to see new sights.

The magnets that drew the gaze of Edo-period provincials were the great urban centers of Edo and Osaka. Although the government bureaucracies were staffed by the samurai, the culture of the times was firmly in the hands of the merchants. These men bought the *chijimi* crepe transported to the city by jobbers like Bokushi, then sold it to retail houses which in turn sold it to consumers. By the early nineteenth century, trade in all sorts of commodities tied the rural producers of handcrafted products to regional and eventually national markets. The men who stood at the apex of these trading systems and their employees were also the patrons of Kabuki, the pleasure quarters, and books. To suit their tastes and meet their needs, there developed a new kind of literary world.

The early years of the nineteenth century are known by the Japanese as the Bunka-Bunsei or Kasei period after the era names chosen for their auspicious connotations. During this time, literature, poetry, painting, and theater flourished for the last time before the end of the Tokugawa period. The nation as a whole enjoyed an unprecedented travel boom. Major shrines attracted thousands of pilgrims annually. Purely recreational travel to hot springs, historical sites, and scenic wonders increased dramatically, and books about travel such as Jippensha Ikku's *Shank's Mare* found an insatiable market. In the cities this Kasei culture was tinged with decadence. Under the rubric of chastizing evil and exalting good, playwrights like Tsuruya Namboku (1755–1829) took the depiction of falsehood, evil, and ugliness to grotesque extremes. The fine arts as practiced in the countryside were fresher, more naive, and performed by amateurs.

By the early nineteenth century, the arts had become cultural commodities in the great urban centers. The number of men who as professional writers, poets, and printmakers tried to make their living from artistic pursuits had increased dramatically to the point where supply threatened to exceed demand. Some of them had to be willing to seek patrons among the rural rich, travel among them, and

INTRODUCTION

accept them as students and disciples. Both Santo Kyozan (1769–1858) and Jippensha Ikku (1765–1831) visited Bokushi in Shiozawa. At the same time, the increased communication between city and countryside brought the peasants to the cities and stimulated their yearning for culture. Soon they came knocking on the doors of well-known artists whose addresses appeared in the guidebooks to the cities, and Bokushi was no exception. Based on this relationship between supply and demand, which presupposed a cultural differential between center and periphery, professionals from the city traveled to the countryside, sponging off wealthy patrons and spreading enlightenment as they went.

Had Bokushi lived several centuries earlier, he probably would have circulated his manuscript to friends who would then have copied it themselves. In the Edo period, however, the widespread use of woodblocks for printing secular texts meant that books reached a large and anonymous audience. Even a man from the provinces like Bokushi could hope to make a name for himself if only he could gain entry into this world. It took Bokushi forty years to get *Hokuetsu Seppu* in print, but before he died he had the satisfaction of knowing that his name had become famous, his book was popular, and his beloved snow country had achieved lasting recognition.

Born in 1770 in Shiozawa, located in the southern section of Niigata Prefecture, Suzuki Bokushi inherited both his occupation and his interest in the arts. In the sixteenth century, his family had served Uesugi Kenshin (1530–78), as who had not in this mighty lord's homeland. When the Uesugi family moved to Aizu, however, Bokushi's ancestors had decided, or had been forced, to return to farming. His grandfather had made himself into a *chijimi*-cloth jobber and opened a pawnshop, but the family continued to hold a few fields, and Bokushi called himself a humble farmer. Then Bokushi's uncle nearly ran the family business into the ground. To save the family from bankruptcy, he turned it over to his younger brother, Bokushi's father, Kouemon. Kouemon managed to gain for the family the privilege of wearing the two swords of a samurai and publicly using a surname, but his real interest was in the writing of haiku.

Kouemon educated his son in both business management and

artistic pursuits. Bokushi attended the local temple school run by a priestly friend of his father's for five years from the time he was seven. There he studied the Chinese classics, Chinese poetry, Japanese poetry, and painting. In an autobiography written toward the end of his life, he claimed that although he studied with other children, he did not join them in play. Instead he preferred to copy pictures by himself. At the age of ten, he desperately desired a ten-volume set of paintings. To earn the money to pay for the set, he massaged his parents every night. At thirteen his doting father sent him to a nearby market town to study with an obscure traveling painter, Kano Baisho. Bokushi then practiced so enthusiastically that he made himself sick. Kouemon himself introduced his son to the writing of haiku.

Like merchants all over the world, his father sent Bokushi away from home for his training. After his coming-of-age ceremony at fifteen, Bokushi spent twenty days with Miya Kuzaemon in Horinouchi, where he observed the buying and selling of *chijimi* cloth. The richest man in Horinouchi, Kuzaemon's connection with the Suzukis was based on both the cloth trade and a love of haiku. His sister's in-laws, the Imanari of Muikamachi, then took Bokushi in and taught him the principles of management, accounting, and inventory. In 1788, at the age of eighteen, he made his first trip to Edo with a consignment of eighty rolls of crepe. Once these had been sold, he stayed in the city to take lessons from the scholar Sawada Toko (1732–96), the first indication of his lifelong infatuation with the famous literary figures of his day. Like tourists then and now, he took side trips to the famous beauty spots of Enoshima and Kamakura. The next year he received two hundred rolls of crepe at Urasa and seemed so well launched on his career that his father immediately turned the business over to him and retired to write poetry. Having devoted a lifetime to haiku, Kouemon died in 1807.

Bokushi apparently enjoyed considerable success as a businessman. By curtailing his studies and refusing to join his friends on pleasure excursions, he managed to triple the family fortune. Indeed, he was so successful that the ruling authorities repeatedly came to him for loans with which to fill government coffers. At the age of fifty-two, in 1822, he was made an elder of Shiozawa, a singular honor. When he retired at sixty, he was a respected member of the community.

INTRODUCTION

In his personal life, Bokushi was not as fortunate. During the winter of his twentieth year, just after he took charge of the family business, an ear infection left him permanently deaf, and he had to use a conch shell for a hearing aid. At twenty-two, he married his first wife, Mine, who gave him a son, but they parted two years later. He then married in succession Hono, Uta, Yu, Tori, and Rita. Some of his wives went back to their parents' homes; some ran away. His three children all had different mothers. Only Uta, who stayed with him for twenty-three years until she died at forty-eight, and Rita, who outlived him, managed to endure his endless search for perfection. After his son died at age twenty, he adopted a son-in-law, Bokuzan, to marry his daughter Kuwa and inherit the family business. His quarrels with Bokuzan, shouting matches so loud that the neighbors could hear, he blamed on bad karma. At sixty-six he was stricken with palsy. Old, sick, confined to the back of his house, almost completely deaf and practically blind, he made life miserable for anyone within earshot. In his last testament written two years before his death, he lamented his misfortunes and vented his spleen at the world. In 1842, six years after his first attack of palsy, he died.

Much of what we know about Bokushi's life comes from the autobiography written when he was fifty-four. Like Benjamin Franklin, he included moral precepts and rules for his descendants to live by, illustrated with events in his own life. At the beginning of the book he admonished his children to reread his writings every year for their own good instead of holding the traditional memorial services in his honor. A typical merchant of the late Tokugawa period, he emphasized the virtues of thrift, diligence, reliability, and fortitude, but he appears to have gone further than many in practicing asceticism. According to his contemporaries, "The master of the Suzuki family talks continually about patient endurance, but in his pursuit of gain, he shows no restraint at all." Not for him were the pleasures of gambling, drinking, or whoring. He lived simply, eschewing fine clothing and fancy foods. In their stead he enjoyed the subtle pleasures of writing essays and haiku.

His autobiography tells us a great deal about how he regimented his life. He never took naps or allowed himself to relax under the *kotatsu* (a quilt-covered table placed over a hole with live coals)

INTRODUCTION

during the day. Unless everything in his store, in the house, in the dressers, even in the needle cases was in its proper place, he could not relax. No matter how late guests stayed, he insisted that the house be put in order before anyone went to bed. If the cleaning was not done to suit him, he would pick up a broom or dust rag and start sweeping away himself. Hating waste, he carefully preserved bits of lumber and bamboo splits. Scraps of paper he saved for his poetry manuscripts. He made his own boxes, repaired his own roof, mended cracks in pots, and crafted his own paper. Until his front teeth fell out, he prided himself on not wasting a second in gulping down his food. He taught his children to read and write and supervised their every waking moment to guard against idleness. He allowed himself the luxury of reading and writing only at night, never during the day. As part of his exercise in self-awareness, he acknowledged that he had his faults—after he turned forty, he began to sleep late in the mornings. Although he tried to be humble, he could not help but take pride in his skill with the brush. Even he admitted that he scolded the members of his household for every little thing.

One activity that he enjoyed was travel. From his first trip to Edo at eighteen to his last at fifty-eight, he took pleasure in seeing new places, meeting famous people, and writing travelogues decorated with poetry as records of where he had been. At twenty-six, he made a pilgrimage to the shrine of the sun goddess in Ise and then went on to complete the thirty-three-stage pilgrimage in western Japan. Pilgrimages were important for a man's salvation and prosperity, but they also afforded an opportunity to view famous sites associated with Japanese history and literature. For his health he visited the famous Kusatsu hot springs in Shinano. He also traveled widely around his own province, collecting materials for *Hokuetsu Seppu,* describing a bullfight for Takizawa Bakin (1767–1848), and doing other ethnographic research. Through letters, essays, and drawings, he shared what he saw with his acquaintances.

For a man living in the provinces, the only way to communicate with the world outside was through letters. Bokushi was no exception, and he wrote numerous letters, many carefully preserved in six volumes with their replies. At the age of fifty-two, he made a ledger of all the people he had ever corresponded with and where

INTRODUCTION

they lived. Fifty-four were from Echigo; the remaining 166 lived in other areas, some as far away as Kyushu. They included people he had met on his travels, people he begged a scrap of correspondence from because they were famous, and people he hoped would help get *Hokuetsu Seppu* published.

Bokushi's list of correspondents reads like a who's who in the artistic world of late Tokugawa Japan. For years the popular writers Santo Kyoden (1761–1816) and Takizawa Bakin encouraged him to think that they could get his manuscript published. Kyoden's younger brother and a well-known essayist in his own right, Kyozan (appearing under his given name Momoki in the present work), went to Shiozawa with his son in 1836 to visit the man he had come to know through letters. Bokushi begged letters from Ota Nampo (1749–1823) and the scholar Kameda Bosai (1752–1826). He met Jippensha Ikku, author of the best seller *Shank's Mare,* on his trip to Edo in 1819, a visit repaid by Ikku in 1826. The next year Ikku wrote requesting materials on Akiyama as he wanted to write about this remote district where the remnants of the Heike were said to have fled after their defeat in the twelfth century. Bokushi could claim acquaintance with the ukiyo-e artists Hokusai (1760–1849) and Toyokuni (1769–1825) as well as the illustrators and painters Okada Gyokuzan (1737–1812) and Tani Buncho (1763–1840). He even wrote to the Kabuki actor Ichikawa Danjuro V and the poetess-courtesan Hanaogi. Some of these people he did favors for, and they did favors for him. Others he apparently sought out simply because they were famous.

Bokushi must have been an extremely busy man after dark, for in addition to his voluminous correspondence, he wrote a great deal. Poetry was his first love, and he edited a volume of his father's poems as well as compiling one of his own. In addition his poems appeared in numerous local anthologies. He wrote seven travelogues which combined haiku with descriptions of places he had seen and people he had met. One of these, *Akiyama Kiko* (A Record of the Akiyama Trip), he did in two versions, one factual and one fictionalized in the style of *Shank's Mare.* Bokushi had apparently hoped to get Ikku to publish it with his name listed as a coauthor, but Ikku died two months before the manuscript was finished. Two novels, *Kodaiji Odori* (A Dance at Kodai Temple) and *Enya Hangan Ichidaiki* (A Life of

INTRODUCTION

Enya Hangan), are works that only modern-day compilers of Bokushi's writings have managed to publish. Then there were the autobiographies and family histories, designed to teach his descendants how to take their proper place in Echigo society. His ethnographic interests appeared in *Hokuetsu Seppu,* in his travelogues, especially *Akiyama Kiko,* and in notebooks entitled *Koshin Jo.* The notebooks recorded the customary chatter of people gathered for a nocturnal vigil when the *ko* and *shin* zodiac signs fell on the same day.

The climax to Bokushi's poetry-writing career came in 1800 when he was thirty. As an offering to the Bishamon shrine in Urasa, he invited poets from his own district, the rest of Echigo, Kozuke, Musashi, Aizu, and Shinano to submit poems for a poetry-writing contest. Each man sent in twenty-five of his best poems for a total of forty thousand. So that handwriting styles would not influence the experts, Bokushi made clear copies of all the poems himself. These he circulated to ten judges in Kyoto, Osaka, Edo, Ise, and Omi. Then he sorted them, putting the best first, had them engraved on plaques, and presented them to the shrine. This was the largest poetry-writing contest that he participated in, but similar events were not uncommon in the provinces.

The climax to Bokushi's literary career was the publication of *Hokuetsu Seppu.* In Edo publishing circles, an unknown writer from the provinces could not simply appear at the door of a printing house and expect to have his manuscript accepted or even read. Even if he were recommended by a famous author, publishers were unlikely to take him seriously. The subject matter too seemed unsalable. The literary world was already crowded with elegantly written novels from the sanctimonious to the salacious, and a factual book about the customs and climate of a remote corner of the country had dubious market value at best. Yet Bokushi tenaciously sought fame in this world; he was determined to have his existence recognized and his writings remembered.

In 1798 Bokushi first announced his intention in a letter to Santo Kyoden. He wanted to publicize the snow in his homeland and the way people lived there, but he felt unequal to the task. Instead he proposed that he provide the materials which Kyoden would then rewrite in his own inimitable style. Kyoden was enthusiastic, and

INTRODUCTION

Bokushi sent him the first draft of his manuscript with pictures of the snow country and drawings of snow tools. Unfortunately the publisher to whom Kyoden showed the manuscript did not share his enthusiasm. How could he invest in an eccentric book by an unknown author? There the matter rested. Bokushi tried to get Takizawa Bakin attached to his cause, but Bakin was Kyoden's disciple and did not want to offend him.

In 1807, Bokushi tried again. To break the impasse in Edo, he turned to the illustrator and writer Okada Gyokuzan in Osaka. He had rewritten one portion of the manuscript, made more drawings of snow tools, and a publisher had been decided when Gyokuzan died. In 1812, the painter Suzuki Fuyo (1749–1816) visited him and expressed interest in the work, but he too died before a commitment could be made. Bokushi's letters to Kyoden ended with that worthy's death in 1816.

Kyoden's death made Bakin the most important literary figure of his time and opened the way for Bokushi to approach him once more in 1818. Encouraged by Bakin's interest, Bokushi traveled around Echigo, collecting more materials for his work, and rewrote the manuscript again. When Bakin asked him to record the bullfight ceremony in a nearby village, Bokushi obliged and his report formed the basis for an episode in Bakin's masterpiece, *Nanso Satomi Hakkenden* (Biographies of Eight Dogs, a long romance about the Satomi family in the Muromachi period and eight heroes who personified the eight Confucian virtues). Between 1820 and 1828, Bakin repeatedly mentioned *Hokuetsu Seppu* and Bokushi in his books, publicity that delighted Bokushi. Nevertheless, the work remained in manuscript form.

Finally Kyoden's younger brother Kyozan came to the rescue. Claiming that he wanted to realize his brother's unfulfilled desire, he offered to get the work published under Bokushi's own name. Bokushi refused once out of regard for Bakin, a regard Kyozan did not share. Finally in 1830 Bokushi asked Bakin to return his manuscript. Bakin refused, and Bokushi had to write it over for the fifth time. Five years later, the first volume came off the presses. The entire work went on sale in the autumn of 1837 with a second edition containing additions and corrections following two years later. The

INTRODUCTION

book achieved unexpected popularity in Edo, so much so that all the lending houses began to stock it. In 1842, the publishers encouraged Bokushi to write a second volume, and he distributed advertisements to all his correspondents just before his death. In a last letter to Bakin, he stated that now he could die without regret.

Hokuetsu Seppu is Bokushi's creation, but without Kyozan's help, it probably never would have been published and read. As editor, Kyozan cleaned up Bokushi's style, put breaks in his sentences, and insisted that words in dialect be explained and readings given for obscure place names. He changed subheadings to make them intelligible and attract the reader's attention. Bokushi liked to use difficult Chinese words and phrases to show off his erudition; Kyozan had him use more Japanese expressions which were easier to understand, less elaborate, and more concrete. Kyozan also explained what had to be censored. Forbidden to print information about the affairs and activities of contemporary officials, Bokushi was forced to omit his depiction of a hunt in Nagaoka. The authorities also insisted that misinformation not be spread to the general public, and Kyozan repeatedly insisted that Bokushi check his facts.

Kyozan also influenced what went into the book. Mistakes in describing the climbing of Mount Naeba and the types of flowers to be found there were made by Kyozan, who never climbed a mountain in his life. Many pedantic allusions to the Chinese and Japanese classics were by Kyozan, who saw no need to hide his own scholarship. Kyozan also insisted that curiosities and marvels be included in the last chapters; the sophisticated urban audience expected these stories, especially in travelogues and books about faraway places. Indeed, in the last chapters, Kyozan included incidents from his own trip to the snow country that stand in sharp contrast to the tales told by Bokushi. The witty description of eating shaved ice with soybean powder, the humorous false etymology of *tempura,* the salacious tales of wolf transformations in China, and the lyrical story of the beautiful *eta* (outcaste), a flower on a dung heap, all convey the detached outlook of a man of the world.

For all his erudition, Bokushi was unaffectedly sincere in his desire to tell the world about the snow country. In both the Chinese and the

INTRODUCTION

Japanese classical tradition, snow was a rare event of great beauty, something to be admired and exclaimed over. The imperial court lady and essayist Sei Shonagon delighted in its sparkling white appearance. The shining prince Genji savored the contrast it provided to the usual rain of Kyoto winters. Centuries later, Edo merchants held banquets for enjoying freshly fallen snow. Well versed in this tradition, Bokushi had a different story to tell. In *Hokuetsu Seppu,* he tried to correct the urban appreciation of snow with his own description of the hardships it caused.

The central and unifying theme of *Hokuetsu Seppu* is snow. For eight months out of the year, the people of Echigo live buried under snow. In that particular area of Japan, cold winds blowing out of Siberia pick up great quantities of moisture as they move across the ocean. Trapped by the mountain ranges that form the backbone of Japan's main island, this moisture precipitates as snow. In contrast, the Pacific-coast side of Japan directly opposite this mountain barrier gets snow only on those rare occasions when the wind shifts from the west to the north. But for people in Echigo, the architecture of their houses, their culinary habits, their customs, their cottage industries, and their very psychology are determined by the necessity of surviving in a cold, hostile environment.

For the people of Echigo, snow is more than an implacable adversary. "Because there is snow, there is *chijimi* crepe." The making of this product brings an income and also beauty into the weavers' lives. In its service as a bleaching agent, snow becomes a friend. Children play in the snow, fashioning great castles and holding snowball contests. People everywhere take pleasure in the coming of spring, but who can rival the joy of people for whom spring brings liberation from months of darkness and misery? Bokushi described the different kinds of snow, the utensils people made to cope with it, and the entire circumstances of their lives bounded by snow. Here we have an encyclopedia of snow.

Bokushi also depicted the flora and fauna that inhabited the snow country. Like the Victorian naturalists, he based his descriptions of plant and animal life on empirical observation, and where he was not sure of his facts, he admitted as much to his readers. For this reason, he did not really believe that bears hibernated all winter because

INTRODUCTION

he knew of no one who had actually seen them do it. Yet he tried to find out what he could of their habits. He was considerably better informed on the life cycle of salmon, a fish he greatly admired. Foxes, geese, wolves, and insects all claimed his attention, making *Hokuetsu Seppu* an excellent barometer of the scientific knowledge available to the local intellectuals of his time.

Hokuetsu Seppu is a "natural history" of the snow country. Taken in its broadest nineteenth-century sense, natural history includes not only animals, plants, and minerals, but also local customs and human activities. Before modern science divided knowledge of the material world into geology, geography, biology, zoology, anthropology, and sociology, a man like Bokushi or the British naturalist Gilbert White would survey it all with equal rigor and interest. Both men were excellent field observers in that they tried to distinguish between things they had observed for themselves and were sure of, and things they had merely inferred or read about. Like his Victorian counterparts, Bokushi promised at the beginning of his book every form of weighty and improving instruction, but much of what he actually related was "fascinating facts, bizarre, curious, and extraordinary anecdotes, . . . long quotations from the poets, personal reminiscence, and pious homilies."[5] The reader was to be entertained as well as edified.

Bokushi studied plant and animal life primarily in its relation to the human world. His descriptions of natural phenomena were always followed by meditations on man in nature. Here was a man who never hunted or fished professionally in his life, yet he found it important to describe in detail just how these activities were performed. Not for him were romantic and largely false stories of man against beast. Some hunters and fishermen were brave, some were foolhardy, but none were sportsmen as we understand the term today. Bokushi judged not; he simply recorded what they did.

Bokushi had a wide field of vision and a coldly observant eye. Nowhere was this more evident than in his ethnographic description of Akiyama district and its inhabitants. To know how the people lived, what they wore, what they ate, and what they believed, he had to see them with his very own eyes. Neither trade nor pilgrimage justified going there; he just wanted to satisfy his curiosity. Like any

INTRODUCTION

good anthropologist, he closely questioned his hosts on their occupation, village administration and taxes, kinship, dialect, legends, and folklore. He wanted to know how houses were built, how agriculture was done, and what people did to worship their gods. The entire range of human activities fell under his purview.

Bokushi also practiced ethnology. He described the hall-pushing ceremony at Urasa not simply to titillate his readers with the sights and sounds of strange customs. Instead he wrote an accurate account of what happened so that this ritual could be compared to others. He preceded his depiction of the New Year's rites in Echigo by what happened in Edo, leading his largely urban audience from the familiar to the unknown. The whole focus of *Hokuetsu Seppu* is explicitly comparative—the difference between life in warm, comfortable climes and life in Echigo.

Bokushi was a thinker. Heretofore the writings of samurai intellectuals have often been translated and much scholarly effort has been devoted to analyzing and explaining the significance of their thought. With the exception of Ninomiya Sontoku (1787–1856) and Ishida Baigan (1685–1744), little attention has been paid to how people like Bokushi, who lived far from the centers of power and whose concerns were not with the intricacies of politics, tried to make sense of their world and their times. This bias has resulted in a view of Japanese history in which those of high position developed elaborate and sophisticated philosophies while the commoners worked hard but thought not at all. Yet Bokushi not only observed the world around him; he fitted it into a conceptual framework. He tried hard to understand what he saw.

Hokuetsu Seppu vividly displays the mind of an early nineteenth-century peasant entrepreneur. In the tradition of Kaibara Ekiken (1630–1714), whose interpretation of Neo-Confucianism emphasized the investigation of things, Bokushi possessed an overwhelming curiosity about the workings of the natural world and the relations of men and women in society. Little escaped his purview, from geological formations to festivals to the experiences of woodcutters. In his attempt to make sense of natural phenomena—snow, rain, and frost—he relied on observation and deductive reasoning. Like Ando Shoeki (1703–62), he then couched his explanations in terms of

INTRODUCTION

correspondences to develop a theory that would account for the world's diversity in the most parsimonious terms. While one might quibble with the details of his conclusions, the manner in which they were reached demonstrates a thoroughly rational and scientific approach to the study of nature, an approach characteristic of the most advanced thought of his times.

Bokushi had one foot in the intellectual camp of late-Tokugawa Japan and one foot in village culture. His education in the Japanese and Chinese classics led him to speculate on and investigate the natural forces that dominated his life. Nevertheless, much of the charm and interest of *Hokuetsu Seppu* comes from the stories about people, and these owe less to contemporary urban norms than to local legends and tales.

All sorts of people appear in the pages of *Hokuetsu Seppu*. Rich peasants, poor peasants, weavers, and hunters throng the book as they thronged the villages Bokushi knew best. For the specialist in folklore, *Hokuetsu Seppu* offers a wealth of information on local customs. Here we see how men cooperate in controlling floods, removing snow, and hunting bears. Yet each woman works alone in spinning and weaving cloth. Even within a single village or a single region, great differences exist in the way they lived their lives, differences that Bokushi sought out and exposed. Influenced by the great haiku poet Basho, Bokushi found pleasure in the minutiae of the world around him. In his concern for the reality of peasant life and customs, he can be seen as a precursor to the Japanese folklore specialist Yanagita Kunio (1875–1962).

Bokushi had a peasant's fatalism. He believed that human beings are naturally good, yet he knew that disasters might strike them without warning. He allowed himself to sympathize with the sufferings of the poor, and he was moved by the plight of those who lost their loved ones, but his stories were not lachrymose. This type of village realism, cruel and unsentimental, appeared in the original European folk tales before they were prettified for children. It signifies a dramatically different way of viewing the world from the modern emphasis which requires either a happy ending or a meaningful tragedy. Folk tales and the stories in *Hokuetsu Seppu* reflect the world of the peasant caught up in an endless struggle to wrest a living

INTRODUCTION

from nature. Modern stories reflect not merely the Christian hope that good will triumph over evil, but a belief in progress.

The stories in *Hokuetsu Seppu* are also quite different from the novels then circulating in Edo. They have nothing to do with the themes of urban literature—money, sex, and the conflict between obligation (*giri*) and human feeling (*ninjo*). This difference appears vividly in the story of the hunter who loses almost his entire family to wolves. Bokushi pulls no punches in relating what happened despite his sympathy for the hunter, but he draws no moral from the tale. In a section added by Kyozan, on the other hand, the emphasis shifts to thoughts on the connotations of wolf-ness. Kyozan ends with a didactic statement: "The wolfishness of man is far more terrible and hateful than that of real wolves." His moral is that one must be on guard against both. Bokushi knows better. Despite man's precautions, one cannot change the implacable nature of karma. What will be, will be.

Not all stories in *Hokuetsu Seppu* end in disaster. Liberated from custom, superstition, and fear, brave men, men willing to confront bears or the supernatural, survive. For himself, Bokushi emphasized restraint and temperance. Like the people around him, he passively accepted the dictates of his fate. But his heroes stood between the supernatural and the human world. The farmer who overcame divine punishment visited on the weaving girl he loved, the priest who confronted a ghost, and the porter who shared his lunch with a monster all exhibited superhuman sturdiness and toughness. Somehow they were able to break out of everyday life and confront the unknowable. They were active, dynamic, manly. In telling stories about them, peasants could vent their frustration at a restricted existence and enjoy vicariously the pleasures of action.

Monsters, demons, inexplicable natural phenomena, and marvels dot the pages of *Hokuetsu Seppu*. Bokushi himself exhibited a keen sensitivity to the divine presence in material objects. This feeling of respect and awe for the mysterious power of nature characterized the outlook of Edo-period Japanese whether they were samurai, merchant, or peasant. Everyone believed in the power of angry spirits (*onryo*). Therefore people in Nigoro Village were fated to remain illiterate because there was buried the minister who exiled

INTRODUCTION

Sugawara no Michizane, transformed into Tenjin, the god of writing. Men who called upon the power of the Buddha to aid them in their endeavors might very well succeed. The weaving women knew that they must not offend the god of the loom if they wanted to become renowned weavers. The gods were everywhere, and they had to be propitiated with amusing stories, festivals, and theatrical fun. Bokushi described how he and the people around him incorporated folk beliefs into the fabric of their everyday lives and in so doing, he disclosed his own reverence for the fearful power of nature.

Bokushi took great pride in the unique qualities of his region. He lamented the hardships suffered by people in Echigo, but he also celebrated the beauties and joys of living in the snow. He knew Edo well, its customs, fads, and literary circles. He also displayed a wide-ranging knowledge of Japanese and Chinese classical literature. To all of these he compared his homeland, placing its customs on the same plane as the great traditions of Asia. This kind of awakening to a strong consciousness of locality accompanied the regional economic and cultural development of the late Tokugawa period. Ultimately it led to an emphasis on particularity that constituted an important intellectual movement in nineteenth-century Japanese villages. Taken as a whole, *Hokuetsu Seppu* constitutes a monument to the provincial literary spirit and to the people whose energy created and supported it.

ANNE WALTHALL

NOTES

1. *Hokuetsu Seppu* has been reprinted many times during Japan's modern era. The most easily accessible versions are the Iwanami Bunko edition, number 30–226–1 and the edition published by Nojima Shuppan in Sanjo, Niigata Prefecture. The Iwanami version was first published by Iwanami Shoten in 1936. It was revised at its twenty-second printing in 1978 and has gone through four printings since. The Nojima edition was first issued in 1970 and has gone through fifteen printings. Both editions include valuable afterwords on Suzuki Bokushi and the writing of *Hokuetsu*

INTRODUCTION

Seppu. Minoru Takahashi's *Hokuetsu Seppu no Shiso* (Niigata: Etsu Shobo, 1981) contains a collection of articles on Bokushi's life, his relations with his wives and Edo literary figures, his beliefs, and the intellectual assumptions that inform his writings. All of Bokushi's writings have been published in *Suzuki Bokushi Zenshu*, 2 vols. (Tokyo: Chuo Koron Sha, 1983).

2. Matsuo Basho, *The Narrow Road to the Deep North*, translated by Yuasa Nobuyuki (Baltimore: Penguin Books, 1966), p. 130.

3. Work on the formation of provincial poetry circles has been published in two articles by Jin Sugi, "Kasei Ki no Shakai to Bunka," in *Tempo Ki no Seiji to Shakai: Koza Nihonshi* (Yuzankaku, 1981), and "Kinsei Makki Echigo Uonuma Chiho no Chiiki Kobunka Ken Shiryo: Horinouchi Mura, Yunodani Mura no Hogaku Kugo o Chushin Ni," in *Waseda Jitsugyo Gakko Kenkyu Kiyo*, 13 (1978).

4. For a fuller translation of this quotation, see my article, "Peripheries: Rural Culture in Tokugawa Japan," *Monumenta Nipponica* 39, no. 4 (Winter 1984): 384.

5. Lynn Barber, *The Heyday of Natural History 1820–1870* (London: Jonathan Cape, 1980), pp. 19, 43, 154.

BOOK ONE

How the Earth's Vapors Become Snow

The four kinds of precipitation that fall from heaven are rain, snow, sleet, and hail. Dew and frost do not fall, but form on earth. Dew is a tiny drop of the earth's vapors, and frost is a frozen crystal of the same; one or the other forms, depending upon the temperature. Rain, snow, sleet, or hail are formed when the vapors of the earth rise into the heavens. When any of these are warmed, they become water, and since the earth is made entirely of water, all of these forms of precipitation eventually return to the earth from which they originally derived.

Now the earth is very deep, and there is warm air in its depths that heats it, causing it to give off vapors which rise to heaven just as a person's breath does. This process never ceases for a moment, day or night. Heaven also gives off vapors, sending them down to earth. This is the breathing of heaven and earth, which is just like the inhaling and exhaling of a human being. The breathing of heaven and earth produces and nurtures all existence. Occasionally heaven and earth become ill, their breathing becomes irregular, and we are subjected to unseasonal hot and cold, typhoons and downpours, and all sorts of other natural calamities.

Heaven is divided into nine levels, and these are called the Nine Heavens. The one closest to the earth is called the Moon Heaven.

It begins roughly 1,180,000 miles from the earth's surface. There are three zones between the earth and the lower limit of the Moon Heaven. Closest to the Moon Heaven is a hot zone, with a cold zone below it and a warm zone nearest the earth. The vapors of the earth extend only as far as the cold zone; they never reach the hot zone. Neither the warm zone nor the cold zone extends very far above the earth's surface. Mount Fuji, for example, reaches beyond the warm zone and approaches the cold zone, which is why the peak is never tempered by warmer air and vegetation doesn't grow there—even in summer it's cold. Thunderstorms and violent rains are quirks of the warm zone and only occur there.

Clouds are produced by the warm vapors given off by the earth, which is why they are shaped like steam—they are formed just as steam is formed when we boil a kettle. Because they are products of warm air, clouds rise. When they reach the cold zone they lose their warmth and become rain, just as steam, when cooled, condenses into droplets. (Clouds which do not reach the cold zone disperse without turning into rain.) If it is very cold when clouds reach the cold zone and they are just about to turn into rain, they may freeze instead and fall to earth as ice particles. The size of these ice particles depends upon the degree of cold. This is the origin of sleet and hail. (Large hail sometimes falls in summer, when it is warm, but I will not discuss that here.)

When the earth is exceedingly cold, its vapors may rise to heaven without taking any form, like the weak steam rising from barely warm water. This results in an overcast sky. As these formless vapors rise and collect in great amounts, the sky becomes gray, and snow prepares to fall. These "formless clouds" first rise to the cold zone and condense into rain. But since the cold zone is not quite cold enough to completely freeze the rain, the vapor falls in the form of flowery powder. This is snow. Whether the vapor becomes ice or snow depends upon the degree of cold, just as the thickness of ice on earth does.

The principle of the three zones is apparent in human physiology as well: our skin is warm, our muscles cold, and our internal organs hot. The production and nurture of all things in the atmosphere is dependent upon the vapors of heaven and earth. None of this is my personal discovery; it is an ancient explanation that I have seen in several works.

Shapes of Snowflakes

There is a limit to the power of our eyesight, beyond which we cannot see. Thus, when we observe snow with the naked eye, it looks like goose down; actually, however, hundreds of snowflakes make up each single downy "feather." When we examine snow under a magnifying glass, the shapes of these creations of the heavens are wonderful and marvelous, as my illustration shows.

The reason each snowflake is different is that the conditions of the the cold zone, in which the snowflakes are formed, are not uniform, and snowflakes form in different shapes in response to these conditions. But because snowflakes are such tiny things that they cannot be seen by the naked eye, today's snow cannot be told from yesterday's, all misty white.

My illustration is based on Lord Kyoroku's work *Illustrations of Snowflakes* of 1832. I have copied it from the fifty-five drawings in that work. Snowflakes are hexagonal: Lord Kyoroku explains that "all square bodies consist of eight parts and all round bodies of six; there can be no disputing this principle," and this is the reason snow has long been known as "six-petaled flowers." Now, it is my humble opinion that roundness is the proper form of heavenly things, while squareness is the true nature of things of this earth, and thus all the myriad living things existing in the flux of the vital forces of heaven and earth are a combination of roundness and squareness. The human body, for example, is square and not square, round and not round. This is because we live between the round heavens and the square earth. Just as a child resembles its parents, our form is modeled after the forms of heaven and earth.

Snowflakes are six-sided because, being made up of water, they are yin, and even numbers are yin while odd numbers are yang. The body

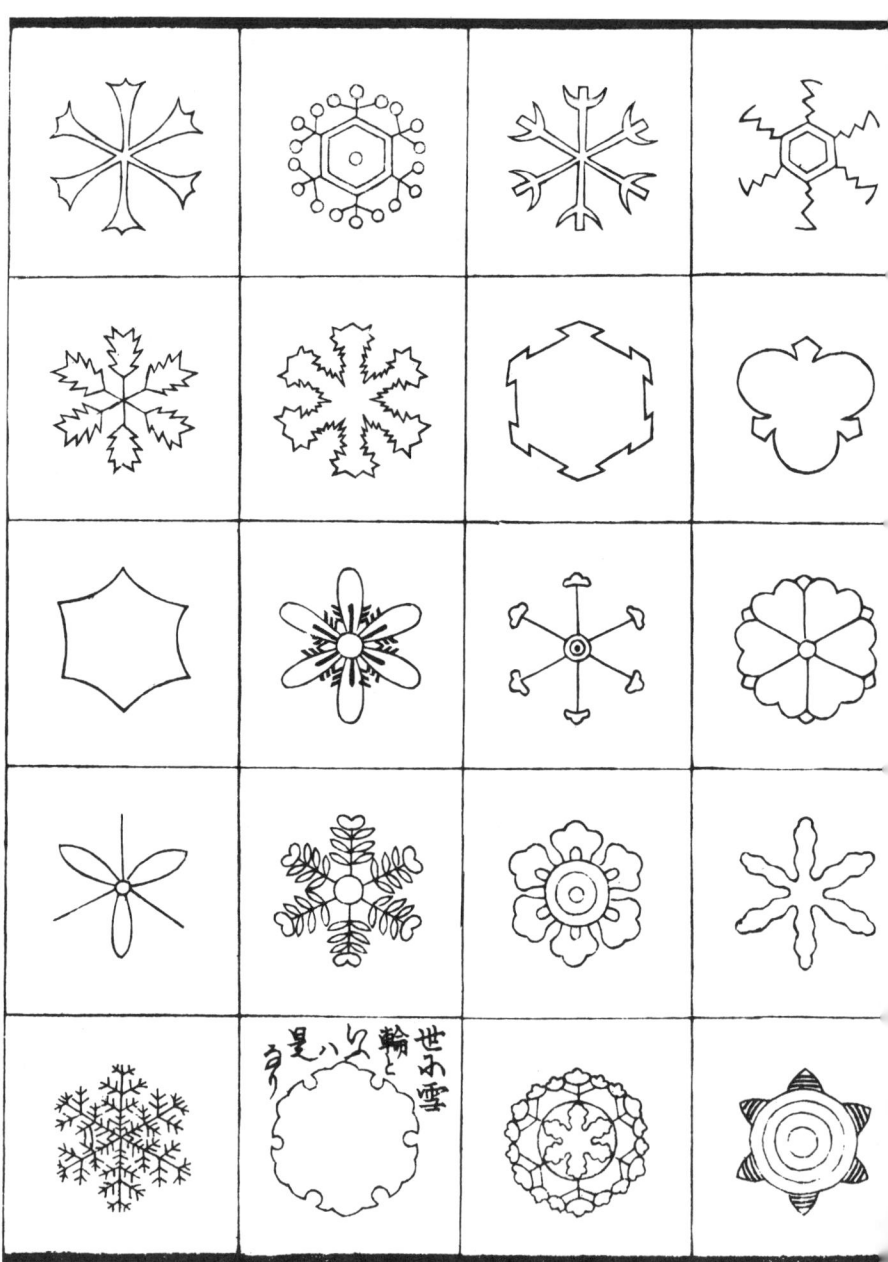

The shapes of snowflakes seen with a magnifying glass.

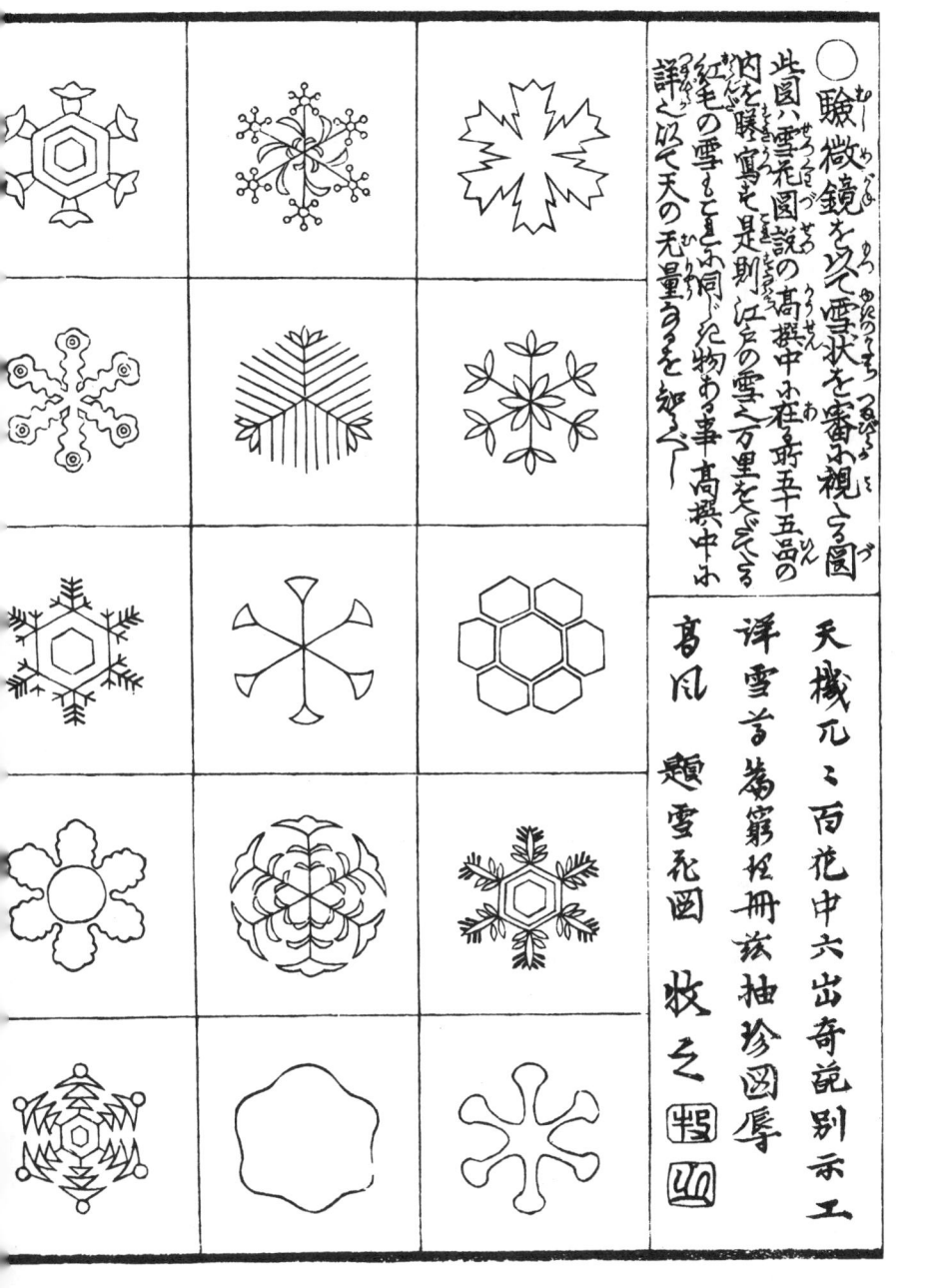

○験微鏡を以て雪状を審ふ視る圖
此圖ハ雪花圖説の高撰中に在る所五十五品の
内を撰ひて是を別に江戸の雪之万里を下てる
紅毛の雪をことく洞ある事高撰中ふ
詳さ以て天の无量うるを知る

天機元之百花中六出奇説別示工
詳雪者爲窮柁冊兹抽珍圖厚
高風　題雪花圖　牧之

of the human male is yang, for it has nine protruberances: the head, two ears, the nose, two arms, two legs, and the penis. The human female has ten—she lacks a penis but has two breasts. Nine is an odd number and thus yang; ten is even and yin. People are a combination of yin and yang, however, so men have two nipples, in the fashion of the female, yin principle (though they don't produce milk), and women have the clitoris, after the fashion of the male, yang principle (though it doesn't produce sperm). All things that move within the influences of the vital forces of heaven and earth follow this principle, without exception.

Snow is not a living thing, but since it does transform and change, it, too, possesses the vital force of activity; thus within many of the hexagonal-shaped yin flakes are rounded portions, after the yang principle. Water is the most yin substance. Yet when a single drop falls, it always creates a round splash. In the activity of falling it takes on the active, yang nature and cannot help but adopt a round shape.

How wonderful indeed is the rule and rank of each and every phenomenon in the atmosphere between heaven and earth; I could never describe them all.

The Amount of Snowfall

Zuo's Commentary on *The Spring and Autumn Annals* refers to a snowfall of one foot in the eighth year of the reign of Duke Yin as a great snowfall because the land of Wu in which it fell was warm in climate. And the remark of the Tang poet Han Yu that snow is the omen of a prosperous year also applies only to a warm land, though *The Five Miscellanies* records that cold regions of the Tang empire saw snow as early as November. When snow falls in these warmer lands, it never amounts to over a foot. The mountains, rivers, towns, and villages are all transformed into a silvery world; entranced by the dancing snowflakes, people liken them to blossoms and jewels. They delight in the lovely landscape, arrange for feasting and music, and amuse themselves by painting pictures and composing poetry on the theme of snow. There are records of many such snow parties in both Japan and China, but these are only pleasures in lands where snow is scarce. What enjoyment is there of snow for us in Echigo, where foot after foot falls year after year? We exhaust ourselves and our purses, undergo a thousand pains and discomforts, all because of the snow. The great extent of our sufferings will be revealed to you as this work unfolds.

Signs of Snow

The signs of snowfall hereabouts are quite unlike those in warmer regions. As a rule, the first frost comes in October. After that it grows colder and colder, and by the end of the month an icy wind chills our bones and tears the withered leaves from the trees. The sky remains a leaden color, and day after day passes without ever seeing the sun's light. These are the signs of snow on the way.

After several days of continuing gloomy weather, spots of white begin to show themselves on the peaks of mountains near and far. This is called "visiting the peaks" (*take mawari*) in the local dialect. In places near the coast, the sea roars, and inland the mountains rumble with a sound like distant thunder. This is called "rumbling bowels" (*do nari*). When we see and hear these signs, we know that snow is not far away. The time varies depending upon the warmth of the year, but visiting the peaks and rumbling bowels occur each year at around the time of the autumnal equinox.

Preparations for the Snowfall

When, observing the signs mentioned above, we know that snow is about to fall, all the weak spots of the house are reinforced to prevent damage. The roof, roof beams, pillars, and eaves (the eaves in front of the house are called in our local dialect *roka,* the same word used for passageways inside the house) and every other part are reinforced and supported so that they will not be crushed under the snow. The branches of the smaller garden trees are gathered and bound tightly together; the limbs of larger trees are strengthened by supports made of cedar or bamboo stakes. Plants that live through the winter must be wrapped and covered with straw mats. A hut is built over the well, and the toilet prepared in such a way that it can be emptied during the long time snow is on the ground.

There isn't so much as a single vegetable during the snow season, so each family must prepare sufficient provisions to last the winter. To keep these supplies from freezing, they are buried in the ground or wrapped in straw and placed in wooden tubs for protection. But as I begin my account I realize that there are so many other things that must be done in preparation for the snow that I can't hope to relate them all here; instead, I will present them one by one in the episodes that follow.

The First Snow

The people of friendlier climates take pleasure in the snow. In Edo, where some years it doesn't snow at all, the first snow is regarded as especially delightful. People set out in little boats, accompanied by geisha, to watch the snow; important guests are invited to tea ceremonies held in the snow; the brothels use the snow as an excuse to encourage their patrons to spend the night; and the restaurants and bars regard snow as an omen of many customers. It is difficult to count the many entertainments in the snow that have been devised. But the great degree to which the snow is celebrated in Edo is a mark of that city's great plenty. The people of the snow country can't help but be envious when they see and hear these things. The difference between the first snow in Edo and our first snow is the difference between pleasure and pain, clouds and mud.

Now Echigo is a northern, yin land, but within its immediate surroundings this effect is reversed. The northwest is regarded as a yin direction and the southeast as yang, but Echigo faces the great sea on the northwest, which tempers the bitter cold, and thus yang energies prevail in that direction; southeastern Echigo is bounded by high mountain ranges, which keep the cold in, and yin dominates there. Because of this odd reversal of the principles of yin and yang, the northwestern districts have less snow, while in the southeast the snow is very deep.

The district of Uonuma where I live is in the southeastern, yin region. Makihatayama, Naebasan, Hakkaisan, Ushigatake, Kinjosan, Komagatake, Usagigatake, Asakusayama, and many other tall mountains and peaks unheard of in other lands range through the southeast like the crests of great waves. Large and small rivers crisscross the area, and the yin energy prevails all about. Since the villages in this area are perched in snow-covered mountain valleys, one can easily imagine how deeply buried in snow they become.

As the sun circles to the south in the winter, our northern land grows even colder. (The same principle can be observed inside a house: the northern side is colder than the southern side.) Although the date of the first snow in Echigo depends upon each year's weather and is not fixed, it usually falls toward the end of October or the beginning of November. The snow in Echigo is not feathery but always powdery in form and easily blown into drifts by the winds. Six, seven, or even ten feet of snow may accumulate at certain places in a single day. From ancient times until the present day, there has never been a year when such snows have failed to fall, and we cannot even in our dreams imagine watching the first snowfall, celebrating and commemorating it in pretty verses as the people of warmer lands do. "Another year under the snow!"—that's the sad thought with which we who were born in this frigid land greet the first snowfall. Are we to be blamed if we're envious of the heavenly blessings of those in prosperous, warm lands who delight at the sight of snow?

The Depth of the Snow

An acquaintance with whom I sometimes exchange poems, the venerable Tenkichi who resides in the neighboring post town

Muikamachi, heard the following anecdote when he was in Tsumari. A certain man of learning living near the Chikuma River measured the amount of snow that accumulated from the first snowfall in 1834 until January 25 of the next year. Each time snow fell he measured its depth in a set place and found that in the end a total of 180 feet had fallen! This is hard even for inhabitants of the snow country to believe, but a bit of reflection shows that if, in the some eighty days between the first snowfall in November and January 25, 5 feet of snow fall per day, 400 feet of snow would have accumulated. Records tell us that 1834 saw an extraordinary snowfall, so we would do well to believe this report.

The actual accumulation of snow cannot be observed in places where snow is cleared after each fall, of course, and it must also be remembered that snow packs as it settles on the ground. It is not difficult to imagine, then—though it may be hard to believe!—the great depth of snow that falls and piles up in the deep mountains and valleys, where many of Echigo's hamlets and towns are nestled.

Snow Poles

In the open square before the main gate of Takata Castle stands a square timber marked at one-foot intervals. This is called a snow pole. It is ten feet tall. Taxes in Takata were once regulated partly by the depth of the snow each year, which is why this snow pole was erected. A letter from my acquaintance Fusekishi, a fellow poet in Takata, reports that in midwinter of 1834 a look at the snow pole showed that more than ten feet had already fallen.

Mention of snow poles as a peculiarity of Echigo appears even in haiku, but aside from this one in Takata, we have no such snow poles, at least today; I cannot vouch for the past. Those who travel to our land for pleasure come only during the three summer months and are careful to avoid the snow. They know nothing of our winters, and when they speak knowingly of the snows of Echigo in poetry and whatnot they make all sorts of mistakes—such as silly blather about snow poles—that only give us cause to laugh.

BOOK ONE

Clearing the Snow

Japanese and Chinese poems often wax lyrical about the elegance of "brushing off the snow," comparing it with "brushing off the fallen flower petals." But clearing away the huge snowfalls of our land is a far from elegant task.

If we let the first fall of snow accumulate undisturbed, the next snowfall will leave us buried under more than ten feet of snow. One snowfall, one snow clearing, that's our rule. (Only if the snowfall is very light do we wait for the next one to get to work.) In our dialect we call this activity "snow digging," because it is no different from digging up earth. We usually dig the snow after each snowfall, counting "the first digging, the second digging," and so on. Unless we dig the snow immediately, the entrances to our houses will be blocked and the houses themselves soon buried in snow, with not the tiniest hole for us to get out! Every family without exception digs away the snow, for no matter how strongly built their house might be, there is always the danger that it will collapse under the weight of its burden of tons and tons of snow.

For digging snow, we use a wooden snow shovel we call a *kosuki*, or wooden spade. It is made out of beech, a light, strong wood, so it is easy to handle and does not break; it resembles an ordinary spade, but the blade is broader. This is the most important tool for life in the snow. People living in the mountains make them and sell them in the towns, and no house is without a supply of them.

I have included an illustration of snow digging, but the number of people engaged in the task has been greatly reduced by the artist. The snow that is dug away is carried to unused land where it will not be in the way, and there it collects in huge mountains that we call *hori age,* or snow piles. Big, prosperous families with large houses and many outbuildings often don't have enough hands to clear all their roofs and hire dozens of shovelers to clear the snow all at once. Speed is so important because if a large snowfall comes before the first snow is cleared away, you will find yourself hopelessly buried, and the task of clearing two snowfalls is nearly beyond human powers. But only the more prosperous families can afford to hire others to help them dig out. This is an impossible luxury for smaller, poorer

Walking in snowshoes (*above, left*); clearing snow from a rooftop (*above, right*); snow gear (*below*).

Snow digging.

households, where everyone pitches in, men and women alike.

And this is how it is, not only in my village, but wherever huge amounts of snow fall. The snow consumes our energy, it eats up our wealth. At the end of a long day one looks back at the places that have been dug out; that night a great snow falls again, and at dawn everything is buried anew. The master of the house and his servants awake and look out at the scene of yesterday's labors; all they can do then is hang their heads and let out a deep sigh.

Foam Snow

The spring snow of warmer lands disappears quickly, so people call it foam snow, likening it to the ephemeral froth on the waves. The fleeting existence of foam snow is often a theme of Japanese and Chinese poetry, but again, the poets speak of the snow of warm climes. The winter snow of cold regions can also be called foam snow, but for the following reason: no matter how much falls it does not freeze, remaining as soft as foam—or more precisely, mud. The only way to walk through this winter snow is to wear snowshoes. In fact, the expression in our dialect for walking through the snow is "paddling through the snow" (*yuki o kogu*)—because it very much resembles paddling across water or slogging through the muck of a flooded rice paddy. By spring the snow freezes and the paths are all as if paved with stone. Travel becomes much easier than in winter; we drive nails into the soles of the wooden clogs we wear to keep ourselves from slipping and sliding. At any rate, our foam snow, which falls in winter, is just the opposite of the foam snow of warmer lands.

Roads in the Snow

The winter snow is soft, and it is usually easy to follow the well-trodden paths that others have made. But when a great snow falls overnight, all paths are buried. A traveler who wakes after a night's lodging may find his road erased; it is especially hard to get one's bearings in open terrain, as everything is covered in white. On these occasions some travelers employ a number of villagers to go out and tramp down the roads with snowshoes so that they may follow in the well-trodden wake, but this amounts to considerable expense, and travelers who cannot afford to hire such help must often spend many empty hours waiting for the roads to be opened. Even strong-legged couriers can only walk five or ten miles a day through the snow because they are hindered by their snowshoes and the snow that comes up to their knees. This is one of the great inconveniences of the winter snows.

But when the snow freezes hard as iron in the spring, sleds (written with the Chinese characters meaning snow car, or sometimes, snow boat) can be used to get about and even to carry heavy loads. Villagers pile the sleds high with goods and ride on top of them, sailing over the snow as if on ships—they even speak of the sled paths as the "courses" of their "snow boats." I will describe the construction of sleds in another place, but suffice it to say that there are many kinds, large and small. The large type are called *shura*. Since the snow won't support the hooves of oxen or horses, sleds do a great service and are much better for carrying goods through the spring snows than beasts of burden could ever be. All in all, sleds are one of the greatest conveniences for life in the snow, though even they are of no use until the snow freezes hard in the spring.

Buried Under the Snow

Snow usually begins to fall toward the end of October, and we greet the spring still buried up to our necks. It is especially deep in February and March; gradually the snow begins to melt in April and May, and by June it has disappeared and the summer roads are visible. The flowers of spring all bloom at once, during May and June. All in

Life buried under the snow.

all, we spend almost eight months of every year under the snow. Only four months are completely without it, and for half of each year we are wholly buried beneath it.

Thus the construction of our houses and, indeed, all things is directed by the need to keep out the snow. It is impossible to record with brush and paper the resources and labor devoted to this task. Farmers must grow their crops in the short time between the beginning of summer and the end of autumn. They are often cutting rice stalks in the snow. The trials and pains of their urgent efforts must be at least one hundred times those of farmers in warmer regions. But those who live in the snow country were born and raised in the snow and, like the beetle that feeds on bitteroot and doesn't know its sharp taste, they think nothing of snow because they have never sampled the easy life of warmer places. Yes, home is where the heart is. All women feel this way, and even most of the men who spend several years' service in prosperous Edo return to their home in Echigo when they've completed their term. "The Mongol horse neighs when the north wind blows, and the bird from the warm land of Yue builds its nest in the tree's southern branch," says the old Chinese saying about homesickness. Longing for one's place of birth is felt the world over.

During the snowy season we hang snow blinds from the eaves that surround our homes and from the window frames. Like the shop blinds of Edo, they are woven from miscanthus reeds. But unlike shop blinds, their purpose is to protect us from blizzard winds. When the snow isn't falling, they are rolled up to let the light in. But when snow falls for any length of time it soon reaches as high as the roofs of the houses, and there is no light to be had whatever we may do; it's pitch black even at noon, and oil lamps must be burned all day. One loses track of day and night during these unceasing snows. When it finally stops and enough can be dug away so that a tiny window can at last be opened—then oh! the brightness that greets our eyes makes us feel as if we were suddenly born into a shining Buddha world!

There are many other hardships in this life trapped under the snow, too many to relate here. Most birds and animals leave the

BOOK ONE

region for places where the snow is not so deep, for otherwise they would be without food. The only creatures that remain to pass their days under the snow are men and bears, dogs and cats.

Creeping Through the Snow Womb

In the post towns that are the stopping points along the government routes, the eaves of the houses large and small extend far out from the roofs. They serve as protected passageways when the snow is deep, and since the streets of the town are no longer necessary, the snow cleared from the roofs of houses is allowed to accumulate there, saving the work of hauling it far away. It gradually piles up until it becomes a great wall of snow dividing the houses on opposite sides of the street. We build tunnels through the wall and pass from eaves to eaves in comfort. The tunnels are called "womb tunnels" in our dialect. They are also called *mabu,* a word borrowed from gold miners' parlance meaning side tunnel. (*Mabu* originally meant a woman's secret love affair.)

In settlements other than post towns, where the houses are not connected by eaves, the inhabitants use the rising and falling snow wall in the streets as their passageway, treading down a single path on its crest to make it easier to walk. When spring comes and the snow hardens, we hew rude steps shaped like boxes piled one on top of the other into the snow wall so we can cross over it. We're quite used to scrambling up and down these snow stairways without ever making a false step, but travelers from afar find them quite frightening, and sometimes lose their balance and take a tumble—only to find themselves buried in a snowdrift. When this happens everyone laughs—except the victim, who naturally loses his temper. But of course these difficult passageways are not built simply to give visitors from more fortunate climates a hard time. Removing the snow entirely would require so much effort and expense that these terraces are built as a less laborious way of keeping the roads open.

SNOW COUNTRY TALES

Floods in the Snow

After the first snowfall, villages near rivers and streams often suffer from floods, which are called *mizu agari* (rising water) hereabouts. Once at about the beginning of November, when eight or nine feet of snow were on the ground, I was staying with a relative, an oil vendor, in the neighboring village of Seki. Suddenly one night at midnight we were awakened by the shouts and calls of people nearby. "What could it be?" I wondered, my heart pounding. Leaping out of bed I saw the master of the house running about carrying things in both hands.

"Quick! The water's rising! Escape to the snow mound behind the house!" he shouted over his shoulder as he ran with his bundles up the stairs to the second story.

When I dashed to the kitchen to see what was going on, every member of the household was racing about grabbing whatever they could carry, lest the household goods be swept away by the approaching flood waters, which were crawling over the low spots on the ground like a tide, creeping higher and higher. They had already soaked the tatami mats, and the garden in front of the house was flooded. Though it was still early winter, a great deal of snow had already accumulated, and the ground was covered with a heavy blanket. Outside, the light of the white snow shone through the dark night with an eerie glow that illuminated the rushing waters, a scene altogether too frightening for words.

The others helped me to escape to an elevated place. From there, looking down on the distant village, we could see a long procession of men carrying lanterns and pine torches, each man with a wooden shovel in his hand. Wading through the sea of water and snow, they approached, shouting. These were the people whom the flood had not yet reached, hurrying our way to cut an opening for the dammed water in order to release it and allow it to subside.

As the night was rather dark, I could not make out their figures, but I could hear the pathetic voices of women and children crying and calling, now nearer, now farther. In the light of the torch he held aloft I could see a man floundering about with a horse, both of them up to their necks in water. Looking closer I realized that the man was trying to lead his horse through the wild current of the flood waters.

In another place, much closer at hand, I observed a woman, kimono untied, clutching a child to her back with one hand and holding a lantern in the other as she tried to climb to higher ground. When lives are at risk, modesty is a luxury. How could I ever describe the many scenes I witnessed that night, some humorous, but most of them terrible and tragic? Only with the arrival of the morning did the flood waters recede and people rest easy again.

In my village, these floods usually take place in either early winter or midspring. In Seki, there are little streams in front of the houses on either side of the main street. They flow into the Uono River. Even during the hottest days of summer these streams run cool and clear. All the families along the street use these streams as their source of water instead of the usual wells. Since clean water can be scooped up by the bucketful anytime from just beyond their doorsteps, these streams are more convenient than a well could ever be. After the first new snow, however, the streams are blocked and buried by snow. To insure their winter supply of water, then, each family digs a hole through the snow cover just big enough to dip a bucket and fetch water. Since the hole is frequently buried again in a night's snowfall, it has to be reopened regularly. This happens even to the small freshets in front of people's houses in town. It is only too easy to imagine what occurs when the major springs of the region are blocked at their sources—not only do the villagers lose their water supply, but they are exposed to the dangers of flooding. Therefore the local people unite their efforts to keep the sources of these streams open.

But with everyone busily engaged in earning a living, the springs sometimes go untended. And if it should happen that during a night's snowfall a certain spring becomes blocked with new-fallen snow, the water is diverted from its usual pathway and rushes into whatever low spots there may be before anyone has a chance to prevent it. Unfortunately, since the snow in the village is well trodden by people coming and going, it is often the lowest place around, so the overflowing springs send water rushing into villagers' homes with the catastrophic results described above. If the blocked waterway is not speedily reopened, often requiring the labor of hundreds, households will be swept away and people drowned.

The flood in the snow at Seki.

The floods in March usually take place around the vernal equinox. At that time, of course, the snow has not yet melted and the slopes and fields as far as the eye can see are still blanketed in white. All the smaller waterways remain hidden beneath the snow, flowing out of sight. Even the largest rivers become frozen snow fields in the depths of winter. This is how it happens: as it begins to get cold, the water along the river banks gradually freezes into ice sheets, on which snow collects after each fall. The snow freezes hard as rock, and as it gathers throughout the long winter, layer on layer, the opposite banks grow closer and closer to each other until they meet and form a solid frozen field of snow arching over the river. With the approach of spring and the lessening of the cold, snow stops falling—usually in about March. Because water responds to temperature changes more quickly than does land, the frozen snow field over the river begins to melt from underneath, where it is in contact with water. First the snow just above the river's rushing surface begins to soften. It falls into the river, the channel grows narrower, and the water flows ever more fiercely. Burrowing through the snow with increasing strength and speed, the river finally comes bursting through its snow crust with all the power of a deluge breaking through a dam.

An old saying, "Like water poured in sleeping ears," means that something terribly unpleasant has happened. The floods of the snow country are surely an extreme and literal case of this, and one that deserves the sympathy of those from warmer climes. I have recorded here only one such disaster. Many variations can and do occur, depending on the lay of the land. It would be difficult to recount or even imagine them all.

Hunting Bears in the Snow

The northwest of Echigo is bordered by the sea and has no mountains. The southeast is crossed by a chain of precipitous peaks that span the five provinces of Etchu, Kozuke, Shinano, Mutsu, and Dewa. This range stretches for miles and miles, one towering summit after

BOOK ONE

another, and countless wild animals dwell there. When winter approaches, some travel to other provinces to escape the snow and some do not, but only the bear holes up for the winter in a cave beneath the snow.

The gall bladder of Echigo bears is considered the best, and the gall of bears in their dens under the snow brings the greatest reward. In hopes of obtaining this rare treasure, groups of five to seven hunters regularly set out from the neighboring province of Dewa as the warmth of spring approaches and snow stops falling. Taking rice, salt, and pots and pans, they lead small packs of hunting dogs. The water and firewood in the fastnesses is theirs to make free use of as they rove from mountain to mountain, living on the game they hunt each day; their nights are spent in the shelter of the roots of large trees or in caves, where they burn green wood to stave off the cold and for light. They sleep fully clothed, and from head to foot they dress entirely in garments made from animal skins. From afar they look like monkeys with human faces. The phrase "with saddle and blade for a pillow" certainly applies to these hunters, whose prey is the Echigo bear.

When the hunters from Dewa have penetrated deep into our mountains they choose a suitable place to build a temporary shelter, which they construct from tree branches bound together with wisteria vines. Then they separate, each with his dogs, and rove in all four directions searching for bears. When one finds a bear cave he marks the spot and returns to camp, gathering the other hunters to join in an attack on the beast.

Their hunting tools consist of a spear with a shaft about four feet long and a mountain axe resembling a halberd, as well as some kind of gun, a mountain knife, and a hatchet. When the blades of their tools grow dull, they sharpen them with the whetstone they are always careful to pack. All of the tools have sheathes made out of animal skins. Hunters such as these do not only venture out in the spring; some even go up into the mountains in the winter.

The bear is the lord of all the beasts of Japan. He is brave and virtuous. He lives on nuts and berries, tree bark, and insects, and never eats animal flesh. The bear will not ravage farmer's fields: when, rarely, that does happen, it is only because he can find no other food. According to *The Book of Songs* the bear is a good omen for the male sex. Elsewhere, he is called General Six Excellences because he is a virtuous creature.

In addition to searching for food in summer, the bear also gathers quantities of mountain ants, which he grinds into a nutritious paste between his paws and licks in his cave in winter to stave off hunger. Male and female bears do not retire to the same cave, but females with cubs take their offspring with them into their dens. Bears may hibernate in huge hollow trees that have been broken by avalanches, or in holes among rocks, or in fact wherever they please, making it difficult to predict their exact whereabouts.

The gall bladders obtained from bears in the snow are one hundred times superior to those of summer because, as mentioned above, bears abstain from eating in the winter. In Echigo we distinguish bear gall according to color: yellow, amber, or black. Among these, amber gall is the best and black gall the least desirable. In fact, much that is sold as black gall is not genuine bear gall at all.

There are several methods for catching bears. Which one is used depends upon the site at which the bear is found. As a rule, the bear retreats to his den about one month after the autumnal equinox and does not come out until about one month after the vernal equinox. Some say that until the day of his reappearance the bear falls into one long sleep, but since no one has witnessed this it is difficult to accept.

The foam snow of winter is soft and difficult to walk in, and so the hunters prefer to set out as the vernal equinox approaches, just before the bear leaves his hideaway—for the surface of the snow is frozen hard then. To catch bears hiding in caves at the foot of cliffs or in the roots of great trees, the hunters use a method called flattening. A platform of sorts is built out of branches and wisteria vines and propped against the bear's den like a lean-to: the edge of the platform closer to the den's mouth is held up with supports attached to crosspieces and the end farther from the den is anchored with stakes. Heavy rocks are then heaped on top of it. From one of the crossbeams, just before the entrance to the den, hangs a rope noose called a trigger that springs the trap.

After the trap is finished, the hunters burn peppers and tobacco leaves, two odors that bears can't abide, and fan the smoke into the cave. Choking and angry, the bear comes rushing out, gets caught in the noose, and springs the trap. The shelf collapses and the bear dies, smashed beneath the heavy stones. This is an excellent means of catching bears without even dirtying one's hands, but it can only be used successfully when the bear's den is located in a suitable place.

Hunters who are especially experienced and daring may station a party in front of the bear's den. One hunter, clothed from the head down in a sedge cape called *hiroro mino* (*hiroro* is the name of a mountain grass; capes made of it are lighter than straw and so preferred by hunters), enters the cave, crawling deeper and deeper, until he is behind the bear. He prods the bear lightly with the prickly sedge grasses, causing the bear to move forward. Again the hunter tickles from behind with the sedge grass, and the bear advances farther. This happens again and again until the bear reaches the entrance of the cave. The moment he becomes visible, the other hunters who have been waiting with spears ready rush upon the bear and stab him. If a hunter misses his mark, though, the bear can easily end his life with a single swipe of his paw.

A man exposes himself to so much danger hunting bears, and all for the love of a little money. Yes, greed undoes many more than lust. Those who long for gold should seek it through proper means, and not attempt to gain it wrongly.

Some bears find a protected spot where no snow has fallen and dig a hole there into the earth. During the winter, snow drifts to some three to five feet over the opening, offering protection from the cold. A small hole in the snow shaped like a tube is always found at the den's entrance. This is created by the warm air the bear exhales. When hunters discover such a den they break through the snow cover and push twigs or grass into the entrance. If the bear pulls the grass into the den, the hunters know he's home. They repeat this until the opening is entirely blocked and the bear comes rushing out. At that moment they stab the bear with their spears. When the hunting dogs see that the bear has been bloodied, they leap on it in one biting, snarling pack. Dogs and men working together finally bring the beast down. This method is also used when bears are found hibernating in hollow trees.

According to the mountain villagers, a horrible storm visits the mountain whenever two or three bears are killed—or even one, if he is old and venerable. We call this a bear's rage. For this reason the farmers of the mountain villages do not hunt bears for pleasure. We even see accounts in ancient records of the spiritual powers of bears.

A White Bear

As snow is white, bears are black. But though that's the immutable law of nature, sometimes the Lord of Heaven plays a trick and sends us a white bear.

In 1832, a woodcutter from Okura Village of Urasa Post Town in Uonuma County where I live went up to Mount Hakkai and somehow captured a little white bear alive. Realizing what a rarity it was, he kept the bear for some time. Later a carnival showman bought it and put it on display at markets and festivals and wherever people gathered. I saw it at one such place.

It was the size of a dog, but the exact figure of a bear. Its white fur was like snow, with a beautiful luster, shining like velvet. Its eyes and claws were crimson. It was so very tame and lovable. The showman toured all around with the little fellow, and I never learned what became of him.

The era name was changed upon the discovery and presentation of a white turtle at court; a white bird is a blessed omen; the god Hachiman's doves are white, as was the flag of the victorious Minamoto clan. Since all white things are blessed omens for our empire, should Heaven see fit to produce a white bear it can only be a fortunate omen of a long era of peace.

Saved by a Bear

One comes across accounts in various books of people who fell into holes and were saved by bears, but first-hand accounts are rare, so let me relate the following story.

When I was younger, I once had business in Tsumari and stayed there two or three days. Since it was summer, straw mats were spread beneath the trees of the garden of the guest quarters, a cool place to relax. The master was quite fond of drink and set out sake and food. Since I don't drink sake, I was holding a cup of tea when an old man passed by. Seeing the master, he bowed deeply and began to head for the garden in back of the house. The master called out for him to stop. Pointing at the old man he said, "This old fellow was saved by a bear once, in his younger days. And thanks to that bear, who saved him from a dangerous scrape, he's lived a long and healthy eighty-two years."

The old man smiled and once again tried to escape. But I called him back. "Saved by a bear? That's a strange story. Tell me about it." At that the master took the teacup that had been sitting before me, filled it to the brim with sake, and offered it to the old fellow: "First down a cup," he said. The old man sat at the corner of our straw mat and with a gleeful smile drank down three cups. Smacking his lips happily, he began, "Well, let me tell you."

"It was in March of my twentieth year. I went into the mountains to collect firewood, pulling a sled behind me. Near the village, all the wood had already been cut, or else the footing was bad and the wood out of reach. But after I crossed a ridge of mountains I found plenty of wood and cut as much as I wished. Singing a sled song I bundled up the firewood without more ado and packed it on the sled. Then I slid my hatchet into its sheath and set out on the sled, following the dips and hills, when one bundle of firewood fell and wedged itself into a crevasse on the edge of a snow-buried valley. (Frozen snow regularly splits into crevasses when exposed to the sun.)

"Thinking it would be a shame to abandon it there, I made my way to the place it had fallen and, grasping the bundle by its end, tried to pull it out of the crevasse, but it wouldn't budge. It was firmly wedged in by the force of its fall, and it was heavy. Trying to pull it from an angle, I lay on my stomach and stretched out my arms. With a loud cry I gave it a mighty heave, but since I was not firmly planted

Saved by a bear. The old man tells his tale (*inset*).

on the ground, I flipped myself over with the strength of my heave and fell down into the bottom of the valley, far below the snow crevasse.

"Fortunately, as I had slid down the snow, I was unhurt. For a while I lay there quite benumbed. Soon I recovered and looked up and saw a huge wall of snow above me that threatened to come crashing down in an avalanche at any moment. I felt more dead than alive, and all around me was darkness. Thinking at least to get out into the light, I made my way slowly through the narrow valley and finally came to a place where I could see the sky. But the snow was viciously cold, and my hands and feet were bent and stiff, so that each step was an effort. 'At this rate I'll freeze to death!' I urged myself on, thinking there might be a path in a hundred steps or so, when I found myself at a waterfall. Looking to the four directions, I saw that I had arrived at a dead end in the valley, like a mouse that falls into a pot, with no place to go.

"There was not a thing I could do, but as I stood there blankly, despairing, I could not even think 'What should I do?' And now begins the story of the bear. But first let me have another drink!"

He poured it himself and took a deep draught; drawing a tobacco pouch from his belt, he began smoking his pipe. I had to prompt him to continue.

"As I looked to one side, I saw a cave that was big enough to crawl into. There was no snow inside, and when I entered I was greeted with warmth. Just then I noticed that the lunch of rice balls I had tucked into my sash had fallen somewhere along the way, and I realized I would certainly starve—though I might survive five or ten days by eating snow. If only I heard the sled song of a villager in that time, I could call out in a loud voice and be saved. But even so I was convinced that my only chance was to entreat the gods of Ise Shrine or the Zenkoji temple, and as I diligently intoned the name of the Buddha and prayed to the gods, the day drew to its close.

"Deciding to make the cave my bed, I felt my way forward in the darkness. It began to get warmer and warmer. As I groped a bit further, my fingertips felt what could only be—a bear! I was frightened to death. My heart threatened to burst. There was no escape—

my last hour had come, I thought. My life or death I laid in the hands of the gods and buddhas. I was resigned to my fate.

"'Sir Bear,' I stammered, 'I am only a fellow who went out to collect firewood and fell into this valley. There is no way for me to return, and I have no provisions on which to live. Surely I must die. If I am to be torn apart by your claws, kill me now; but if you have any mercy, help me.' And I stroked the bear all the while, most fearfully.

"In the darkness, it seemed to me that it got up. In a moment it was beside me and nudged me with its rear end. When I sat down where the bear had been, what warmth! It was like a hearth, and as my whole body grew warm and I forgot the cold I thanked the bear profusely and begged it again to save me, repeating the details of my sad story. At this the bear raised its paw and softly pressed it to my mouth several times. Recalling that bears live off a store of crushed ants in the winter, I licked the paw and found the taste sweet, but a little sharp.

"After licking the paw several times I felt refreshed and my thirst was quenched. The bear began to snore; it was asleep. Realizing that the bear was going to save me, I was greatly relieved. I lay down back to back with the bear and thought only of returning to my village, not the least bit sleepy. Then before I knew it I was asleep, too.

"Later I awoke as the bear began to stir. Looking toward the opening of the cave I could see that dawn was just arriving and, crawling to the entrance, I looked about for a path leading home, or at least a wild wisteria vine with which I could pull myself up the valley's steep slope. There were neither. The bear came out of the cave, too, and went to drink at the bowl of the waterfall. For the first time I saw it—and a great, huge bear it was, seven times the size of a dog. It returned again to the den, while I waited at the entrance, straining my ears for a sled song. But there was nothing, not even the call of a bird, only the sound of the waterfall.

"That day ended sadly, and as it grew dark I once again entered the cave to spend the night. Staving off starvation with the bear's proffered paw, I passed several days without hearing any song, and it is hard to describe my despair. It was during this time that the bear gradually grew tame and quite lovable."

Here the host interrupted the old man and, slightly tipsy, declared, "It must have been a female bear!" upon which we all roared with laughter. What with the drinking and exchanging cups that followed, the story got lost, so I asked what happened next.

The old man continued: "Well, the heart of man changes with events. When I first encountered the bear I was certain I was going to die, and I was resigned to it. But after having been saved by the bear, I began to entertain hope again and believe that even if no one passed my way, I might pull myself out of the valley by scrambling up tree roots and overhanging rocks and find my way back home, if only the snow would melt.

"And waiting for that I spent day after listless day—I lost track of how many. The bear became as tame as a dog and learned, I think for the first time, that man could be a friend. The snow in the valley melted even more slowly than that in the villages, and the only thing that gave me pleasure was that time was passing. One day, while I was picking my lice in a sunny spot at the cave's entrance, the bear came out of the den and began pulling at my sleeve. Wondering what this was about, I followed, and we reached the place where I had first fallen into the valley.

"The bear went ahead of me, easily opening a path with its paws and allowing me to follow. I followed the bear this way and that until we finally came upon human footprints. At that, the bear looked about in all four directions and raced away, I know not where.

"I thanked the bear for leading me there, prostrating myself in the direction in which it had fled and repeating my grateful praises. 'This is all due to the kindness of the gods and buddhas,' I declared and bowed toward Ise and Zenkoji. Joyfully I returned to the post town, hardly knowing where I walked, and arrived at home just before it was time to light the tapers. The people in my neighborhood had all gathered and were reciting the Buddha's name. At first my parents were so surprised that they thought I was my own ghost, and they made quite a fuss. That was to be expected. My hair had grown and was sticking out like a straw cape, and my face was as thin as a

BOOK ONE

fox's. Gradually the cries of surprise became laughter, and my parents and everyone else rejoiced. Exactly forty-nine days had passed since I had gone out for firewood, and so it was the eve of the service for the rest of my soul. Thus the solemn Buddhist ceremony became a welcome-home party." And with that the old man ended his narrative.

His name was Kyuemon and he was a farmer. I went home and by the light of an oil lamp wrote down everything exactly as he told me, but that was long, long ago.

Snow Insects

Snow lies deep on Mount Omei in Sichuan of the land of Tang, even in summer. *The Mountains and Seas Classic* records the existence of an insect called the snow bug living in the snows on that peak. I am sure this is the truth, for we have snow insects in Echigo as well. They begin to make their appearance in the snow at the beginning of the year, and when the snow melts they, too, disappear, their life cycle bound to the snows.

The five elements of wood, fire, earth, metal, and water all nurture

Snow insects.

insects. We frequently see wood insects, earth insects, and water insects, and there is nothing remarkable about them. Flies are produced by ashes, and ash is the burned residue of fire, so the fly is a fire insect. A fly that has been killed (as long as it hasn't been crushed) will come to life again if placed in ashes. Lice are produced by the warmth of the human body, and warmth is fire, after all. This is why both flies and lice like warm places.

People are ignorant of metal insects because they are so small that they cannot be seen by the naked eye. But when metal begins to decay metal insects appear, and the places they appear change color. Metal does not decay if you polish it regularly, for this kills the insects. Rust is the first sign of decay, and metal insects are always to be found in rust. It is only because we cannot see these insects that we are ignorant of them. (This is the theory of a Dutch writer.) If insects are to be found even in metal, there can be no doubt that there are insects in the snows! But because this is out of the ordinary, it is recorded in the annals of China as an oddity, a wonder.

The snow insects of Echigo are as tiny as a mosquito. There are two kinds. One has wings and flies; the other also has wings, but always crawls. Both have six legs and resemble a fly in color, though one is darker. They are found both in towns and in the fields, just like mosquitoes, but they do not sting. I have drawn them as they appear under a magnifying glass. Further discussion of the creatures waits upon the conclusions of naturalists.

Blizzards

A blizzard occurs when the snow that has accumulated on trees and on the mountain peaks is whirled and blown about by the wind. Since in some cases the wind is a gentle one, in many ancient poems the snow has been likened to the scattering cherry blossoms, but such a thought is only possible in lands to the south and to the east, where no more than an inch or two of snow ever falls. The blizzards of our northern land of Echigo, deeply buried in foot after foot of snow, are whirlwinds and snow twisters; the cruelest trial of our snowy land, they take the lives of many, year after year. Let me relate just one such tragedy to let those who gaze at the gentle snow breezes of warmer climes know the terror those winds bring to our land of snow.

In a village not far from Shiozawa, where I live, there was a farming family. They had one son, a good fellow who always served his parents well. In the winter of his twenty-second year he took a bride of nineteen from a village some two miles away. She was quite good-looking, had a sweet disposition, and was skilled at the loom, all of which endeared her to her husband's parents. Husband and wife were devoted to each other, and the whole family looked forward to spring in a happy mood.

That same year at the beginning of October, the wife was safely delivered of a fine boy. The whole family was in high spirits; they felt as if they held a precious pearl in their hands. The new mother quickly recovered from childbirth. She had more milk than her baby boy could drink, and he grew plump and strong. They christened him with an auspicious name to insure long life.

Everyone in this family was industrious, and they worked hard in the fields and at the loom so that, though they were just small farmers, they were not poor. With a good son, a fine daughter-in-law, and a beautiful grandchild, they were the envy of all the others in the village. Why is it that Heaven sent suffering to this virtuous family?

A good time after the birth, when the snow that had been falling continuously stopped and the skies brightened and cleared, the young wife said to her husband: "Today I would like to visit my parents in my home village. Would that be all right?" Her father-in-law, seated next to her, answered, "That's a fine thought. Your husband should go with you. Make your good old mother happy by showing her her new grandson, and you two can act the proud parents." The daughter-in-law beamed at this. When she told her mother-in-law of the plan, that good woman began to gather together gifts for the couple to take with them, while the young mother dressed her hair and joyfully changed her clothes. The wadded cotton headgear that is always worn in the cold suited her well.

As she tucked her child into the breast of her kimono, her mother-

Hunting bears in the snow (*above*). The youn

uple struck by the snow whirlwind (*below*).

in-law came up to her and said, "Give him plenty of milk now. It will be hard for him to drink on the road," showing with every word her love for her grandson. The husband wore a cape, hat, and leggings made of straw and put on snowshoes and slung the bag of gifts over his shoulder (farmers always wear straw capes when they go out into the snow, even on clear days). Begging their parents for their leave, the couple started off happily on their journey.

But this was to be their last parting, for what followed was a tragedy.

For a time the husband led and the wife followed behind. He said to her: "Today is such splendid weather. That really was a wonderful idea. Your parents will never suspect that today we are coming and bringing their first grandson to meet them! They'll be so happy when they see his face." She answered: "Though Father saw the child when he came to visit last, Mother hasn't seen him yet. If it gets late, may I stay the night? You stay, too." "No, no—if we both stay my parents will worry. I'll return." And while they talked about this the baby began to cry, so his mother pushed her breast to his mouth and they pressed on.

When they had arrived at an open plain called Misashima, the color of the sky suddenly changed as it grew covered with black clouds. The husband looked at the sky and was startled—"A blizzard's on the way!" And while he hesitated, a roaring wind blowing snow fell upon them like a great wave crashing over the boulders at the seashore, and a whirlwind of snow funneled up into the sky like white dragons storming up a mighty peak. A moment before, everything had been quiet and peaceful; in a flash heaven raged and earth ranted, the cold wind slashed the skin like a lance and the frozen snow pierced the flesh like arrows.

The wind tore the cape and hat from the husband and blew the wife's hat away, whipping her hair about wildly. In an instant, snow was blown into their eyes and mouths, down their collars, into their sleeves, and even up the hems of their kimonos! They began to freeze, and breathing grew difficult. Already half-buried in snow, they called out with all their might, for life was at stake: "Halloo, halloo!" But no one passed by, and they were far from human habitations. Their hands and feet soon grew stiff and useless and they were toppled as easily as withered trees by the blizzard winds; side by side they died, in the snow where they had fallen.

The blizzard ended with the day, and the following morning four or five men passed by the scene under a blue sky. The corpses of the couple went unseen, for they were buried in the snow, but the men happened to hear a strange sound: the crying of a baby, *under the snow*. At first they were gripped by fear and ready to flee, but a stronger-minded fellow among them began to dig through the snow. The first thing he came upon was the young wife's hair. "She must have been felled by the blizzard!" Some of the men ran off to get help, and everyone began to dig in earnest.

Soon both bodies were found. Buried in the snow they seemed as if still alive, and several people easily recognized them as man and wife who had perished side by side. The babe was still tucked in his mother's breast, his head covered by her sleeve, shielding him from the snow—that was how he had survived and sent up cries from between the corpses of his parents. How all wept as they looked at the scene, imagining the young wife lovingly covering the child's head with her sleeve before she and her husband had died hand in hand. One of the villagers tucked the child into his clothing while others wrapped the corpses in straw capes and carried them back to the home of the husband's parents.

Now the parents had supposed all along that the young couple had only stayed the night at their in-laws' house. When the frozen corpses were brought to them, at first they could find no words to speak, no sound to make; then they threw themselves on the bodies, pressing their own faces to the cold faces of their children, wailing at the tops of their voices. Their misery was a pitiful sight. One of the men finally brought the child out from his breast and passed it to the grandmother, who wept with tears of grief and relief to see her grandson alive.

Deaths due to snow winds are usually of the sort described here. The difference between this and the snow winds of warmer regions, likened to falling flowers and praised prettily in verse, is as great as the difference between sporting in the surf and drowning in a tidal wave. And those in warm lands should know of the difficulties of life in the snow country. It is quite common for a spell of bright, clear weather to change in an instant to a blizzard strong enough to uproot trees and crush houses, and it is difficult to calculate the harm done to men and their dwellings.

If you are caught in a blizzard, the best thing to do is dig a hole in the snow and crawl into it. In a very short time you will be covered with snow, and, surprisingly, this is the warmer place to be. You can breathe and thus escape death. Men traveling through the snow always wrap their testicles in wadded cotton cloth, otherwise they are the first part to freeze, and a man's vital energies are lost.

Those who have been frozen may sometimes be revived with warm water or heat, though very hot water and high temperatures must be avoided or, with the first warmth of spring, the victim will be afflicted with swellings that even the best doctor will be unable to cure. The first thing to do for those who have been frozen is to apply heated salt wrapped in cloth to their navels. Then they should be gradually warmed with a straw fire. This way there will be no complications later. (It is best, you see, to warm such victims of freezing to body temperature and no warmer.) If great heat is applied to frozen hands or feet, they will swell up like a burn when they come into contact with natural warmth, only to rot and later fall off. No medicine can prevent this. I am writing here of what I have actually seen.

Both freezing to death and frostbitten hands and feet are the result of the blocking of the veins by yin poisons. If a frozen person is warmed quickly by intense heat, his vital energy will assist the flow of blood, but though the yin poisons temporarily dissipate, they are not completely eliminated. Since yang is stronger than yin, the presence of the yang drives the yin poisons into the flesh, where they start to fester. No, people who are frozen when out walking in the snows should never be warmed too suddenly; it is far better to wait until the body heat returns on its own. This is one of the arts of insuring long life.

BOOK ONE

Fires in the Snow

One of the famed wonders of Echigo is the fire that burns out of a hole in a stone mortar in a farmer's kitchen in the village of Nyohoji, Kambara County. Everyone considers it a wonder, and its fame has been spread by word of mouth as well as by mention in a variety of sources. Since the first record of this flame's appearance is in the Temmon era (1532–55), it has been burning continuously for some three hundred years, which is itself a miracle of miracles.

But Heaven has not produced just one wonder; there is another such fire in our land, in Uonuma County. Since everyone knows of the former, but no one from other lands has heard of the latter, I would like to introduce it to the world.

There is a low mountain to the west of the post town of Itsukamachi in Uonuma County of Echigo. At the foot of the mountain is a small pond. One day in March, sometime during the Temmei era (1781–89), a group of children had gathered about the pond and were playing all sorts of games. Bored with their play, they decided to make a fire of twigs. After they lit it and were just about to gather round and warm themselves, they were startled to see another fire flare up and burn merrily at a place a little distance from their own. Frightened, they scattered in the four directions, but one lad, after returning home, told his parents what had happened. Being smart folks, they returned to the scene and observed the burning flame. A hole large enough to insert a hand had been made in the snow, and a flame was burning about four or five inches above it.

After carefully observing the flame, they concluded it was like that at Nyohoji Village. Placing a stone over the hole, they extinguished the fire and returned home without saying a word to anyone. When the snow had melted they returned to the scene and were able to see that the flame had burned from a place in the pond's bank. They ignited it once more with tinder, which they then tossed into the water: flames, for all the world like little garden bonfires, ignited and danced over the pond's surface! This sight was even more wonderful than the flame at Nyohoji Village, and people gathered from all over the area to watch.

Later a money-minded fellow built a bath near the edge of the pond. He drew the fire from the ground with a pipe, just as one draws water from a river, and used it to heat and illuminate the bath. Warming the water drawn from the pond, he charged admission to his bath, which was quite popular for a time because the water contained sulphur and was beneficial in treating skin diseases.

There are veins of both fire and water in the earth. Because the earth is the Great Yin there are nine water veins for each fire vein, and fire veins are very rare. The veins of fire in the earth never cease to flow, for the earth breathes just like a human being does, though we cannot see it. The breath of the earth burns when we ignite it with the ordinary sort of fire we use every day. This burning breath of the earth is known as yin flame or cold flame. The reason that the pipe used to draw the cold flame does not burn is that the earth's breath has not yet been ignited as it travels through the tube; untouched by yang, it remains in its breath state. When it comes into contact with yang at the tube's mouth, it burns with a flame an inch or two above the mouth, proving that it is the earth's breath that is burning. The flame at Nyohoji Village is of the same sort. This is not my discovery, but based on the writings in classical works.

Crevice Mountain

There is a mountain more than two and one-half miles high and the same distance around behind the village of Shimizu in Uonuma County. Since the mountain is riddled with great crevices, it is called Crevice Mountain. The lower half of the mountain is clothed in a web of ancient trees; above are rocky peaks of boulders stacked one upon another like twisting dragons and raging tigers, a scene too strange and wonderful to describe. Mountain streams rush down about the base of the mountain, where they come together and form an indescribably beautiful waterfall. If during a drought one prays for rain at the basin of this waterfall the heavens will not fail to grant the plea, it is said.

One year, in May when the snow was just beginning to melt, some twenty farmers of Shimizu Village gathered to hunt bears on this mountain. Certain that many of the creatures lived in the caverns of the numerous mountain crevices, they burned firewood mixed with tobacco and hot peppers and blew the smoke into the caves to drive the bears out. But the caves were so deep that the smoke did not penetrate to the back, and not a single bear was flushed. The next day the farmers decided to increase the firewood as if to burn the entire mountain, but still no bears appeared. Instead, the smoke began seeping out from the crevices here and there on the mountain, forming a great black cloud hanging over the eerie peak. So very strange was the sight that the farmers abandoned their bear hunt and returned empty-handed—that's how the farmers of Shimizu Village tell it.

The upper half of the mountain is a skeleton of stone, with very little earth. The shallow veins of earth allow vapors to pass through, and it was from these veins that the smoke billowed forth. This is certainly a wonder of the natural world, far beyond our comprehension.

Avalanches

Avalanches, together with blizzards, are our greatest tribulation. The snow on the mountains is both deeper than that in the villages and freezes much harder—as hard as rock, in fact. In the mountains of the southeastern part of Echigo, fourteen or fifteen feet of snow fall even near the villages; yet this is considered a light snowfall. When warm, yang air begins to rise from the earth in March and the snow begins to melt, fissures form in the mountain snows because of the difference in the temperature between the air and the land. One section breaks off, then another and another, with a crack like the sound of giant trees falling. This is the unmistakable portent of an avalanche. Avalanches occur in some places but not in others due to the topography and the position of the sun. And avalanches always take

Crossing the blocks of snow that fell in an avalanche on Mikuni Peak.

place in March. Since the villagers know the places, times, and signs of avalanches, people are rarely killed in them; but since the heavens are unreliable and changeable, some are still crushed beneath the falling blocks of snow.

The sections of frozen snow that fall in avalanches range in length from more than sixty feet to smaller ones only five to nine feet in length. Thousands of such snow blocks, all as square in shape as if they had been carefully cut (why they are always square is discussed below), fall at once from the mountaintops several thousand feet above. The sound is as loud as a thousand thunderclaps, breaking giant trees and loosing great boulders. A fierce wind always rises at this time, driving the broken bits of snow, like gravel, into the sky; the brightest day becomes the darkest night. It is impossible to describe how frightening this is. In the next book I will recount anecdotes I have heard or describe events I have witnessed of people who lost their lives in avalanches and those who survived them for the information of the residents of warmer regions.

A certain person asked me: "Earlier you explained in great detail that snow is hexagonal. Avalanches are caused by falling heaps of snow. Why is it that they break into square blocks and lose their original, hexagonal shape?" I replied thus: "The vapors of the earth are transformed in the heavens into snow, which is hexagonal because it is a combination of the round principle of the heavens and the square principle of the earth; a hexagon is a combination of roundness and squareness. When snow falls from heaven back to the earth, it ceases to form according to the yang principle of roundness and begins to mold itself after the earthly square yin shape. This is why the blocks of snow that fall in an avalanche are all angular in shape. When the snow of the avalanche begins to melt, the angular blocks become rounded. This is due to the influence of the roundness of the heavens in the form of the sun's heat. The most certain of all truths is that yang contains yin within itself and yin contains yang. Laozi says in the forty-second chapter of *The Classic of the Way* that 'All things bear the yin and embrace the yang. This is the principle of harmony.' By this principle, a wife who does not contain within her yin self a bit of the yang is not in accord with heaven. Unless from time to time she speaks up in place of her husband, family affairs will be a mess.

On the other hand, if she speaks out too much—if the hen crows to greet the dawn—yin and yang will be at odds in the household and the family will perish. The heavenly principle that governs all things must not be trespassed."

And my inquisitor left with a hushed "I see, I see."

Not all blocks of snow that fall in an avalanche are square in shape, but at least seven or eight out of ten are, and so I offer this explanation. The blocks of snow illustrated in the avalanche picture are all square because they have been modeled after the most commonly found blocks.

BOOK TWO

The Story of an Avalanche Victim

Let me relate the story of a man from Uonuma County who met a tragic death in an avalanche, as told by the people of his village. Since it is such an unfortunate story, I will omit the people's names.

There once was a farmer's family in a certain village. The household included some ten members, masters and servants. The master of the house was fifty years old, his wife not yet forty. Their son was just over twenty and their daughters eighteen and fifteen, all of them obedient and respectful. One year at the beginning of March, the father left the house in the morning on an errand. Three o'clock came and went, and at five o'clock he had not yet returned. Since the business he had set out for should not have taken very long, his family thought his long absence odd, and the son and a manservant were sent to the house that the father was supposed to have visited; but no one had seen hide or hair of him. The son and his servant tried to imagine where the father might have gone, and asked of his whereabouts here and there, but learned nothing. Sad at heart they set out for home as the day drew to a close.

When the son related these circumstances to his mother, she refused to believe him and sent servants running off to locate her delinquent husband. But they learned nothing either, and though it was well past midnight, the master had still not returned home. The people in the neighborhood heard about the matter and gathered

The old man borrows chickens to find

...e master buried beneath the snows.

to discuss it. No one had anything to offer until one old man arrived and spoke up, "What? No one has seen the master? Well, I have, and I've come to tell you about it." The wife was overjoyed to hear that someone had indeed seen her husband, and together with her children she thanked him, asking him what tidings he brought. So the old fellow began, "Yes, I met the master of the house this morning as I was on my way to Nishiyama Pass. He said he was going to Inakura Village, and continued on his way. Then later, on my way back home, I heard the familiar sound of an avalanche in the far distance, coming, sure enough, from the mountain I had passed. How relieved I was to be safely across the pass! And as I was wondering whether the master of this house had gotten by the foot of the mountain safely too, or if—heaven forbid—he had been struck by the avalanche, I reached home. Now, since the master's not back yet, perhaps after all . . ." and he knitted his brows.

This was hardly the news that the mother and children had so eagerly begged for. They looked in each other's eyes to see tears welling up. The bearer of these worrisome tidings saw this, too, and left in a hurry. The younger folks decided to go to the place where the avalanche had fallen, and with cries of "Torches!" made noisy preparations to begin the search. But another old man said, "Now, now, just wait a minute. Those sent to ask after the master have not even come back. How do we know that he won't return? The master isn't the careless sort who would be caught unawares by an avalanche. That old busybody with his unwanted babble has only succeeded in worrying everyone terribly."

This comforted the family somewhat, and they brought out sake and offered it to their visitors, who sat around the hearth drinking merrily, and time passed. One by one the servants sent afar returned, yet not one of them brought news of the master.

Dawn came and not only the people of the village but indeed everyone who had heard of the matter gathered at the house. "There's no use waiting any longer," was the general opinion, and with shovels in hand a file of people headed for the place where the old man had said there was an avalanche, the members of the household following behind. When at last they reached the spot, they saw that the avalanche had not been so large: there was a wall of snow about 120 feet long blocking the road. Even supposing the master was buried beneath the snow, there was no sign where they should start digging. People milled about wondering what to do when the old man of the night before reappeared and said, "Let me show you how this is done." Taking several younger men with him, he went to the nearest village, borrowed some roosters, and brought them back. Then he scattered feed over the bank of snow and let the roosters wander about as they wished, pecking at it. One of the roosters suddenly rose up, stretched its wings, and crowed, whereupon the others all flocked together and began crowing at the same place. (Now, a similar method was used of old for locating the drowned; the roosters were rowed about in a boat until they began to crow over the spot where the corpse lay below. Forever after people talked about the cleverness of the old fellow who had adapted this method to find someone buried in the snow.)

The old man turned to the young men holding shovels and said, "That's where he is! Start digging!" And everyone dug at once. Working furiously, they soon made a hole six or seven feet deep, but found nothing. Digging deeper, they suddenly came across a patch of snow dyed red with blood. Digging still deeper, they found the body, with one arm and the head ripped off. Next they found the arm but not the head. Finally, after enlarging the hole and digging here and there in the wall of snow, the head, too, was found. Buried all this time in snow, the poor fellow looked as if alive.

At this sight, the wife, who had been standing nearby with her children the whole time, grasped her husband's severed head and held it in her arms, while the children threw themselves over their father's body, crying and lamenting. Everyone who witnessed this pathetic scene was reduced to tears. But they couldn't go on like this forever; the wife finally wrapped the head in the *haori* overcoat she was wearing; the son removed his padded cotton gown and, with tears flowing down his cheeks, carefully blanketed his father's body and arms in it. As he was about to lift the corpse onto his back, a number of men who had hurried away earlier came running back with a door and rush mats on which to carry the body home. They took the head from the wife and placed it with the body, and the procession started back, with villagers in the front and rear, and the wailing wife and children following.

I was told all this by someone who took part in the sad story when he was young. It is not an unusual event; many are those who lose their lives in avalanches. Sometimes houses are crushed as well. What frightening things avalanches are, hitting with such force that, as in this story, their victims may have their heads and limbs torn right off.

A Temple Avalanche

Avalanches are not by any means restricted to the mountains; why, they are likely to happen anywhere snow builds into a peak. In the first years of the Bunka era (1804–17), my uncle, Abbot Shitchu, was the chief priest of the Tenshoji temple in Omoigawa Village. One day very near the end of midwinter he was seated at his desk writing in a second-story room and was bothered by the five- and six-foot-long icicles that hung from the eaves over the windows, blocking the light. (Icicles, by the way, are known as "ice nails," *kanakori*, in our dialect, as they were by people of old.) Climbing out on the roof, he grasped a shovel that had been left there by the servants when they were shoveling snow from the roof. The reverberations from his very first blow to the icicles loosed a mass of snow from one wing of the roof of the main hall, and it fell with a roar, sweeping the abbot along.

By rights, he should have fallen into the reservoir of water next to the earthen-walled storehouse on the temple grounds. But the strength of the avalanche tossed him like a ball beyond the reservoir into a bank of snow that had been cleared from other places. He was half-buried; his cries brought the servants who had been clearing snow away from the temple's domestic quarters running with their shovels in hand, and they soon set to digging their abbot out.

The abbot was laughing uproariously. A hasty examination showed that he had not been hurt in the least, and even the eyeglasses he had been wearing were unscratched. His life had been saved as if by a miracle. At this time he was over seventy years old.

When we compare his fate with that of the avalanche victim described earlier, it can only be regarded as a blessing from heaven. The abbot lived on in fine health until he was over eighty, finally passing away at the end of the Bunsei era (1818–30). He often recounted this incident to me. "I had just taken a brush in hand to copy a scripture when I was hit by that avalanche. Since I was invoking the name of Amida Buddha with each Chinese character I copied, it was his wonderful powers that saved me from what was otherwise certain death. Yes, people will escape from harm by arousing constant faith in the gods and buddhas. No evil can come from a heart that believes in them. The most important thing in escaping evil and harm is to be without an evil mind." Thus he often instructed me, and even now those words ring in my ears.

Of course even though the greatest efforts and wisdom are expended, we sometimes meet with unfathomable disaster. Such are the workings of karma, beyond our ken. And though I know of many other stories, of houses crushed by avalanches, of deaths and injuries, I will stop here, and record no more.

Gyokuzan's Illustrations of Snow

In a woodblock edition of a certain war tale printed some years ago by the artist Gyokuzan, there is a picture showing a battle in the snows of Echigo. Though the text calls it deep snow and the battle is supposed to be taking place in January, the way the warriors are depicted certainly suggests very light snow. For one thing, the snow in Echigo in winter is too deep for horses to walk in. Even dray horses and oxen are no use in the snow. War horses are out of the question. To describe a battle on horseback is an obvious error by the author; the artist, too, is mistaken. Since he is from a place with little snow, of course he knows nothing of what snow is really like here.

A true picture of the snows of Echigo would be very different.

Of course a picture must take some liberties or it is likely to be dull, but this illustration was so far from reality that it threatened to be a flaw in the jewel of Gyokuzan's reputation. Since I had been in correspondence with the artist for some time, I decided to take up my own clumsy brush and draw some snow scenes for him. I wanted to show him some unusual scenes as well, so I took the trouble to travel to a hot spring at the foot of Hoshi Peak, which is close to Mikuni Peak, to view the snow in the middle of spring.

Avalanches had fallen from the high peaks. Large triangular and square blocks of snow from 30 to 40 feet in size extended for some 120 to 150 feet. They had fallen into a valley and several layers of them, large and small, lay at the bottom. It was a strange sight even for the eyes of one born in the snow country.

I drew this on the spot, and sent it with the other drawings to Gyokuzan. In his response he said that his eyes were as dazzled as if the snows of Echigo had fallen on his desk. He suggested that I collect many more such pictures and compose a text to accompany them, binding them together in an illustrated book which, he said, he was sure would take the country "by snowstorm." And this is the book that I am writing now. What a pity, what a terrible pity, that Gyokuzan crossed the river to the other world before this work was completed.

Echigo Crepe

Although it is known throughout the land that crepe is a famous product of Echigo, most people believe that it is produced throughout the entire province, though this is not so. In fact, it is limited to Uonuma County. Though it can be found in a few other localities, the quantity is negligible and the quality cannot compare with that of Uonuma County.

Only recently has it been distinguished by the name crepe. In olden times it was called simply cloth (*nuno*). The old expression is still used, and you often hear an old woman say, "Take the cloth to the market today." There is a record in *The Mirror of the East* as well that states that in 1192 the Lord of Kamakura presented one thousand rolls of Echigo cloth to an imperial ambassador as a farewell gift on his return to the capital. There are even older records, but I will not go into them here. A later mention than the first, the various annals of the Ise clan, which record the glorious prosperity of the rule of the Muromachi lords, frequently speak of Echigo cloth. Thus it is clear that crepe has been a famous product of Echigo from ancient times.

In my opinion, the Echigo cloth of olden times was simply high-quality cloth. As time passed, weaving skills advanced and the thread was twisted tighter to produce a crimped (*shijimu*) weave that absorbed perspiration. Perhaps the words "crimped cloth" (*shijimi nuno*) were gradually shortened and slurred to "crepe" (*chijimi*). Over the years, skills and techniques have improved greatly, and in the attempt to weave ever more beautiful cloth, the crimping survives in name only.

The crepe woven today far surpasses what I recall from my youth, and rivals brocade in its designs. All sorts of difficult patterns are woven, stripes and checks and plaids all done with great accomplishment, and many wonderful effects are produced. All this is the result of the ingenuity of the weaving women.

Varieties of Crepe

The same kind of crepe is not produced everywhere in Uonuma County; each village weaves certain distinct types. This is because from ancient times each locality has concentrated on one sort. The places and the varieties of crepe are as follows.

White crepe is produced in the villages of Horinouchi District. It is also produced in the villages of Urasa District and Koidejima District.

Patterned crepe, *kasuri* checks and plaids, and the indigo design called *aisabi* are produced in the villages of Shiozawa District.

Indigo-striped crepe is produced in the villages of Muikamachi District.

Red-and-purple-striped crepe is produced in the villages of Ojiya District.

Light blue-striped crepe is produced in the villages of Tokamachi District.

Navy blue "Benkei-checked" crepe is only produced in the village of Takayanagi.

All of these are villages in Uonuma County. Two or three other villages weave crepe, but since they do not do so as a specialty, we will pass them by.

Women weave crepe during the months they are buried under the snow. The thread for the crepe to be sold the next year is spun in November of the previous year. By the middle of March the bleaching of the cloth is completed. It might seem as if white crepe is the easiest to weave, but as a matter of fact it is considerably harder than weaving patterned crepe, for each movement of the weaver's hands shows up quite clearly in the finished cloth. It would be impossible to tell of all the pains the village women take to weave fine crepe, but I will provide at least a glimpse below.

Ramie

Ramie from Aizu in Oshu and Mogami in Dewa is used to weave crepe. Only ramie from Aizu is used for white crepe. The ramie known as shadow ramie (*kage so*) is the best. Select ramie (*eri so*) from Yonezawa is also of top quality. The ramie merchants of Echigo travel to various provinces in search of the fiber to sell back home.

Spinning Ramie

One year when I was staying in Edo I heard a fellow say that when it was time to spin ramie in Echigo, all the women of the village gathered first in one house and spun all the ramie needed there, then went from house to house, working together, to spin each woman's ramie in turn. Why would anyone want to make up such a ridiculous story? Still, Uonuma County is a big place and, who knows?—perhaps somewhere that *is* how ramie is spun. But even so, it could only be ramie for the lowest quality of crepe. Leaving that aside, let us turn the discussion to crepe of middle quality and above.

To produce this, the spinner sits at her workplace in a straight posture and coordinates her hand movements with her breathing. If she works just anywhere, without preparing a proper place, she won't be able to concentrate and the thread will vary in thickness and be entirely useless. Most weavers use spittle to wet the thread, but for spinning crepe thread a bowl of boiled water is kept at hand. Crepe weavers are very careful to always wash their hands and keep the weaving area clean.

Twisting the Thread

Just as in spinning, a special place is prepared and good posture is a necessity in twisting the thread. The names of the tools, the techniques, and their order vary greatly, and it would be a great bother to list them all here, so I refrain.

All the work of weaving crepe, from spinning the ramie to bleaching the cloth, takes place in the snow. Were it not for the natural humidity of our life under the snow, it would be impossible to pull and twist the thread to the thinness—finer than a hair—that is necessary to weave the finest crepe. The fibers break if the air is too dry, and when fibers break the thread is weak and likely to snap. No sources of heat are allowed near places where the highest quality of crepe is being woven, for this reason. If crepe is being woven late in the season, after the middle of March, when the dampness has lessened, a big pot filled to the brim with snow is placed in front of the loom to provide humidity.

Upon careful consideration, we can see that silk, because it is made from threads of the cocoon of the silkworm, responds favorably to yang warmth, while crepe, because it is made from ramie, responds to yin cold. And silk is used in the cold to keep us warm, while crepe is used in the heat to keep us cool. Surely this is due to the natural disposition of the principles of yin and yang.

The thread is spun and twisted in the snow, the cloth is woven in the snow, it is washed in snow waters and bleached on snow fields. There is crepe because there is snow. Echigo crepe owes its fame to the combined powers of man and snow, working hand in hand. In Uonuma County, we say that crepe is a child of the snow. Crepe is also produced in regions with little snow, it is true, but the thread is made differently, and it can't compare with the crepe of Echigo.

The Weaver Women

Many establishments that produce cloth of one sort or another employ a staff of professional weavers. Though crepe is the unrivaled specialty of our snowy region, the odd fact is that there is not a single establishment employing weaving women to make it.

The reason for this is that it is impossible to calculate the value of the hand labor that goes into the production of a single bolt of crepe. Crepe weaving simply cannot be compensated with money; it is unprofitable. What it is, in fact, is a pastime for the womenfolk who are buried under the snow for so many long winter months with nary a thing to keep their hands busy.

In weaving crepe, the basic unit of thread is the *yomi,* which consists of forty working threads. The very best crepe has a warp of twenty to twenty-three *yomi.* Actually, each working thread that is passed through the reed is made up of two strands, so one *yomi* consists of eighty threads. The weft threads are arranged to match the warp. (There may even be more weft threads, though I don't believe so.)

Thus some 920 individual movements are required to weave a single foot of crepe. To weave an entire twenty-seven-foot length requires 24,484 hand and foot movements. Of course, this is just a rough calculation. (The standard length of a bolt of crepe is fixed according to an old measure, a whalebone yardstick, at about ten yards.) At any rate, it is literally impossible to describe all the pains and care that the weaving women devote to the long process from the spinning of the thread through the weaving of the final length of bleached cloth. Of course to a certain extent this is true of all clothmaking, but I speak of what I know close at hand.

In places where crepe is manufactured, skill in weaving is the first requirement in the selection of a bride; appearance takes only second place. Naturally, parents see to it that their daughters are well tutored in this skill at an early age. At twelve or thirteen, a girl is started weaving rough crepe. From the middle teens to the mid-twenties is regarded as the peak of a woman's crepe-weaving abilities; the crepe woven by older women lacks luster and is thought inferior in quality.

Orders for crepe by people of rank as well as other orders for crepe of the highest quality are given to those women who are renowned for their skilled and accomplished weaving. Usually the person who is to do the work is specified: "Have so-and-so of such-and-such a place weave this." All the weaving women try very hard to be included in the select group to which special orders are entrusted.

Yet all this trouble and labor are ill-rewarded and for the benefit of strangers. How true were the verses of the Tang poet Qin Taoyu about the village girls:

> Over the years, my greatest bitterness
> Is that I weave with golden threads
> The bridal gowns of others.

The Mad Weaver Maiden

Several years ago, a young girl in a certain village in our area received her first order for high-quality crepe from a person of rank. Overjoyed, she never paused to ask what her reward would be, but determined to make a name for herself by showing everyone just how skilled she was. She completed each step of the process on her own, refusing the help of others from the spinning of the thread to the final stage of finished cloth. After many days of utter devotion, she lifted her crepe from the loom and sent it off to the bleachers.

When her mother later brought the bolt of cloth back from the bleachery, the girl was so eager to see it that she put aside what she was doing to unroll the cloth and inspect it. For some unknown reason, the crepe was stained with a soot-colored spot the size of a coin.

"What shall I do, Mother, what shall I do? How terrible!" the girl cried out, burying her face in the crepe and falling to the ground in tears.

The weaver maiden went mad then and there. From that time on she would suddenly burst into foul language and run wildly about the house. As her parents observed her in her distress, they couldn't help but recall the pure-hearted devotion she had given to weaving her crepe, and the tragedy of it always sent them into tears, as it did all who saw her and heard her story.

I was told this tale by a friend.

The Loom Chamber

When crepe is being woven for noble or imperial use, great care is taken to dig away all the snow around the house, and a brightly lit room, far away from the hearth and its smoke, is made spotlessly clean, spread with new rush mats, and hung with ceremonial ropes. In the center of the room stands the loom. This room is called the Ohataya, or Honorable Loom Chamber, and it is treated just as if a god were present in it. Only the weaver may enter. She eats meals prepared at a separate hearth; when she is to enter the room she changes into fresh apparel and purifies herself quite thoroughly by bathing in salt water, washing her hands, and rinsing her mouth. Of course she may not enter the room when she is menstruating.

Women often say things like, "I think today I'll go to worship at Lady So-and-so's Honorable Loom Chamber," using this kind of language to show respect. For only very skillful weavers are accorded the honor of setting up an Ohataya, and other women envy

BOOK TWO

them just as the petty officials envy the nobility who are allowed to enter the imperial palace.

The Mysterious Power of the Spirit of the Loom Chamber

It is often said that a god's power is increased by the act of worship. Any insignificant object, if it is sincerely believed in as an amulet or a charm, will become efficacious. Why, even discarded old straw sandals have, by the faith of the multitudes, later come to be worshiped as the God of Straw Sandals, according to *The Five Miscellanies*. When a truly holy object is worshiped, its mysterious heavenly powers are far beyond human comprehension.

In a certain village near here there was a weaver girl. While she was working at the loom with calm and devoted concentration, she heard a soft tapping noise at the window of the weaving room. Thinking "Oh, it must be him!" she got up to see what it was. And, indeed, there was the young man who had won her heart. Since there were no forbidding glances to bar their way, the girl slipped out of the weaving room and led her lover who had been standing at the window into a small shed nearby.

A short time later the girl's mother returned. She grew suspicious when she saw that her daughter had deserted the loom, and began calling and searching for the girl. From the little wooden shed the two heard her calls and were greatly alarmed. The young man managed to escape, but the girl was so flustered that she dashed back to the weaving room totally oblivious to the fact that she was now, of course, impure. She hurriedly sat down at her loom to continue weaving, but the next moment blood gushed from her mouth and she fell over unconscious.

Her mother, aghast, rushed to her side. Carrying her child out of the weaving room, she tried all sorts of things to revive her, but the girl's shallow breathing was the only sign that she was still alive. The woman immediately sent for her husband, who was visiting at a certain house in the village. He returned home and then sent for a doctor,

The unclean weaver girl is struck dow[n]

the Spirit of the Loom Chamber.

who dosed the girl with potions, but to no effect. How grief-stricken were the parents! Neighbors came running and sat at the girl's bedside, weeping and wringing their hands in anticipation of her certain and imminent death. Just then a young man entered the house and, as if ashamed, sat behind the others. Though he remained silent, he seemed to want very much to say something as he sat with his head hanging and tears falling from his eyes. People turned to look at him and recognized him as the second son of a certain man from the same village.

Bit by bit this young man edged his way to the mother's side. In a low voice he said to her: "I do not want to hide anything any longer. As a matter of fact, your daughter and I have promised ourselves to each other in this life and the next. This morning when I saw that no one was near, I persuaded her to leave the weaving room. When you suddenly returned and I heard your voice, I became frightened and ran away. Afterwards, when the terrible news reached me that your daughter was thus afflicted, I thought everything over carefully, and I realized that she must have forgotten that she was impure when she sat down at the loom and had been struck by divine punishment. This is all the result of my offense. Although no one else knew of this, I could not bear to pretend as if nothing had happened, for that would be breaking the life-and-death vows we two have exchanged. I have come to offer my life for the life of your daughter. I will take her punishment upon myself. If in spite of this she is bound to die, I will follow her. May this assembly be my witness!"

With this he tore off his clothes and undid his bound hair. Naked, he ran outside to the well and doused himself with icy water. Then he squatted in the snow and began to pray with all his might. Gradually the cold began to claim his body, and it looked as if he might freeze to death.

Now, the girl's parents and the others gathered there were hearing this story for the first time. Realizing that this indeed must be the punishment of the god of the loom chamber, they too stripped and went over to the well, dousing themselves with water and joining the young man in his prayers. Perhaps the god took pity on the youth, was moved by his good heart, and listened to his prayers and those of the people, for the girl arose as if she had been asleep and called for her mother. All knew her recovery to be a miracle, and they thronged around her, while she looked about and asked what all the fuss was.

Joyfully, her mother told her everything that had happened, one event at a time. The daughter could only remember up to the point when she had approached the loom, and nothing more. In her great happiness and relief, the mother now wanted to bring the young couple together, but the youth had slipped away in the meantime and could not be found.

After resting for four or five days, the daughter recovered completely. Since she was already seventeen, it was time for her to think about a husband anyway, and as her young man loved her truly, they quickly sent a go-between to make the marriage proposal. A felicitous wedding ceremony was held, and in no time at all they had a fine son. The family is flourishing even today.

How strange that the punishment of the spirit of the loom chamber should have been the tie that bound this happy couple together. This all happened, by the way, when I was a child. I have recorded it here to remind young people of the power of the spirit of the loom chamber. Yes, yes, indeed—how we should fear and revere it.

Bleaching Crepe

Crepe bleaching is a special occupation, and it is a rare weaver that bleaches her own crepe. The bleacher first spies out a suitable place near his home; there he builds a temporary shed to store supplies and to serve as a rest area. Bleachers, men and women together, purify themselves just as the weavers do.

Crepe bleaching takes place from February to the middle of March. At this time the rice paddies and vegetable fields are still a uniform blanket of white, and some bleach the crepe by laying it out on the fields. If a bleaching field becomes all trampled during the

Bleaching crepe on the snow.

day, the bleachers take a board with handles and smooth the surface of the snow, for otherwise it would freeze as hard and fast as rock again at night, all full of holes and uneven patches. The bleachery is spotless, without a speck of dust, and looks like a salt-drying beach, vast and white and smooth.

White crepe is bleached after it is taken off the loom, but other kinds of crepe are bleached as threads, hanging in skeins. The threads are stretched from the ends of a thin piece of bamboo some three or four feet long, bent into the shape of a bow. These bow-shaped skeins are then hung over a bamboo pole. White crepe is often bleached layed out on the snow, but sometimes a wall of snow is built and the crepe draped over this to bleach. The wall is usually some three feet high—or tall enough to drape the crepe full length, and long enough to line up several bolts of cloth. This prevents dogs or other animals from running over and dirtying the crepe. Skeins of thread may be draped over these snow walls as well. Everything differs from place to place, depending upon the peculiarities of the site. In addition to snow bleaching, the finished crepe or the thread is soaked in a weak lye solution overnight and then rinsed again and again and wrung out the next day before being bleached in one of the ways described above.

Crepe destined for imperial or noble use is not bleached like ordinary crepe. A separate bleaching place is marked off and special precautions are taken, just as in the weaving.

It very rarely rains in Echigo during the snowy season, because it is simply too cold. Rain is especially rare in spring. That is why the type of bleaching I have described is possible, because clear day follows clear day. After the crepe has been soaked in lye night after night and bleached in the sun day after day it becomes whiter than white, and the bleaching process is completed. It is impossible to describe the beauty of the crepe as it reaches the final stages; the lengths of crepe draped in rows over the glittering snow glow with an iridescent scarlet as the red dawn breaks. How I wish I could show this rare snow scene to the literati of warmer climes!

There are many techniques involved in bleaching crepe, and I have only given a broad outline of them here.

BOOK TWO

Crepe Markets

The Crepe Market is held in four towns: Horinouchi, Tokamachi, Ojiya, and Shiozawa. The first market of the year is called "raising the snow blinds" (*sudare aki*) in our dialect. This refers to lifting the reed blinds that serve as protection against the snow, which takes place at about the same time, the beginning of May. The market starts in Horinouchi. Next it moves to Ojiya, then Tokamachi, and finally Shiozawa. Each market lasts for three days; an interval separates one from the next. (This all varies from year to year.) There are no other markets. In Tokamachi there are official lodgings for the cloth dealers of the three major cities of Kyoto, Osaka, and Edo, and they do their buying there.

On market days everyone, men and women alike, brings their crepe carefully labeled with name and address to the market. They show their work to buyers, and once the price is agreed upon the buyer gives them a coupon that is redeemable after the market is finished. All their labor and pains over the past half a year have been for this day. Not only those who buy and sell crepe but people from all around gather in a great throng, wave after wave of market goers jostling each other and treading on each other's toes. Stalls and shops selling everything imaginable are set up. Those who come from afar seek lodging, and all the houses of the village are full of people. The sideshows of traveling showmen and the spiels of patent medicine hawkers draw great crowds, and there is barely room anywhere to so much as drive a nail. The excitement and activity of the first market day is a match for that of the great prospering cities.

Even after the four markets have come to an end, people bring crepe to the crepe dealers every day, and the dealers also travel here and there to buy crepe. Crepe disposed of by the fifteenth day of July is called summer crepe. That from the seventeenth of July to the first market of the next year is called winter crepe.

The quality of crepe is ranked as number one, number two, and so on. Prices are generally fixed, but they rise and fall a bit from year to year. The mood of the market as well as conditions of the previous year determine these variations. If the demand at the market is high, number three crepe will bring the price of number two, and number two sell for the price of number one. But as I mentioned earlier, it is useless to talk about a fair price for the labor of crepe weaving; the real interest lies in talking about who sold their crepe at the highest price at the first market and in tallying the praises of the weavers' skills. Since it is very likely that a girl's weaving skills may attract a husband, fame comes before profit. And the weaving maidens march out to the first market like warriors to battle.

One interesting fact is that, in any given year, the market for crepe is the exact opposite of the grain market. In a bad year the price of grain rises, while the price of crepe drops. In a bountiful year grain is cheap and crepe is expensive. This is just one example of the way everything is related to good and bad harvests. And so it is that everyone everywhere prays for years of plenty.

Powder Avalanches

Powder avalanches, which we call *hora* in Shiozawa, are a natural calamity resembling avalanches. The *hora* occur around January and come about when great amounts of fresh snow fall on top of the already very deep and frozen snow of the high mountain peaks. Because of the weather conditions, the new snow does not freeze and remains in a fluffy, powdery form. Blown by the wind or dropping under its own weight, the snow falls in lumps from the branches of the great trees on the heights and begins to roll down following the contours of the mountain slope. More and more snow collects on the downward course, and the *hora* grows larger and larger until it weighs several tons, crashing down the mountainside like giant boulders, carrying with it a great tidal wave of snow that uproots mighty trees, looses huge rocks, and, with horrible regularity, crushes any human habitation in its path.

A violent wind always accompanies the *hora*: the sky grows covered with frozen gray clouds and it becomes pitch dark at noon, just as when an avalanche occurs. As I recorded earlier, there are signs that precede and warn us of avalanches; but the *hora* comes without warning, and those caught unawares have a hard time escaping in the tide of soft powder snow. Only one in ten manages to flee. It is beyond human powers to dig through the hundreds and hundreds of feet of snow to search for the victims; and in April or May it is not unusual to come across the corpses of the *hora*'s victims as the snow melts.

There are many words in our dialect for *hora*: *ote*, *waya*, *awa*, and *hawatari*. Houses in the mountains are built in places that are thought to be safe from avalanches and *hora*. Yet I hear every year of entire villages being destroyed by *hora*, and it happens so frequently and the details are so much alike that there is no use in recording every such instance here.

The Blossom-Water Celebration in the Snow

The tutelary Ugachi Shrine in the old village of Ugachi in Horinouchi, Uonuma County, is devoted to the worship of the god Hachiman. It was built in ancient times, and there are many writings about its origins, but I will not go into them here. The miraculous events connected with this shrine are known throughout the land, and in the household of the shrine master, Miya, are records of them dating back to the fifteenth century. The present master of the shrine is a cultivated fellow and a prolific poet. He has adopted the pen name Masaki. We share an interest in literature and correspond with each other regularly. The shrine is an important one, with many shrines in other places affiliated as branches.

For every follower of this shrine who marries, the Blossom-Water Celebration, in which water is cast over the bridegroom, is performed by divine order. This religious event takes place every year on February 15. A messenger of the god visits every newlywed couple, and when there are many, he is busy from early in the day until evening.

My friend Bokusai (that's his pen name; his real name is Miya Jihei, and he is from Horinouchi) says that the Blossom-Water Celebration derives its name from an anecdote in *The Chronicles of Japan*. Mock-orange blossoms were said to have fallen from heaven into the water of a well at Awaji no Miya Mizui as a good omen; thus the name Blossom Water. At any rate, dousing the bridegroom with water is one of the sacred rituals of this shrine.

First a messenger of the god must be chosen to visit the homes of the newlyweds on the festival day. The rule is that this messenger must be selected from among the oldest and most established of the farmers' households. Even these households are quite strictly winnowed, eliminating families in which there has been the slightest accident or unpleasantness in the past year. The entire family, including distant relatives, must be free from illness, evil omens, and most of all, death. The candidates for messenger are finally chosen from households that have passed a completely safe and peaceful year.

The morning before the ceremony the shrine master performs ablutions, purifies himself, and dresses in new robes. Climbing up to the main shrine he announces the names of the candidates and writes them on paper prayer slips, leaving the selection of the divine messenger to the will of the god, by sacred lottery. The one chosen as the messenger then purifies himself before assuming his duties. He is called Tayu, meaning Great Man. (Bokusai says that he is properly called "man of the god who practices with purity," and that "great man" is simply the local phrase.)

Now then, the procession of the messenger of the god leaving the shrine on February 15 is a fine one: first come bearers carrying lacquered gift boxes on poles over their shoulders, sacred implements, standards, and parasols; then two messengers carrying bows, and others shouldering lances, all dressed in official costume and wearing the ceremonial court hats called *eboshi*. Next come long swords, spears, and more parasols, a man carrying the messenger's sandals, and a lancer. (All of these objects are taken out from the shrine storehouse.) Behind follows a great crowd of the shrine's worshipers, also wearing formal clothing.

Pathways are cleared through the snow in advance to allow the procession to reach the houses of families with newlyweds. Snow steps are cut into the steep slopes, and sometimes bleachers of snow are built along the route for those who wish to watch the procession pass. All of this requires no small amount of labor.

BOOK TWO

Those waiting for the procession to arrive at their home bustle about making everything immaculate. They choose a special room as the "reception hall" for that day's rite and purify it by sprinkling salt. A seat of honor made of colored straw matting spread with fine blankets is set out for the messenger of the god. They set up a sword rack, just as one finds in the reception hall of a samurai mansion. The antechamber next to the reception hall is stacked with gifts from relatives and friends and decorated with a *shimadai*, a festive altar hung with salutary verses—all sorts of special preparations are made!

Next they turn to the outside and hang a curtain across the entrance to the house, gathering and tying it in the middle, and lay down a dais for removing footwear just behind it. They arrange the entranceway of the house in the fashion of a proper entrance hall of a grand samurai mansion. Then everyone in the family changes into fresh clothes and waits for the arrival of the messengers.

When the word comes that the messenger of the god has arrived, parents and children alike go out of the house in their ceremonial dress to greet the procession. The sandal bearer comes running ahead, stops and stands at attention, and cries in a loud voice, "The messenger from one of the three official first-ranking shrines!" At the appearance of the messenger, the head of the house prostrates himself and then rises and leads the messenger to his seat in the reception hall. The rest of the members of the procession align themselves like a file of troops on either side of the house.

Now the master of the house offers tobacco, tea, and tray after tray of fine dishes to the messenger. Then the groom is given a cup of sake (offered in an unglazed cup on an unfinished wood tray), and with many delicacies to eat between rounds, seven cups are filled and drained in turn. Each exchange is toasted with celebratory songs. The duty of the divine messenger is to announce the bestowal of the "blossom water" from the god to his follower. Thus the ceremony ends. The first part of the festival is over and the messenger departs for the homes of other newlyweds, where he performs the same rite and makes the same announcement.

Before returning to the shrine, the messenger stops for a feast of sake and accompanying dishes at the village chief's household.

When the people see that the messenger's procession is about to return to the shrine, the second part of the festival begins. A parade of dancers forms. In the lead two men carry a special kind of parasol tipped with a halberd. Brocade cords, a festive drum, and hanging bells ornament the halberd tip; many-colored strips of cloth dance and bob from the parasol's edge. The men tie purple crepe scarves under their chins and bind back their sleeves with tie-dyed scarlet bands of cloth.

Following the two lead dancers comes a masked dancer in the role of Usume, the goddess who brought laughter to the heavens and drew the Sun Goddess from her cave. On her shoulder she carries a broom, on the tip of which appears a piece of paper depicting the female sex organs. Next comes a masked dancer in the role of Sarutahiko, wearing a linen hat and carrying a wooden pestle, the tip painted red in the fashion of a phallus. Third come the mountain ascetics called *yamabushi* in resplendent religious robes, blowing conches. Fourth follows a troupe of little children dressed as guards in costumes of their own devising, followed immediately by the adult guards in formal samurai dress, bearing staffs and ready for any emergency. Last dances a great and lively crowd, all wearing bright summer kimonos tied with colorful thin sashes (though it's only February, the excitement and the throngs of participants make it warm enough for summer wear). This procession is called the *gorinsho* here, which means "imitation of the honorable descent from the heavens." Bokusai says the name came from the imitation (*sho*) of the descent by the ancestor of the imperial house to Takachiho Peak at Hyuga. There are other explanations, which I omit here.

In the meantime, as the procession back to the shrine is forming, the groom spreads out a straw mat anew, fills two buckets full of water, ties pine branches and seaweed with ceremonial paper cords, and, placing these things on the mat, puts them, together with a tray of sake bottles, in front of his house in preparation for the dancers' approach. Two "water carriers" and two assistants stand on either side of the groom, their sleeves rolled up in manly fashion. Clothed in his summer kimono tied with its thin cloth belt, the groom waits for the procession of dancers. As the line approaches the house, it splits and surrounds the straw mat, everyone dancing and singing festive songs:

> Happy, happy be the young pine tree.
> Your branches flourish,
> Your needles grow thick.

or

> *Sanya!*
> The felicitous blossom water, *sanya!*
> Pour the water on his back,
> On my husband's back.

Alternating the verses as they repeat these songs over and over, they sing and dance. The guards and the two water carriers, who are experienced in the performance of this rite, wait for the right moment and then toast the groom with three toasts of three cups each. When this is finished, the water carriers on left and right take the buckets in hand and douse the groom like a waterfall spilling over his head. The throng of well-wishers clap their hands as they dance and shout "Rejoice! Rejoice!" The drenched groom dashes into his house and the dancers follow, singing and dancing their way after him, coming and leaving as many as seven or eight times, finally departing in a thundering herd, reforming their ranks, and heading for the next groom's house. When they have visited and properly doused every groom, they head for the house of the post-town chief or to the houses of others who might like to see the dance. Since there are so few interesting sights in the country, young and old, men and women come from afar to watch this festival. The way they swarm about like ants, pushing and shoving each other and throbbing with excitement, is beyond description.

The ceremony of dousing the groom with water is obviously a spell to encourage childbirth by drenching the yang fire of the male with the yin water of the female. It is a rite to put a stop to the bride's menses. The custom arose in the samurai households of the

Dousing the groom in the Blossom-Water Festival.

Muromachi age, and was gradually adopted by farmers and merchants as well. (Master Kaibara says in his *Almanac* that the custom originated when Matsunaga Danjo gave his niece in marriage to one of his retainers.) In Edo this ceremony always took place on February 15, up to about 1710, when it was outlawed. It seems that enemies or people who bore grudges against the bridegroom would play all kinds of pranks during this festival, sometimes resulting in death. The details of this are to be found in the book *A Long, Long Time Ago* (a book about customs from the founding of the country to the middle of the Genroku era, 1688–1704). But the Blossom-Water Celebration I have described here has a divine meaning quite separate from this, which is why I have told of it here amidst all this talk of snow, for I know it will interest all who love ancient customs.

Oddities at Hishiyama

Matsunoyama is the name of a great manor in Kubiki County in Echigo that includes many villages. All of them are perched in the mountains, and there are no level places even within the villages, with the exception of a place called Matsudai. Matsudai is flat, and row upon row of farmers' houses line its streets. This Matsudai is the one in the Noh chant about the mirror of Matsuyama recorded in the book *Another Hundred Verses*. The Mirror Lake mentioned in that chant is here, too, though now it is filled in and only traces remain. Come to think of it, since the chant about the mirror of Matsuyama is actually based on *The Broken Mirror Picture Scroll,* we can expect that our manor of Matsunoyama is mentioned there as well.

Now in this Matsunoyama Manor, there is a mountain called Hishiyama, or Water Chestnut Mountain. It was so named because the mountain looms up in a great triangle, just the shape of a water chestnut leaf. Near the mountain are two villages, Sukawa Village (named after the river) and Shobu Village (named after the wild iris). Every year in March there are avalanches on Hishiyama—always and only at night, the crashing sound echoing for miles and miles. It is said that a venerable old man in a white robe and with a head of long white hair comes riding down these avalanches, holding high his sacred staff. It is also believed that when the avalanche falls down a straight course of a mile or so in the direction of Sukawa Village, it will be a rich year; when it falls crosswise down towards Shobu Village, the year will be lean. Never has this sign proved false. On this mountain and this mountain only do avalanches predict the fortunes of the year to come, certainly an oddity worth noting.

This reminds me of a friend of mine, Maruyama, who lives in Teradomari. His is a doctor's family, and his grandfather had quite a reputation as a man of learning. Twenty years ago, when I made a brief stop at their home, my friend showed me a book he said was from the Horeki era (1751–64) called *Names of Echigo*. It was a copy he had made with his own hand, in three hundred rolls. Though it was called *Names*, it was actually an account of Echigo's history and customs. It was illustrated and organized so as to be of great convenience, divided into sections on Shinto shrines, Buddhist temples, famous places, ancient ruins, mountains and rivers and other geographical features, people, and local products and medicines. I found several mentions of Hishiyama there, but I have not repeated them in this account. I just happened to remember that great work as I was relating stories of Hishiyama; what a shame that such an important tome is shut away and unknown to the world.

The Ancient Ways of Akiyama

At the border of the provinces of Shinano and Echigo is an area called Akiyama. The original settlement there is called Oakiyama, and the region is comprised of this and fourteen smaller villages. The fifteen villages are located on the east and west banks of the Nakatsu River, which runs down the mountain and eventually flows into the Chikuma River in Tsumari in Uonuma County. On the east bank are Shimizukawara Village (though there are only two houses, it is called a village), Mikura Village (three houses), Nakanotaira Village (two houses), Oakasawa Village (nine houses), and Amasake Village (two houses), all in Echigo; in Shinano, Koakasawa Village (twenty-eight houses), Uenohara (thirteen houses), and Wayama (five houses). On the west bank are Shimoketto Village, Sakamaki Village (four houses), Kamiketto Village (twenty-nine houses), and Maekura Village (nine houses) in Echigo; and in Shinano, Oakiyama Village, Yashiki Village (nineteen houses), and Yumoto (with a hot spring). As I said earlier, Oakiyama is the original settlement, and some of its villagers possessed famous swords and weapons of old, but during the hard year of 1783 they sold them for provisions, and when even those provisions ran out, the entire village died of starvation. I have heard that now all that is left are the grasses of the fields.

To the east of this region the peak of Naebasan stretches to the heavens, followed by peak after peak. To the west, the great summit of Akakura pierces the clouds, and a host of other mountains range into the distance. Shimizukawara is the entrance to Echigo; Yumoto the single perilous passage into Shinano. Well guarded by even one soldier, the passes could keep back thousands of troops, so tightly sealed are these provinces.

The local story has it that the fleeing Heike soldiers hid in this region long, long ago. And I say, who knows? After all, from the time of Okuyama Taro, the grandson of Jo no Kikuro Sukekuni and the fourth-generation descendant of General Taira no Koremochi, to the time of the legitimate heir Jo no Taro Sukenaga, the Heike ruled the land of Takata in Echigo from their castle at Torisakayama. The Kamakura government, suspecting treason, sent Sasaki Saburobei Nyudo Seinen to defeat them, and only after a long, drawn-out battle was the castle taken. Some of the nobility may have hidden away in the hinterlands of Akiyama; and so it seems there is some reason in the popular belief that the descendants of the Heike are there.

I had heard that ancient ways were preserved in this Akiyama, and had always wished to visit there. Finally finding a knowledgeable guide to the area, I decided to go, and, following his advice, I readied rice, miso, soy sauce, dried fish, tea, and candles. We had a bearer carry these provisions as we set out on the eighth day of October, 1828.

We stopped the first night at a temple lodging, the Fudo Hall in Mitama Village, not far from Akiyama. The next day we entered the region, feeling as if we were entering the forgotten Peach Valley

BOOK TWO

of Chinese legend. Now, as I said before, Shimizukawara is the entrance (from the Echigo side) to the region. Just as the road was approaching the village, we came across a sign made of two logs driven into the ground and joined by a straw rope, from which hung a placard. As we drew nearer to see what it could be, we found the following message written in the simplest script, as if by a child: "Let no one from a village with smallpox enter here." The guide explained that the people of Akiyama fear smallpox like death. When someone contracts the disease, even one's own child, he is driven from the house and abandoned in a little hut in the mountains. Food is brought to him, but nothing more, though some families with a bit of cash may call a mountain ascetic to pray for the sick one. Nine out of ten die. Thus when people from Akiyama go to another area on some sort of business and hear that smallpox is about, they drop what they're doing and flee like the wind. As a result, of course, smallpox is almost nonexistent in Akiyama. There may not be even one case in ten years, my guide told me.

Now then, when we arrived at Shimizukawara Village, we found only two houses (and I will describe below just what they looked like). We rested there for a while, and just as we rose to go on, my guide said, "First let us look at Sarutobi (Monkey-Leap) Bridge," and went on ahead. The roads of Akiyama are quite primitive, cleared just enough to allow the local people to pass. Since they don't use oxen or horses in those parts, narrow paths suffice and, grown over with the low, spreading bamboo called *sasa,* one spends a good deal of time searching for their traces. And in this manner we finally reached the banks of the Nakatsu River.

The bridge connects this side with Sakamaki Village on the opposite cliff. It has been given the name Monkey-Leap Bridge, but when I gazed at it all I could think was that even monkeys couldn't leap the chasm it spanned—unless they sprouted wings! Both "banks" of the river were sheer walls of rock, standing as stiff and straight as giant folding screens. Ledges of rock projected from both sides about ten feet below the top of the cliff. On these rested the bridge. A ladder of sorts had been devised to descend from the cliff's edge to the bridge.

The bridge itself was made of two straight logs laid next to each other. On top of them small branches were tied with wisteria vine to

The sheer cliffs of Akiyama (*above*). Monkey-Leap Bridge (*below*).

serve as footholds. It spanned some 120 feet, but was only 3 feet wide and there were no railings. A wisteria-vine rope hung down from a great tree at one end of the bridge to help you climb the cliff after successfully crossing the bridge.

Just looking at the bridge was terrifying. It was an easy match for the plank bridge at Kiso, about which Basho composed the haiku:

> Even the butterflies teeter
> Above my reed hat.

I asked tremulously whether we would cross it. The guide replied no, we would stay today on this side and visit the villages on the east bank; we would probably reach Koakasawa in good time, and since he had a friend there we would have lodging for the night. My poor heart calmed when I learned I would not have to cross the bridge, and sitting down on a rock, I pulled out my brush and ink box and began to paint it. As I was looking all about, a flight of geese rose over the peak inscribing their sign on the clouds; the frolicking monkeys leaping from branch to branch left their likenesses in the water below. I saw strange trees twisted about the rocks like sleeping dragons and weird stones blocking the path like tigers stretched out in slumber. The forests spread out before me in the distance like dyed brocade and the roiling waters below ran deep and wild like an indigo ribbon. How could I capture the golden peaks, the green slopes, in a painting? My eyes were dazed, and I was lost in the wonder of it.

As I rested, two farmers drew near, each shouldering a wicker basket, and made to cross the bridge. While I watched from the bank, they stomped down the ladder like it was a stone stairway and trudged across the bridge as if it were any ordinary road. As they reached the middle, the bridge began to sway in a way too terrible to say—just looking at it made my hair stand on end. When they reached the other side they pulled themselves up the cliff with the wisteria-vine rope, just like monkeys. Without in the least expecting to, I had been able to witness people crossing the bridge, and I must say I was astonished.

We then left that place and went back to our narrow mountain road, following it up and down until, after a good long while, we arrived at Mikura Village. There were three houses here. We entered a house thinking to open the lunches we had prepared in Mitama Village, where we had stopped the night before, and an old woman greeted us with "Welcome!" in her mountain dialect. She was combing some long plants set out on a wooden tray. When we asked her what the plants were and what she was doing, she replied they were *ira* (nettles) picked in the mountains. She was spinning them into thread, from which she would make *amikinu*. When I asked her about the meaning of this strange word, she only laughed. According to the guide, though, *amikinu* is the name of the garment the old granny was wearing. A better look at it showed that it was like a sleeveless coat made out of rough cloth.

When we asked for tea, the old woman first asked us if we carried the pox. The guide announced, "We have come from Shiozawa to see the sights of Akiyama. There has been no pox there since last year." The old granny said, "Everyone in this house has spent the whole year huddled like frogs in a well. We haven't been out of our village even once," and poured us some tea, which had the appearance of boiled soot. We asked for ordinary hot water and finished our meal.

While looking closely at my surroundings I saw that the pillars of the houses did not even rest on foundation stones, and the beams that connected them were attached by no more than wisteria-vine rope. The walls were made of woven sedge, and the windows were very small. The door was built from the bark of a great tree. It had been pressed flat and attached to a frame of poles. There was no lintel; it was secured by wisteria vine. The thatched roof was very low. Though it was only a rough grass hut, it must have been very strong, for the snows of Akiyama are much deeper than those of the towns. Scraps of rice-straw mats were spread inside the house (since neither rice nor barley can be grown here, rice straw is rare, and the mats in all the houses are old and worn). No decent shelves or storage closets were to be found, though hanging nets had been woven out of sedge rope.

The open hearth was a square five feet by five feet, and it was at least two feet down to the layer of ash at its bottom. This is because they have plenty of firewood and build raging fires in the hearth.

The only really noteworthy objects to be seen were several large wooden bowls, a local product. There are no kettles, teapots, or mortars in any of the houses of the people of Akiyama.

We had seen five households since entering Akiyama on the first day, but no men were in sight. They were all busy cutting millet, since it was the season. While we were resting, though, a girl came back from the mountains where she had been gathering horse chestnuts. Her hair was not, like that of most women, dressed with oil, but gathered in a bun and tied with a string, and an old hand towel served as a sweatband. Her dirty cotton robe was at least a foot shorter than usual and tied at the back with an obi only two inches wide. In fact, we frequently see women wearing these sweat bands and narrow obi in old paintings, and it was the ancient style: short robes, too, were the style for those of low station. All of the women of Akiyama dress like this. We asked the old woman about the customs of Akiyama, but she didn't seem to understand, so we left her something for her trouble and headed on.

Treading our way over the steep mountain trails, we passed through Nakanotaira Village, Amasake Village, and Oakasawa Village, until, between four o'clock and five, we arrived at Koakasawa Village. This is one of the two large settlements in the Akiyama region, with twenty-eight houses. (Kamiketto has twenty-nine houses.) The head of the most important family in this village was named Ichiemon and fortunately he was a friend of my guide and agreed to provide us lodging. Upon entering, we saw that his house was six bays by four bays, or thirty-six feet by twenty-four feet. The master of the house and his wife were old, with a son about twenty-seven or twenty-eight and three daughters. A four-mat room at the back of the house was curtained off by hanging straw mats. (Hanging straw mats were once used in the houses of the nobility as well, and this ancient practice can be seen in many old paintings.) Among the many utensils scattered about the kitchen were three or four of the large wooden bowls mentioned earlier. The hearth, too, was large and deep like the one described above.

Well, then, we took out our rice and miso and other provisions, and my guide offered to make our dinner with mushrooms he had procured at Shimizukawara Village that morning and potatoes from

Koakasawa. When he asked the youngest daughter for the mortar, she reached up to the back corner of the shelves and brought it out. It was obviously not used regularly, for it was covered with soot. We later heard that this family and the main house of the same clan were the only houses in all Akiyama that possessed mortars. In recent years the people here have begun to grow beans and make miso, though they do not add yeast to ferment the beans and make only a rough soup by adding the chunks of bean paste—hence they have no need for a mortar to grind the bean paste to a fine consistency.

There was no separate hearth for cooking in the house, and all the dishes were prepared at the open hearth in the main room. As it grew dark, torches made from thin pieces of split pine were lit, and they filled the room with light brighter than any candle. The guide heaped the ill-matching bowls with his concoction and brought them out on a rough tray. The master of the house urged us to enjoy some of their miso soup, which had potatoes, turnip greens, and a strange-looking substance floating in it. The guide anticipated my question and said "That is the famous tofu of Akiyama." They had at least ground the beans this time, but they had not been pressed through a sieve, and the resulting bean curd was quite tasteless.

After dinner the master addressed me, "Master of the Tearoom" (in Akiyama they call someone Master of the Tearoom as a sign of respect, perhaps because it suggests he might have the means to possess his own tearoom), "How about a *doffuri?*" I had no idea what a *doffuri* was and asked my guide, who told me I had just been invited to take a bath. Here a bath is called *doffuri* or *oriyu*. (The only ones in Akiyama to own a bath are this house and the main branch of the same family. Everyone else takes only occasional splash baths, even in winter. When they come home from the mountains or the fields they step directly onto the matting on the floor, without washing their feet.) Well, I got into the bath with no further ado, and left the weariness of my travels behind.

After the bath I returned to my seat at the side of the hearth (the side seat is the seat of honor according to the country custom). Our host announced that he had a tea kettle, so I had one of our bearers make tea for us all; I gave sweets that I had packed to the three girls, who came out and sat at the edge of the hearth with us,

BOOK TWO

stretching their legs and letting their feet dangle into the ash. They ate the little cakes as if they were rare treasures. Here they burn logs the size of pillars without a second thought; and in the light of the fire I saw that the youngest girl was round and dark and ugly. From time to time she rolled up the hem of her robe and picked a louse, without the least embarrassment. The two older girls were light-complexioned beauties, and next to their sister they seemed two jewels. As they laughed and talked and ate their sweets, they were a very pretty sight. How sad that these two jewels will become the wives of Akiyama farmers, a waste as lamentable as burning a gracefully shaped harp to boil soup.

Our host knew a great deal about the region and knew, too, what sort of things might interest us. What I record in rough form here is what he told us about the customs of Akiyama.

"Only recently has this area been subject to taxation. But since we don't grow rice or barley, the tribute is very light. (The tax is called *kannayaku,* and is paid in local products.) The villages of Akiyama are under the rule of various other villages in Shinano and Echigo. Parishes, too, have been designated, but since almost twenty feet of snow may fall in winter, the dead cannot always be sent to the proper temple, so we must often hold private funerals. In the house of Sukesaburo—his family name is Yamada—there is a painted scroll called *Prince Shotoku on a Black Steed (Kurokoma Taishi)* that has been handed down through the ages. When someone dies we borrow this and pass it over the body two or three times, to lead him safely to the land of the dead. This has been the custom for a long time, before any parish temples were decided on." (In Akiyama there are only two family names: Yamada and Fukuhara. Sukesaburo is the head of the main line of the Yamada clan. The painting of Prince Shotoku is a scroll of fine cloth showing a figure who looks like Prince Shotoku riding a black steed through the clouds. I went to Sukesaburo's house and asked to be shown this scroll, but was told that it was only unrolled during February and August, and I was not allowed to view it.)

"The festive dish here is millet mixed with beans. The usual fare is millet bran mixed with millet and dried vegetables. The people of Akiyama also eat horse chestnuts.

"Marriages are made from among the fifteen villages of Akiyama, and thus marriage partners are not sought elsewhere. From ancient times, families have disowned and refused to ever see again daughters who took husbands from outside the mountains.

"There is not even a single hermit's hut in Akiyama, not to mention a temple, but there is one small shrine to the god Hachiman. It's because there are no temples where children may learn to read and write that the people are illiterate. From time to time someone with a will to learn might acquire a primer from far away and learn the syllabary, thus earning respect and a local reputation as a scholar.

"There are no mosquitoes here, and rare is the one who has even seen a mosquito net.

"The mountains are too dark and deep for the cultivation of silkworms, or even cotton, and that is why the clothing of Akiyama is so rough and poor. The plant called *ira* grows in the mountains, and its bark is used in place of ramie to make cloth." When the old man told me this I did not ask for particulars, but upon thinking it over I decided this must be the nettle referred to in The Herbal Encyclopedia under the name *tamma*. The fact that the second character of the compound *tamma* is the character for ramie is a hint that this nettle can be woven like ramie. Still, that book records that this nettle is poisonous. A plant called the mountain scallion (*yama nira*) also appears in that work; it, too, can be woven like ramie. Perhaps *ira* comes from *nira*? Since I did not inquire about the plant's appearance, it is hard to know.

The people of Akiyama all sleep with their kimonos on even in the winter, our host told me, and there has never been anything like bedclothes. A great fire is built in the hearth before going to sleep, and everyone sleeps nearby. When it is very cold, they tuck themselves into sleeping bags made of straw, which must be obtained from other places. A married man makes a straw sleeping bag large enough so that he and his wife can sleep together inside it. Besides our host's house, only one other family in all Akiyama had any bedclothes, and even these were for the use of guests. They were made from nettle and stuffed with nettle scraps, just a bit thicker than the usual wadded cotton. I slept in this bedding the night I stayed there, and the stuffing kept slipping down to the hem. There were many scratchy places, too, and in general it was not very comfortable at all.

Sleeping around the open hearth in Akiyama (*above*).
Hunting geese from a snow blind (*below*).

Since they lack straw, there are no straw sandals, and men and women alike go off barefoot to work in the mountains.

When someone falls ill, they are fed rice gruel as a medicine. When the illness is serious, a mountain ascetic is called to pray for the sick one. Praying for a sick person is an ancient custom that appears even in *The Tale of Genji*.

They say that only five women in all of Akiyama own mirrors, which reminds me of the old story of the mirror of Matsuyama.

The people of this region are sincere and warm. They do not fight among themselves, are not given to sensual pleasure, and never gamble. Since there are no sake shops, they do not drink. It is said that from ancient times no one has stolen as much as a straw. It's like a land of Taoist sages—except that the people eat meat!

The next day we crossed Yabutsu Bridge and stayed at Yumoto and bathed in the waters of its hot spring. Following that we toured the western villages and stayed at Kamiketto; then we crossed Monkey-Leap Bridge and stopped overnight at Mitama Village, after which we returned home. I saw so many things that I cannot record them all here, for my account would grow too long. I have written everything down in my *Record of a Journey to Akiyama* in two volumes, which I have stored away in my home.

But at least I would like to record the use of horse chestnuts for food, described to me by my venerable host, as a precaution for lean years. Horse chestnuts can be picked up as they ripen and fall in September. First they should be steamed, then dried. Next, you crush them with your hands and put them through a rough sieve, to separate out the inner layer of skin. The fine powder resulting is then heaped on a small split-bamboo mat over which a cloth has been spread, and smoothed out. After sprinkling it with water, the mat and the cloth full of horse-chestnut powder is rolled up and tied and the whole thing is left sitting in water for four or five days. The water is wrung out and the powder dried. It is now as white as snow. This powder can be mixed with millet, eaten as it is, or made into a sticky cake by pounding, though actually the horse-chestnut powder usually made into cakes is from a different type of horse chestnut. Acorns can also be eaten prepared in the same way.

I know that there are mountain villages in other parts of Japan that are not unlike these of Akiyama; though Akiyama is not unique, I write of it here because I have observed it so closely.

The products of Akiyama include wooden bowls, round wooden boxes, wooden trays, vine rope, and timber. Though there is much fine lumber in Akiyama, the Nakatsu River that flows down the mountain is full of twists and turns, runs deep and shallow, and so it is hard to send rafts down it. Of course, horses and oxen cannot be used either, and the fine wood stays where it is, making the people poor as if by nature.

Foxfire

In *The Youyang Miscellany* we read that the fox, worshiping the north star, places a skull-crown on its head and thumps the earth with its tail, sending sparks flying here and there. Though I am unable to judge what happens in faraway China, I would like to relate what I have seen with my very own eyes.

Foxes dislike the cold, and for this reason are only rarely seen near human habitations in deep winter. However, when the snowfall ceases with the returning spring and a heavy layer of snow many feet high still blankets all their food, they begin to prowl near the houses of villagers to steal whatever they can snatch away. Thus, they become a great nuisance.

People all know this, of course, and do everything in their power to keep the smart fellows out. But at the slightest lapse of vigilance, the foxes sneak in and make off with something edible. Their cunning is a marvel absolutely beyond understanding; they manage to get into places where only mice can enter. Of course, in both China and Japan, the fox is well known as a supernatural creature, so this is hardly surprising.

Living as I do, many months under the snow, I used to push my desk as near as possible to the window to get even the least little bit of daylight. One day my friend the late Bosai sent me a box of cakes. As I was about to go to sleep that night, I thought of the hungry foxes. I took pains to close the box of cakes particularly carefully, tied it tightly with a hemp string, and hung it from the ceiling, far from the desk and out of reach. "Now the cunning fellows will scarcely be able to make use of any of their tricks," I thought, and, satisfied, fell asleep. When I awoke the next morning I couldn't believe my eyes. The cord was hanging from the ceiling as I had fixed it—but the box was gone! And what was worse, there it sat neatly on my desk, just as if a person had placed it there. All the sheets of paper were still inside, but the cakes had been devoured to the last. This trick was strange indeed, and still puzzles me.

Sometimes foxes imitate the cries of cats, calling the creatures to them, mating with them, and then killing and eating them. Wily and venerable foxes may trick women or girls in a similar fashion and then rape them. Such pitiable victims can always be recognized by their disheveled hair and the deep trance in which they remain lying at the spot where it happened. When asked, they can never tell anyone the least thing about it—they all say that they have absolutely no memory of what occurred, before or after the event. That they really don't know anything at all is difficult to accept. Most likely they are ashamed and can't bear to talk about it.

The Youyang Miscellany also says that the fox knows how to divine the strange sounds made by the ice in winter. There are cases of this in Japan as well. When the people living in the Lake Suwa area see a fox running across the frozen lake, they, too, dare to cross it—just as in China.

There are quite a number of different explanations of just how the fox ignites the fires that are his trademark, but they are all rather difficult to accept. Yet even I have actually observed this phenomenon. It took place in the early predawn hours when I was looking out of the same second-story window I described above. I clearly saw the light of a fire outside through the crack of the window, and thinking it strange, peeped through the slit. A fox was standing on the snow wall and sending flames out of its mouth. The flames burned a little above his mouth, just as did the fire in the snow at Myoho Village, described earlier. A closer look revealed that it was exactly as if his breath were burning.

It was fascinating to observe, I must say. Sometimes there was flame, sometimes not. Most likely this depended upon the air in the fox's stomach from moment to moment. Of course, the fox's breath did not burn with a continuous flame. Sekitei speaks of the shining "fox jewels" in his *Cloud-Essence Annals,* because the jewels shine like foxfire, but the glowing of these fox jewels is quite a different thing from foxfire itself.

To Catch a Fox

A friend of mine once told me the following anecdote. "Someone I know was returning one evening from a neighboring village where he had been visiting when he spied a tea kettle on the side of the road. Since it was the middle of summer, he thought a farmer may have left it there after finishing his lunch. Fearing that some dishonest type would make off with it or hide it, he picked it up intending to take it into town and inquire after its owner. After he had walked a few hundred yards, the kettle swinging by its handle at his side grew heavier and heavier, and suddenly a voice came from it asking 'Where are you taking me?' A chill ran down his spine; as he tossed the kettle away and began to run, a fox dashed in front of him and disappeared in the grass by the roadside. All the while the fox had been playing a clever prank on him. But why is it that foxes can be duped by men and captured even though they possess such powers of bewitchment?"

And here was my response. "Let's first put aside the subject of hunting foxes with a gun. By any other means, foxes are caught with some sweet-smelling bait. Though they know very well that they are being tricked by men, they simply cannot control themselves. In fact, don't they get fooled and captured precisely when they try to beat men at their own game, to take the bait and run? This is because foxes are too wily for their own good. But not foxes alone; the same applies to people.

"The wily ones, knowing well that something is wrong, go ahead and do it if they think no one will find out. In the end, their wits are the end of them. Lust, greed—all the passions are that sweet-smelling treat. A good man may find a thousand pieces of gold on the road, or meet a great beauty in her chamber, but his heart doesn't quaver because he knows how to control himself and make his own decisions. The heart of such a one is a bright mirror, it illuminates good and evil, knows evil, and conquers it. This is called the mirror of bright virtue and was given to each of us by the Lord of Heaven, but it doesn't shine unless you polish it. I was taught this by a Confucian teacher when I was young." And thus I used this story of foxes as bait to trap my young questioner into a lesson from *The Great Learning,* for though he was still young, he was on the path to ruin. But my useless tongue wags; I have simply followed recollection.

Now then, of all the tricks for catching foxes in my village, there is one by which the hand never leaves the pocket. During the spring, the snow that has accumulated softens during the day. The trapper selects a place where foxes roam at night and then, with the sort of pestle used for pounding barley, he makes two or three holes—just the size of the pestle and no larger—in the snow. At night these holes freeze as hard as stone. The oil cake that foxes love is scattered about and placed at the bottom of the holes.

As the night grows late and all human noises cease, the foxes come out. After they have finished the cakes near the holes, they are still not satisfied, and so they always try to eat the ones at the bottom of the holes. They squeeze their bodies into the holes head first, but when they try to pull themselves out again after they have finished the bait they cannot. The holes are made so deep that only a bit of their tails stick out, and there is no way for them to pull themselves up. As the night grows older and colder the snow freezes harder. No fox has the strength to break out of the hole, but they try and try, and finally succeed only in exhausting themselves. The trappers wait for this and come with buckets of water to pour into the holes. The frozen holes hold the water for some time, and the foxes wave their tails about furiously as they suffer. Their hunters watch from a good distance away, for the foxes fart just before they die. When the tail stops moving the fox is dead, and it is pulled up like a radish.

Two or three holes are usually made, and on a good night, two or three foxes are plucked out. This method only works because the snow freezes stone-hard at night—if it were a hole in the earth the fox could easily escape. Since this is a practice peculiar to the snow country, I have included it here, with all this talk of snow.

Signs of the Geese's Feeding Grounds

When snow abounds in our land there is not the tiniest speck of food for birds, and they disappear from the mountains and fields. Only when spring approaches and the snow stops do we see them again. Finally in March, though the landscape remains blanketed in snow, the water in the flowing freshets begins to warm and melt the snow in places, clearing the way for waterfowl to land.

When geese discover such a place, one or two birds land. First they look for food; if they are successful, they leave their droppings as a sign to later arrivals. In the native dialect these are called the signs of the geese's feeding grounds. The geese do this to gather their companions and lead them to food, it is said, a kind of friendship that might well make people ashamed.

Now some heartless men go looking for goose droppings, and when they find these signs of the geese's feeding places they wait for the geese and bag them using all sorts of tricks. After several birds have been caught at a place, though, the geese grow wary and begin to bury their droppings so that people will not find them. At feeding places where there is little to eat, they leave their droppings unburied—but they never return, either. You see, the geese are just as smart as people are.

But then the people find this new trick out, too, and when they discover droppings covered with earth they build a shelter nearby out of snow in the shape of an overturned bowl. The entrance is in the back and the inside is like a cave. A hole is made in the direction the geese are expected to land from, and there the hunter watches and waits. (Geese feed at certain times and do not come to the feeding grounds otherwise. I will discuss this below.) When the geese alight, the hunter pushes his gun out of the hole and shoots. This kind of blind is called a snow house (*yukindo*). This is not the only way geese are hunted, for the methods are many and various. Geese move about at dusk or during the late night or early dawn. The hunters know this and wait for them, catching them with all sorts of clever methods.

Heaven's Net

We speak of heaven's net because a man can no more escape divine punishment for his evil deeds than a fish can the fisherman's net. Some seven miles north of Niigata is the village of Akazuka. There are many small dips and dales in the mountains nearby, and across them hunters string nets to catch birds. In our region these are called the heaven's nets of Akazuka.

There is a lagoon near this village that is much favored by waterfowl. As they come over the mountains toward the lagoon, they fly through the dips and are inevitably caught in heaven's nets. The most frequent catch is the *aji,* a bird that looks like a duck. They are delicious eating and are praised far and near as the "winter solstice fowl" of Akazuka. Their proper name is *ajikamo,* a word that can be found in many ancient poems.

When Geese Take Flight

In general, land birds are blind at night, while waterfowl see well in the dark. Geese, especially, have keen eyesight at night. I don't know about other places, but the geese of our land sleep during most of the day and fly at night. They gather far away from men to sleep, and two geese stand watch, gazing in the four directions. These are called the guard birds (*bandori*). Guard birds are also posted while the flock is feeding.

The file of geese in flight is called *ganko* and is mentioned in works on military strategy. Geese also form an orderly file as they land. When they feed, they feed together; when they play, they play together. Among the geese there is one that all the others follow, like soldiers after their general. When people approach or when something startles them, the guard birds beat their wings and the other birds, whether they are eating or sleeping, stop and listen. They all break suddenly and take to the air in seeming confusion, but soon they form an orderly file. We call this "the breaking of the flock."

A flock of geese is as alert as a military unit, unlike flocks of any other type of bird. The geese of other lands are no doubt the same as ours in Echigo, and this sort of talk is of little interest to country folks, but I thought it might be amusing for city people.

Crossing the Iceplank of Shibumi River

The Shibumi River springs from a source at the border between Shinano and Echigo provinces and flows one hundred miles through Echigo, joining the Chikuma River before it enters the northern sea. My first thought was that the river was named Shibumi because it flows through the four counties of Kubiki, Uonuma, Mishima, and Koshi, interpreting the name as "four(*shi*)-counties(*bu*)-seeing(*mi*)"; but that is not so, for in ancient sources we see it written with the characters meaning "bitter sea" or sometimes with others meaning "new flow." I'd be hard put to describe the bends and twists, the broads and narrows of this river. In winter much of it is closed over with ice and piled up with snow and cannot be told from the snowy plains around it. Yet where the current rushes against its rocky banks or flows with tremendous speed, snow does not accumulate, and in fact sometimes waves can be seen!

A crossing can be kept open with an axe for some time, but eventually the ice becomes too thick, and the task grows beyond human powers. Then the boats are pulled up on the shore and people cross over on the ice. We call this "crossing the iceplank."

The ice over the river begins to melt from the warmth of the sun at the end of February or the beginning of March, looses itself, and flows downstream. These sheets of ice range up to forty-five feet in length, varying in size depending upon the place in the river they came from. The ice always flows away in one day, or at most a day and a night. If it begins to crack in the morning, by evening the ice of one hundred miles has emptied into the northern sea. The noise it makes as it does so is as great as a thousand thunder claps, enough to make the mountains tremble. On this day people living near the river stay quietly inside their homes and do not go out; but people come from afar to watch the ice of the Shibumi River as if it were a blossom-viewing party, bringing sake and spreading colorful mats and blankets on the river's banks. And indeed, the thousands of sheets of crystalline ice riding the indigo waves of the rushing river are a wonderful sight. Certainly no one in warmer lands can boast the pleasures of ice viewing.

There is a miraculous story about this river and butterflies, which I will save for the next book.

We are caused great difficulty by the snow, but there are also some benefits it brings us. One is the convenience of sleds; snow makes crepe production possible; we can build snow houses, and, in the case of our amateur theatricals, the stage, the boxes, and the *hana-michi* ramp can all be made out of snow. The stalls and shelves of street-corner vendors are made from snow and called *satsuya*. Snow assists in the capture of birds and beasts. Snow-buried houses keep out the cold. In the snow that remains in the mountain valleys even in summer we can pack fish and fowl to prevent them from spoiling. The snow feeds the rivers and streams. If I went into detail, the list would be much longer.

All of this only leads us to conclude that there is nothing among the myriad things of heaven and earth that should be shunned—except for the evil of man.

BOOK THREE

The Butterflies of Shibumi River

In the local speech, butterflies are called *betto,* and those living near the Shibumi River are called *sakabetto.* Butterflies are the winged form of many different sorts of insects. The larger ones are called butterflies and the smaller ones moths, and there are a great many kinds. Even plants and flowers may turn into butterflies, according to The Herbal Encyclopedia. The ancient Japanese reading for "butterfly" is *kawabirako,* according to The New Mirror of Collected Characters; *sakabetto* does not appear there.

Now at the Shibumi River, mentioned earlier, at just about the time of the vernal equinox, millions and millions of butterflies flock together so close that their wings rub against each other, hovering and flitting some two or three feet over the river's surface. The layer of butterflies between the two banks is more than ten feet deep as they make their way upstream like a blizzard of falling flower petals. The river seems draped in mist for mile after mile. From dawn to evening the unending trail flits upstream, so dense that the river itself cannot be seen. Then, when the day comes to a close, the butterflies all drop into the water and drift downstream, and the river looks like bolts of white silk are being rinsed in it.

These butterflies are white in color, similar in shape to a tiger moth. Though there are many large and small rivers in our land, the Shibumi River was the only one that boasted this strange phenome-

Viewing the butterflies of Shibumi River.

non, year after year; but since the flood of the Temmei era (1781–89), it no longer occurs even there.

While flipping through *The Herbal Encyclopedia* to write about the butterflies of the Shibumi River, I noticed that it gives "sand flea" (*suna shirami*) as an alternative name for the caddis fly and says that it builds a cocoon on the stones of mountain streams. In the spring and summer it sprouts wings and hovers above the river's surface, says the encyclopedia. The *sakabetto* I have described must have been the caddis flies of the Shibumi River, and they are no longer to be seen because during the flood their eggs were all washed away, though no doubt they are found in rivers in other parts of the land that provide a home for the caddis fly. Now I must admit that I myself have never seen the butterflies of the Shibumi River; but when I asked an old woman from my neighborhood who came here in marriage as a young girl from a place near the banks of the river, she related all of this to me, and I have recorded it just as she told it.

Thoughts on the Chinese Character for "Salmon"

The dictionary *The New Mirror of Collected Characters* was compiled by the monk Shoju some 940 years ago, during the Kampyo and Shotai eras (889–900). From ancient times the scholars of the world have handed down copies of this work devoted to the scrutiny of Chinese characters, and it has been regarded as a priceless treasure. Only recently did the scholar Murata Harumi purchase this work in Kyoto, and later, in 1803, first have woodblocks of it carved for printing. Truly, Harumi's great gift to the scholars of the world was to place this treasure on their desks for the first time since it was written.

Some twenty years after the composition of *The New Mirror*, we find *The Thesaurus of Japanese Names* by Minamoto no Shitago, another lexicon. This was first printed in the Genna era (1615–24) by Naba Doen. Five hundred years after the appearance of the *Thesaurus*, *A Collection of Everyday Expressions* was written, and this, too, was printed

BOOK THREE

in the Genna era—in 1617. Fifty-three years after the composition of *A Collection of Everyday Expressions,* in 1496, Hayashi Soji (a merchant from Osaka) wrote *A Collection of Handy Phrases.* It was printed in the Bunki era (1501–4). This was the first dictionary of phrases arranged in alphabetical order. One hundred and eighty years later, in 1698, the Hermit of Komagai, Makinoshima Terutake (from Edo) wrote *A Reference of Works, Words, and Characters,* also known as *The Supplemented Collection of Handy Phrases.* This was an expansion of Muneji's work, again arranged in alphabetical order. (I will not mention other works that I do not cite below.)

These by and large are the lexicons of our land. All dictionaries and phrase books in popular use today can claim *The New Mirror of Collected Characters* and *The Thesaurus of Japanese Names* as mother and father; all the later works are their progeny. Now what I really want to talk about is the Chinese character for "salmon," but I thought I'd say all of this first for the sake of the little ones, who may not know it.

In the "Fish" section of *The New Mirror of Collected Characters,* 鮏 is given for "salmon." The main entry in *Japanese Names* is also 鮏, and the character 鮭 is decried as a vulgarism. But, in fact, it also has been in use since ancient times. In the latter work, a passage from *The Food Classic* by Sai Useki is quoted: "Salmon roe is as red and shiny as a strawberry; the fish is born in the spring and dies before the year is over, and so is also called the year fish." The appearance of the character 鮭 for 鮏 may be merely a copyist's error that has been passed down through the ages. Perhaps the character 鮭 refers to the blowfish? *A Collection of Everyday Expressions* gives two instances of 鮭, and Muneji in his work does the same. These, too, could well be copyists' errors. The Hermit of Komagai gives at least four different ways of writing "salmon," but quotes *Japanese Names* and states that 鮏 is the original character. In Reverend Daiten's *Dictionary* the character 鱖 is given, but that is properly read *asaji* and means "perch." Chinese dictionaries tell us that this perch has a large mouth and fine scales, and those points of resemblance to salmon may have led the Reverend Daiten to borrow this character. *The Collection of Chinese Characters* states that 鮏 derived from the character 鯹, which means "smelly"; and come to think of it, the reason may be that

113

fresh salmon is a particularly smelly fish. Since the character 鮭 is a synonym for "blowfish," its use for "salmon" is pretty far-fetched.

At any rate, when all is said and done, we should know the character 鮭, but probably use the character 鮏 for daily use. As I have taken pains to explain above, it has been used from ancient times and is in general use in Japanese literature. On the other hand, the character 鮏 is much less frequently seen, so I will use it in the following entries.

Salmon Dishes

Salmon can be eaten raw as sashimi, *namasu* (vinegared fish), or sushi. Salmon can be baked, boiled, and prepared in any number of other ways. From ancient times, salmon has been salted and dried, too—in fact, one of the old lexicons I mentioned in the earlier passage gives "dried salmon" and "salted salmon" as entries under the character. The "*kokomori* salmon" mentioned in *The Codes of the Engi Era* probably refers to salted salmon stuffed with salted salmon roe.

Salmon is even listed in the same book as an item of tribute to the imperial court from the provinces of Tango, Shinano, Etchu, and Echigo, so we know that in ancient times it was eaten by the emperor, empress, and the nobility at court. This must have been salted salmon, since it was brought from so far away. The transparent cartilage inside the fish's skull was called the *hizu* and was particularly relished as a vinegary *namasu* treat. Salmon roe is called *hararago* and is delicious when cured in salt.

The Herbal Encyclopedia states that salmon is slightly sweet in taste, mild flavored, and without poisons. Its main effect is to warm the body and activate the vital spirit, but eating too much of it will cause a phlegm buildup. In Echigo, there is not a single house that does not feast on salted salmon on New Year's Eve. Salmon is also offered to those who are ill. I can only imagine that salmon is shunned in other countries as causing boils because the inhabitants are not accustomed to eating it.

BOOK THREE

Where Salmon Are Found

Salmon are unknown in the five provinces nearest the imperial capital as well as in the western provinces. They are only found in the great rivers of the northeast that lead to the cold seas. Salmon are most numerous in Ezo and Matsumae, and these lands supply many places with salted salmon. Next in abundance are the salmon found in our Echigo, as well as in Shinano, Etchu, Dewa, and Mutsu. I have heard that they are also caught in Hitachi. But the number of salmon caught in all of these provinces (except Matsumae and Ezo) is only enough to supply the local people, not enough for sale outside. There are even said to be a few salmon in the Tone River that runs through Edo, but they are so rare that the price of the first salmon of the year is comparable to that of the first bonito!

In Echigo, the first salmon fishing takes place on the day after the Festival of Suwa, held hereabouts on the twenty-seventh day of August, and it only comes to an end when the weather begins to grow really cold at the end of January. When the first salmon taken by the fishermen of Kawaguchi in Uonuma and Nagaoka in Koshi are sent to the lord of Nagaoka, he usually offers seven measures of rice for one fish. There are prescribed payments in rice for the five largest sizes of salmon, the amount dropping accordingly. The largest salmon are some three feet four or five inches, and the smallest a foot shorter (though certainly there must be even smaller salmon).

Salmon are divided into *ona* and *mena,* written with the Chinese characters for "man fish" and "woman fish," rather than simply "male" and "female." The females are more valuable because their bellies are filled with roe.

All of the first five sizes of salmon are presented to the lord; the others are brought to market. By this we may imagine the value of the very first catch: it is certainly not any less celebrated than the first bonito in Edo. The first salmon shines like silver, with a faint blue gleam, and its meat is as if painted with scarlet. By midwinter, in December, the body is blotched and the meat is paler; the taste is less delicate, too.

The best salmon in Echigo are caught in the rivers of Kawaguchi and Nagaoka—their flavor is ten times more exquisite than any others! The salmon caught just a short distance away no longer taste so delicious. The flavor of the former is superior because they have made a long and strenuous journey up the rivers from the northern seas, and fish that have fought hard currents always have a sweeter, more delicate taste. In a similar fashion, the fishes of the northern seas are said to be more flavorful and those of the southern seas more bland in taste.

The Life Cycle of Salmon

The salmon of Echigo leave the northern seas at the beginning of autumn and begin to make their way up the two great rivers of the region—the Chikuma and the Aka—to spawn. The male salmon follow the females upstream. The entire journey is some 125 miles, and the salmon are in the rivers for more than five months. During that time (from September to January) many end up as some fisherman's prize. Those that are not caught return again to the sea, and that's why larger and smaller salmon can be found.

The fish make the journey upstream in search of a place to spawn. Though there are exceptions, usually they select a place below the point called Kawaguchi where the Chikuma and Uono rivers join, because at that point the combined flow of the two rivers mixes sand and gravel together, making a fine bed in which the salmon can lay their eggs. The returning salmon seek out a clear flowing stream in which the current is not too strong. Pairs of salmon preparing to spawn are said in fishermen's talk to be "digging troughs" or "flirting," for the salmon dig troughs of all shapes, and "flirting" describes their behavior just before spawning time. Both the female and the male hollow troughs in the sand at the river bottom with their tails. Each trough is roughly one foot wide, ten inches deep, and nine feet long. It takes the pair several days to finish one trough. When they are done, the female lays her eggs, one at a time, in the trough. The male watches her and follows behind, secreting his milt over the eggs.

Immediately afterward male and female together cover the eggs with the sand and gravel they have piled up at the sides of the trough, pushing it in with their tail fins. They are so careful that not a single egg is washed away with the current.

When one trough is filled with eggs and covered over again, they start on another next to it. After they dig, they lay; and after they lay, they dig again. They continue until an area nine feet square is neatly lined with trough after trough, and the female has laid every single egg in her belly. Sometimes they make troughs at several different locations. The fishermen insist that salmon will not spawn unless they can find a place where the river bottom is made of a mix of sand and gravel. At any rate, the salmon show a wisdom of their own not in any way inferior to man's.

The pains and difficulties of spawning leave the salmon exhausted and ragged, their fins torn and bodies thin. They drift downstream again with the current to seek refuge and to recuperate in deep pools. Once they are fine and fat again, they return upstream. Fishermen never catch salmon during the spawning period; oh, it may happen by accident, but that is an exception. The male salmon will not desert the eggs as long as the female is not caught. The whole purpose of the salmon's long trek upstream is to spawn. The male follows the female upstream to help her for the sake of their offspring; and here there is no difference between their hearts and our own.

One strange fact is that if, for example, a broad portion of the river where salmon have laid their eggs floods, overflows its banks, and the old riverbed dries out, the eggs do not die. If the river returns to its course, the eggs will hatch and the salmon fry will be born. A friend of mine tells me that several years back when some villagers near the Uono River dug a well, they found fresh salmon eggs!

Fishermen call the hatching of salmon eggs "quickening" (*hayakeru*) or "embodying" (*miyokeru*). The eggs hatch after being submerged for fourteen or fifteen days. The fry are shaped like a thread and are only an inch or two long. They look like they have an open slit (*sake*) across their bellies instead of an intestine—and some people say this is the origin of the word "salmon" (*sake*). By spring the fry are three or four inches long, and everyone is careful not to fish for them at this stage. The fry ride the rush of the melting snow to the sea; by this time, the fishermen tell me, the slit has closed and they have a stomach and bowels like any other fish.

As mentioned earlier, salmon are only fished for in the winter months, and it is believed that anyone who catches them after winter is over will be punished. There was, when I was young, a certain fellow in a fishing village who stole and ate the salmon that a river otter had caught. He was afflicted with a terrible fever and died after three days, so it certainly won't do to make light of this belief. Another belief has it that the family line of anyone who dares to rob the salmon of its eggs will be cut off at that generation.

There are some large salmon over three and one-half feet in length—these are the clever old fish that have managed to avoid the fishermen's nets year after year. The largest female salmon carry as much as two quarts of roe in their bellies. Smaller females may have only one pint. When I was young, salmon were plentiful and cheap; the catch has lessened considerably of late, and their price has, quite naturally, more than doubled. Year after year the methods of catching salmon have improved, and so their numbers have decreased. According to a naturalist of repute, the salmon pickled in salt that are in great demand in Edo are actually a different variety from those we catch here in Echigo. Salmon are born in the rivers and grow to maturity in the sea. Still, from ancient times they have never been caught in nets set in the seas.

When you consider the life cycle of salmon, there can be no doubt that they are one of the most marvelous members of the family of fishes.

I have always thought that it would be an excellent idea to collect, during the winter months, some roe and some of the male salmon's milt, mix the two together, and place them in a large jar with the gravel and sand of a river in which salmon are found. This jar could then be brought to the clean upper reaches of a mountain stream that flows to the sea and the eggs buried in the stream bed just as a pair of salmon would do. Then, if a three-year prohibition on fishing is observed, the river will surely produce salmon. If this plan were successful, it would greatly benefit the land. The eggs of the white fish of Edo were brought there long ago in just this fashion.

BOOK THREE

Weirs and Traps

Two great rivers, the Aka and the Chikuma, empty into the Japan Sea at Niigata. I will not talk about the Aka River here; the Chikuma River (Thousand-Bend River) is also known as the Shinano River in some parts; sometimes it is written with the Chinese characters meaning "Thousand-Nook River." Many small and large rivers from Shinano, Echigo, and Hida flow together to create the Chikuma River. It crosses the two old manors of Tsumari and Ueda in Echigo, joining the swift Uono River. After flowing through all of Uonuma County and old Yabukami Manor, it reaches Kawaguchi Post Town and joins the river coming from Shinano. Passing through Koshi and Kambara counties, it empties into the sea. The Shinano current is dirty and the Echigo current is clean; the Shinano currents run with the dirty water of the Sai River, and that's the reason.

In early autumn the salmon leave the sea and begin to head up these rivers. At Kambara, the river is shallow and broad, and salmon can be caught with large nets. But from Kawaguchi Post Town upstream, and especially in Ueda and Tsumari, salmon are caught with weirs called *uchi kiri*. This is how it's done:

Work begins in the late summer. A line of posts is driven into the riverbed from bank to midstream. These posts are crossed with horizontal supports, and a fence of bamboo-weave blinds is strung across the river on this framework. Rocks from the riverbed help to support the structure, which may be as long as four hundred yards. The exact shape of the wall depends on the conformation of the riverbed and banks. A passage, illuminated at night, is made for boats to pass freely through.

Traps called *tsuzu* are set at the bottom of this bamboo weir, tied in positions so that salmon might easily enter. The bottoms of the traps are tied to the posts. *Tsuzu* are made by tying one end of a bamboo basketwork while making inward-pointing teeth out of bamboo at the other, "mouth" end of the trap. The bottom, buried in the riverbed, is flat and the top rounded. The body of the trap is round, and the whole thing exactly five feet in length. It is made quite cleverly, for the mouth stretches open as a salmon enters only to close immediately to keep it from escaping.

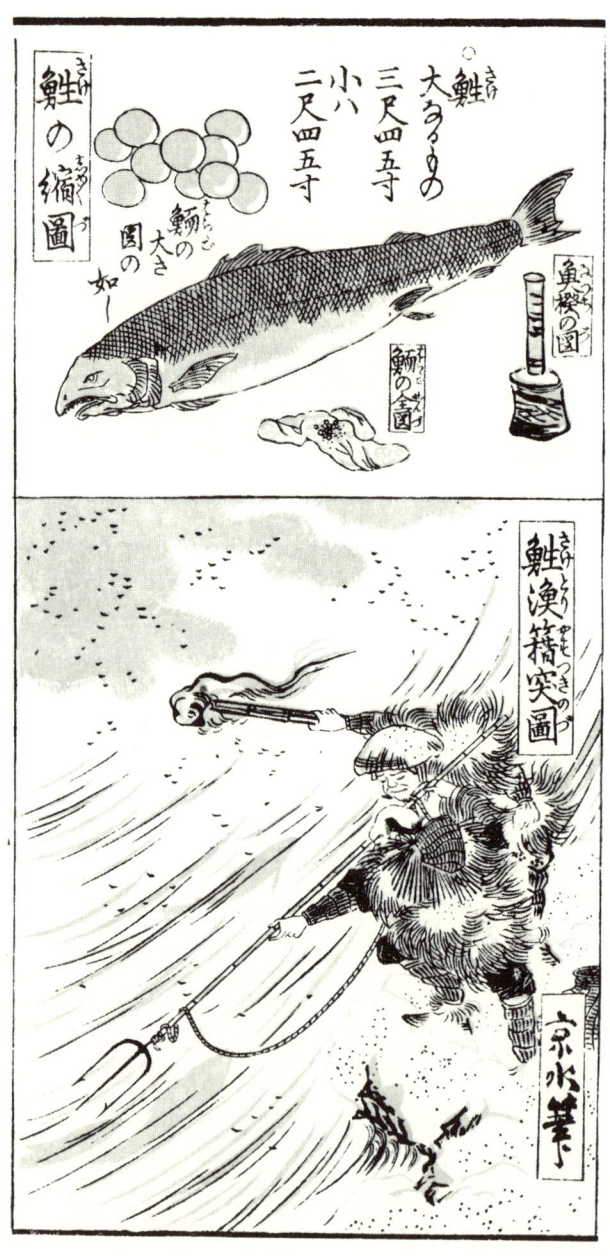

Salmon, with roe and horse-hoof hammer (*above*). Spearing salmon (*below*).

BOOK THREE

(*Tsuzu* is obviously a local pronunciation of *tsutsu*, which means "tube." There are many words in our country dialect that are pronounced as they were in ancient times, but there are just as many plain and simple mistakes and corruptions, where "t" is pronounced "d" and "k" is pronounced "g"—for example, the Aka River is called by many the Aga River.)

Now then, since a considerable amount of labor and expense goes into building these weirs, it is a joint venture that all the fishermen undertake together after much discussion. They also build huts on the riverbanks to which the weir is attached, and there they stay night and day, never sleeping, waiting for the salmon to swim into their traps. From August to the bright cold days of January, these groups of fishermen man the huts in shifts, catching salmon all the while. Kawaguchi is regarded as the first spot for this kind of weir. Another fourteen weirs are set at intervals in the river above Kawaguchi. The divisions of the river lengths into territories and the guarding of the boundaries are extremely strict.

The salmon come swimming up the river until they reach the weir. Water spills through the passage for boats like a waterfall, pushed through with great force by the wall that slows the rest of the current. The salmon wish to avoid these rapids and head for the quiet pools near the weir. When they run into the fence they start looking for places to squeeze under it, and soon chance upon a trap. In an attempt to squeeze under the weir, they enter the trap. Their hopeful passage is blocked by the trap's sturdy bottom, and when they try to go out again they are stopped by the bamboo teeth that line the trap's mouth.

The fishermen waiting in the huts say they have a feel for when their traps are full. They set out in a boat called a *hanakamasu* (made out of a log split in half and hollowed out; in shallow places no boat is used). Without a thought for the cold, even on freezing, snowy nights, they strip down to their loincloths and leap into the river, untying the traps filled with salmon and tossing them into the boat. Once in the boat they shake the salmon out of the traps. Some of these wildly flopping fishes are more than three feet long, and the only way to kill them is to hit them with a single blow on the head with a "fish mallet" (*natsuchi*). Now the truly odd thing is that the salmon don't die unless they are hit with a mallet made from a horse's hoof. "No other hammer will do," insist the fishermen, "you can hit them again and again with a hammer of your own making, but they refuse to die. And there's a special place on the head where they must be struck, too." Wherever salmon are fished, this hammer—always made of a horse's hoof—is used.

A buyer called a *sukego* comes to these riverside huts to purchase the salmon that he will later sell at market.

Scoop Nets

Kaki ami are scoop nets for catching salmon. To make one, you select a branch that has a sturdy fork and bend the two prongs round together in a ring. To this you attach a net. Another long branch becomes the handle. In parts of the river flanked by high banks, salmon press close to the shore as they make their way upstream. A fisherman builds a little platform just big enough to hold him, plants himself firmly on it with his fish mallet tucked in his belt, and scoops up fish from the river below. In places where the banks are absolutely sheer cliffs, fishermen sometimes hang their shelf-platforms by wisteria-vine ropes from the roots of large trees. Perching perilously over the cold depths of the river, their lives suspended from one thin rope made of twisted vine, it's a wonder they are not terrified; but in fact they seem to be quite used to this and do not think to be afraid.

A Fisherman Drowns

In a certain village, a husband and wife lived with their son of five, their daughter of three, and the husband's aged mother. (Since what I am about to recount is a sad event, I will keep their names to myself.) They made their living mainly as farmers, but the husband went out fishing during the salmon season every year to make their life a better one.

Fishing with a net from a suspended platform.

Now, since the riverbanks near the village that this family lived in were quite steep, all the local fishermen built little platforms and fished with scoop nets. But in places with especially straight, sheer banks, no one dared to build a platform. No one, that is, except the fellow whose story I recount here. He was tempted by the guarantee of a big catch and made himself a hanging seat in one of those dangerous places. There he sat, pulling in salmon one after another, just as if his life and limb were not hanging by a thread.

Snow was falling and fish were biting one day in November as he hung from his perch. Undaunted, he sat from morning on his shelf, wrapped in a rush coat, a rush hat on his head, fishing without stop. When his creel was full, he shinnied up the lifeline that held him aloft—for he was as accustomed to climbing up and down his rope as a monkey is his tree—and pulled his catch up after him with another rope he had attached earlier. The only other times he climbed up to the cliff's edge were to eat his meals.

As this particular day drew to a close, the snow began to fall more thickly, and, since fish bite more eagerly during a heavy snowfall, he decided to return to his hanging seat after the evening meal and resume fishing. He wouldn't listen to the pleas of his wife and mother that he stay home; instead he readied pine torches and returned to his perch hanging from the cliff. Netting away, he caught a great harvest of salmon, and began, as in the cormorant fisher's song, to "forget about sins, forget about punishment, forget about the next world"—so engagingly did the time pass.

Now the wife put her mother-in-law and children to bed and began to worry about her husband: "He'll freeze in this snowstorm! I'm going to go and bring him home." And she put on her rush cape and a hat, lit a pine torch, and stuck two spare torches in her sash. When she arrived at the spot she waved her torch this way and that until she finally discovered her husband far, far below. She called out to him, "You must be so cold! The first watch of the night has already passed, and it's past eight o'clock. Quit right now and come home. Dinner is warm and sake is waiting. Come home, come home! You must be out of torches by now. There's so much snow already that you'll have to wear snowshoes. Look, I've brought them."

But the strong west blizzard winds made it very difficult to hear.

BOOK THREE

When she raised her voice even louder, her husband at last seemed to hear. "You should be happy! I've caught so many salmon! I'll be back tomorrow and drink that delicious sake. Just let me catch a few more. You go home first." "Well, at least let me leave this torch here for you," she said, and wedged the burning torch into the fork of the great tree to which her husband's perch and lifeline were tied. She lit another torch from the first one and left for home. And this was the final parting of husband and wife.

When the wife got home she kindled the fire in the hearth and set about preparing all sorts of treats so that her husband would have something warm to eat when he got home. Then she sat down and waited. But time passed and he did not return. Finally her patience was exhausted and she went back to the spot where he was fishing. The pine torch she had stuck in the tree was no longer there. Though she held the one in her hand low over the cliff, she could not make out her husband's form; and when she raised her voice and called and called him, there was no answer. "Well, isn't he down there any longer?" she thought, but quickly stilled her worst thoughts. Instead she waved her torch about, looking for signs in the snow that he had climbed up the bank again. She found none, but she did see that the pine torch she had stuck in the tree fork had burned down and fallen to the ground. "What if . . . ?" she thought, and when she looked even more carefully by the light of her torch, she found the burnt remains of the rope from which her husband had been suspended.

Her heart froze in her breast. The pine torch had burned and fallen, singeing and cutting the rope, and her husband had fallen with his platform into the deep river—there could be not the slightest doubt. For no matter how fine a swimmer he might be, falling into the rushing current in the depths of night, hands and feet frozen, and with no help in sight—he could not have survived. "What shall I do, what shall I do?" she lamented and wept, "What shall I tell my mother-in-law?" She threw her pine torch into the river and was about to throw herself after it when she thought again. "But if I die, who will care for my aged mother and my babies? She will be forced to lead them out on the road to beg. No, it will be greater punishment for me to go on living than to die. Forgive me, my husband!" she cried and threw herself down in the snow. Clasping the burnt slip of rope, she raised her voice in wails of lamentation.

After some time, she began her return home, clutching the burnt piece of rope, weeping, weeping, as she stumbled through the blizzard-blown night without any torch to guide her, tears streaming down her face. They never found her husband's corpse—or so I was told some years ago by a friend who lives in the area, who said then that this had happened only recently.

So Waterfall

So Waterfall is about one hundred miles upstream from Niigata Harbor, on a stream leading into the Chikuma River near a village called Warino. This is the only waterfall on the entire river, from its source at Tambajima in Shinano to its mouth at Niigata. The river is at least two hundred yards wide at this point; the waterfall is created by a huge rock like a sleeping dragon lying in the water across the surging current.

When the salmon reach this point in the river, they leap this way and that as they try to scale the rushing falls. The fishermen take advantage of this and lay bridges of tree trunks and brushwood tied with vines from the banks to large rocks near the river's edge. After hacking the frozen snow off the rocks, they settle there to begin their scoop netting. Because they value their lives, each one of them ties a rope about his waist; the other end he anchors to the point of a rock. They try to clear footholds in the rocks for easier scrambling back and forth, but if anyone takes just one false step, he will tumble into the falls and be pulverized. How dangerous is this work!

When I was in Edo some years ago, I related this story to the late Santo. His comment—delivered with a wry chuckle, I might add—was that the whirlpools of this world were more perilous than So Waterfall, yet we could hardly afford the luxury of carefully picking our way through life. I know I thought those wise words at the time

BOOK THREE

and remembered them then—as I just happened to now once again, which is why I have set them down here.

Methods of Catching Salmon

Casting nets. This refers to catching salmon with a hand-cast triangular net.

Anchored gill net (*oikawa*, literally, "driving up the river"). Posts are driven into the riverbed and nets stretched across them. Then the salmon are driven into the nets by fishermen beating the water with bamboo poles.

Four-handed net. This is the usual square sunken net used in other parts of the land as well.

Gaff hooks. It is curious indeed to watch these being used.

Floating gill nets. Also called drop nets, such nets may be more than four hundred yards in length. They are used in Kambara County.

Spearing. The fisherman spots a salmon in the river and pierces it with a spear. Again, the skill with which they spear their catch, never letting a fish evade them, is marvelous.

There are many other methods, but it would be tiring to describe them all in detail, so I will let them slip through my nets.

The Sandbank Race of the Salmon

The sandbank race of the salmon often occurs on riverbanks and sandbars before the snow begins to fall. Blocked by nets and chased by fishermen, the salmon leap up onto the riverbanks, make their way on land past the nets, and slip into the water again. A large fish takes the lead, and his smaller companions follow him ashore. Though they are only on land for eight or ten yards, they shoot straight and swift as arrows, faster than any man can run. If the lead salmon bumps into some obstacle and falls on its side, the salmon following behind all do so, too. Since they cannot right themselves again, they lie there just waiting for fishermen to come along and pick them up—without lifting a finger or wetting your hands you've made a fine catch of two or three fat salmon! They walk on land though they have no feet, but once they fall over they cannot get up again. Truly, when we compare these salmon to other members of the fish tribe, they are curious, curious beasts.

Icicles

When I traveled to Edo years ago and visited the homes of various writers and painters, seeking to purchase their writings and works, I grew quite friendly with the late Hermit Santo and was in his company frequently. In those days, Kyozan, Santo's younger brother, was still in his youth. One day we were talking about snow, and Kyozan told the following anecdote.

"Some friends of mine and I decided to pass by the gay quarters on our way back from viewing the plum blossoms during February of this year. As dawn broke it began to rain, though it stopped again of a sudden. As we left the quarters and reached the bank of the surrounding moat we saw several willow trees at the moat's edge strung with little two- and three-inch icicles all along every branch where the early morning rain had frozen. The graceful green threads of the new willow branches were as if draped in crystal. As this spectacle shining in the red of the dawn was such a wonderful sight, we decided to stop at a teahouse nearby to gaze at it, rest ourselves, and compose some poems on the theme."

These icicles were the result of the brief rain while the cold of the night still held sway. Kyozan talked about it as if it were a very rare sight, and indeed it is for warm places like Edo; I thought his excitement was amusing, though, since compared to the icicles of our land, those he raved about were as inconsequential as a duck fart.

Before I say anything else about the icicles of Echigo, let me start by describing those on my own house. Many icicles—or should I say ice pillars?—form on the eaves of my house around the start of spring.

BOOK THREE

The front of the house is fifty-four feet wide, and icicles line the entire width. Some are long and some are short. The long ones may be as long as six or seven feet and two feet around at the base—though some are flattened rather than round. The front of the house is as if enclosed by crystal bars. But the people of our land are used to seeing such icicles from childhood and would never think of writing poems about them! We knock them off each morning with a shovel because they block the light.

The dips of the roof are called *dagi* in our local dialect, and here much larger icicles than those of the eaves form, because in spring, as the snow on the roof starts to melt, it all drips down through these little valleys. If there is nothing below to obstruct their growth, the icicles may end up almost twenty feet long. We let them grow long and fat provided they are not in the way. When the time comes to knock them off, a strong man whacks away at them with a large stake. After they finally break and fall, these giant icicles become the playthings of children, who cart them around on their sleds. The icicles of my own house that I have described here are not at all unusual. They certainly do not compare with the much larger icicles that form on temple and shrine roofs or those of the deep mountain fastnesses.

The Icicles of Oikake Rock

A bit over seven miles to the southeast of Shiozawa is the village of Shimizu. There is a rock on the mountain near that village called Oikake Rock (Overhang Rock). It stands more than 100 feet high and runs 125 feet from side to side. Below it flows a river (the source of the Nobori River). The rock spreads out like a huge folding screen in shape, the peak of the rock looming over to cover the river like a roof. This overhang is so large that forty or fifty people can easily be seated under it. Oikake Rock is one of the many famous boulders of Upper Echigo.

The icicles of Oikake Rock are so astonishing that even we take note. I learned of them from the village head of Shimizu, Old Man

A salmon weir across the river (*above*).
The sandbank race of the salmon (*below*).

Abe. According to his tale, some of the icicles hanging down from the rock's overhang are as long as 100 feet and as wide around as the outstretched arms of two men. They drip down like giant candles, but unlike the rather ordinary icicles of our villages, these twist and turn in fantastic shapes like fanciful crystal creatures. Sparkling like diamonds, they reflect and glow in the red light of the dawn, creating a truly wonderful sight.

Old Man Abe of Shimizu Village is a descendant of Abe Uemon no Jo, who was famous long ago. Through the generations, the family has been guardian of the pass at Shimizu. The ruins of the castle of Nagao Iga are also to be found here.

Icicles Round the Waterfall

Since so many mountain ranges run through Upper Echigo, there are also many waterfalls. Deciduous trees of great size are always found around waterfalls, flourishing in the spray. As spring approaches and the snow on their branches melts, exposing a leafless forest, the spray from the waterfall drenches the branches and freezes into icicles. The trees then are a singular sight, as if draped in jeweled curtains. Icicles also form around the waterfall itself, and the entire cage of crystal is set against a backdrop of sparkling, jewel-like snow, reminding one of Mount Kei in China, the famous source of precious gems. Yet rare is the person other than the passing farmer or woodcutter who enjoys this scene.

Those of warm lands would no doubt be thrilled by the rarity of this sight. I was fortunate to witness it myself as I crossed the mountains from Kashiwazaki to Tsumari once.

Winter Ascetics

There is a manservant in my house who was in Edo for two years. He tells us of religious practitioners there who observe the winter nembutsu, reciting the Buddha's name as they make their way during the thirty days of the cold winter season to the execution grounds at Suzugamori and Senju to pray that those executed may be reborn in the Pure Land. The practitioners wear long underwear and straw sandals, and so are relatively warm, but there is another practice carried out in the winter called the naked pilgrimage. All of the young men in the carpentry trade participate. As they run quickly to the places where they will chant Amida Buddha's name, the naked young men ring bells and carry long lanterns with the characters "daily worship" written in bold letters. At each place they worship, they douse themselves with water. According to my servant, you are likely to see several of these practitioners running through the streets on any cold winter night.

Though we are like Edo in having winter ascetic practices, the practices themselves are quite different from those of the capital. First of all, as I have described many times before, Echigo is blanketed with snow all through the winter and is terribly cold. Our practitioners tramp over the snow every night for one week or for three weeks, whatever their vow might be, to visit the shrine they have chosen or to practice the winter chanting of the Buddha's name. Most of them are young farmers or servants in merchant's houses and must work during the day, restricting their wandering practice to the night, but they douse themselves with water at least three times during each of their busy days, and some choose to do so even more frequently. It is forbidden for them to wipe themselves, and so they dress again while still wet. As part of their practice they allow themselves only a rough bundle of rice stalks for a seat, tied together at one end so that it can be spread open like a fan. (The rice straw is said to represent the sacred Shinto *shimenawa* rope.) To prevent themselves from lapsing into their usual behavior and sitting any other way, they tuck this rice straw into their belts.

All practitioners take a vow of silence, and they are not permitted to receive food prepared by any woman's hand, not even from their wives. The only exception is their own mothers. Of course they observe all of the usual abstinences, purifying their bodies with water and salt and abstaining from eating meat. Everyone can see from the straw tucked into their belts that these men have taken a vow of silence, and no one addresses them, for if someone talks to a practitioner, he may thoughtlessly answer, breaking his vow, and then he would have to start his practice all over again from the beginning. Some practitioners do not take a vow of silence, though.

As night falls the practitioner performs ablutions while chanting the Buddha's name one thousand times. On every hundredth chanting he douses himself head to toe; all in all, then, he douses himself ten times during his practice. He dresses again in clean clothing—without wiping himself—and, whether it's snowing or not, wears a rush cape and hat. No matter how thickly the snow is falling or how fiercely the wind whipping, the practitioner then sets off beating on his bronze pilgrim's bell. There are always fellow practitioners to travel with. One calls to another by standing outside the door and tapping his bell. The one inside answers by tapping his bell in return, and so they gather without breaking their vow of silence. The practitioner cannot enter the house, for if he were to meet a woman he would be defiled and would have to purify himself again by bathing in a river or dousing himself with well water before continuing on his pilgrimage. Thus, when they hear the ringing of the ascetic's bell, women stay inside their homes; or, if they hear the bell from afar when they are out on the road, they duck behind a corner and hide until the ascetic has passed.

Whenever one of these ascetics hears of a death, he makes a visit to the house of the deceased, whether it be five or ten miles out of the way, on the rounds of his pilgrimage. He never asks whether he knows or doesn't know the person; he only goes to pray for his rebirth in the Pure Land, for this is a part of his practice. The sad families who have been visited recently by such misfortune thus wait for the arrival of these ascetics, offer them food, and serve them in a pure manner.

I do not know whether the austere practices of the winter nembutsu or shrine pilgrimages that I have described above occur in other parts of the land, but I do know that they are very different from the winter nembutsu or naked pilgrimage of Edo. I will record in the following entry the wonderful virtues acquired through this harrowing

The merits of the winter ascetic. The icicles of Oikake Rock (*inset*).

asceticism. For the benefit of ignorant children, I will tell how any god or buddha will respond to the prayer of one who undertakes austerities.

The Merits of Winter Asceticism

What I am about to recount happened only recently. A little more than one-half mile to the southwest of Shiozawa is a place called Tanaka Village. In Tanaka Village there was a certain man who was engaged in the winter asceticism I have described above. One day he shouldered a bag of rice and set out for Naka Village, only one-quarter mile away. He was walking along the Mikuni Highway, a well-traveled road; but though I say well traveled, it was a narrow track, for those who walked it always followed in the footsteps of others, and aside from this thin, well-packed passage, the rest was deep snow. One false step and you found yourself up to your waist in it. Now it is the custom of the snow country to step back and make way for those carrying a heavy load. Even samurai are expected to do this. (You can see tracks in the snow showing where people have stepped back to make way, in fact.)

While proceeding on his way, this fellow from Tanaka Village happened to meet a samurai coming from the other direction. Though the practitioner was carrying a bag of rice, he took one step back for the samurai. But the samurai bellowed in a loud voice, "Get to the side!" Realizing that if he took another step back he would be hopelessly mired in the snow because of the heavy bag of rice, he was puzzling what to do when the samurai shouted "You arrogant bastard!" and shoved him so that he fell sideways into the snow. As soon as he fell, the samurai, too, went flying into the snow as if thrown there by someone. The man from Tanaka quickly pulled himself out of the snow and hurried off without looking behind.

Some time later another person from Tanaka happened down the road and saw the samurai lodged in the snowbank, seemingly unable to get up. Thinking this strange he approached and asked, "Are you ill?" And the samurai answered in a pitiful voice, "Please, please pull me out." Though he was certainly pale he did not seem sick; but when the man extended his hand to the samurai, he could not reach out to grasp it. When the traveler tried to lift him bodily from the snow, he would not rise. Though he pulled and struggled with all his strength, the samurai was as heavy as some great boulder and unable to move his body at all.

Seeing that his would-be helper was bewildered and beginning to grow frightened, the samurai told him everything that happened. "And now my limbs are paralyzed and I cannot move at all," finished the once-arrogant warrior. When the man from Tanaka heard the samurai speak of the fellow carrying a bag of rice, he understood what had happened at once. "This is your punishment for mistreating an ascetic," he said, and proceeded to explain to the samurai his error and his plight. "I am going to the same village of Naka the ascetic went to. I will find him and bring him back. You must apologize to him. It's not far, so just wait." And off he ran.

Soon he came back leading the ascetic behind him. The samurai did the best he could to rub his palms together, begging, "Forgive me, forgive me," but the ascetic did not seem in the least bit angry. Without a word he took off his robe and hung it on the branch of a willow tree growing beside the road. He doused his naked body with water, making obeisance in the direction of the shrine to which he was making his winter pilgrimages. Then he took the samurai's hand and pulled, and the man rose out of the snow as if light as a feather. Terribly ashamed, the samurai thanked him and made a hasty departure.

A man from Tanaka who frequently comes to my home told me this tale.

A Ghost in the Snow

Just a short distance away from the nearest post town, Seki, is the village of Sekiyama. A bridge leads from this village over the Uono River. The current is so quick that the slightest rise in water would wash away the sturdiest bridge, and so a temporary one of planks is thrown across the river—which is not narrow by any means. When it snows, the villagers clear a path over the middle of the long bridge, but since from three to five feet of snow may accumulate in a single night, and since the villagers cannot clear the bridge every day, the bridge can be quite treacherous. Narrow as it is and covered with slippery snow, cases of someone making a false step, falling into the river and drowning are not rare, even among villagers who cross the bridge daily and are quite used to it.

A certain monk who went by the name of Genkyo lived in a grass hut on the outskirts of Sekiyama Village, devoting himself to chanting the name of Amida Buddha. Well over sixty, he was an unpolished and rustic man who could not boast of great learning; but of his practice of the meditation on the Buddha's name the most elevated monk could not find fault. As a matter of course he practiced the winter nembutsu each year, though he did not take a vow of silence and thus recited the Buddha's name each night to the accompaniment of his pilgrim's bell. On his way back from his pilgrimages to temples or from the homes of the bereaved, he made sure to stop on the bridge at least every other night and pray for the victims who had slipped and drowned during the past year.

On the night of the completion of his vow he stopped as usual on the bridge, but this being the last night he prayed for the rebirth of the poor drowned ones in the Pure Land with great fervor, ringing his bell and chanting the name of Amida. Suddenly the bright moon clouded over: "This is strange," he thought, and just then a flickering blue flame rose out of the water. "Ah, this is the ghostly flame of the dead!" he thought, and closed his eyes, though he continued to ring his bell and chant the Buddha's name as before. When he opened them again he saw, some fifteen feet away, the form of a young woman. She appeared to be thirty years old, and disheveled black hair framed her pale face. She stood before him adjusting the sleeves of her kimono—which were dripping wet, as if she had just risen out of the water.

Most would have let loose a cry and fled, but our monk did not. He faced the woman and looked her over carefully. Though it was dark, he realized as he inspected each feature and form that she was not an ordinary woman. In fact, her body was nearly transparent, and he could see the landscape behind her, faintly, through her form. From the waist down, it was as if she was both there and not there. The monk knew now that he was confronting a ghost, and he repeated his invocations with an even greater fervor.

Without taking a step, she was upon him. In a thin voice she said: "I am Kiku, from Koshi County, the village of . . ." but he failed to catch the name. "My husband and my children all journeyed to the shades long before me, and left me here alone. I could not make even the meagerest living for myself and was heading for a relation in Igarashi Village for help when I slipped on this bridge, fell into the river, and drowned. Tonight is the forty-ninth-day anniversary of my death, but there's not a soul in the world to pour a dipper of cleansing water on my grave—such is the sadness of being abandoned in this world. By the virtues of your constant prayer, however, most worthy monk, I too should be able to attain buddhahood, were it not for this long black hair. It is an obstruction to my deliverance, forcing me to wander in this world. All that I beg of you is that you cut these tresses!" With a final exclamation of sadness, she buried her face in her sleeve and began to weep bitterly.

Genkyo replied, "That is an easy thing to do. But I have nothing to cut them with here. Come to my hut in Sekiyama tomorrow night and I will grant your wish." And he saw her nod in a manner that seemed to indicate happiness, as she disappeared like smoke and the moon came out again, its bright light illuminating the snow.

And Genkyo returned to his hermit's hut. The next morning he sent someone to call Konya Shichibei, an old friend of his from the same village. When Shichibei arrived, Genkyo told him the story of the visit of the ghost of Kiku in great detail. "The ghost of Kiku will most certainly come to my hut tonight. Her story would be a very good means of converting those who have strayed from the Buddha's path, but no one will believe it unless there is a reliable witness. That is why I have called you. Everyone knows that you are honest and truthful, and your testimony would never be doubted. You would be performing a wonderful service for all." Shichibei was the same age as the priest and a devout follower of the Pure Land faith. He nodded eagerly and replied, "How could I refuse your request? I will come at the lighting of the tapers. Hide me in some

Genkyo performs the tonsure for the ghost of Kiku.

inconspicuous place and I will watch the event and report on it." "Beneath the Buddhist altar will be the perfect hiding place!" responded Genkyo. "But do not mention this to anyone. If you say anything, all the young folk of the village will come running to see the ghost." "I understand," said Shichibei, and he left to return at dusk.

And later, as the dusk fell, Genkyo paid his respects to the Buddha with more than usual care, purified the altar, and began to recite the sutras. Shichibei was there early, and after reciting the sutra Genkyo offered him an evening meal. When it was finished, Genkyo said, "It's growing dark. You'd better hide in the cupboard beneath the altar. There is a crack in the doors that you can peep through." Then Genkyo purposefully lowered the lights before the altar and throughout the house to a dim glow and spread a mat before the image of the Buddha for the ghost to sit on. He opened the door to his hut just a bit and prepared two sharp razors. There was nothing to do now but sit and wait for the appearance of his ghostly visitor.

Snow was falling and the wind that blew in through the slightly open door was about to extinguish the lights, so Genkyo closed it and said to Shichibei in his shelf by the hearth, "There is bedding laid out in the cupboard. Don't you go to sleep!"

"How could I do that? When I think that I am about to meet a ghost, the only thing I want to do is chant the Buddha's name! You just be certain that you don't start up with *your* usual snoring."

"Be quiet! You're too loud! Make sure not to make a sound when you see the ghost."

And so this banter went on. Genkyo tired of smoking the rough-cut, home-grown tobacco that he had received from a believer and he started stroking his chin and pulling hairs to pass the time, as he droned the Buddha's name, stopping now and then to stifle a yawn. The only other sound was the soft flutter of snow falling on the blinds, and since there were no other dwellings on any side, the hours of the night passed with a lonely stillness.

There was no sign of the ghost, and Genkyo, warmed by the hearth, began to doze where he sat, until he fell over and awoke with a start to find the ghost of Kiku seated on the mat he had laid out for her facing the Buddha, her head bowed. Though Genkyo was startled, he addressed her with a quiet "I'm so glad you came." She did not reply, but she looked just as she had the night before. Genkyo rinsed his hands and, dipping some water from a bowl, rose and approached her with a razor in his hand. Her wildly disheveled hair, he saw, was wet, but there was not the slightest trace that she had traveled through the snow falling outside. Then Genkyo decided that he would try to save a few strands of her hair as proof of her visit, and he began to carefully cut her locks, but as soon as he cut a handful of hair it flew into the breast of her robes as if pulled by a string. When cutting the next handful, Genkyo wrapped some hair around his fingers in an attempt to hold on to a few strands, but it flew into her breast all the same. Genkyo recalled the old saying, "A woman's hair is her life"; in the end he only managed to save a few strands, and he finished her tonsure. The ghost brought her pale, thin hands together in a gesture of worship before the Buddha and grew paler and paler until she disappeared from sight at last.

The Hair Mound at Sekiyama Village

Then Konya Shichibei crawled out from his hiding place in the cupboard and said, "What a frightening scene we have witnessed! I was amazed that you were able to shave her head, even if you are a monk. I was terrified just looking at her. I couldn't bear to return to the village alone. Let me stay here tonight."

"By all means, by all means! Stay here with me! I have nothing to do now that the one I was waiting for has left. Look at this. Thinking that it would make excellent proof, I was finally able to save these few strands of hair. No doubt she knew my purpose and let me have them." But though Shichibei looked at them, he could not bring himself to reach out and touch the strands, which Genkyo soon wrapped in paper and set in the altar.

Some sake from the evening meal remained, and though there was nothing substantial to eat, they decided to drink it and sat cross-legged near the hearth, warming themselves.

Shichibei eventually spoke. "Though I have often heard of ghosts, this is the first one I have seen. 'Even the passing brush of another's sleeve is the result of karma,' the saying goes, and it would be a great shame were I to let this opportunity slip by. Tonight for the first time I truly feel the great worth of the Buddha's teaching. Tomorrow I shall begin to recite his name one million times in this hut, that Kiku may attain buddhahood."

"Ah, that will be a great deed," said Genkyo. "Tell everyone that you have seen the ghost of Kiku of Koshi County, and that you and I are witnesses. The story of her ghost will be a means of leading people to the Buddha's way. There are lots of old stories of this sort," he went on, and recalling the rough outlines of some of the ghost stories from *The Sand and Stones Anthology* and other stories that he had heard from people, he related one or two. Soon the night grew very late, and they both drifted off to sleep cuddled up in one set of bedding.

The next morning Shichibei returned home, accompanied by Genkyo. He gathered his neighbors about and told them the story of Kiku's ghost, upon which Genkyo took out the hair from the breast of his kimono for all to see. There was none who did not look at it in wonder. When Shichibei announced his plans to recite the Buddha's name one million times, everyone agreed that it was a wonderful deed.

"Let's hold the assembly this very night."

"We'll bring the tea cakes, and you, honorable monk, provide the tea."

"Since you don't have a 'million-nembutsu' rosary at your hut, we'll borrow one from the temple."

"Let's go and invite everyone else to join."

Shichibei's wife, who was seated at his side, turned to him and suggested, "It's such a special event, why don't you pound some rice cakes for the guests?" "What a wonderful idea!" he said, and he began his part of the preparation for what promised to be a lively gathering.

So that night a great crowd arrived at Genkyo's hermitage and chanted the Buddha's name with admirable fervor. The news of the success of this ceremony spread far and wide, until someone with a thought for these things suggested that Kiku's spirit in the shades would certainly rejoice if her hair were entombed in a mound and a stone monument built over it. Many agreed with this sentiment, and plans were made. When the time had come to actually build the monument, Genkyo deferred and said that it was beyond his capacities to carry out the ceremony. He suggested that the Zen master of the Saijozan Kangoji temple be invited to conduct it instead, and so some set off to make this request and attain as well a posthumous name for Kiku. Kiku's hair was buried, then, like any person would be, in a mound near the bridge where she had drowned, and a monument of stone built over it. Everyone gathered on this occasion, too, and a Buddhist ceremony was lovingly carried out.

This event inspired Konya Shichibei to enter Buddhist orders later, it is said. And as all of this happened not so long ago, the hair mound of Sekiyama still exists today.

Hunting Deer in the Snow

People from other parts of the empire think that all of Echigo is a land of great snows, but this is not so. As I have stated earlier, the region near the coast has comparatively little snow, in fact. Uonuma, Kubiki, and Koshi counties have lots of snow. Kariwa and Mishima counties might be included with either group, for they have deep snow in some parts, light snow in others. Kambara County is large and in general has light snow, but it borders Oou on the southeast and is ringed by high peaks; and so in some parts it, too, has deep snows. In places with deep snows, neither horses nor cows can be allowed out during the winter. Although people have developed different kinds of footwear that make walking over the snows easier, these can't be adapted for beasts of burden. If they were let out to run through the snows, they would soon find themselves buried up to their necks—which is exactly why they are of no use in the winter. So from November until May of the next year there is nothing to be done with them but lock them up and feed them. This is certainly one difficulty that farmers of warmer parts don't face.

As I wrote earlier, most wild beasts head for places with light snows at the first sign of winter, following the mountain chains. Some, however, are late in departing and, trapped by the snows, become the targets of hunters. (Bears were discussed in Book One.) Wild boars are ferocious animals and hard to catch even in the deep snow, but deer and antelope are weak and easy to bag in the snow. Deer, especially, have long legs and thus have a harder time running in the snow than even humans do. Deer avoid the deep mountains and prefer the meadows at their feet.

Now whatever the skill or science may be, its secrets only speak to those who know it well. To experienced mountain hunters, the tracks of animals in the snow tell stories: they know what beast has made them, and when—"These were made this morning; those were made just now." When I asked a man from Futai, north of Mikuni Pass, about deer hunting, he told me that hunters thereabouts go on deer hunts together. First they dress in warm clothes, for they will have to paddle (and that is the word we use for trudging through deep snow) through the mountain snow, taking short hunting knives, rifles, spears, and staves. Once they come upon the deer tracks, they simply follow along until they spot the deer. When the deer see the hunters they try to flee, but they cannot outrun them, for they soon sink neck-deep in snow and are eventually chased down and slain. Some brave hunters, it is said, wrestle a buck down by the antlers and then kill it with their hunting knife. This type of deer hunter is certainly unique to the snow country.

The Giant Cat of Tomariyama

To the east of Iijizan, a mountain close to the neighboring post town of Seki, there is Amida Peak, where woodcutters go to cut timber. (The portion that each village may cut is decided.) When March arrives and the snowfall stops, the farmers begin to talk about going to cut timber on that peak. But before heading up the mountain they prepare several days' provisions. The first thing they do on the mountain is to select a spot and build a hut to sleep in. For several days they wander about as they like, felling trees and then chopping them into firewood. They pile these bundles of firewood around the hut, and when they think they've cut enough they leave the bundles and head back home. This is called staying in the mountains (*tomari yama*), and the origin of the phrase is obvious.

Now by the time summer and fall come around the firewood has dried properly, and the farmers drive oxen and horses up into the mountains to carry the firewood down to their homes for use. This is a clever plan necessitated by the deep winter snows, which make it impossible to go into the mountains during the winter, and is an example of the pains we must take all because of the snow.

There is no water on Amida Peak. Well, actually, there is a stream, but it runs at the bottom of a sheer-walled gorge several hundred feet below the mountain. There is no way to draw water from it— unless one has wings. But ancient wisteria vines growing round the great trees by the river cliff hang down into the gorge, and when men stay in the mountains they draw water by clambering down these wisteria vines with a bucket tied to their back. After filling the bucket, closing its lid, and tying it to their back again, they climb up the wisteria vines as if climbing up a ladder through the clouds. Without these wisteria vines, those who stayed on the mountain would not be able to draw water. The strongest rope is not as strong as these vines, and thus for those who chop wood here, wisteria vines are a great treasure.

A man who once stayed on this mountain had an interesting story. "We went there in March that year, like always, seven of us. As we were cutting wood here and there, we suddenly heard the thunderous roaring and spitting of a cat. Everyone was afraid, and ran back to the hut. With axes in hand, we listened intently. The cry was first very near, then very far, then near again. At first we thought there might be many cats, but no, it was the voice of a single beast. Yet it never made an appearance. After the cries stopped, all seven of us went to one of the closer places from where the cry had come and saw there, in the frozen snow, the paw print of a cat—only it was as large as a platter."

It is not impossible that such a creature exists, after all. A friend from Shinshu tells me the story of a fellow who went fishing in the Chikuma River one night and spotted a fine, large rock in the river that would easily support three people. Half-projecting from the water, it looked like it would make the perfect fishing spot. He climbed onto it and dropped his line. From time to time, two shining things the size of a large ball would appear on the rock's surface. As he was wondering what they could be, the moon passed out from behind its screen of clouds, and he saw that he was not sitting on a rock, but a giant frog. The shining spots were its eyes! The fisherman was nearly startled to death and in an instant dgrpped his poles, his lines, and his catch and fled like the wind. Or so the story goes.

Mountain Talk

Camping in the mountains goes on at other places besides Amida Peak. It takes place in the region around Koidejima, and the men of the villages at the foot of the mountains in north Echigo frequently camp in the mountains, too. Wherever men work deep in the mountains, they use a special mountain talk, and the legend has it that if they forget and use the ordinary village word, the mountain god will punish them. Here are some mountain words, unknown in other lands: rice is called "grass berries"; miso is "little balls"; salt is called *kaename*; fried rice is called *zao*; rice gruel is called *zoro*; good weather is called *taka ga ii*; wind is called *soyo*; both rain and snow are called *soyo ga mau*; straw raincoats are called *yachi*; sedge hats are called *tetsuka*; when a person dies they say he *magatta* or *heneta*; the female sex organ is called "a bear's den." There are many more such secret words, and these are just a sample. The last example suggests that these words are like the secret code merchants use on their price tags. It is hard to believe that the mountain gods would punish anyone who fails to use these words while camping in the mountains, but it would certainly be foolish, with our limited powers of understanding, to make light of what the gods may desire.

BOOK THREE

Snow Games

As I have repeated again and again, we here spend almost half the year under the snow, from November to April of the following year. Born in the snow, raised in the snow, the children here have all sorts of snow games, most of which are not to be encountered in warmer parts of Japan, and some of which could scarcely be imagined by people from those climes.

One of these pastimes is building snow castles. First the children build tall snow mounds. They pat them down with toy shovels and make the tops smooth and flat by stamping them down with their feet (children in the snow country always wear straw boots when playing in the snow). Next the children gather snow to make a great wall around the mound, just like the earthen wall that surrounds a village. Inside this main enclosure they build smaller walls, all of snow, and make entrances in them that lead from one "house" to the next. In the great wall a main entrance is opened, and a "shrine" is constructed inside the compound. Steps leading up to its "main hall" are made from snow, as is the figure of the god of the shrine—Tenjinsama, Ebisu, or Daikoku. The children spread mats on the floors and make a cooking place in the snow as well, for you can start and keep a fire burning in the snow by scooping out a hollow and spreading a layer of rice bran in it. The entire construction is called a snow hall or a snow castle. The children gather inside the walls of the snow hall and cook food. Some of this they also present to the deity, and the rest they eat together.

They play house in the little walled areas they have made, visiting other "families" and playing all sorts of imaginative games. When they become tired of their snow castle, tearing it down becomes yet another great game. Sometimes they rally together and launch attacks on neighboring snow castles, built by other children in the same way; sometimes they live in peace.

I was a great one for these snow games when I was a boy, and quite a little general during an attack. But now the years have slipped by, and those days seem as distant as a dream.

SNOW COUNTRY TALES

A Blind Man Snows In

As I have mentioned time and time again, the New Year always finds us still buried beneath the snow. Special efforts are made to dig away the snow and let in as much light as possible through the windows to brighten the New Year's festivities, but everyone is so busy with the rest of the holiday preparations that there is no time to haul away the accumulated snow. It is packed hastily on to the elevated snow pathways that run between the houses, higher than their roofs in many places, and naturally many slippery dangerous spots are bound to appear.

One year on New Year's Eve I set out with my fellow poet and friend, Tokakushi, to pay a visit to the editor of a collection of poems that I had read and commented on, the book tucked safely in the bosom of my best kimono. Our host was delighted to see us and went on and on about how auspicious a visit like ours was on the eve of the New Year. He urged us to stay and have a leisurely chat and called in his wife, his daughter-in-law, and his young daughter, who proceeded to entertain us royally.

As the talk wandered pleasantly from topic to topic, my host's wife addressed a question directly to me: "I've heard that in Edo there are exorcists who go from house to house on the eve of the New Year and warn that demons are bound to make their appearance that night. Then they offer to tell interesting stories about driving off demons in return for money. Is this an ancient custom? And is not the superstition that demons make an appearance on New Year's Eve an idle tale passed down from ancient times?"

I replied that the poet Gozan discusses just that in *Toshinamigusa*, a copy of which her husband possessed, and urged her to read it. But Tokakushi, who was already more than a little drunk, interrupted and began to tease the mistress of the house. "So you think that demons are just an old superstition, do you? As a matter of fact, you know, they say demons are especially drawn to gatherings of women. Why, it's precisely because demons really do appear on New Year's Eve that the custom of tossing dried beans out of the house on New Year's Day is called 'demon chasing.' Now that even appears in *The Almanac of Poetry*, my dear."

BOOK THREE

The thirteen-year-old daughter, seated next to her mother, interjected: "Have you ever seen a demon?"

"Sure I have, of course I have. Quite a variety of them exist, believe me," Tokakushi replied. "In general, demons are either red or blue. Those with white faces are a little less frightening and are called white demons. The roly-poly black ones are called black demons. When I lived in Edo, I saw an exorcist catch a demon and toss him into the western sea with a big kerplash!—that was a black one, by the way. Now if demons are around and about on New Year's Eve even in bustling Edo, you can be sure that there are plenty of them here for our snowy New Year's Eve. Why, one might be peering into the window at this very moment," he hinted darkly, and glanced up at a high window that was directly above where the three women were sitting.

Although both the daughter and daughter-in-law pretended not to believe a word he said and told him to stop telling such silly lies, they both crouched close to the mistress between them and were visibly frightened.

Just then there was a great crash as the window behind them burst open and an avalanche of snow came thundering into the room, carrying with it a dark figure amidst the heaps of packed ice and snow.

At this the women shrieked and threw themselves prostrate on the floor, shaking in terror. We men all leapt up utterly surprised, while the servants came running from the back of the house, alarmed by the uproar.

And now, as all stared at the strange creature buried in the heaps of packed snow from the collapsed pathway outside, they recognized the little blind masseur Fukuichi (whose name, you must know, means "Good Fortune"), a frequent visitor to their home. Luckily, he didn't seem to be hurt. He sat just as he had landed, benumbed, rubbing his head and patting his sore behind.

"Well, if it isn't Good Fortune!" they all shouted, laughing—as Fukuichi did, too. The servants immediately set to work removing the mountain of snow that had carried him in and repairing, at least temporarily, the broken window.

The mistress of the house, however, was terribly upset and scolded the blind man mercilessly. "Fukuichi, you rascal! Tokakushi

Fukuichi snows in.

here was just telling us stories about demons, and we thought you were one. You gave everyone a terrible fright. What bad fortune to have a blind man come tumbling through your window, on today of all days! Get out, get out at once!" she screamed hysterically. But our host calmed her down and asked the blind masseur, "Fukuichi, tell us how it happened that you tumbled through our window. Are you hurt?"

"No, not at all," Fukuichi responded with a grateful grin. "I left home tonight with the intention of conveying my New Year's felicitations to you all. I don't know whose doing it was, but when I was walking on the snow pathway I noticed that something was different from yesterday, and as I was feeling my way along I took a wrong step and slipped and tumbled in here. I didn't mean any harm, believe me! Please, please, forgive me."

But the daughter-in-law and the young girl were of one voice: "We thought you were a demon! How dare you scare us so, you horrible blind man!" Nor had the mistress's anger abated. "And you had to fall in from a perfectly good window that is, on top of everything, facing this year's felicitous direction. Out with you! Be gone, quick!" she scolded him passionately.

At this Tokakushi intervened, telling Fukuichi to first return home and then make a fresh start and come here again—in order to cancel the inauspicious jinx he may have cast on his patrons. "In the meantime, I'll make your apologies for you." But Fukuichi just sat there, his head hanging down as if he were lost in thought. Suddenly he lifted his head and said to Tokakushi, "I've composed a poem. Would you please write it down for me?"

Now little Good Fortune, though he was still young, frequently composed poems and comic verses, so the master of the house thought it might be interesting if Tokakushi obliged him. Fukuichi had Tokakushi take down the poem. The master read it, thought it interesting, and had Tokakushi read it to everyone. This was done. Fukuichi's verse went like this:

> Out of the lucky direction,
> Fukuichi
> The little blind man

BOOK THREE

> Comes tumbling—
> With a foolish thump
> On his rump.

But the poem could also be read to mean:

> Out of the lucky direction
> Good fortune!—
> A rice barn appears,
> With the festive pounding
> Of rice cakes sounding.

Everyone was immensely entertained by this, and they applauded Fukuichi, chanting, "Good Fortune, Good Fortune!" as the sake cups were passed round again.

The host asked his daughter-in-law to bring a cloak with his family crest, which he presented to Fukuichi for his fine verse. Tenderly the blind man placed the cloak on his lap, stroking it ever so gently with his right hand. "What a lucky mistake," he said, beaming. "And how fortunate I am to have this cloak to wear during the New Year festivities." With these words, he put the cloak on, pulling it into shape and continuing to stroke it ever so gently. Now, wearing the lovely cloak, he was happier than ever.

It is quite possible that this strange occurrence was indeed a sign of good fortune, as Fukuichi had hinted in his poem. For during the next year, the daughter-in-law delivered her first son, who grew into a healthy child. Even when he contracted smallpox at age three it was a light case, and he soon recovered. He is now a fine little fellow of seven.

As for Fukuichi, who was able to keep his wits about him, he is now said to be in Edo, where he is a promising government official. So much good fortune, worthy of felicitations!

BOOK FOUR

Castle Towns of Echigo

In ancient histories it is recorded that Echigo is wedged between Dewa and Etchu. There are at present seven counties in Echigo. In the east are Iwafune County, on the sea, and Kambara County, which includes the harbor of Niigata. In the west is Uonuma County, far from the sea. And in the north are Mishima County, on the seacoast, and Kariwa County, which is near the sea. In the south, there is Kubiki County, near the sea in some places, and Koshi County, which is far inland. These are the seven counties of Echigo.

The castle towns in Echigo are Murakami in Iwafune County, ruled by Lord Naito, with a stipend of 302,000 bushels of rice; Shibata, ruled by Lord Mizoguchi, with a stipend of 256,000 bushels; Kurokawa, ruled by Lord Yanagisawa, with a stipend of 51,000 bushels and a battalion of troops; and Mikkaichi, ruled by Lord Yanagisawa Danjo, also with a stipend of 51,000 bushels and a battalion—all in Kambara County; in Mishima County, Yoita, ruled by Lord Ii, with a stipend of 102,000 bushels; Shiiya in Kariwa County, ruled by Lord Hori, with a stipend of 51,000 bushels and a battalion; Nagaoka in Koshi County, ruled by Lord Makino, with a stipend of more than 379,000 bushels; and in Kubiki County, Takata, ruled by Lord Yanagiwara, with a stipend of 768,000 bushels, and Itoikawa, ruled by Lord Matsudaira, with a stipend of 51,000 bushels and a battalion of troops.

In addition to the above castle towns, there are several prosperous cities: Ojiya in Uonuma County; Sanjo in Koshi County; Teradomari and Izumozaki in Mishima County; Kashiwazaki in Kariwa County; and Imamachi in Kubiki County. It goes without saying that Niigata in Kambara County, as the main port of the north sea, is a flourishing region as well. I will not mention other well-to-do settlements here. Snow falls in all of these places from November, the depth depending upon the topography and the location, which I will discuss below.

Ancient Sites in Old Poems

The most famous ancient site in Echigo is Iyahiko (or Yahiko) no Yashiro Shrine on Iyahiko Mountain. The deity enshrined there is Amanokagoyama no Mikoto, the child of Nigihayai no Mikoto. He is said to have manifested himself, through the compassion of the Buddha, in 710, during the reign of Emperor Gemmei. The shrine estate amounts to 2,560 bushels of rice annually. Iyahiko is not an especially tall mountain, but it sits in the very middle of Echigo's two-hundred-mile coastline, unconnected to any other peak. With Mount Kunikami to its right and Mount Kakuda to its left, it seems as if it sits with folded arms facing the rest of Echigo's mountains. It is more prominent than any other mountain and truly deserves its fame as the guardian of our province; no wonder the god chose to make his appearance there. Since there are simply too many stories of the deity's wondrous deeds and powers, I will not record them here.

There are two ancient poems that mention Iyahiko Mountain. One is in *A Collection of Ten Thousand Leaves*:

> How awesome
> Is Iyahiko!
> Even in the cloudless sky
> It stands wrapped in rain.

BOOK FOUR

It is anonymous. The other, from the same source, is by Yakamochi:

> At the feet of
> The god of Iyahiko
> Frost is fallen again.
> Peacefully the young deer
> Rub each other's antlers.

The ancient town of Nagahama was in Kubiki County. (Some say it was in Mishima County.) Yakamochi mentions it in one of his poems:

> The beach of Nagahama:
> Here it is, they say,
> The geese rest their wings
> On the long journeys to and fro.

Nadachi (Reputation) was in the same county, in Nishihama. A post town now bears the name. Emperor Juntoku, on his way to exile on the island of Sado, mentions it in his poem:

> I who have lost my way
> Far from the capital
> Once more tonight,
> Desolate,
> Gaze at the moon of Nadachi.

The place once called Naoenotsu was located along the shores of what is now Takata. Emperor Juntoku also composed a poem about it:

> It cries; I hear it.
> And I long so for the capital.
> Fly, fly from this village,
> Mountain thrush.

Another ancient site in Echigo is Lake Koshi—"Koshi," meaning to cross over, being the ancient name for Echigo. In Kambara County there are many small lakes called *kata*, for that is our local word for a lake. The largest in that area is called Lake Fukushima. It is nearly seven and one-half miles in circumference. Near the lake is a mountain called Samidareyama—May Rain Mountain. There are several famous poems about this place. One is by Ki no Tsurayuki:

> The rising tide of Lake Koshi
> Lies so near at hand
> That I can see the glistening clam shells
> Dancing on the waves.

Another is by Fujiwara Toshinari:

> However much I languish
> What can I do?
> Unless
> Stranded on Lake Koshi's shores
> I should meet you.

And a third is by Fujiwara Tamekane:

> Over the years it gathered and grew
> Until the forest dew
> Of May Rain Mountain
> Created great Lake Koshi.

There is a post town in Kubiki County called Kakizaki, or Persimmon Cape, and here it was, according to tradition, that Saint Shinran composed this poem:

> At Persimmon Cape
> Bitterly I searched for lodging.
> Finally, a landlord's heart
> Ripened.

BOOK FOUR

Shinran was exiled to Echigo when he was thirty-five, because of slanderous charges laid against his master Honen in Kyoto. That was in March of 1207. Though he was pardoned five years later, he remained another five years in Echigo to spread the Buddha's Law, and it is because of his long stay here that many old sites are associated with him. It was only after twenty-five years of teaching, at the age of sixty, that he returned to the capital. (In the meantime he had spent five years in Echigo, three years in Shimotsuke, ten years in Hitachi, and seven years in Sagami.) He died at the age of ninety, on February 28, 1262. The poem about Kakizaki was no doubt composed during his stay in Echigo, propagating the Buddhist teachings.

There are also poems that mention such ancient places as Ariake Bay, Iwade Bay, Seba Ford, Ikuri Wood, and Koshi no Matsubara. Places of this name existed not only in Echigo but in other parts of the land as well, and it is impossible to be sure the poems refer to Echigo.

Some 541 years ago, in 1298, when Fujiwara Tamekane was on his way to exile on Sado, he was forced to wait for favorable winds at a place called Teradomari in Mishima County. He was joined there by a courtesan called Hatsugimi, who composed for him the poem:

> Oh yes, I've heard
> That even the white waves
> Breaking on the coast of Koshi
> Will certainly, will surely, return.

This poem must have served as a good omen, for five years later Tamekane was pardoned and he was allowed to return to the capital. Nine years after his return, he was called on to edit *The Jewel Leaf Collection,* an imperial anthology of verse, and he decided to include Hatsugimi's poem. This was a great credit to Echigo. An ancient site connected with Hatsugimi remains at Teradomari, and it is called locally Hatsugimi's Mansion. There was a stone inscription of Hatsugimi's poem, dated 1684, in the hand of the priest Mangen, but it fell into disrepair. Later, in the Kyowa era (1801–4), it was restored by the local people.

SNOW COUNTRY TALES

New Year in the Snow

From times of old people have quite rightly spoken of Echigo as the place in all Japan with the deepest snow. And of all Echigo, snow is deepest in Uonuma County where I live, more than twenty feet accumulating in the winter. The next-deepest snow falls in Koshi County, and then Kubiki County, while the accumulation of snow in the remaining three counties is comparatively less. The natural conclusion, then, is that my homeland of Uonuma has the deepest snowfall in all Japan. Born in Shiozawa, I have seen nothing but snow from November to April or May for more than sixty years; and it was to pass the days spent buried under the snow that I began of late to compose this book.

Shiozawa is only some 135 miles from Edo. If measured by a straight road, the distance is even less. A strong runner can make the trip in four days during the snow-free season. Now of the New Year of the wealthy and the highbred of Edo I know nothing; but before the thousand gates and ten thousand doors of the common people throughout that town one finds at the New Year the luck-bringing pine and fine, straight bamboo, around which are wrapped the sacred straw ropes, symbol of peace. Holiday well-wishers promenade in the streets in ceremonial clothes, and dancers singing congratulatory verses mix with the crowds. Female entertainers warble festive songs to the bright strumming of their shamisens. Young girls bat their shuttlecocks back and forth, and the boys send their kites aflying. All sights and sounds conspire in joyful celebration as the sun rises gloriously on the first day of the New Year, and the jewel of spring has arrived.

Though the New Year of Edo and the New Year here in our land of snow are the same New Year, the contrast between the bustling holiday of the capital and our white hinterlands couldn't be greater. On New Year's Day, our pastures, our mountains, our fields, and our villages, too, are buried in a great white blanket. The plum and willow in the garden, which should greet the spring, are bound and staked for their own protection as they were before the snow began to fall in late autumn; they do not know it's spring. Until April or even May people have still not seen plum blossoms. The poet Basho composed the poem:

> Spring gradually
> Prepares its landscape
> Of moon and plum blossoms.

on the fifteenth day of the New Year, in the city. And the poem:

> The festive New Year's dancers come late
> To the mountain village
> Plum blossoms.

refers to April.

We in Echigo must set up our ceremonial pine decorations in the snow; we fix our sacred ropes from the snow-covered eaves. Since snow still falls in spring and the sun's light is blocked by the immense snow walls in the streets, we may well sip our festive New Year's soup in a dim house and a gloomy mood. The New Year's well-wishers brave enough to venture out may wear geta, but their servants still wear high straw boots. And when, traveling the snow ways, they come to a set of crude steps cut into the snow walls, even the master changes to straw boots. Not only these masters and their servants, but everyone wears geta or straw boots, for straw sandals are impossible until the beginning of summer, when the snow has finally melted.

The first rays of the New Year's-day sun illuminate a silvery world. There is not a single sign of spring. The ancient poem:

> If I could only show
> Those who long for blossoms
> The spring of this green shoot
> That breaks through the snow
> In the mountain village.

must speak of the meager snows of the capital. For the people of

New Year's Day in the snow.

Echigo live and die never knowing such a spring, and for them, to enjoy the spring of the rich and prosperous cities, graced year after year with the bright green and white of willows and plums, seems a great gift of heaven.

Snowball Contests

The children of Edo have lots of New Year's games: the girls play with brightly colored balls and battledore and shuttlecock, and what little boy doesn't have a kite to send aloft? Yet even in spring the children of Echigo can't run about freely, for the ground is covered with snow, and they rarely play in the streets. But here we have a game called snowball contests. (Of course it's not limited to spring, but can be played anytime in the snow.)

First you make a snowball about the size of an egg, squeezing it and slapping it until it is quite hard and compacted. To make it even harder, you pack more snow around the outside and stamp on it or slap it against the pillar of a house. This is called fattening it. When you have fattened your snowball to a ball the size of a fist, you and your playmates place your snowballs on the ground under the eaves. The object of the game is to throw your snowball against those of your rivals, one by one, to see which is the strongest. The snowball that breaks, loses. This game is known by many other names in many other places: *kombo, koma, jikoma, ikindama* (for in the local dialect, *yuki*—snow—is *iki*), *zuzugo, tamagoshio, kachiai* (contest), and more.

If you add a little salt to the snowball, it will become hard as a rock, and so the children agree that it's unfair to do so. This is just another example of the nature of salt as a hardener. Since salt preserves things, salted meat doesn't spoil. It's also said that if you rinse your mouth with warm salt water morning and evening, you'll harden your teeth and prolong their use. The snowball contest may be a child's game, but it's also fine proof of this hardening principle of salt, which is one reason I have recorded it here.

BOOK FOUR

Shuttlecock and Battledore

According to those who have spent the New Year in Edo, the sight of lovely young girls batting shuttlecocks back and forth with gloriously colored battledores beneath the pine and bamboo decorations that fill the streets is a typical spring scene in the capital. But because ours is a shuttlecock game of the countryside, it lacks this gentle loveliness. During the New Year even the servants have permission to rest and to play a bit, and it is then that they decide upon a game of shuttlecock. First they select a place and tramp all the snow down, forming a ring like that used for sumo wrestling. The shuttlecock is made out of a short stem of the deutzia, cut like a tube to a length of two inches and stuffed with three pheasant tail feathers. It is much, much larger than a shuttlecock of Edo and is batted back and forth with the wooden shovels that we clear our roofs with. It often flies high, high into the air, since the players bat the shuttlecock with all their might.

This isn't children's play. Young men and women mix and tumble about roughly in the straw boots and leggings that they wear when they play the game. All line up and hit the shuttlecock back in turns, and anyone who misses is dealt with in a way agreed on beforehand: pummeled with snowballs or showered with snow. Everyone has a great laugh when the snow goes down the loser's collar and into his breast. Watching this from the window is one of the entertainments in the snow.

Kyoden quotes *A Collection of Everyday Expressions* in his own *Collection of Curiosities* to say that the battledore existed as long as 370 years ago, in the Bunnan era (1444–49), though its history before that is unknown. Some in our region also play the same game as enjoyed by the little girls of Edo.

A Sale of Roasted Rice Balls in a Blizzard

The most terrifying things in the snow country are the blizzards and

The blizzard at Tsukanoyama Peak.

hora during the winter and the avalanches during the spring, the strange facts of which I have already recorded here. But I have heard another odd story that I would like to include here, so that it may be known in other parts.

Now Lu of China said all there is to say about the value of money, and I have nothing to add. But years of bad harvest have been with us from the beginning, and when people are starving, the belly can't be filled by licking a gold piece, and a bowl of rice glitters far more brightly than a coffer of coins. It is said that during the last famine, some fifty years ago, one hundred pieces of gold were found in the breast of a man who had died of starvation.

A certain farmer was traveling from Yabukami Manor in Uonuma County to the post town of Kashiwazaki, a distance of just twelve miles. On the road he met a ramie dealer, and they traveled on together. It was the beginning of January, and the snow of the last several days had made way for blue skies, so both of them trudged along in good spirits. Just as they came to the small peak known as Tsukanoyama, the snow country played its usual trick: the blue skies grew covered with cold clouds and a violent wind blew from the four directions into a spiraling snow twister whirling the snow about until it blocked the sun's light and you couldn't see your hand in front of your face. The two men found themselves caught in the midst of a snow country blizzard, and as the wind blew the snow up their sleeves and down their collars, they began to freeze. (Since these blizzards start up all of a sudden without any sign, it is the custom of our land to wear sedge coats and hats whenever we go out, even while the sky is clear.)

The two continued to paddle through the snow in their snowshoes, calling out to each other and helping one another along until they finally, thankfully, made it over the peak. Then the salesman said to the farmer, "When I set out this morning for Kashiwazaki with the blue skies overhead, I never thought to pack a lunch. But now I am so hungry that I cannot bear the cold, and soon I will not be able to keep up with you as we paddle on. Just a while ago you mentioned that you had a lunch tucked away in your kimono breast. Would you consider letting me have it? Of course I'm not thinking of receiving it for nothing. Here, I have six hundred coppers. What are six hundred coppers when it's a matter of life and death? Sell me your lunch and take the money."

Now the farmer was a poor man, and when he heard the figure six hundred coppers he could not help but rejoice at his luck and in an instant pulled out the two roasted rice balls he carried and exchanged them for the purse. The salesman ate the two big rice balls, still warm because they had been tucked in the farmer's breast, quenched his thirst with a mouthful of snow and, refreshed and strengthened, once again set out, paddling through the snow.

While they hurried on the blizzard grew fiercer, and hampered by their snowshoes, they were still on their way as the day drew to its close. Now the farmer who had sold his lunch grew hungry and tired, while the salesman who had eaten it proceeded with a full stomach and a strong stride. Eventually the farmer dropped behind, and the salesman left him and went ahead, arriving at the nearest village alone. He entered the house of an acquaintance and, as he sat and warmed himself by the hearth with a cup of sake, he felt as if he had come back from the dead.

Some time had passed when those inside the house heard "Halloo, halloo," the cry of someone caught in a blizzard and in need of help—for it is our custom to cry thus. "Someone has been felled by the blizzard! We must help him!" And they ran out to gather others from the neighborhood. All ran off with shovels in hand to dig out the person who had been buried by the blizzard, another custom of our region. After a time a large group of people returned, dragging the corpse of a man into the earth-floored entranceway to the house. The salesman rose to see who it was, to find none other than the farmer who had sold him his lunch earlier.

This merchant of ramie fiber once stopped at the house of one of my poet's circle and told the story that I have recorded here. He concluded his account with the observation that if he had begrudged the six hundred coins and not bought the rice balls, it would have been he who was claimed by the blizzard, not the farmer. "I owe my life today to those six hundred coppers," he said with a laugh—according to my poet friend.

SNOW COUNTRY TALES
Theatricals in the Snow

When the five grains have ripened and a rich harvest has made it possible for us to pay our taxes with easy hearts, and we greet the spring with bellies full and plenty of provisions to spare, we hold theatricals around the time of the festival of the local clan gods. The actors are all amateurs from the area or towns and villages nearby. An actor from some traveling country troupe is hired as a director.

First, everyone gathers in the local temple or some other place and decides on the play. After that, parts are cast. This debate is quite roisterous and even vehement, and matters are never settled in a single meeting. But when things are finally decided to everyone's satisfaction, the cast regroups in the temple and rehearsals begin. After all the parts and business are learned, the opening day is set. There is no problem with such things as wigs and costumes, for they can be rented from a local shop that makes that its business.

The performances are held in March or April, when our world is still a silver one, encased in ice. The actors' families, of course, take a hand in building the stage, and their relatives and friends join in. Occasionally help is also hired. First the place for the stage is tramped down and the snow made flat and even. The stage, the raised runway leading to it, the dressing rooms, and the stands—all are made out of snow. The picture shows just how well they are made, in fact.

The heavens lend a helping hand to all this human endeavor, for each night that day's work is frozen hard as stone. No matter how full the house becomes, the seating area is never in danger of collapsing.

By April, it snows less frequently, and with a hopeful glance at the clearing skies, the builders go from house to house to borrow the snow fences made of logs and the snow blinds (made of miscanthus reeds and measuring about eight or nine feet by twelve) to make a temporary roof for the theater. The stage and runway, which are built of snow, are covered with boards. In a single night the boards freeze to the snow and are stuck faster than if nailed. There is certainly nothing to compare with this in the warmer parts of Japan. Teahouses selling refreshments are also built. Since the ground is stamped down flat, hollows can be dug for cooking. Some bran is spread on the bottom, and one has a rare sight indeed as the little fires burn here and there in the snow without melting it.

Sometimes spring snows continue to fall after the theater has been built, the weather refuses to clear, and the opening day has to be postponed. Not only is this a terrible disappointment for the actors and their families, but also for the relatives and other people come from far away to see the plays, and actors and audience together peer at the skies waiting for them to clear. Finally, tired of attending to all of these waiting guests, the actors gather together and go to the river to pray for clear skies by breaking through the ice and dousing themselves with the icy waters.

Momoki relates the following story: In the summer of 1837 I was traveling through north Etsu and found myself at Shiozawa. Hearing that a play was being performed in the neighborhood, I went to the location, a temple, with my son Kyosui. To one side of the temple gate a billboard had been raised and strung with lanterns. On the billboard was written, "In order to raise funds to repair the roof of this temple, a play will be performed for seven days in the main hall. The title of the play is *The Forty-Seven Loyal Retainers.*" The actors had all given themselves names in the theatrical style on the cast list that appeared on the billboard. The temple grounds were crowded with stalls selling all sorts of things, and people were milling about.

Large wooden doors had been collected to fence off the theater area, and an entranceway had been built. A ticket taker stood at the entrance to collect everyone's admission, which was of course going toward the repair of the temple roof. The stage had been built attached to the steps leading up to the temple's main hall, and the raised runway extended to the left. The good seats on the left and right were made of low bamboo platforms, and roped off. The gallery had only cloth or rush matting over straw mats placed on the ground. I have heard from the actor Ichikawa Danjuro V that most traveling theater companies use this sort of arrangement. As a gesture of extravagance and finery, bright-colored mats had been spread out in certain parts of the gallery and colorfully painted screens set up at the rear.

Preparations for theatricals in the snow.

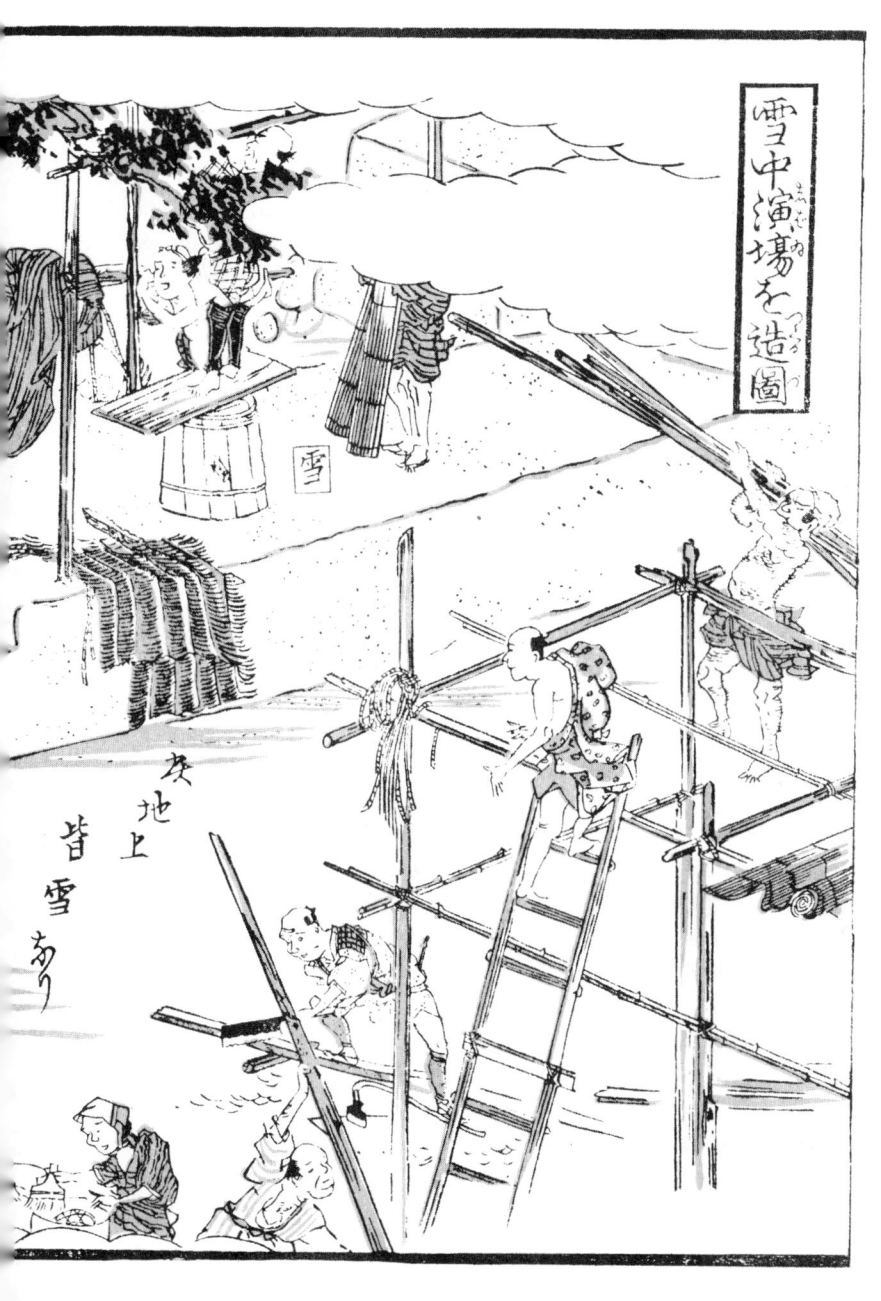

The audience rushed in and packed the house. Some small children climbed up into the trees like monkeys, to get a better view. Little girls carrying baskets plied the crowd calling "Ice, ice!" Green leaves lined their baskets, which were filled with lumps of frozen snow that they were selling as a refreshment. How marvelous, I thought: selling ice instead of tea! (Shaved ice is discussed in another entry.) The wadded hoods of four or five women in the audience showed that ancient customs had not completely disappeared in these parts.

Finally the announcers came out and proclaimed the names of those who had donated goods to the temple or gifts to the actors, whether sake or rice, calling out the names, the gift, and the amount. With "And now *The Forty-Seven Loyal Retainers* begins," the curtain parted.

"Iwai Tamanojo" (his stage name, of course) played the part of the beautiful Okaru. He was extremely lovely, and a fine reputation as a traveling player preceded him. The fellow who played Yuranosuke was a man of some learning whom I had met on my travels. He was young, which is, no doubt, why he had time for these frivolities. I hardly recognized him from our earlier meeting, for now he resembled Bando Hikosaburo, and he was both handsome and a fair actor. The barber who served the customers at the inn where I stayed played the role of Teraoka Heiemon. He, too, was quite different in his stage persona, with a naturally fine voice that resembled Seki Sanjuro's, as did his acting style. I turned and looked at Kyosui, who seemed to be thinking the same thing, for he shouted out Seki's stage name, "Owariya!" But no one there seemed to understand, and no one else paid our barber that compliment.

We had decided beforehand to leave after the first act, but the ticket taker would not open the door. "If you want the toilet, it's around back. If you're hungry, buy a box lunch." He was quite stubborn and wouldn't relent. We were not the only ones prevented from leaving, either. He must have feared that if he let anyone leave the seats would empty out and the theater would become rather sorry-looking for the actors.

When I asked whether there was any exit, I was told that the four sides of the temple grounds were firmly enclosed, and not a crack had been left open. Just when I was about to give up, I saw some children break in through a hole in the fence. Kyosui and I managed to escape from the same hole—the first time I ever sneaked *out* of a theater!

Ice Pillars in the House

By spring, the snow that winter has piled around our houses is higher than the roof, and inside all is dark and gloomy. I have written earlier about how we clear away the snow before the high windows, to let some light in. The roof of the house is inevitably damaged by the wooden shovels we use to clear the snow time after time during the winter. Most of our homes are roofed with boards, thicker and broader than those used in other parts of the land. Wooden supports are laid over and across the roof boards, and stones are set on these to hold them down and protect the roof from high winds. We can never, therefore, clear the snow away completely. Then in the spring a new layer of snow falls on what remains from winter and freezes. Because of all this, there is no way to know whether the roof has been damaged.

But as spring advances, the snow begins to melt where the sun strikes it and around the area over the open hearth. All of a sudden one night melted snow from a damaged portion begins to run along the rafters and to drip furiously inside the house, and the tatami mats must be taken up and every bucket and pan we can lay hands on is put out to catch the leaks. Since most of the snow still hasn't melted there's no way to repair the roof for the time being, and as the leaks begin to freeze, we find great icicles growing right inside the rooms of our houses. I would love to show these to people from warmer climes.

Momoki adds: In my travels to Echigo I observed the construction of the large houses. The stairways were as thick as those of a fireproof storehouse in Edo. The ceilings were high, and the space between the lintels and the peak quite large, all to let in more light during the snowy season. The doors are heavy and well made, and the doorframes wide and thick. I was surprised that everything was made from large beams and boards and was told that this was to prevent the house from being crushed by the snows. The front overhang of the roof that is called *tanashita* in Edo is called "staggered overhang" (*ganki*) or "eaves" (*hisashi*) in Echigo. There is enough space under the overhang to lead a small pack horse, and that is because this area is used for passage during the time of the deep snows.

On my way back to Edo from Echigo, I passed through the castle town of Takata, the main market of the region. There I found row after row of shops, and there was nothing one could not purchase. The eaves stretched for nearly a mile, and it was most pleasant to stroll under them. I also heard that there were many men of literary talent there, but, unfortunately, my travels took place during a very bad year, and I hurried for home without exchanging calling cards with anyone, a fact which now I much regret.

Snow Gear

Though I illustrated equipment for walking in the snow in the first book, I did not explain its manufacture, which I plan to do in detail here.

Straw shoes. These are woven from a single length of straw. The straw is held in a round bunch at the start, and towards the end

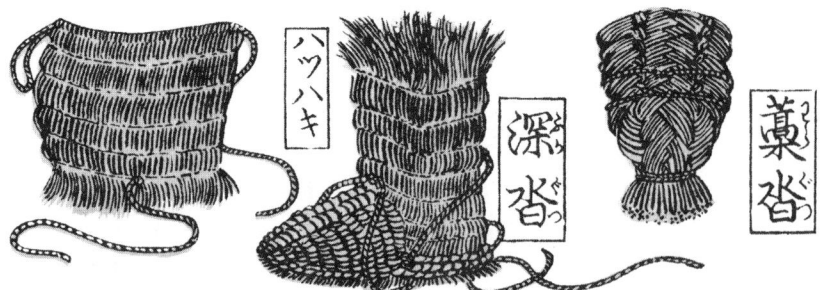

Straw legging; straw boot; straw shoe.

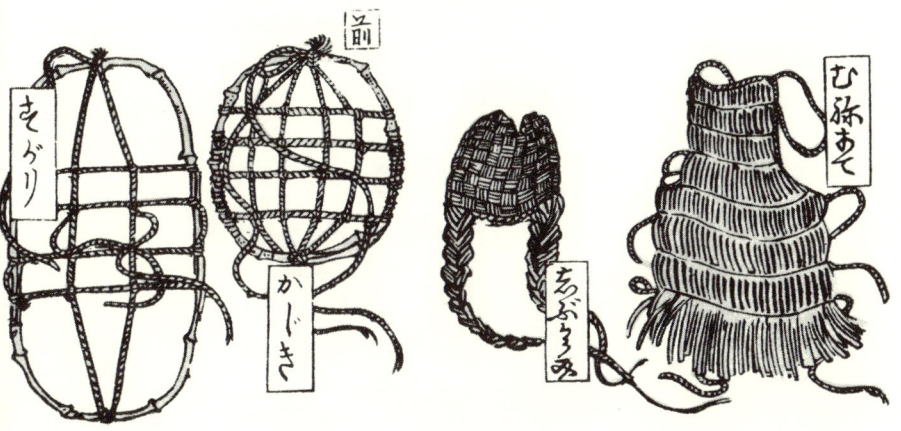

Snowshoes, *kajiki* and *sugari*; straw foot cover; snow vest.

the amount of straw is increased, divided in two, folded under, and the ends tied at the middle. This is the most common footgear in the snow. Children wear them, too. Straw shoes of the best quality are woven with white paper at the front of the shoe, and the instep is covered with a piece of reed matting cut from a floor mat.

Straw boots. These are woven from beaten straw. They are worn over ordinary socks. If you wear these, there is no need to wash your feet when arriving at someone's house even after walking through the snow. The weaving process is extremely complicated, and I only show the general appearance here.

In other countries, we find footgear made of leather, which is useful for muddy roads. There is, of course, no mud on the snow-covered roads of Echigo, which is why all footwear except for geta is made of straw. There are types of geta known as "horse's hooves" and "cow's hooves," and they are different for men and for women, but I have not illustrated them here.

Straw leggings. These are called *happaki* in our dialect, a variation on *habaki,* meaning leggings. They are made of either straw or bulrushes and are always worn in the snow and by people working in the mountains. The general method of their construction can be seen in the illustration. To put it simply, they are a kind of straw

Bokushi's manservant demonstrates snow gear.

knee pad. Since straw keeps out the cold, most winter footgear is made from it.

Snow vests. These are made from the bark of trees from the deep mountain forests. The measurements are adjusted to fit the wearer, but a vest is roughly twenty-eight inches in length and two feet around. Also called chest covers, they are designed to protect you from snow blowing from the front. Farmers always wear them, and they are found in other parts of the land as well.

Straw footcovers. These are woven by wrapping the socklike portion, which is made first, around your heel and then weaving the bindings, left and right, on either side of your ankle. They are worn, of course, in just the reverse fashion, as a cover to keep your toes warm and dry in the snow. Soft straw scraps are called *shibi* in our dialect, and since these footcovers are made of *shibi* and wrapped (*karami*) around the ankles, we call these, with some slurring of sounds, *shibugarami*.

Snowshoes. The ancient word is *kanjiki,* but we say *kajiki*. They are made of twigs from the *jagara* tree, in the shape illustrated, measuring about twenty-seven inches by seven and one-half inches. On the reverse side of the front tip, vines such as *kumaibu* are sometimes used. The twigs are all wrapped with the sticky bark of the mountain lacquer tree. Snowshoes are worn, as an earlier illustration shows, bound under the shoes to allow you to walk through the snow.

The large snowshoes known as *sugari* measure from thirty to thirty-six inches in length and are about fifteen inches wide. They are made by bending mountain bamboo stalks into the proper shape. Both types of snowshoes are for walking through the soft snows. Unless you wear them, it's difficult to take even one step; yet those who are well accustomed to wearing snowshoes can even chase down game in them!

In addition to the items listed above, there are all sorts of snow headgear and snow geta, but since they are also found in other parts of the land I will not describe them here.

Momoki adds: While I was staying at Bokushi's house during my visit to Echigo, he was kind enough to have one of his servants dress up entirely in gear used for walking through the snow, and Kyosui made the accompanying sketch. For amusement, he tried to walk in snowshoes, but was unable to take so much as a single step—yet the servant was running all about as swift as a steed.

Sleds

When Yu Wang settled the waters and founded Chinese civilization, four methods of transportation were ordained: boats for the waters, carts on land, sleds for swamps, and snowshoes in the snowy mountains. Thus we know that sleds have existed from ancient times in the land of China, but since they were to be used for traveling through muddy swamps, they were no doubt different in construction from those we use to travel in the snows. There are many different Chinese characters for "sled," and phrases such as "snow cart" and "snow boat" are in common use.

Now, sleds are the most important convenience for life in the snow, as useful to man as boats and carts. They are very easily constructed, too, as the illustration shows. We know that sleds have been used in our land from ancient times, for we have the poem by Minamoto Kanemaki in *A Hundred Verses of Emperor Horikawa's Reign*:

> The first deep snow
> Must have fallen,
> For the travelers ride on sleds
> Over the high pass
> Of Arachi Mountain.

As I have said many times before, the winter snows of Echigo do not freeze. If we tried to use sleds in the winter, they would sink in the snow and we would be unable to pull them out. Sleds are used, then, during the spring—February, March, and April—when the snow has frozen hard as iron. At that time we speak of "sled paths," which are in fact the only way to get about. Thus the use of "sled" as a seasonal word indicating winter in poetry is in error; but since sleds are things of the snows, the word is hardly suitable as a reference to spring, either, and in many ancient poems, "sled" is used as a reminder of winter. Even if it does not exactly fit the facts, then, I suppose it is appropriate.

Since sleds are of simple construction, every farmer's and merchant's house has one. Though the size of sleds ranges considerably depending upon what is to be carried, large and small sleds are built the same way and they are all called sleds—except for a giant sled called a *shura,* used to carry massive boulders and huge timbers.

Although in spring the great trees on the mountains are still buried in snow, the tops of their branches remain visible. It is a very easy thing to collect firewood at this time, and here is how it's done. The farmers pull their sleds up into the mountain forests (though some leave the sled at the foot of the mountain). Now they can cut the highest branches as they please, for the snows that have buried the trees serve as a natural platform to reach the treetops that normally they can only gaze up at. Six bundles of firewood usually make one sledload. Three bundles are laid on the bottom, two in the middle, and one on top, all bound tightly with rope. To lead his prize home, the farmer aims his sled for the foot of the mountain and sends it gliding down over the frozen snow, covering hundreds and hundreds of yards downhill in a flash. If there are twists or obstacles in its path, he rides on the sled himself, using one foot as a rudder just as a ship's captain steers a ship through the waves. With amazing skill he guides the sled around difficult places, making the long descent without a single mishap. I find it a marvel that the farmers are able to do this without any special study, quite on their own.

When two or three set off to cut timber together, they pack their lunches in bags woven of grass, which they tie to their sleds. The mountain crows are very good at spotting them and gather in a flock to break open the bags and devour the contents. "Well, that's about it for today," someone says, "It's time to eat!" But when they reach their sleds they find themselves mocked by a flock of cawing crows in the treetops and not a grain of their roasted rice balls left. Curse and glare as they might, it's no use; they return home with an empty stomach and no sled song to announce their arrival. "Yes, that sometimes happens," said the person who related this to me.

For otherwise they always sing a song as they lead their sleds, and these are called sled songs—also known as woodcutter's songs. The verses of these sled songs are of ancient grace. A father has gone off into the mountains to cut wood; when his wife and daughter hear the sound of his sled song from afar, they know he has returned and rush out to meet his sled. They set the father astride the piles of firewood and pull the sled on, singing the sled song too. Simple ancient customs such as this have survived here till today because ours is a hinterland that has not known the advances of prosperity.

As "spring begins to prepare its landscape," the plums and willows are still heavy with snow, and as the days pass gradually we have no idea if flowers and green are hiding beneath the white. Yet the skies of March grow a lovely blue, and as one sits by a bright window reading a book and hears from afar a sled song, one can't but be elated by the powerful feeling of spring. Nor is this my feeling alone, but the feeling, I know, of all who live in the snow country.

Momoki adds: When I was young I recall that from the day after New Year's Day, the streets would be full of voices hawking "Fans, fans!" and others calling "Sweet sake, sweet sake," cheering us and making us feel that spring had arrived. You don't hear those voices anymore, nor even the songs of the female entertainers who customarily made the rounds at the New Year. In faraway country towns built around a samurai mansion one still hears the calls of the sushi vendors selling their shad and sea bream. These, too, were reminders of spring. "Primroses, buy my primroses!" in April brought first thoughts of flowers, and the blossoms of the deutzia hedges followed on the cries of the dried tuna vendor in June. The hawker's call "Bamboo, bamboo" before the Tanabata Festival cooled and refreshed the heart in summer, while the same cry (but this time for bamboo dusters to clean the houses with) in the last days of the old year filled us with busy anticipation.

Everything calls according to its season, and it is only natural that these sounds should shape our feelings. The grass flute of China evoked such melancholy by the same power. Though here I have spoken of men's voices, how much more evocative are the song of the nightingale or the trilling of frogs in spring, the cicadas' drone in summer, the cry of the first autumn goose, the deer, or the crickets, the plover in winter. So if hearts swell with spring at the sound of the sled song, is it in the least strange? Because I have felt this myself I have spoken of it here. For the people of Edo, the idea that a sled song could be a herald of spring is probably strange beyond imagining; yet in each province there must be such things, that have a very special meaning for the people there.

Some sleds are used for fertilizing the fields. They are smaller, just the right size for this task. In March and April, of course, everything is covered with an unbroken layer of white snow, and it is very difficult to guess where one paddy stops and another starts. Yet the farmers of our region come with their manure sleds and, with no mark or sign to guide him, each digs out a hole in the snow as if he were digging a well, where he deposits the manure. Never does he miss his own paddy by so much as one foot. When I asked one farmer what he takes as his sign amidst the white, unmarked snow cover, I was told, "I don't depend on any sign. Something just tells me 'This is it' and there I dig. I'm never wrong, either." Though the task itself is a lowly one, I have written of it here because it represents the highest mastery of a skill, and I wish to encourage those engaged in perfecting their arts and crafts to pursue a like mastery.

The largest sleds are known as *shura*. When big timbers or boulders are carried on these sleds it is called a Great Load, or Daimochi. One year when the Honganji temple in Kyoto was being built, huge zelkova timbers ninety feet long with a diameter of more than five feet at the top were carried on such sleds. Two or even three sleds were tied together for this task. The trees were cut in autumn, before snow had fallen, and left in the mountains to be brought down when sleds could be used. The snow, you must realize, freezes hard enough even to support such massive timbers as these! Since everything, including all the paddies and fields, are covered with frozen snow, a direct path can be taken, which is a tremendous convenience. A mighty rope was tied to the *shura* to haul it, and many smaller ropes attached along the sides to help steer it. In the fore stepped two men carrying banners that read "Beams for the Honganji," and believers young and old, male and female, together with a swarm of children, gathered like an army of ants to pull the load. Seven song

Children playing Great Load by carting an icicl[e]

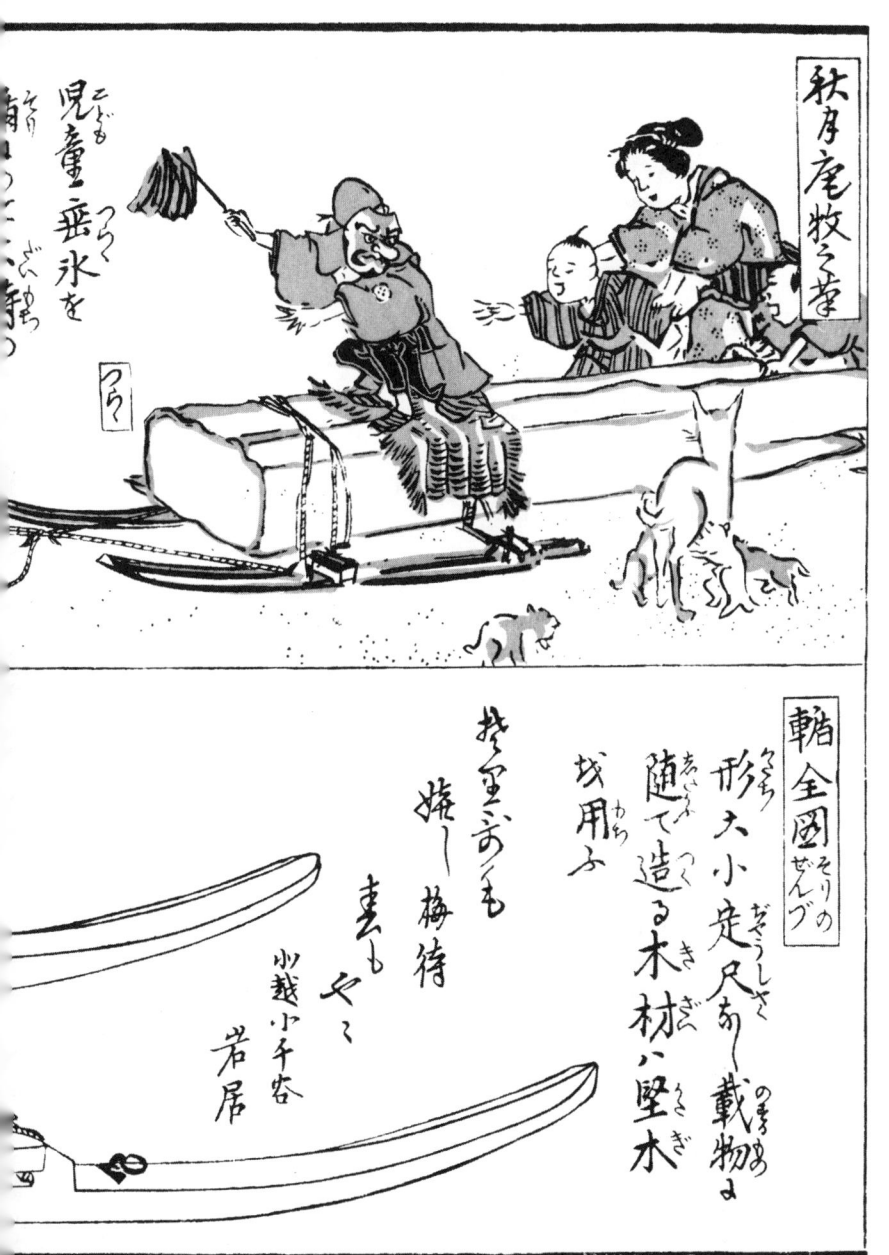

out on a sled (*above*). A sled's construction (*below*).

leaders, dressed in colorful costumes and waving batons with tassels of colored paper, rode atop the load and led the people in a woodcutter's song. It went like this:

> Rabbit, rabbit, little rabbit
> Why are your ears so long?
> When you were in your mother's womb
> She ate bamboo grass leaves, that's why,
> That's why your ears are so long.
> The Great Load made its way
> On to the glorious capital.
> (*One hundred voices sing the next together:*)
> Heave, heave!
> Everyone sing together and pull!
> Heave, heave, heave!

There are also sleds designed for children's play. The young ones pile big six- or seven-foot icicles on their sleds and play at Great Load, singing songs and pulling their sleds. Certainly this must be unheard of in warmer parts of the land. There is always more that can be said about sleds, but I will pull to a halt here.

Hoarfrost

Not only in winter and spring, but whenever evaporating snow touches things, they are as if covered by frost. This is called *shiga*, or hoarfrost, in our region. Often hoarfrost even makes its way indoors and forms inside the rooms of our homes, though it melts away when the morning sun falls on it. In spring the lower branches of the trees of mountain and meadow are still buried in snow, but the snow on the treetops has already melted. They are covered instead with hoarfrost, so that they look like branches made out of jewels, a truly wonderful sight. Hoarfrost even forms on the hair of people working near a river. Actually, hoarfrost is rare in Shiozawa. It is frequently seen in Koidejima in the same county, because that place is near a great river, the moisture of which easily forms frost.

Early Summer Snow

The snow in our land, at least in the villages, begins to melt as April approaches. Though each morning it is frozen again as hard as iron, it melts from both the top and the bottom during the day. By the end of the month, the snow melts so quickly that the daily difference can be recognized. When it seems that it won't snow again, people begin to remove the snow supports here and there and to dig the snow out of the garden and dispose of it. But since the snow is still frozen hard, it must be sawed into blocks with a great saw (called a *daigiri,* or "big cutter") and taken away. The sight of people carrying off these large square blocks of snow on their backs and on their shoulders is certainly not one to be seen in warmer climates.

The supports and ties that kept the branches of the garden trees from being snapped by the snow are removed and undone, and we see that the plums have bravely put on buds while beneath the snow, waiting for spring—though that season has already reached its end! Now, at last, the rooms of our houses that have been dark since November grow gradually lighter, and we feel like a blind person who regains his sight. Though we set out the dolls for the Peach-Blossom Festival, we know it in name only, for the peach blossoms are still tight in their buds.

By May the snow on our fields begins to melt in patches, and the vegetables that we planted at the autumnal equinox the year before have sprouted beneath the snow. The plums are past their peak, and the peaches and cherries make the summer their spring. When we now dig out our springs and ponds, the goldfish and carp that have been dwelling in a world of blackness for two hundred days, since the first snow last year, swim about happily as if to say "At last, at last! How happy we are!"

Yet even in June, the snow that has remained untouched by human hands and lies in the shade lingers in the mountains, just as before. There are places in the deep mountain valleys where the snow never melts, even during the hottest part of the year.

Shaved Ice

Momoki recounts: It was late summer in 1837 that I traveled to Echigo with my son Kyosui. On the fifteenth of July, we crossed Mikuni Peak, and from the bottom of the valley heard the song of a cuckoo.

> At our feet,
> The cuckoo's cry
> As we, too, crossed the deep valley
> Wandering through the mountains
> Of Koshi.

Though a humble effort, the poem so truly expressed the moment that I record it here. After crossing the peak we walked for some four miles along a mountain road so steep and twisting that we were never on level ground for even a single stride. We stayed that night in a post town called Asakai. Then we crossed Futai Peak and stopped overnight at Mitsumata, a mountain post town. As we were descending Shibahara Peak the next day on the road to Yuzawa, we spied in the distance a little teahouse.

Underneath the eaves was an elevated verandah, and on it a shallow box containing some white squares. From afar we took them to be *tokoroten,* a kind of jelly, that they must be selling. Though neither of us could imagine getting it down our throats, we were overjoyed at the very thought of a teahouse, for we were no longer in the mountains and it was terribly hot. Drenched with sweat and tired from walking, Kyosui and I rushed under the eaves and sat on the verandah, where we saw that the white substance we had seen was not *tokoroten* but frozen snow!

Now the sight of snow in July was a great wonder for us from Edo, so we went nearer to see that the box, about five inches deep, was filled with water in which floated blocks of frozen snow the size of small stepping stones. When we asked the old teahouse keeper about this, he told us that it came from dark mountain valleys, and he urged us to try it, so we ordered some. We watched as the proprietor took a large kitchen knife and shaved off the ice with a rasping sound, putting it in bowls. He then sprinkled it with yellow soybean powder and served it. Although it was quite odd for us from Edo to see ice served sprinkled with soybean powder, my son and I caught each other's eye and did our best to stifle our chuckles. "This is quite something. Let's have another plate—this time without the soybean powder, though, please." We sprinkled it instead with sugar that we had carried with us. It's difficult to say how rare this experience was; eating that shaved ice so cold it made our teeth ache, we forgot entirely about the summer heat.

Among the references sprinkled through ancient books to the rare delights of eating shaved ice, Lord Teika's *Bright Moon Diary* says: "On the twenty-eighth day of August, 1204, we were on our way to the Poetry Bureau. Fujiwara Karyu ordered two Chinese chests to be brought along, containing lacquer lunch boxes, melons, sake, and, of all things, ice. Taking his sword in hand, he began to shave the ice himself, certainly an astonishing scene." Some six hundred years have passed between this event and the one I describe. It is remarkable that we were able to enjoy shaved ice here in a mountain village of Echigo, just as in times of old, and it was an opportunity bound to delight those who love the old ways.

The original reading of the character for "ice" seems to have been *hi*. The present reading *koori* derives from the word "to freeze": *kogoekooru*, according to *The Dictionary of Japanese Readings* by Tanigawa Kotosuga. The term "ice chamber" (*hi muro*) is among the seasonal words used in Japanese poetry and so known to all. We know that ice chambers existed in ancient China as well, for they are mentioned in *The Rites of Zhou*. We may know how old they are in our country by the fact that they are mentioned in *The Annals of Nintoku*. In *The Codes of the Engi Era* we read of five ice chambers in Katsuragi County of Yamashiro. Ice was taken from these on the first of July every year and offered as tribute to the emperor, who then

Selling snow in July.

六月賣雪圖

divided it among his ministers. The ice mentioned in *Bright Moon Diary*, however, was not such a gift from the emperor, since it was enjoyed on the twenty-eighth day of August. Ice presented to a minister on the first of July would surely have melted by the twenty-eighth of August. Even if a copyist's error in *Bright Moon Diary*, which has been copied thousands of times, mistook August for July, ice taken from an ice chamber on the first of July won't last even one day. Nor is it at all likely that the guardian of the ice chamber would permit more ice to be taken out for private individuals.

Ice chambers were underground places in the coldest, deepest shade of the mountains where thick blocks of ice were stored. A house was built next to the ice chamber for the one assigned to guard it. In old poems we read of these guards of the ice chamber. Several books also comment that frozen water was stored in the ice chambers, but frozen water makes for impure ice, and it is very unlikely that anything impure would be offered as imperial tribute. At any rate, ice formed from water would melt too easily if stored underground, simply because as an extremely yin substance it is very susceptible to the yang principle.

The ice shavings of Echigo are probably from a natural ice chamber deep in a cold, dark valley, and the ancient ice chambers were no doubt chambers of frozen snow as well. First a hole was probably made in a very cold, yin place, and a roof was raised over it. Then a separate location, a naturally clean place, was fenced off to prevent either humans or animals from entering and dirtying it, and the snowfall was awaited. After falling, the snow from this clean place was carried to the hole, pushed in, and buried. A man was set to guard it, and to open it only on the first day of July, when the purest pieces of frozen snow were presented to the emperor as tribute. This is my reasoned explanation of the ice chambers of antiquity.

I could never hope to cite all the ancient poems that mention ice chambers, but from Fujiwara Teika, who himself tasted the delicious ice shavings, we have (in his *Collection of Foolish Scribblings*):

> Though summer, the autumn winds
> Rise on the ice-chamber mountain:

BOOK FOUR

>   Here, for certain
>   Winter remains.

And Minamoto Nakamasa (in *Poetry of a Thousand Years*):

>   The gently descending blossoms
>   Of the late cherries
>   On the ice-chamber mountain!
>   Or is it only
>   The last remaining snow?

This poem means that the late-blooming cherries of the ice-chamber mountain could be mistaken for some lingering patches of unmelted snow, strongly suggesting that in fact ice chambers were storage places for frozen snow. And today, the snow that the lord of Kashu sends to the emperor on the first of July is frozen snow, which also supports the same conclusion.

Impressed with the rarity of the frozen snow served me in this teahouse, I arrived the next day at Bokushi's house in Shiozawa. During my stay there an old woman from a mountain village came by every day with a cry of "Ice, ice!" A handful cost a mere three pennies. At first I was amazed at the rarity, but afterward I began to forget it was ice at all. I'm afraid it must be human nature that what is rare is valued, what is common is not. When I recall how ice in July soon grew so familiar while I was in Shiozawa, it occurs to me that the people of Yoshino must barely see the famous cherry blossoms there, and the people of Matsushima never once look up at its much-vaunted moon. Perhaps the only two things that people never tire of are the shining faces of devoted children and the glint of gold in the storehouse.

Differing Amounts of Snow

In the south of Echigo, bordering Joshu, is Uonuma County. To the east, bordering Oshu and Dewa, are Kambara and Iwafune counties. There is much snow along all of these borders, which are ranged by high peaks. The road to Nezumigaseki in the northwest (in Iwafune County on the border with Dewa) and to Ichifuri in the west (in Kubiki County on the border with Etchu) pass along the north seacoast for nearly two hundred miles. Because of the ocean's influence, this region has no more than six or seven feet of snow, varying, of course, from year to year, and melting rather quickly. Takata in Kubiki County, on the other hand, though not far from the sea, has deep snows. During the great snow at the beginning of the Bunka era (1804–17) they had in the city of Takata such a fall of snow that it buried the entire town. All and everywhere it was totally dark. For ten days, the people didn't know whether it was night or day! Soon all the oil for the lamps had been used up, so the governor of Takata had oil distributed to each household.

Here in Shiozawa, too, we have great snows and lose track of day and night. Sometimes we spend as long as two weeks under the snow without any light at all, for blizzards rage day after day and we are unable to clear away the snow that blocks our windows and plunges our homes into blackness. People's spirits sink dangerously, and some even fall ill.

Momoki comments: When Bokushi was adding a few additional comments to this work in preparation for publication, he wrote in his letters to the printer: "The snow was late this year, and at the start of winter no more than a foot of snow lay in the town. If things continued like this, everyone thought, we'd have relatively little snow this year, and there was considerable rejoicing.

"Then on the twenty-fourth of December it began to snow in the evening; it continued for five days, through the twenty-ninth. In that time, some fourteen or fifteen feet of snow accumulated. Normal as this was, it was also totally unexpected, and the town was a mess as from the twenty-seventh to the twenty-ninth everyone rushed to clear the snow off their roofs. Suddenly walls of snow rose up around and under the eaves, making it difficult to even enter and leave our houses. Today, too, another great blizzard is blowing; the house is dark and I write this by candlelight. It is difficult to predict how much more snow will fall, and all of us are very anxious."

The letter is dated December 29, 1839, and serves as eloquent testimony to the snows of Echigo.

Yet when I visited Echigo in summer, there was no evidence that the snows damaged cereal or fruit crops. The scenery of the mountains and fields was untouched by traces of winter and appeared just as that of any other land. The "Heaven" chapter of *The Five Miscellanies* states that plants do not fear snow so much as they do frost, because snow is born of clouds and therefore yang. Frost is born of dew, and is yin by nature. The summer of Echigo is certainly ample proof of Xie Zhaozhi's theories.

The Hall-pushing at Urasa

Two towns down the road to Lower Echigo from my home in Shiozawa, past Muikamachi and Itsukamachi, is a post town called Urasa. Here there is a temple called the Fukoji, of the Shingon sect. In the Fukoji complex there is a forty-foot-square hall known as Bishamon Hall, said to have been built in 807. Ridgepole tablets, still preserved, mark each rebuilding or renovation. The image of Bishamon is three feet five inches in height; it is supposed to have been carved from a giant camellia tree in a village called Tsubakizawa (Camellia Brook). The name of the sculptor is unknown.

The holy image being made of camellia wood, anyone in the region who cut camellia for firewood was visited by divine punishment, and as a result no one planted camellias thereabouts. The divine spirit also prohibited the catching of birds. Flocks of them gathered in the temple precincts, without the least fear of people. If any of the inhabitants of this area were to catch or eat a bird, divine punishment descended upon him directly, even if the person went in marriage to a far distant place and after long, long years ate a bird. This is a clear case of the powers of spirits, and many people far and near are believers in the power of this Bishamon.

Devotees on their way to the Hall-pushing at Urasa.

Every year on the third day after the New Year an event called the hall-pushing occurs in the Bishamon Hall. Although it has never earned the rank of an officially declared ceremony, it has been from ancient times a holy event. The roads at this time are all snow paths, but people come from as far away as twenty-five or even fifty miles to Urasa, where they spend the night; of course those nearer by are certain to be there.

First, all who have arrived for the hall-pushing, men and women, enter the Fukoji temple and undress, tossing down their clothes and possessions in disarray. Women wear only a thin cotton robe tied with a string belt, and sometimes they even strip to the waist. All the men are naked except for loincloths. Just at the hour when the torches are usually lit, these women in light robes and men in nothing at all press into the hall, which grows so tightly packed that there's not room to drive a nail. When I was young I once participated in the hall-pushing myself, and I recall that we were so closely jammed together that it was impossible to bring a lifted arm back down to one's side.

No one in particular gives the command to push, but as all are chanting *"Sanyo, sanyo"* in a loud voice, suddenly the young men and women packed in the hall cry *"Osai, kosai!"* and begin to push vigorously from north to south; then the cry is given again and they all push from west to east. It is very startling to see the hair of men and women alike fall wildly askew as the cords that keep it in place break during the first push. The great number of naked people in the hall can be easily imagined: enough to pack the forty-four-square-foot hall so tightly that no one can even turn around. On that cold night of the third day of the New Year, the exhalation of this multitude is like smoke or fog. It dims the sacred torches and rises up to the roof, where it condenses and falls like rain; the steam pouring out of the open peaks of the gables billows into the sky like a cloud.

Rarely, a mother will bind her child to her back and join the crush. It is a fact, and a most incomprehensible one, that the child never cries. Nor has anyone, from ancient times, ever received the slightest hurt during this hall-pushing. Though the women are wearing only the flimsiest clothing and all are pressing together in the dark hall, there has never been a case when anyone was molested. This is because all fear the punishment of the god Bishamon.

The reason that everyone is naked is that, with the heat of human bodies, the interior of the hall soon grows burning hot. Some, having undertaken a special vow, come to the hall-pushing from as far as five miles away, enduring the cold of the New Year, so cold it pierces the skin, and carrying huge icicles the size of pillars on their backs. After two or three pushings, you're as hot as if it were the middle of summer, and some douse themselves in the great stone basin near the hall, only to return for another turn at pushing. It is a rule that a person should catch his breath after each pushing and quit after seven pushings and seven sessions of the dancing that follows—though dancing is barely the word for it, for everyone is covered with sweat over every inch of his body, and it's more like potatoes being washed by rubbing them together in a tub.

After the seventh dance, the "mountain chief" (that is, the leader of the farmhands) of the Fukoji, with a bamboo rasp in hand, is carried on interlocked arms to the center of the throng, where he chants in a loud voice: "A black cloud came down in front of Bishamon." And the crowd replies with the question: "What did it come down to say?" "It came down to say that rice would rain!" answers the mountain chief, rubbing his rasp. Since it is thought that if the rasp is rubbed to the inside, a bad harvest will result, he rubs to the outside, to the outside with every stroke.

Those who have made special vows notify the Fukoji in advance and offer a cask of sanctified sake and a set of sake cups. The mountain chief, carrying the sake and cups, proceeds into the hall, his way cleared by a vanguard of twenty men who carry lanterns as they press through the crowd. Everyone has been told that good fortune will come to those who manage to grab a cup, and so the people jostle and push each other, trying to make one theirs. The holy sake is sprinkled over the heads of the crowd as an offering to the god and the cups thrown into their midst. Whoever catches a cup takes it home and enshrines it, and that household is always blessed with unexpected good fortune. The lanterns, too, are soon torn apart in attempts to grab them, and it is said that even a single rib of a lantern, inserted at the mouth of a paddy irrigation ditch, will guarantee a rich harvest and freedom from pests. Everyone knows of the great power of this god.

When the rite comes to an end, the people all return to the main hall of the Fukoji, where they first undressed. Looking about at their scattered belongings and valuables they find that not so much as a single piece of tissue paper has been taken; and this is because whoever might attempt to steal anything would be punished by the god on the spot.

After all the people have left the hall, it is customary for the mountain chief to toss hemp stalks about the building. The next morning he brings blessed sake and other offerings, walking backwards as he presents them—to walk in the usual forward-facing manner is forbidden by the god. The hemp stalks that he scattered the night before are all broken into little bits; it is said that this is because after the mountain chief departs the gods gather and dance on the stalks, breaking and bending them. Many of the gods' actions seem like the play of children, yet we must not try to understand them with our limited powers of mind. No doubt there are rites similar to this hall-pushing in other parts of the land. I record it here so that it may be compared with others like it.

BOOK FIVE

Bagging a Bear in an Avalanche

In *The Youyang Miscellany* it is recorded that the bear's gall bladder is to be found in its neck in the spring, in its abdomen in the summer, in its left foot in the fall, and in its right foot in the winter. When I questioned hunters to see whether this was true, they replied, "A bear's gall is always in his abdomen, whatever the season." Perhaps the bears of China, though, have the traveling gall bladders described in *The Youyang Miscellany*.

The bear is the most sought-after prey of the hunters who prowl the mountains, and the reason is that the hide and gall of a large bear may bring as much as five gold pieces. But bears are both fierce and intelligent, and not an easy catch. In the winter, the skins and gall bladders of bears fetch twice the normal price, and so hunters search out their dens in the snows; the ways in which hunters cooperate in this venture, employing a variety of wiles, is described in the first book. Should they chance to catch a bear, the reward must be divided and becomes smaller, but it is almost impossible for a man alone to bag a bear in the snow.

In the village of Goya, not far from where I live, there was a farmer by the name of Mizaemon who lived with his two aged parents. It was their wish to make a pilgrimage to the Zenkoji temple in Shinshu Province, and he was kind enough to make it possible for them to do so. One day, during their absence, he found that he had to make a short trip some five miles away from home. In his absence, a person of the neighboring household started a fire by accident. Sparks leapt to the eaves of Mizaemon's house, and Mizaemon's wife just managed to escape with their two small children. All of their possessions were reduced to ashes before her very eyes. Mizaemon heard that there was a fire in his village and dashed back to find the house that he had left in the morning reduced to a heap of ash. Yet he rejoiced that his wife and children, at least, had been spared.

Since they were widely known as an upstanding couple—and often held up as models of filial piety—several well-to-do farmers offered them temporary lodging in their homes. "We would be more than willing to show our gratitude and repay your hospitality by working on your farms, but we cannot bear the thought of our parents returning to find that they must squeeze into a stranger's house." And so they refused all such offers. Secretly instead they mortgaged some of their paddies, and with that money built a house that would serve at least temporarily. Their parents returned and to the young couple's relief had a place of their own to stay.

They had to replace everything, of course, even down to a scythe to cut the grass. The fire thoroughly impoverished them, but they never spoke so much as a word against the neighboring household, where the fire that burned their home down had started. In fact, they stayed on the same friendly terms as before. Thus the year drew to a close.

At the beginning of March of the next year, Mizaemon went up into the mountains to gather firewood. On his way home he spied in the heaps of snow from an avalanche that had fallen into a valley something black, distant but distinct. Gazing at it from afar, he feared that it might be someone who had been killed by the avalanche and started down the valley toward it. But when he approached it he discovered that it was an enormous bear that had been killed by the falling snow. Mizaemon was overjoyed to have discovered this wonderful prize and was about to skin it and remove the gall bladder when he noticed that the sun was already well down toward the west. "I'll return tomorrow," he prudently decided and covered the bear with heaps of snow to hide it from anyone else who might happen to pass by. After clearly marking the place in his mind he headed home, and there he delighted his parents with news of his great find.

The next day he prepared the tools he'd need to skin the bear and made his way back to the place. The gall bladder, he found, was twice the normal size, and he put it in his lunchbox for safekeeping as he carried it home. The skin was sold for one gold piece and the gall for nine. With this windfall of ten pieces of gold, Mizaemon was able to redeem his mortgaged land. From that time good fortune was his, and soon he was able to properly rebuild his house, more prosperous and grand than before. Mizaemon's discovery of the bear killed by an avalanche is not unlike the tale of the filial son who found a pot of gold when digging a hole, and, according to my friend Kokuo, who told me this story, people praised him as proof that Heaven loves those who are kind to the elderly.

Funerals in the Snow

I have described before the blizzards of Echigo, how all of a sudden a fierce wind arises, how it whips about the snows of the high mountains and the flat plateaus, swirls in the four directions, and how the frozen snow is pitched like thousands of tiny daggers. I have related how anyone out walking at this time is struck down, and how they are half-buried in the snow in no time, and how they quickly freeze to death. Though a blizzard may arise in an instant, without warning, out of a blue sky, it may also continue for two or three days, and every year all travel is brought to a halt by blizzards. When someone dies it is usually possible to wait for the end of the blizzard to hold funeral services, but sometimes it cannot be helped and the coffin is brought out in spite of the raging storm.

The family of the deceased, of course, must somehow bear this. But it is a shame that others, too, must be so inconvenienced. Certainly this is one of the great difficulties of life in the snow country. When I was staying in Edo, there was a death once in a house near the inn where I was staying. On the day of the funeral, a fierce storm arose. The proprietor of my inn was to go out to the funeral, and while wrapping himself up tightly in rain gear, he grumbled, "What terrible past karma the dear departed must have had—enough to send people out in this storm and to make himself the object of their complaints! I doubt he's on his way to the Pure Land, indeed." And thus he took his leave. As I watched and listened, the comparison with the blizzards of our land came easily to mind, and I thought what a small difficulty he actually faced.

Dragon Lights

The so-called mysterious lights of Tsukushi are often referred to in the poetry of ancient times and are quite widely known. Shunki, in his *Travels to the West,* describes in detail how they shine, having seen them with his own eyes. These mysterious lights belong to the category of phenomena people elsewhere have come to call "dragon lights."

In Kambara County there used to be a lake called Yoroigata (*gata,* or lagoon, means "lake" in our local dialect). It stretched two and one-half miles from north to south and three and one-half from east to west. Year after year, in the middle of March, people made pilgrimages to this lake to watch the strange lights that between six in the evening and two in the morning would dance above the surface of the water. They were known as the ten thousand lights of Yoroigata.

When I heard that a friend of mine had actually seen these lights, I questioned him and found that they were no doubt the same phenomenon as the mysterious lights of Tsukushi mentioned in Shunki's work.

Recently, however, they have drained Yoroigata, channeled its water into the Sea of Japan, and made paddies in its place. The ten thousand lights of the mysterious lake have become the million lights of human homes.

The same occurrence has been reported at Hakkaisan—Mount Eight Seas—which has on its summit eight ponds, after which it is named. On the peak of the mountain there is also a shrine dedicated to the deity of the mountain, Hakkai Daimyojin. Many people climb the mountain to worship there on the first day of September.

On this night only can one see the dragon lights, though even then no one has ever seen where they come from. In general, dragon lights can be observed in spring, summer, and autumn.

Studying the almanacs of various lands, we learn that there are dragon lights in all countries. Their appearance is always the same, whether they rise out of the sea or seem to descend from the mountains. The strange thing about them is that they always, year after year, show themselves on the same day at the same hour. A popular explanation has it that the dragon lights are the offerings of the dragon kings, the *nagas,* to the gods and buddhas, but I have a more interesting story to relate about them.

The government post road leads over Mount Yone Pass toward the Sea of Japan, and along this road one finds many historical remains and ruins. When I traveled to southern Echigo to visit these last year, the village chief of Shindo Village, Iizuka Tomoyoshi, told me of his pilgrimage to a temple at the foot of Mount Yone called Iosan Beisanji. This temple was built during the Wado era (708–14). On the summit of the mountain is a little hall dedicated, as is the temple, to Yakushi, the bodhisattva of healing. Women are forbidden entirely to set foot on this sacred mountain.

There are two huts at the top of the mountain, he said, at a place called Ohachi. They were built for pilgrims who make overnight stays. A year ago in summer he climbed Mount Yone with other villagers to pray for rain. They decided to stay overnight in the huts, and it happened to be the twelfth day of July, the day the dragon lights customarily rise over Ohachi in the evening. Delighted at this unexpected chance to see the lights, the villagers quieted down in anticipation of their visitation.

In the early evening hours the dragon lights began to gather out of nowhere. The larger ones were the size of a football, the smaller ones as small as an egg. Both sizes mingled, hovering over Ohachi, flitting about, some slower, some quicker. They moved as if they were living things gamboling in the dusk.

The color of their light resembled that of fireflies, glowing stronger and then weaker, as they danced tirelessly around the summit, never stopping for a moment. There were so many that it was impossible to count them.

From the start, the villagers had kept the hut doors tightly shut and no one uttered the least sound. All watched silently. Two or three smaller and larger lights danced to within some fifty feet of the huts, as if they were unaware of the pilgrims' presence. Thanks to this, the farmers could see clearly that the dragon lights were shaped like birds and the light seemed to shine from a place below their throats. Just when the entranced viewers thought they could make out clearly the shapes of the dancing lights, they would halt their approach and drift lightly away again.

Since the group had gone up the mountain with the intention of spending the night, they had taken their guns along as a precaution. Suddenly one of the villagers, a young sharpshooter, lifted his gun and aimed at one of the lights, ready to shoot it. A village elder standing nearby stopped him.

"Wait!" he cried angrily, "Don't be a fool! These are the offerings of the dragon gods to Yakushi Bodhisattva. You will invite divine punishment!" he scolded sharply.

At that very moment all the dragon lights vanished, as if frightened by the angry voice of the speaker. And this is what the village chief told me.

Poems in Basho's Hand

Though there are many poems that make mention of the snows of Echigo, few are the poets who have ever actually seen them. There is no sign of Echigo's snows in Saigyo's *Mountain Hermitage Collection* or Tona's *Grass Hut Collection,* and it is doubtful that either of these poet-monks knew of them. Minamoto Toshiyori has composed a poem that is a perfect description of our snows:

> All traces of the valley
> Are buried in the snows.
> The very tips of the trees alone
> Mark the mountain roads in winter.

BOOK FIVE

But Toshiyori was never in Echigo. As they say, poets can recreate famous places simply by virtue of their art.

Date Masamune has composed several poems on snow:

> No need to bar the barrier gate,
> Tonight no one will breach it.
> It lies buried in white
> In the snowy dusk.

> On and on
> The serpentine path,
> Until its traces vanish.
> And there in the snow,
> The neighboring village.

Because Masamune was such a well-known and well-loved poet, his compositions—including the two above—have been passed down through the years. He was able to describe such scenes so truly because his own land was one of deep snows, too.

Basho stopped in Echigo on the return portion of his wanderings to the north, and at Niigata he composed this poem:

> Rain falling on the sea
> And I find myself longing
> For lodging and ladies.

At Teradomari he wrote another:

> The wild sea.
> Reaching for Sado,
> The Milky Way.

These are poems of summer and autumn, and it is certain that Basho did not see Echigo under the snow. Even today, when many literati visit our province, they come only in the temperate season. As fall comes to an end, they flee back to their homes, in terror of the snows. They write no poems of Echigo's snow, pen no travel diaries of our winters. On the rare occasions when an outsider happens to spend a winter here, he inevitably has no literary talent and leaves no record.

A man from Sanjo in Echigo, a certain Hermit Konron, has published a work called *Strange Tales of North Etsu,* but it contains not a single mention of snow! (The work appeared in 1811, in six volumes with illustrations.) Nowadays everyone's writing a book, and new ones appear as if bubbling out of the ground, but no one has seen fit to describe the greatest snows in all of Japan. And so I have been bold and put my ignorance behind me, daring to record here the oddities and wonders of our land for future generations, to provide a few bits and pieces of information about this region for those of active curiosity.

But to return to Basho, there was in the Genroku era (1688–1704) in the castle town of Takata a certain doctor by the name Hosoi Shoan. He excelled at poetry and used the pen name Toun. One year, Basho, on his way back from the north, came to see Toun, opening his visit with the poem:

> Which flower shall I pick
> From the garden plot
> To be my grass pillow?

Toun replied:

> Lifting the blinds
> Of the bush clover:
> The rising moon.

Basho took down both poems, on separate sheets of paper. One has light overwritten brushstrokes suggesting that it has been revised. Both autographs were formerly held by Shoan's family. Later the unmarred one was kept by a relative of Shoan, Misakiya Yoshibei, and the corrected one by the Gochi Nyorai temple. But in the Bunsei era (1818–30) they were given to Lord Sakakibara of Takata, who is devoted to literary pursuits. Yoshibei received in return two paintings by Kano Tsunenobu and five pieces of silver, and the temple was also richly rewarded. Now both autographs are in the lord's collection.

Petrifying Valley

In *Travels to the East* there is a description of the petrifying valley in the mountains of the Ono estate in Echizen Province. If anything—it doesn't make any difference what—is left in this valley for one month, it turns to stone. The work relates that its author saw several vessels and containers that had turned to stone, and even a sheaf of paper that had been wrapped in straw.

We have our own petrifying valley in Echigo. My friend Kitei has told me that if you rinse rotten silkworm cocoons in the Hane River at Koide in Uonuma County, they will turn to stone in a single night. The petrifying valley of Ono is known to all the world because of its appearance in *Travels to the East,* but our petrifying valley remains obscure.

We also see in *The Cloud-Essence Annals,* in the section on transformations, "A certain person said: 'There is a waterfall called Cold Water Falls in Oi County in Echigo. It is located in the deep dark cold mountains. Anything tossed into the bowl of this waterfall turns to stone after one hundred days. The branches and the fruits of trees around the base of the waterfall, as well as other living things nearby, are all petrified.' Once, in the past, I had a person bring me stones from this waterfall. A look at them showed that they were not ordinary stones, but stalactites. Inside them were visible the leaves of trees and other things. *Stones of Clouds and Forests* says that stalactites gradually develop from stones."

I know, of course, that there is no Oi County in Echigo. Nor have I heard of Cold Water Falls. Though "a certain person said" these things, there was obviously an error in the transmission of this tale. There does appear, however, in *Strange Tales of North Etsu*, a place called Petrifying Valley, said to be located some seven or eight miles down the deep valley of Koma Peak, next to Aizu. Insect or bird,

Examining the petrified tortoise.

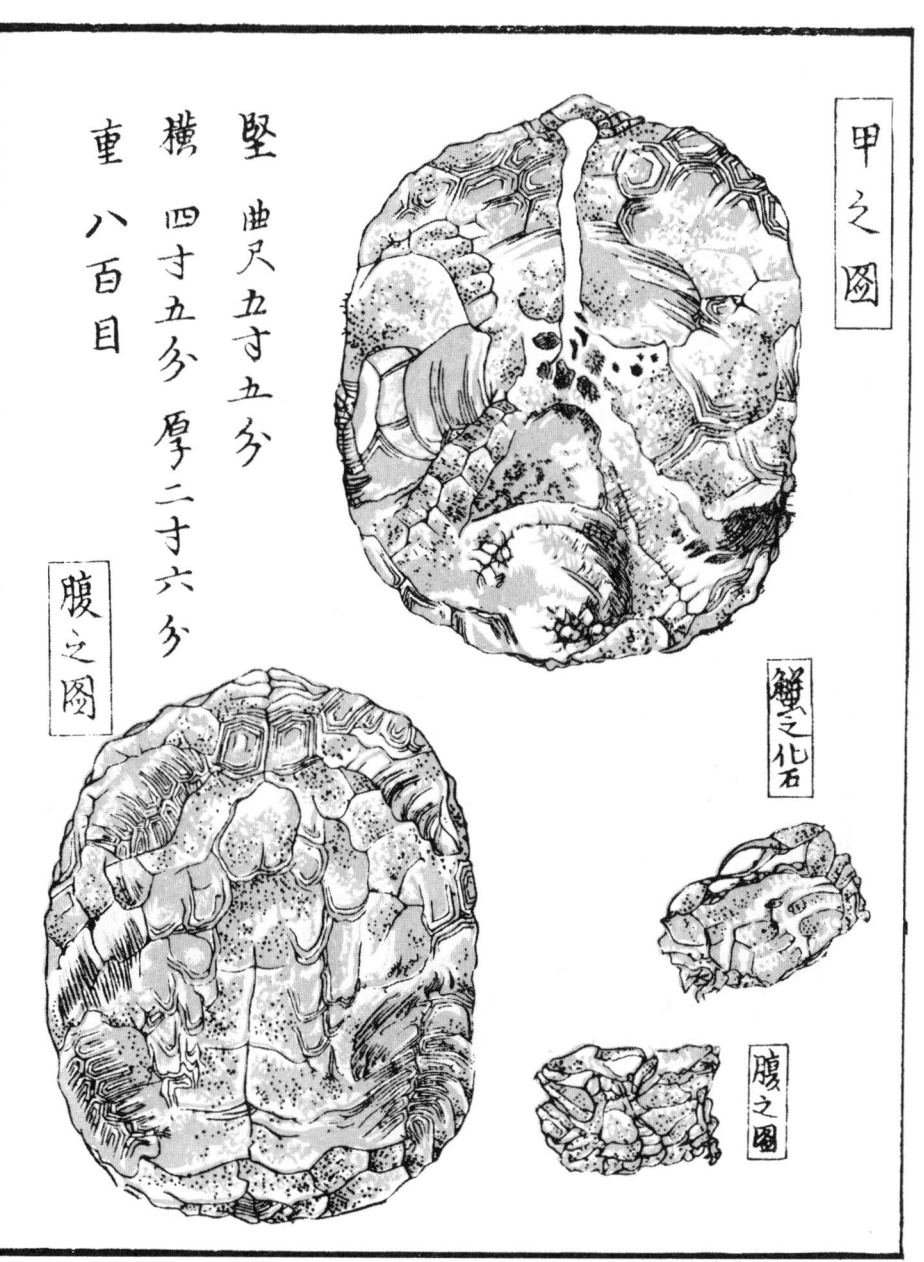

The shell of the petrified tortoise and a petrified crab.

tree or plant, whatever enters that valley petrifies after one year. The river that runs through the valley is extremely cold and cannot be forded, even in summer. It is also said that there is a petrifying valley deep in the mountain recesses of Shitada, north of Somon Peak. Perhaps the passage in *The Cloud-Essence Annals* mistook these places for the ones it mentioned.

A Petrified Tortoise

Murayama Fujizaemon, of an old family in the village of Oka, is the brother of my son-in-law. His family treasures a petrified tortoise that has been passed down over the generations. Legend has it that the petrified tortoise was excavated from the mountains nearby. It is truly a rare specimen of a petrified object. I provide an illustration here and await the conclusions of connoisseurs of such things.

Momoki adds: The illustration shows that this object is a little different from the ordinary tortoise. Perhaps it is what is called a Qin tortoise in *The Herbal Encyclopedia;* there the synonyms "diviner's tortoise" and "mountain tortoise" are also given, and in common usage it is often called a stone tortoise. A Qin tortoise is found in the mountains, which is why it is often also called a mountain tortoise. In spring and summer it roams the valley streams and in fall and winter it hides in the mountains. It is said to be a very long-lived tortoise. The reason it is also called a diviner's tortoise is that the divination described in *The Book of Changes* was originally carried out by heating the shells of tortoises and reading the cracks that appeared. The petrified tortoise described here, should it actually prove to be a Qin tortoise after being examined by an expert well versed in the *Herbal,* would be even more valuable. The fact that it was discovered in the mountains seems to suggest that it is a Qin tortoise after all. Most petrified objects are small, and even then, not complete. The petrified tortoise in the illustration is not only complete but rather large, increasing its rarity.

When I made a trip around all Japan years ago, I stayed for half a month in Kyoto and visited many well-known figures with my artist friend Shunkin. Once while visiting Doctor Rai, the famous Confucian scholar (his name is Ki, his pen name Sei, Sanyo his honorary name, and he is commonly known as Rai Tokutaro), the subject of the discourse turned to petrified objects. Doctor Rai was kind enough to bestow on us a petrified crab. It was not in the least faded and resembled a living crab in color, but was as hard as stone. The stone crabs mentioned in *The Qianque Anthology,* the *Herbal,* and *The Illustrated Three Levels* had all turned to stone embedded in the mud in which they were found. When we placed this crab beneath a miniature wild iris on a tray landscape, it looked as if it might move at any moment. I have included it with the illustration of the tortoise so that experts might get a look at it as well.

Luminous Stones

The "Supernatural Events" section of *The Cloud-Essence Annals* says: "There was a brave fellow named Yoshibei who lived next door to me. One time he traveled to a place called Tagami Valley, deep in the mountains. It was quite late at night when he began his trip back. He saw from the bottom of the valley across the way a blue light rising like a rainbow into the sky, mixing with the lights of the heavens. He was a very courageous and curious sort, and so without a second thought he parted the grasses and climbed over the mountain, crossing down to the valley in search of the source of the light. All he found was a stone, with nothing at all peculiar about it. He picked it up and put it on his back, and while he walked along the road, it shone just as before. It helped ease the difficulties of traveling the night roads considerably, and at dawn he arrived at his home. He placed the stone down beneath the eaves of the house and had his breakfast. When he went back to look at the stone afterward, however, it was no longer there. Trying to discover what could have become of it, he asked and looked about, but to no avail."

According to the account of the head priest of the Choonji temple in Koka County, Ishihara, a farmer nearby upturned a stone about the size of a fist while he was plowing his fields. This stone was ever so much more beautiful than most stones, and so he brought it home. At night it shone just like a falling star. A friend of his said "This is a supernatural stone, and should not be made a possession. As long as it is in your house, some misfortune is sure to befall you. Quickly, destroy it and throw it away!" Hearing this, the fellow took an axe and split the stone into pieces, which he then discarded in a stand of bamboo. That night the bamboo forest glowed as with the light of thousands of fireflies. The next morning people thereabouts heard of this and all gathered to see, but on visiting the bamboo grove they found nothing, not the slightest trace or fragment of the stone.

Here is another similar incident. Once a man of Agatsuma County in Chikugo found himself on an errand to a neighboring village at night. He came to a narrow stream, which he was crossing on foot when he noticed a shining object. He reached down, picked it up, and saw it was a little stone. The next day he offered it to the lord of the region, and shortly thereafter it was lost.

These incidents all took place in other places, but we in Echigo have luminous stones as well. There is a Koshin Mound in a field near the road between Kaji and Chujo, two places in Kambara County, northeast of Shibata. A round stone one and one-half feet in diameter sits atop the mound, guarding it. This the farmers worship. The stone was discovered when a farmer was putting the bamboo grove behind his house in order, digging out bamboo clumps and roots. The stone was black with a bluish sheen, and very smooth, so the farmer used it as a base on which to beat and soften straw.

That night when his wife stepped out into the garden she came upon a brilliantly shining object. She thought she had encountered a ghost and screamed in surprise. The master and the young son came running with several servants to drive the ghost off, only to find that it was the stone that was shining. They threw it quickly back into the bamboo grove, thinking it terribly strange. The stone continued to glow night after night. All the people of the village were terrified and refused to go out of their houses after dark. Thus this stone came to be worshiped at Koshin Mound, plastered with mud to prevent it from shining. Now it is covered with moss. Collectors of curiosities have sought this stone time and again, but the people of the village fear that they will be punished if they part with it, and so they have refused all offers.

The river that runs between the villages of Oyu and Tochio at the foot of Koma Peak is called Sanashi River. Once a few years ago when this river was low because of a drought, a glowing point of light became visible in its waters. It seemed as if a firefly sat beneath the river's surface. Its position did not change for several days; then a sudden great rain fell, the river waters rose, and the glimmer was no longer visible. But soon after, another brilliant object was seen several hundred yards downstream, again shining with a firefly's light. This is an isolated mountain region, and the people there are ignorant. They had never heard of luminous stones. They didn't even bother to ask anyone about them, and in the great flood that autumn, the stone was washed away and its whereabouts became unknown. (This anecdote is from *Strange Tales of North Etsu*.)

Here, at last, is an authenticated story about luminous stones. In March of 1819, while traveling through Lower Echigo, I entered Mishima County to worship at Yahiko Shrine. I stopped to visit my old friend Takahashi Mitsunori, who was happy to see me and kind enough to offer a night's lodging. This old gent excels at Japanese poetry, likes ancient things, and is a fine and learned fellow. Refined conversation flowed as from a spring, and before I knew it I had stayed my traveler's staff for four or five days.

One night my friend related to me the story of a sparkling object that, some forty or fifty years ago, glowed night after night from the Otori River valley near Yoshida, in Mishima County. People were afraid of it and didn't dare to approach. There was a village near this river known as Tominaga, where lived two brothers who worked as blacksmiths, supporting their old mother. The family was very poor. But both brothers were adventuresome types, and one day they decided to find out just what that shining thing really was. If it truly was some sort of monster, they would drive it away and astound all the villagers.

So that night they went to the spot from where the light came. It was autumn and the river waters were high. There was no reflection of the moon on the river's surface, and all that could be sensed was the sound of the current. Though both of them stretched their pine torches out here and there looking for the shining thing, they did not find it or anything else suspicious. Just as they were grumbling, "Well, what everyone has said is a lie; let's go home," suddenly there appeared a shining brilliance above the water's surface. With a shout of "Hurry!" they stripped off their clothes and dived into the river, swimming toward the light in search of its source. It was coming from a stone the size of a small pillow. They took hold of it and brought it back to their home; when they put it down by the cooking hearth, it illuminated the entire room. They recounted the details of the event to their mother and the entire family rejoiced at finding the wonderful treasure. Neighbors also came to see it, but since they were uneducated folks they didn't realize that here was a prize equal to the famous jewels of Zhao and Sui. They merely gawked and left.

Later the younger brother made plans to move to his own house, and the mother said that the household goods should be divided so that they each might have their proper share. The younger brother, however, said he didn't need anything but the shining jewel, which he planned to carry away. The older brother insisted, "It was my idea to look for the stone. All you did was help. Mother has no right to give it to anyone. It's mine. When parents divide household goods among their children, they can only parcel out what they have provided. I won't give up the stone. I won't let you have it."

But the younger brother said, "Oh, no. That stone is mine. You made no plans to bring back a treasure—your idea was to drive away a monster, that's why we went to the river. I jumped into the river before you, I'm the one who found the stone, and I'm the one who carried it home. Why shouldn't I be able to take what belongs to me?"

"No, it's mine!"

"It's not. It's mine!"

And so the two brothers argued back and forth, with no end in sight. Soon they were pushing and pulling at the stone. Their mother then stepped in to calm them down, saying, "Divide the shining stone in half."

At that the younger brother took the stone, set it on the anvil they used in their labor, and brought the hammer down with all his might. Unfortunately, the shining stone broke, revealing a white jewel inside, which was smashed to pieces as well, and liquid sprayed in all directions. That night everything that had been splashed glowed with the light of a swarm of fireflies. After two or three days, though, the light faded and disappeared.

No matter what excuses are made for their foolishness, it is a great shame that this rare jewel should have perished under the mallet of a bumpkin. A disaster for both man and mineral—or so my host told it.

When considering this story, I am reminded of a passage in *A Chain of Stories from a North Window* by Tachibana Shunki, from which I quote: "In recent years, there have been a great many famous collectors of stones and gems such as Kinouchi Kohan of Yamada Bay in Omi, Yamanaka Tansaku from Ise, Kajimaya Gentabei of Osaka, and other dilettantes of the cities and literati of the provinces. I have had an opportunity to view many of these collections, some of them ranging up to three thousand or even five thousand varieties of stones. Only after five or sometimes ten days of uninterrupted viewing could I finally lift my gaze. Yet among all these there were few that were particularly startling or arresting.

"Kajimaya Gentabei tells the story of a man who once came from the north country claiming that he had a stone about the size of a fist that glowed at night. He vowed that it could illuminate a room and that he would sell it if he could get a good price. Right then and there Kajimaya charged the man with selling it to him. 'I want the stone. Should it, on a dark night, illuminate the inside of the box it is kept in, I will pay you fifty pieces of gold; should it, on the same dark night, give enough light to read a large Chinese character, I will pay you one hundred gold pieces. If the light is bright enough to read a letter by, I will offer three hundred pieces of gold; and if it lights the entire room, I will give everything I have, devote my life and fortune to acquiring it.'

"The man promised to act as a go-between for the purchase, but there was no word from him after that. 'I can only conclude that it was all a hoax,' were Gentabei's final words."

The stout-hearted brothers find a luminous stone.

This story of Kajimaya was current in the world of collectors during the Temmei era (1781–88) and Shunki recorded it afterward, just as he had heard it. I heard the story of the blacksmiths who found the shining stone in the spring of 1819. Since the event as it was told to me was supposed to have taken place forty-five years ago, the blacksmiths' stone broke into pieces at the end of the Anei period (1772–81) or the beginning of the Temmei. That was a period when collecting stones and gems was quite popular, and it may well be that the man from the north country in Kajimaya's story, who was offering for sale a stone that illuminated an entire room, was a crepe merchant of Echigo smooth-talking Kajimaya with the story of the blacksmiths' stone. The reason that he never replied to Kajimaya was that he soon learned that the stone had been smashed.

It was only when the king of Chu received it that Bien He's jewel was known to the world. Of the five stories of luminous stones related above, three take place in Echigo, but are unknown to the world at large, a most unfortunate circumstance.

Momoki says: There is a story similar to that of the blacksmiths in the section titled "Things" in *The Five Miscellanies*. At the beginning of the Ming reign, there was a man in Minzhong Lienjiang who found a jewel when he was shelling clams. Ignorant of the worth of his find, he boiled it in the pot with the clams, upon which the jewel leapt about in the roiling pot, and flaming lights burned up into the sky. The other villagers thought it was a fire and rushed to rescue the fellow. When they learned what had happened, they opened the lid of the pot and saw that the treasure had already grown half dim. The jewel was just an inch in diameter, but it was a true example of a luminous stone. The account concludes by lamenting the harm done to the jewel by the ignoramus.

The Five Miscellanies continues with another story, the ancient tale of King Hui of the Wei dynasty, who, with a jewel only an inch in diameter, illuminated some twelve carriages, front and back. Finally, Xie Zhaozhi, the author of this Ming-dynasty work, states that such jewels that glow in the night are no longer in the imperial possession.

BOOK FIVE

A Record of Supernatural Events and *Penetrating Darkness* also mention these glowing jewels, but they only appear in the "Doubtful" section. In *Notes on Things Ancient and Modern* it is recorded that the eyes of especially large whales are luminous stones.

About Bien He's jewel it is said "when it was split, there was another jewel inside it"; thus it resembles the jewel found by the blacksmiths, which also revealed another jewel inside it when split open. And the offer of King Zhao of Qin to exchange fifteen castles for the luminous stone of King Hui of Zhao is just like Kajimaya's vow to do everything in his power to buy the jewel from the north country. In *The Sequel to The Guixin Collection of Miscellaneous Facts*, there is a story of a weaver woman who was soaking her threads in water one night when she saw a large white spider. As the spider drank the water its body gave off a light. The weaver thought this was very strange and caught the spider by covering it with a basket. When she looked at it closely she found a glowing jewel the size of a pellet inside its stomach. (This incident also appears in the "Jewels" section of *Strange Tales of North Etsu,* quoted above by Bokushi, not a whit different in detail, as an event that took place in Echigo. Yet *The Guixin Collection* is a rather rare Chinese work, hard to gain access to, so it is doubtful that the author of *Strange Tales* simply copied the anecdote from the Chinese source with the intent of entertaining his readers. Rather, this tale was probably extensively known.)

In the *Agon Kyo* it is recorded that the kingdom of a Great Sage Ruler will be illuminated for a distance of twelve *yojanas* by a shining *mani* jewel one and one-half feet in diameter. Since there are so many passages to this effect, I will not quote them. One *yojana* equals one hundred miles, and so twelve *yojanas* is equal to twelve hundred miles. That a jewel one and one-half feet in diameter could illuminate an area twelve hundred miles in every direction is certainly a marvel. It is also recorded that a certain Great Sage Ruler, obtaining this gem, placed it on top of a tall banner at night, and it so brightly shone that his subjects, thinking that dawn had come, began to go about their daily tasks. Hearing of this from the great scholar Ryoa, I borrowed the scripture and read it myself. This, certainly, is the great ancestor of all luminous stones.

SNOW COUNTRY TALES

Rice-Cake Blossoms

> At night, the mice
> At Yoshinoyama
> Have their own flower-viewing
> Of rice-cake blossoms.

So goes the verse of Kikaku. The words "rice-cake blossoms" signal winter in poetry because in Edo and other places, rice-cake blossoms are made at the same time that rice cake (*mochi*) is pounded, in the last month of the old year, and set on the special altar made at that time. But in our province, rice-cake blossoms are made in spring. The first two weeks of the New Year are called the Great New Year, and then the period from the fifteenth to the twentieth is known as the Little New Year. This is, at least, what we are accustomed to calling them.

On the thirteenth or fourteenth day of the Great New Year we take down the sacred rope and pine decorations from our doors (in Naga-oka, these are removed on the seventh, and another decoration, of shaved wood, is put up until the fourteenth) and make our rice-cake blossoms. Branches of rice-cake blossoms are presented at the household shrine, one each to the Great Shrine, to the god of the year, and to Ebisu, the god of good fortune.

Rice-cake blossoms are made by cutting switches of dogwood or willow and then sticking rice cakes cut out in triangles or the shapes of plum or cherry blossoms on the branches. Sometimes little balls of rice cake are mixed in with these flower shapes, and these are called cocoons. "Rice ears" made by stringing together rice-cake balls on these switches in tight rows and paper ornaments resembling little packets of coins are also made to decorate the tree. In the homes of crepe merchants, people make miniature models of crepe bolts out of paper, and in farmers' homes they carve tiny wooden plows and other farm implements and hang them from the branches. Each household hangs miniatures of the things related to their trade, as a ceremony to insure blessings and fortune in the coming year. Usually it is the young people who make the rice-cake blossoms. It is a mixed celebration, and men and women join in singing rice-planting songs. Hearing these melodies, one can't help but long for the summer to come, and everyone sighs and wishes that the snow still higher than the rooftops would melt away soon; such are the hearts of the inhabitants of the snow country.

Since rice-cake blossoms are mentioned in old glossaries of proper seasonal words for poetry, it's clear that they have been made in various parts of the land for at least two hundred years. I have heard that in Edo these days they are made and sold as children's toys.

Contributions for the Way Gods

It is the custom in the Shiozawa area where I live for young boys from the age of seven or eight to about thirteen to solicit contributions for the Way Gods (Sai no Kami) just before the fifteenth of February.

Boys from well-off families carve themselves swords from branches of the sumac tree, fashioning a sword guard by shaving back bark from both sides. They call these magic wands, and insert two, a short one and a long one (just like a proper samurai), through the sash of the formal garb they wear for the occasion. A boy servant accompanies each of them, carrying a measure. Some carry the measure around their neck on a string. Inside the square wooden measure are two little dolls some five inches in height. Their heads are made of wood, and they have painted features. One doll is a male deity, the other female. She wears a cloth wrapped around her head, and her paper robes are painted with red plum blossoms. He wears a court hat, and has a beard made of curled shavings; his paper robes are painted with young pines and other felicitous designs. With both these dolls in the measure, the boys walk from house to house calling, "Contributions for the Way Gods! Contributions for the Way Gods!" They do this not for their own gain but as a New Year's game that all the boys take part in, and they receive offerings of rice cakes or coins from the people of the village.

Boys from households that are not so well-off do the same, on a more modest but far merrier scale. They form parties of five to ten, each wearing a rosy red hood with sky blue borders and carrying a single magic wand. They place their pair of gods in a rough willow basket that they hang from their necks as they go from house to house singing, "Contributions for the Way Gods! Contributions for the Way Gods! Give a penny, give gold!" and making a merry fuss and uproar. People give the boys coins or homemade sake, paint black marks on their faces with charcoal, and laugh and have a jolly time. This is a custom we never fail to observe.

In Nagaoka the magic wands are some three feet in length and painted with symbols of luck and long life. Instead of the children soliciting the contributions, in Nagaoka this becomes a rowdy adult activity. They sing:

> Give us pennies, give us gold,
> And next spring you'll find a wife, find a husband,
> So that your life will be
> Like a spring bubbling from its source.

In this guise they gather funds for the celebration in honor of the Way Gods (which I will describe below).

Large groups of children also gather at dawn in front of houses where there was a marriage ceremony the year before and tap on the gate with their sticks, calling, "Send out the bride!" (or "Send out the groom!") together in a loud voice. Since this is a local custom, every house invites the children in; sometimes they are given treats as well. There are many examples of similar customs in other parts of the land, I know.

I had thought all along that this was all nothing more than a simple children's game until I discovered a passage in *A Collection of Curiosities* by Kyoden referring to the *kayu* (rice-gruel) tree. The *kayu* staff or celebratory tree or *hoitake* stick referred to there is the same magic wand described above. Kyoden explains the origin of the name rice-gruel stick. Apparently, a staff was made of the firewood used to cook rice gruel on the fifteenth day of the New Year, and childless women were beat with it on the buttocks so that they would conceive a male child. He finds references to the rice-gruel stick in a great many writings, including *The Pillow Book, Sagoromo,* and *The Diary of Ben no Naishi,* and investigates in great detail all mention of it from the ancient court to present-day cities. This is how I discovered that our magic wands are in fact the ancient rice-gruel stick. In some parts of our province it was also called the celebration staff or the honorable celebration staff.

The works quoted by Kyoden reveal that this custom has been carried out on the fifteenth day of the New Year for seven or eight hundred years. Of the works he quotes, the description in *The Customs of Japan* most resembles the custom as practiced in our land. This is a record of things of Japan composed by a Ming Chinese over three hundred years ago and shows that what is now a children's game is a reflection of customs of long ago. The passage from *The Customs of Japan* quoted by Kyoden is as follows: "Village youngsters from fifteen to nineteen and even older take willow branches, from which they strip the bark. They carve these branches into swords, then wrap them once again with strips of bark and hold them in a fire until they become black with soot, taking off the bark a last time to reveal black-and-white flower patterns. These swords are called *kobarami*. Then they place the thorny branches of wild roses before their family altars and make offerings. Next the youngsters go out in groups carrying their wooden swords and visit the houses of childless young wives. They beat them on the buttocks with their wooden swords, shouting '*Kobarami, kobarami!*' The woman always bears a male child that year." The present custom by which children stand outside beating on the gate shouting "Send out the bride! Send out the groom!" is obviously a remnant of that ancient practice. Momoki thinks that the sentence "Then they place the thorny branches of wild roses before their family altars and make offerings" is actually a description of the offering of rice-cake blossoms before the family altar that has been mistakenly inserted in this description of the *kayu* stick. If that is so, it speaks as well for the ancient origins of rice-cake blossoms.

The Festival of the Way Gods

Our Festival of the Way Gods on the fifteenth of February is based on the ancient court ritual, the Sagicho. In China it was called the Bamboo-Firecracker Festival. The bamboo firecrackers were set off on New Year's night, as the verses of the Chinese poet Hu Ye tell us: "A thousand gates echo with the explosions of the bamboo firecrackers, and their light illuminates ten thousand homes." At the Japanese court, green bamboo was set afire on the fifteenth day of the New Year in the garden of the Seiryoden, in a ceremony in which the first poems of the year were burned and offered to the heavens. On the eighteenth there was another celebratory offering, in which fans were tied to bamboo decorations that were then burned in the same garden. The common people imitated this practice and on the fifteenth gathered together all the New Year's decorations and burned them. This, too, was called the Sagicho, and was performed from ancient times; it has also been called the Festival of the Way Gods since long ago. Both the Bamboo-Firecracker Festival and the Sagicho are discussed in detail in *Toshinamigusa,* a glossary of seasonal words for poetry, with quotations from many sources.

Ojiya in our district is a prosperous town of a thousand houses. The Festival of the Way Gods (also called the Gods of Good Fortune) held there is grand and glorious. Places in various neighborhoods of the town are selected to celebrate the festival, and at each one a space is tramped down in the snow and a round platform eighteen feet around and six or seven feet high is built out of snow. Steps leading up to it are made in two places; they are also of snow, of course. This whole thing is called the castle. A freshly felled cypress tree is placed in the very center of the platform as a pillar, and all the New Year's decorations are tied to it or piled up around it. Sacred ropes lead from the top of the tree to the ground, coming down on all sides and creating the appearance of a straw raincoat (reeds are stuffed in at places to shape the tree). At the very top, to the right and left of the sacred rope decoration called a radish rope (*daikon shime*), two open fans are attached, making the form of a bird with its wings spread. A shelf is carved out on the platform, on which holy sake is readied, and the elders of the town gather in their formal dress. They worship, asking for blessings for the region.

After the worship is finished, a purified flame is set from the four sides. A trail of oil cake has been spread to make it burn well, and as the flame reaches the center the tree and the decorations begin to burn lustily. (Rice cakes are toasted in this fire and eaten; from times of old these have been thought to guard those who eat them against illness.) This is our Bamboo-Firecracker Festival, our Sagicho, though the same ceremony is carried out in other parts of the country as well. Someone told me that until about one hundred years ago it was also held in Edo, but was forbidden because of the danger of fires there.

Another custom is to make a thing called an *ombe,* attach it to the Sagicho decoration, and burn it during the ceremony. *Ombe* is our local word for *gohei,* the paper or cloth streamers used in Shinto worship. We make them by bundling together several hundred sheets of white and colored papers, anchored at one end, and then cutting them in narrow strips to form streamers, fan-shaped at the end. Thousands of these are then hung from a pole of green bamboo, split at the top to hold them. Each household makes *ombe* as they wish, long or short, large or small—but people pride themselves on making the fullest ones they can. Four open fans are attached to the top end of the pole; on them are painted the family crest and other colorful designs. Since it's all made out of colored paper, it's a beautiful sight.

After the *ombe* is made, everyone sets one outside their gate, just as they do the carp streamers on the fifth day of May. Then on the fifteenth they carry them to the designated place, attach them to the Sagicho tree, and burn them, which is regarded as a celebration and a blessing. Large crowds gather to watch the fire, and after it's over banquets and drinking parties are held here and there. All of this is a reflection of the power and glory of our ruler. The Sagicho Festival is held in other places in our region, but that of Ojiya is the most splendid by far.

Momoki relates: During my travels in Echigo with Kyosui, I stayed some fourteen days in Ojiya during the month of September at the home of a relative of Bokushi by the name of Iwabuchi. His son was twenty-four or twenty-five and went by the artist's name of Gankyo. He was an excellent calligrapher and was exceedingly kind to us during our stay. Ojiya is the major market town of Echigo.

The Festival of the Way Gods.

Its streets are lined with shops and there is nothing you cannot buy there. Since it is only seven miles from the sea, fresh fish are available in plenty. I also stayed in Shiozawa for some forty days. It is far inland, and during the summer there is little seafood to be had—for an Edoite like myself that was a long forty days without the taste of fresh fish! I can't tell you how wonderful it was to finally eat it again when I arrived in Ojiya. The town faces on a great river that runs to the sea, so during the salmon season, fresh-caught fish can be under the chef's knife in a matter of minutes. The taste surpasses that in Edo. One day I was served salmon tempura. When I asked Gankyo what this dish was called here, he answered, "Tempura. It's difficult for a young man like me to understand the word's meaning, though. I've asked several older people about its origins, but no one seems to know. Could you enlighten me, perhaps?"

"Let me finish my meal first," I answered. "Then I'll tell you about the origins of tempura," I said, as I continued to eat my fill of the delicious stuff.

Explanations of the Origins of Tempura and Steamed Bean Sweets

And so it was that I related the following to Gankyo. "About fifty years ago, in the early years of the Temmei era (1781–88), there was in a prosperous household of Osaka a second son named Risuke. He was about twenty-seven or twenty-eight and in love with a courtesan some two years older. They ran away together to Edo and took up residence in lodging behind my house in Kyobashi. From the first time he came to my house one day on an errand of some sort, I let him have free reign of the house, employing him as if he were my own servant. As a man who had sacrificed his fortune for a woman's love, he had many interesting stories to tell and considerable intelligence, showing good judgment. 'What a shame that he has no means of his own!' my late brother often jokingly remarked of him.

"One day Risuke said to my brother, 'There are so many street-corner vendors selling sesame-oil-fried food here in Edo. In Osaka we call it batter-fried food. You know, batter-fried fish is really good, but there aren't any night-time snack stalls selling it in Edo yet. What would you think if I tried selling it?' My brother Kyoden said, 'What a wonderful idea. But first, I think we should try this treat ourselves.' And he had Risuke prepare some right away. It was truly delicious.

" 'When I sell this at a night-time snack stall, I'll have to write something on the lantern, so people will know what I'm selling. I'd hate to have to write "Fish Fried in Sesame Oil"—it's so long and clumsy. Can't you come up with a clever name for me?' begged Risuke. After thinking for a moment, my brother took up his brush and wrote the Chinese characters *ten pu ra*. When he showed it to Risuke, the latter looked at it dubiously and asked 'What on earth does *ten pu ra* mean?' My brother explained, smiling: 'You are a runaway (*ten*) wanderer who has meandered (*bura*) down to Edo to start a business, and so *ten-bura* (tempura) is a fine name for your product. I've used the character *fu* that means wheat because it's coated with flour, and *ra* that means thin. Your creation is dipped in a thin coat of flour, and that's the reason for these characters.' Risuke was fond of this sort of verbal play and thought it a wonderful concoction. He greatly enjoyed the description of himself as a runaway wanderer who had meandered down to Edo, too.

"Eventually he came around to our house with his large lantern and asked that I write the characters *ten pu ra* on it, which I did in my inexperienced hand and returned it to him. His tempura was four coppers a piece at that time, and his stall was sold out every night. In less than a month there were tempura stalls all over the neighborhood, and the name soon spilled out of our area to the world at large. It's a small miracle of sorts that it's even known here in Ojiya. But none of the great scholars or brilliant minds have the faintest idea that my brother was the godfather who christened Risuke's baby. Yes, I'm the only one who truly knows the origins of tempura . . ."

I said with a smile, and Gankyo, delighted at my yarn, clapped his hands and laughed.

When I related this story to my friend Seiro last year (he's a great scholar of the classics), he mentioned that there was a name similar to the word tempura listed in *The Deep Blue Memory Jewel of All Things* (by the Ming-dynasty Chinese Huang Yizheng, in twenty-four volumes), in the chapter "Barbarian Foods." I borrowed the book and took a look at that section, where I found the entry *ta bu la* (in Japanese pronunciation, *to fu ra*), with a note describing how to prepare it: "Fry leeks, pepper, and miso in oil. Then put in duck, chicken, or goose and cook at medium heat until done." It also mentioned deep-fried crabs.

The night that Gankyo made us tempura, a friend of his named Yogaku (who was the owner of a sweet shop called Sakuraya) stopped by as well. Having heard that I didn't care for alcohol, he brought along some homemade steamed-bean sweets for me. They tasted just as good as those of Edo. I was greatly moved to be able to have something so nice as this in Echigo and said to Gankyo, "This, too, is a recently invented food. It's better tasting than the usual bean sweets. When I was a boy, even ordinary bean sweets never found their way into the mouths of the common people. That I can today find these special steamed-bean sweets in a place as far away as this from Edo is certainly a virtue of the glorious period of peace we now enjoy." Yogaku also excelled at both calligraphy and painting; he was well read, and had a great native curiosity. So when he heard this he pressed his knees together, leaned forward, and asked, "Sweets are my family business. I would very much like to hear of the origins of these steamed-bean sweets that you say are a recent invention." And so I told him the following tale.

"In 1789, there was a tiny little store without even its own signboard—the walls of the shop were just flimsy lattice frames—on a side street called Shikibu Alley off of Nihombashi Street in Edo. It was run by a fellow by the name of Kitaro, who was helped by his wife and one assistant. The story was that Kitaro had originally worked at a sweet shop that prepared sweets for the nobility. He left their service, though, and set up shop here, where he made only the very best sweets and sold them to connoisseurs of the tea ceremony and to the wealthy. When Kitaro first invented steamed-bean sweets and began to sell them, people called them Kitaro's steamed-bean sweets, and they were all the rage. And since he was the only one making them, when he was sold out there was nothing to be done. Many's the time I watched servants sent by their masters with boxes to have filled with sweets leave his store empty-handed. In the next year or two, one or two shops began to make steamed-bean sweets in imitation of Kitaro. Since they were still very much in demand, they soon became available in all the sweet shops of Edo—and now they are to be found even here in faraway Ojiya. Surely they are available wherever there are markets in this province, as well as in all the rest of the provinces of the land." Yogaku laughed and said, "For your information, we have *ogura* sweets and eight-layered sweets as well. You must stop by tomorrow."

Such things do not really belong in a collection of snowy tales, but they came to mind at the mention of Ojiya earlier on, and I think they'll interest people. There are, of course, many more things that could be said about the origins of foods, ancient and modern, but since I have written about that in *A Study of the Development of Foods,* I'll not go into it here.

Wolves in the Snow

As explained in the first book of this work, the wild animals of Echigo migrate during the winter, wandering over the mountains to regions with less snow than ours. This they do because they can no longer find sufficient food; all is buried deep under the snow. In spring, however, the animals return to their native haunts. Still, even in spring not all the snow has thawed and disappeared, and food remains scarce. It can happen then that wolves approach human dwellings and carry off a dog or, on occasion, even attack men. This usually happens in small mountain settlements; wolves are afraid to approach villages of larger size.

In one of these mountain hamlets, there lived a certain poor farmer with his old mother, his wife, and two children. I will withhold their names because their story is so tragic. The daughter was thirteen and the boy seven. The man was both a very good father and a good son.

One year toward the end of March, the farmer had business in a place five miles distant. The way he had to travel to get there was all narrow mountain paths. "Be careful," warned his old mother. "When you go, be sure to take your rifle along." "You're absolutely right," he said, and he left with his rifle slung over his shoulder. He had an official license that permitted him to carry a gun, for he hunted as well as farmed for a living.

Soon the day was spent, his business completed, and he hurried home. On his way, just as he was approaching his village, he saw in the distance, in the shadow of the snowy mountain, a wolf. It seemed to be chewing on something. He crept within shooting distance, struck the fuse of his flintlock, and, right on target, felled the animal. When he walked over to where it had fallen, he found that the wolf had been gnawing on a human leg. Stunned, it flashed through his mind that the wolf might have sneaked into his own house, and fear befell him for his family. He left the dead wolf where it lay and raced home.

Outside his cottage the snow all around was dyed crimson with blood. Wildly alarmed, he leapt into the cottage just as two wolves bounded past him in escape. As he scanned the scene, he saw his mother lying by the open hearth, gnawed off on all sides, one of her legs totally gone. His wife, swimming in blood, lay near the window. She, too, was mauled and chewed. Threads of her cotton crepe weavings lay scattered and trampled everywhere. As for his seven-year-old son—he found, outside in the garden on the snow, only half of his little body.

His wife was still breathing. At the sight of him, she tried to sit up but could not, for all the strength had left her. All she could do was gasp "Wolves!" Then she was gone. The good man, not sure whether it wasn't all a horrible nightmare, stood clutching his rifle. Then he remembered his daughter and began to call her name, half in tears. At this the hapless girl came creeping from underneath the floor and, with an anguished cry, threw herself on her father's neck. The father clutched his daughter to him and wept.

Since houses in these mountain settlements lie rather far apart, set here and there, no one else knew of the tragedy. During a single day the farmer had lost his mother, his wife, and his son, all torn to pieces by the fangs of wolves. The stricken man gnashed his teeth in torment, and father and daughter moaned ceaselessly and raised their voices in wails of agony.

By and by the other villagers heard about the awful happening. They came one after another, each screaming in horror when they saw what had happened. As more and more neighbors arrived, they asked the poor girl how it had happened. "Suddenly three wolves came leaping in through the window. I was tending the hearth, and at once crept under the floor of the house. I heard the screams of Mother and Grandma and my little brother, but I stayed where I was, chanting "Save us merciful Buddha!"

The event was reported to the authorities. At evening the next day, the farmer laid his wife and little son in one coffin and carried it along with the one for his mother to the place where the villagers burned their dead. There was no one among the assembled villagers whose eyes remained dry. Because, on his mother's suggestion, the farmer had taken his gun along and so was able to kill the wolf which was feasting on her leg, one could think that he somehow avenged her. Yet it was a terrible shame indeed that the other two wolves escaped him. After this blow, the farmer abandoned his homestead and left with his daughter on a pilgrimage. Since all this happened very near here, it is a well-known story.

Momoki adds: Here in Japan people do not believe—as they do in China—that wolves can transform themselves into other shapes. In China, wolves are thought to have the same powers of transformation as foxes do.

In the "Beasts" chapter of *The Great Record of the Taiping Era* by Li Fangdeng of the Song dynasty, we read about a wolf that changed itself into a beautiful woman and had intercourse with a young man. Another wolf was said to have changed itself into someone's mother, only revealing the transformation when she turned seventy, at which time she fled in her beast form.

Another wolf, so says the chronicle, devoured a certain man's father and subsequently assumed the victim's shape, passing several years in this manner, no one the wiser. One day the young man went

The wolves leap into the farmer's house.

into the mountains to pick mulberry leaves. He was surprised when a wolf that stood upright like a man began to gnaw at his garment. The man struck the animal on the forehead with the axe he carried, and the wolf ran away.

When the man returned home he found his father sitting there with a fresh wound on his forehead—just in the place he had struck the wolf earlier. In a flash he realized that this was the wolf he had encountered before. He struck his father down where he sat, and at once the creature appeared in its true shape, as an old wolf. The man reported this incident to the authorities since he had, at least officially, killed his own father.

These stories were drawn from *Reports of Weird Occurrences* and *Tales from the Imperial Chamber*.

The Chinese character for "wolf" is used in many compounds with malignant meanings, including: "a wild dog or wolf's heart" (*sairo no kokoro*), meaning to be cruel; "a wolf's voice" (*rosei*), meaning a frightening voice; "wolf poison" (*rodoku*), meaning a very virulent poison; "wolf-wolf" (*roro*), meaning chaos of the worst sort; "a wolfish look" (*roko*), meaning a shifty or menacing glance; "a mountain wolf" (*nakayama okami*), meaning a savage; "to wolf food" (*rozan*), meaning to be voracious; a terrible sickness is called "a wolf sickness" (*roshitsu*); and there are other words, too, such as violent disorder, or "wolf mess" (*rozeki*); greed and cruelty, or "to revert to wolfishness" (*rorei*); and "to run wild" (*robai*). All of these phrases are based on the hideous character of the wolf. (These definitions are given in *Grains of Sand from the Sea of Words*.)

All of this shows without a doubt that wolves are the most hated of animals. Ah, but consider for just a moment: at least a wolf is a wolf and acts like a wolf. When men act like wolves they hide their wolfishness, and do not dare to show it openly. Indeed, there are a great number of men who fall victim to "wolf poisoning" in this way.

The wolfishness of man is far more terrible and hateful than that of real wolves. Men who give themselves the appearance of honest persons but inside are full of insatiable greed we call "wolf men" (*okami mono*), and a mother-in-law who treats her daughter-in-law badly is an "old wolf wo... (*ami baba*). Well they might be able to hide the wolfishness i... earts; yet the wise man's eye still sees the truth's reflecti...

Wolves! Wolves! Ho... e, how disgraceful! Be on guard against wolves!

BOOK SIX

Bird-chasing Towers

In both country and town the New Year's custom of bird-chasing towers is observed each year. Various books record the details of the event, which is held in many places and differs with each one. The bird-chasing of Edo is observed in the following manner. Outcaste women entertainers known as *onna taiyu* don lovely cotton robes, make up their faces, wear woven hats, and to the accompaniment of the shamisen and the two-stringed fiddle, prettily sing festive songs as they wander from house to house begging alms. This begins on the first day and continues as long as the New Year's pine decorations are up, in some places even longer. In Echigo, we begin to make bird-hunting towers during the Little New Year (which starts from the fifteenth of the New Year). We pile snow on top of the mounds of snow that we have cleared during the last year to a height of eight or nine feet, or even higher, and make a watchtower out of the snow. We build a stairway, also of snow, leading up to its peak and flatten the top of the tower and set up pine and bamboo branches at the four corners, linking them with sacred ropes. (This area can be as large as one wishes.) Within the rope boundaries we lay mats, and children play here, eating all kinds of treats and singing bird-chasing songs. One of them goes like this:

The bird-chasing towers of the New Year.

正月鳥追櫓之図
図中 山をあす所
皆雪なり

> Lo! Those birds down there!
> Where have they been chased from?
> From Shinano they've been chased here.
> With what in hand have they been chased?
> With firewood bundles they've been chased here.
> Birds of the fields, birds of the rivers,
> Away, away, be gone!

And another:

> The birds from my rice-seedling beds behind the house
> Chase them, chase them, sparrows and cuckoos,
> Away, away, be gone!

Sometimes, instead of a tower we build a square snow hall on top of the snow mound, making shelves out of the snow to put things on and, as before, spreading mats. Then pots, tea kettles, trays, and all sorts of cups and bowls are placed on the snow shelves, and we cook festival foods and drink home-brewed sake. Great groups of children play in the snow hall and sing together the bird-chasing songs, staying there all day. This is a New Year's game certainly not to be found in warmer places. There are several of these bird towers in the town, as different groups band together to make them and play in them.

Snow and Frost

As I have repeated many times, of all the northern provinces, Echigo has the most snow. The three counties of Uonuma, Koshi, and Kubiki have the deepest snow in Echigo Province. "Although we must spend the winter under ten feet of snow, the temperature is not that much colder than an Edo winter," remarked a person who had spent a winter there.

In *The Five Miscellanies,* frost is defined as a yin substance created by the binding together of dew, while snow, which is formed from clouds, is said to be yang. Since snow is yang, the vegetable seeds sown in summer still germinate and begin to sprout under their blanket of snow, and though this happens more slowly than in warmer climes, there is no basic difference. An example of the slowness is the plum tree: we first see ours bloom in April; the first gourds and eggplants only appear in June. In the deep mountains the cherry blossoms only reach their peak at the end of May or the beginning of June.

The Fires of Hell Valley

In the first book of this work, in the entry on fires in the snow, I mentioned that a flame burned out of the ground at the foot of the mountains in Itsukamachi, Uonuma County. It is quite well known around here and counted as one of the seven wonders of Echigo. It burns from the ground on the land of Souemon, a farmer of Nyohoji Village in Kambara County, and also on the land of Shichibei Magoroku. But a flame that burns even more lustily than these is to be found in Hell Valley in Ojiya. In China such fires are called fire wells. In recent years an inn has been built in Hell Valley. The fire is used to heat baths for its guests, of which there are a great many in summer and early autumn. I have never heard of these fire wells in any other part of Japan, but they are very numerous in Echigo.

Last year a certain family in Kambara County was digging a well. A doctor visited them one night and, hearing that they were sinking a well, went out to have a look at it on his way home. When he lowered his lantern into the well to have a good look, a great flame leapt out, burning so brightly and fiercely that people all around came running thinking a house was on fire. When they saw that the fire was coming out of the hole, they accosted the owner of the well, saying that it was all his fault: if he hadn't dug the well, there would be no fire. The man who dug the well grew fearful of it, too, and filled it in again, it is said.

This sort of earth fire is also called a yin (potential) fire. The yin fire at Nyohoji Village sprang up when the wind blew a spark from a fire being set nearby over to it and ignited it. Without a yang (active) fire and the breeze to carry it, it could not have leapt into flame. It is said, too, that the first fire at Nyohoji Village, long ago during the Temmon era (1532–55), only started when farmer Souemon was at work with a forge and bellows. And the well fire talked about earlier was kindled by the flame of the doctor's lantern as he lowered it into the well for a better look.

There is a post town called Nosho on the official post road that runs along the coast in Kubiki County. Just five miles farther inland is the village of Masekuchi. An earth fire just like that at Nyohoji is said to be found at a farmer's house there. This region suffers from a lack of water, and during droughts people dig wells into the side of the mountain to obtain water. Once, when digging such a well, they reached the mountain wall and stuck in a torch to illuminate the hole only to have flames suddenly shoot out, burning several people to death.

All of these incidents lead to the conclusion that there are many places in Echigo with veins full of earth fire that have yet to meet with an active flame and be set to burning.

Momoki relates: While I was in Ojiya, Gankyo arranged for me to see Hell Valley. He had servants prepare and carry drink and food for us and five other friends, and the ten of us (for Kyosui was with me of course) left Ojiya and headed west. Passing through Shinho Village and Yabukawashinden, we arrived at a village called Ichinomiya. The trail traced its way between the mountains and around terraced paddies, winding and curving, and we traveled three and one-half miles before we arrived. But it was an especially clear and bright day, and the autumn scenery of the farming villages was breathtaking.

After crossing a flat-topped mountain we came to a downward slope, which was the road that led to Hell Valley. Looking down from the top of the hill, a single thatched cottage was visible. This is the bathhouse mentioned by Bokushi. When we were halfway down the slope we could see, on the second-story balcony of the cottage, four or five lovely women. Each was leaning on the railing, and one was pointing to us, still far in the distance. They were laughing, calling our names, clapping their hands and waving us toward them. What a startling sight it was to see such beauties in this isolated place surrounded on all sides by mountains and dark forests of ancient trees.

"These must be badgers or foxes!" I exclaimed, and as I did so Gankyo exchanged looks with his friends, who also clapped their hands and laughed. For, in fact, these women were all geisha from a teahouse in the entertainment district of Ojiya. Gankyo and his friends had planned the entire thing, having these girls sent out here to entertain me. I was not deceived by a fox at all, but by the foxy Gankyo. By now we were down into Hell Valley. The others climbed up to the balcony to join the ladies as Gankyo took Kyosui and me to see the fires.

Many wild cherry trees grow in the valley, and it was once called Cherry Valley (Sakuradani) after them. The earth fires burn in a flat place about forty or fifty paces square (one pace being about six feet). The fires are used to heat the baths, which are for the purpose of entertaining guests. How the cherry blossoms must lament that their lovely Cherry Valley has had its name changed to Hell Valley!

A close look at the fires showed that they burned from a shallow well in the ground, with a flame stronger than that usually found at bathhouses. Above the flames was a bath six feet on each side. A narrow pipe led from the mountains nearby, carrying clear water into the bath, which overflowed on all sides, so that the temperature was regulated and it was neither too hot nor too cold. Since the earth fire born of heaven was never extinguished, the bath, made by man, was never cold. Needless to say, it was also extremely clean.

Next to the bath was a kitchen. The hearth was fueled by the earth fire, too, and all sorts of dishes could be cooked there. Next there was a middle room. A bamboo pipe led up from underneath the floor, and at its tip was inserted a one-inch copper tube from which burned a little flame. From above hung a hook on an adjustable pole, and using this one could warm sake or make tea; at night the flame served as a light.

Closely observing the flame, one notices that it actually burns about one inch above the opening. If you fan it, it goes out just like an ordinary flame. If you put your hand over the tube then, all you

255

can feel is a slight breeze. When you strike a flint and send a spark near it, it suddenly begins to burn just as before. The owner of the placc said that the flames burn stronger at night and make people's faces look bluish. The owner's wife wanted to show us flames burning out of the water and led us to a paddy field terraced on the mountain slope just out behind the bath. Little bubbles were coming up from various places in the water of the paddy. When she struck a flint near one of these, a flame began to burn in the water, glowing like a candle. The old woman said, "There are other places that burn like this as well. If you should end up near one at night, you can light all the fires and keep wild beasts away."

All of this was quite strange for me, a man from Edo. In China they call these fire wells; the fire wells at Yuntaishan described in Chinese encyclopedias must be the same as these at Hell Valley, but they can't match Hell Valley's in scale: ours must be the most extensive in all of both China and Japan. This was really one of the most marvelous things I saw in my travels. The fire wells of China are in the northern province of Sichuan; since the fire wells of Japan are also in the northern province of Echigo, their presence may well be related to geography.

One of the geishas called down to Gankyo from the stairway and Gankyo, thus called, went up to her. Kyosui and I went straight to the bath, and soon we heard the sounds of the shamisen coming from the balcony. By the time we finished our baths and went up the stairs ourselves, everyone had had plenty to drink and the party was quite boisterous. The lovely sleeves of the geishas' kimonos filled the room with color, as they plucked the strings with their soft hands and songs fell from their ruby lips. They looked for all the world like lovely bodhisattvas, and their presence seemed to turn this Hell Valley into the paradise supreme. The geishas' master had also come along and brought with him a chef, who prepared for us delicious fish and vegetable dishes, making the party even livelier. This master, though his profession was the most worldly, had something refined about him and was always pining for the company of men of letters. It was Gankyo's promise that he would meet me that brought him here today, he confessed. A measure of his wit is the name he gave his establishment: Two Hills Terrace, a pun on his two very prominent protruding front teeth, for the name could also be read Two Buck Teeth. He was an easygoing and pleasant person, loved by all, who just happened to have two little hills on either side of his house.

Mr. Two Buck Teeth proceeded to take his fan from his sash and ask me to write a verse on it, and hearing this one of the geisha also produced her fan. Kyosui painted a picture and I improvised a poem, inspiring Gankyo and his friends to begin writing their own verses on the paper walls, and the party progressed with other elegant pastimes. Soon the day was nearing its end, and we prepared to make our way back. The geishas had worn straw sandals. "Those are mine!" we heard as they quarreled playfully over the sandals they had discarded in haste. Everyone was a bit tipsy, and we walked along the rural path making considerable noise. When we came to a narrow stream, the geishas with their red lips and white faces raised the scarlet hems of their under kimonos and waded across. The sight of these lovely, willowy flowers crossing a stream in straw sandals was utterly fascinating, a sight I never expected to see with these Edo eyes. The drunken fellows sang folksongs as the tipsy geisha pranced along after them, half dancing, half walking. Someone frightened one of the geisha into thinking an old rope was a snake, and in her surprise she took a step into a muddy paddy—which sent everyone into an uproar of laughter.

Since the road was no more than a farmer's path, there were no teahouses or other places to rest along the way; about halfway home, we stopped at an ancient shrine to catch our breath. One of the geisha disappeared behind the shrine and then came back and dipped a bit of the little remaining water from an ancient stone basin to wash her hands. Then she went and crouched in front of a statue of Jizo Bodhisattva that stood underneath a large tree, pulled a mirror from her breast, and began to apply powder to her face where it had rubbed off, redo her lipstick, and in general repair her makeup. As she did so she rested her powder box and other things on Jizo's head! "A bodhisattva on the outside, a demoness inside"—so runs the old warning. "What could the bodhisattva be thinking?" I wondered with some distress. And as the sun had already begun its downward course, we each hurried our steps back to Ojiya. (Another book of mine describes this journey. It's included in my record of my travels in Echigo.)

Famous People of Echigo

Hangaku, who married Osanotaro Sukemori, the lord of the castle of Kaji Myojinzan, was born in Koshi County. Shuten Doji, known to every three-year-old, was from Sunagotsuka Village in Kambara County. Even today there are traces of the house in which he was born. At first he was the disciple of Gyohoin, of the Unshozan Kokujoji temple. High Priest Geno was born in Yahagi Village at the foot of Iyahikosan.

Though in recent generations there has been no lack of people of Echigo who were virtuous monks, lofty Confucian scholars, poets, and painters, the fame of few of them has spread in the four directions. (The painter Go Shummei only became well known because he went away to Edo.) But we have seen, of late, many famous sumo wrestlers from Echigo: Koshinoumi and Washigahama of Niigata, Kumonryu from Imamachi and Sekinoto from Shidaihama, both in Takata. And everyone has heard of Nakano Zenyuemon from Kubiki County, Chobei from Tateishi Village of the same county, and Sangoyuemon from Sanjo in Kambara County. These great champions, without match in strength, are known to all. Chotokuji from Yokoto Village near Yoroigata and Gyokoji from Tanine Village are also famous for their superhuman strength. Both of these men were strong enough to easily lift a great temple bell by themselves.

In ancient times there were several people from Echigo famous for their deep filial piety: Murakami Kojiro, Kikume from Shibata, and the monk Chiryo from Kubiki. Recently there has been Yurime, daughter of the farmer Ibei, in Murata Village of Mishima County; Monzaemon, the son of the farmer Tatsunosuke of Arakawa Village in Shibata; Harumatsu the tofu vendor, son of Kamasuke, in Tsuk'ahara; Shinroku, the farmer of Shakatsuka Village in Kambara. All of them were known throughout the province for their filial piety, and some of them are still alive today.

Momoki says: I visited the old sites associated with Hangaku and Shuten Doji during my travels in Echigo, and took a look at Niigata as well, to worship at famous temples and shrines. I was planning to visit, in Teradomari, sites associated with Emperor Juntoku, Yoshitsune, Muso Kokushi, Honen, Nichiren, Lord Tamekane, and the courtesan Hatsugimi, but the weather was bad, and since the harvest was poor, the price of rice kept rising day after day, and the people were restless. I began to wish to return home, and my journey lost all its elegant air as I passed sadly from site to site and found myself reduced in spirit to an ordinary traveler. I regret to this day that I did not call on all the literary men that I had heard of. Ah, how regrettable is a year of bad harvest!

Jointless Stupas

About two and one-half miles east of Muramatsu in Kambara County is the village of Raiko; there you will find a temple called the Eikokuji, of the Soto sect of Zen. Near the temple runs a river called Hayade River. Some one-quarter mile downstream from the temple is a little hall to Kannon Bodhisattva. Where the river flows just below the hall is called Toko Abyss. There is a precedent that when someone becomes head priest of the Eikokuji temple, he is to throw a copy of his dharma-lineage certificate into this abyss. Then, a year before the head priest is destined to die, a naturally shaped rounded stone suitable for a tombstone will appear along the banks of this abyss. This is called a jointless stupa because it is in one piece instead of made of several stones stacked on top of each other as are most stupas. The head priest of the temple has always, from ancient times up until today, died in the year following the appearance of his tombstone. Many times the head priest has not been satisfied with the size of the stone, and he has returned it to the waters; that night they flow in reverse and always succeed in turning up a stone that pleases. Once the head priest, seeing the stone, grew afraid and ran away. Though he was in a faraway province, the next year death caught up with him all the same, it is said. It must be that there is a spirit in the abyss who warns of the abbot's upcoming death.

My friend Master Hokuyo (of an old family of Kambara County; he loves literature and excels at calligraphy) has seen the temple and described it to me. The main hall is sixty feet wide, with a priest's residence on the right and a meditation hall forty-eight feet by thirty on the left. There is a bell tower to the left of the path leading up a slope to the main hall. Behind the meditation hall is a lotus pond, above which sits another hill. By climbing this last hill, one reaches the graves of the head priests. They consist of the round stones thrown up from the abyss, each set on a stone base shaped by masons. The grave in the center is that of the temple's founder, and, in order, to left and right are the graves of his twenty-three successors. The largest stones are one foot two or three inches across, the smaller eight or nine, or even only six or seven inches. The size of the stone is said to depend on the head priest's merits. Hokuyo told me that the bases of the gravestones were all one foot high.

The following story is told about the spirit of the abyss. There was once a certain lord who lived near the Eikokuji. His wife, jealous of her husband's mistress, threw herself into Toko Abyss to spite him. She was transformed into an evil dragon who harmed people until the founder of the temple (I didn't catch his name) threw his dharma-lineage certificate into the depths, converting the evil spirit, who attained enlightenment. As a token of thanks, the spirit tossed up a tombstone to warn the head priest of his death. This is the reason that even today those who assume the rank of head priest at this temple throw their dharma-lineage certificates into the abyss.

There are also jointless stupas in neighboring Shinano. Sekitei of Omi says in his *Cloud-Essence Annals:* "There is a wide river called Hoshi River running in front of the Yokoi Onsenji temple in Shibuyu Village, Takai County, Shinano Province. One year before the head priest of the Onsenji is to die, from nowhere in particular a naturally shaped square tombstone two feet high, of beautiful luster, is washed up. Though natural, it is as prettily formed as if it had been carved.

When such a stone appears, the local villagers inform the Onsenji: 'Next year the head priest will leave this world. This stone stands here as proof.' This began nine generations ago, and the stone stupas of all nine head priests are to be found there, lined up together, the same shape, size, and type of stone.

"One priest entreated heaven the year his stone appeared: 'I have made a vow to read *The Lotus Sutra* one thousand times, a vow it will take me at least another full year to complete. Please, somehow, permit me to live one more year and fulfill my promise.' And with that he tossed the stone back into the river. He lived for the next year and completed his reading without event. The month he finished, the same stone appeared again in the river, and the year after that he died at last. When the stone of the next head priest appeared, he threw it back into the river without any special vow. But however many times he tossed it in, it appeared again the next night, and he died the following year. These tombstones are called jointless stupas hereabouts."

It is indeed very strange that the happenings at the Eikokuji in Echigo and the Onsenji in Shinano should be so very much alike.

Momoki says: When Bokushi was going over the manuscript for this section, he sent a messenger asking if the character *ho* (seam or joint) was not mistaken, for the meaning seemed obscure. I explained the reason for this writing of the word. *The Cloud-Essence Annals* writes *ho* with the character for "cap," but "capless" is just as puzzling as "jointless." Perhaps the proper character for *ho* is "hope"—for hopeless tombstones? Certainly the priests must feel hopeless when they learn their death is near. I close here with a little humor of my own, hopeless as it may be, and await the conclusions of knowledgeable experts.

Abbot Hokko

The Undoan in Undo Village of Uonuma County is one of the four great temples of Echigo. The other three are the Jikoji of Muramatsu

Abbot Hokko confronts the hellcat.

Village in Takiya, the Kounji at Murakami, and the Shigetsuji at Yahiko.

The virtues of the thirteenth abbot of the Undoan, Tsuten, who was a relative of Lord Sotai, are still talked about. It is said that Kagekatsu, the lord's nephew, also studied at this temple. As the Undoan is the most important temple in Echigo, it keeps many old documents, books, and treasures. Among them is a certain surplice called the hellwagon-repelling surplice. It looks to be made of linen dyed in the boiling sap of the clove tree, and it is sprinkled with blood.

The surplice is a treasure because it belonged to the abbot Hokko, who lived here during the Tensho era (1571–91). He was the tenth abbot of the temple and a great scholar, standing high in the esteem of the people. Once during midwinter, someone in nearby Saburomaru Village died in the midst of a period of extremely heavy and continuous snowfall. His relatives delayed the funeral for several days, waiting for the snow to clear up, but squalls continued to blow and there was no sign of improvement, so they finally had no choice but to hold the ceremony and went out to fetch the head priest of the parish: Hokko. Accompanied by him, they left the village for the funeral, carrying the coffin through the snowstorm. Not only relatives but many neighbors, too, had joined the procession, and all were wearing straw capes and straw hats.

When they were still only halfway, a great wind arose suddenly, and in no time heavy black clouds covered the entire sky, so that it became dark as night. As they pressed onward, an immense fireball came floating toward them out of nowhere and hovered in the air over the coffin. In the center of the fireball they saw a huge and unbelievably horrible hellcat with two tails. It was baring its fangs, hissing, snarling, and spitting, trying to tear the coffin open.

When the mourners saw the monster they scattered in every direction, fleeing for their lives. Abbot Hokko alone stayed by the coffin, never ceasing to chant his sacred mantras. Suddenly he shouted at the monster in a thundering voice, raised his holy staff, and with a mighty stroke he struck the flying cat-demon on the skull. It split open and blood spurted out, soaking the abbot's robe. In an instant the beast vanished, and the raging storm ceased. Thanks to

Abbot Hokko's courage, the people were able to carry out the funeral.

This event has been recorded in the old books of the temple, and the surplice that he wore is kept as a holy relic and known as the *kasha otoshi,* or hellwagon-repelling surplice.

Momoki adds: With Bokushi I went to the Undoan, which is about two and one-half miles from Shiozawa. There we talked with the head priest, who kindly showed us the relics and other treasures of the temple. We saw the surplice of Abbot Hokko with our own eyes.

The Undoan is indeed a large temple. Two huge Chinese characters reading "prayer" on a vertical plaque fixed to the wall are said to be in the hand of Emperor Juntoku himself. He is supposed to have written them on his way to exile on Sado Island.

Before the temple gate is an announcement on a wooden bulletin board of sorts, put there by the governor of old, Naoe Sanjo, prohibiting fires and the cutting of trees without a permit. There used to be a tombstone for the good general Usami Suruga, who died a martyr, near the pond in the garden. Last year Bokushi had it re-erected, which was certainly a good deed. (In my opinion, the reading *kasha,* or hellwagon, is an error for *yasha,* a demon. There are many Chinese accounts of these *yasha.*)

Congratulatory Poems

When I reached my sixty-first birthday, I collected many felicitous writings and paintings, of course from people of my region, but also from literary men of many provinces and great writers and artists, courtesans and actors, of the three great cities of Kyoto, Osaka, and Edo. I even received one poem from a man of Qing China who had crossed the seas to come to Japan. All of them signed their pieces "Dedicated to Bokushi." I asked one person after another to write something for me, until I had over one thousand, upon which I had them bound in an album and placed them in my storehouse.

One year, thinking to air this album, I opened the sliding paper doors of the large room adjoining the shop and unpacked my collection, spreading the pieces out on the floor. Just as I was doing this a friend arrived, and we began to pass the time in discussing the various poems and appreciating the paintings. A husband and wife on a pilgrimage arrived under the eaves of the house just then. We always have straw sandals prepared to give to such people, which we did, along with an offering of money. But instead of leaving, the old fellow of the couple stayed where he was, looking at the spread-out album leaves with great interest. Finally he said, "Though it can't compare with what I see here, I'd like to add a rough pilgrim's verse to these. Please bring me some paper." I have to admit that I was rather displeased, thinking such words did not befit someone who appeared to be a beggar, but I had paper and ink box brought out.

> I will first to the River of Death
> And, so you may greet your hundredth year,
> Stay its flow for you.

Thus he wrote, with a masterful brush as well. It was certainly a unique sort of congratulatory poem; both my friend and I were rather impressed, and I offered him lodging for the night. My friend, too, urged him earnestly to stop and talk with us at length, but he refused to stay his staff any longer and left. All he said was that he was from the western provinces. To this day I wonder what sort of fellow he really was.

The Strange Thing About Nigoro Village

About two and one-half miles toward the mountains from Ojiya is Nigoro Village. There are two burial mounds in this village, called Large Mound and Small Mound. Local legend has it that Large Mound entombs Fujiwara Tokihira, the villainous minister of the left who is known for his persecution of his virtuous rival, Sugawara Michizane. Small Mound is said to be that of Tokihira's wife. Of course there

BOOK SIX

is no truth at all to this claim, which is nothing more than a popular belief.

Still, there is one strange thing about the village, and in the light of it, it may just be possible that someone related to Tokihira was exiled to this place and ended his life here. The strange thing of which I speak is that, from ancient times, whenever people of the village tried to learn to write, they were struck by the punishment of the god Temmangu (the spirit of Michizane and the god of learning). As a result, the entire village is illiterate. If someone from Nigoro goes to another village and learns to write, there is no punishment. But after he returns to his own village, he forgets, day by day, the Chinese characters he learned so diligently until he is unable to read or write again. So, when the people of Nigoro have a need to write something, they ask someone from another village to record what they dictate. Also, when the illustrated books that children sometimes receive as presents from those who have come from Edo contain any picture of Temmangu, it always provokes punishment by the god. It seems, then, that there is after all some basis for the old story that the large and small mounds are those of Minister Tokihira and his wife.

Michizane died in Tsukushi on March 25 of the third year of the Engi era (901–922), 915 years ago. Yet even now the brightness of his spirit is deserving of fear and respect.

There is another event similar to this, recorded by Nankei in his *Travels to the East*. When he was in Tsugaru, a great rain and wind continued for six days without stop. An official went from inn to inn grilling each innkeeper, "Is there anyone from Tango here? Anyone from Tango?" Nankei asked his innkeeper the reason for this inquiry, and the innkeeper replied, "Iwaki of our province is the birthplace of Princess Anju and her brother Prince Zuiomaru. The people of old worshiped these two as the gods of Mount Iwaki—the shrine still stands. Since this brother and sister were kidnapped by people from Tango, who then sold them to the villainous Sansho the Bailiff, under whom they suffered so greatly, all people from Tango were abhorred by the gods. Since ancient times, if even one entered the province a great rain would fall and a fierce wind blow for days and days. If they returned to the border and crossed out of our province, the storm would stop almost instantly. And that is why they are searching for a person from Tango."

The father of the prince and princess was the rightful lord of Iwatsuki, but while in the capital he was slandered and his clan was destroyed. This occurred in the Eiho period (1081–83), more than 750 years ago. It is beyond human understanding that the anger of the gods has not yet relented, but Nankei actually experienced its effects and was moved to record them.

Travels to the West relates a similar occurrence: "Kagekiyo's grave mound is in Hyuga, as everyone knows. His mother is entombed, however, in Kiribata Village, about thirteen miles to the east of the castle town of Hitoyoshi in Kuma of Higo Province. The tomb of Kagekiyo's daughter is in Kiribata as well; together they are worshiped as the clan god of the village. Blind people are forbidden in this village, and there is always divine punishment should a blind person venture in. The people of Kiribata believe Kagekiyo's mother hates blind people because of Kagekiyo's tragic blinding."

Both of these phenomena are similar to the strange thing about Nigoro Village. In one, there is a shrine that despises people from Tango; in the other, a tomb that despises the blind. Nigoro Village has a grave mound that forbids the presence of the holy spirit of Michizane, the god of writing. The more one considers these things, the more likely it seems that the grave mounds are those of some relative of Michizane's nemesis, Tokihira.

The Seven Kettles of Tashiro

Seventeen miles to the south of Tokamachi, the official post town in Uonuma, in the midst of the mountains of Tsumari (the area called Upper Tsumari), there is a village called Tashiro. Another one-quarter mile out of the village is a place called Seven Kettles. (We call the bowl of a waterfall a kettle.) It earned its name from the seven-tiered waterfall there. The seven falls have different names, like Sake-Flask Spout and Fudo Falls; they are so wonderful and weird that they defy description. I have painted the surroundings of the bowl of the seventh and last waterfall, which should provide a general idea. The cliff walls are called Tate Ogo (vertical collection box) and Yoko Ogo (horizontal collection box). We call the collection boxes carried by the servants of Ise Shrine *ogo,* and the fissures of the cliffs resemble the vertical or horizontal slots of the boxes. A close look at one of the stones fallen from the cliff shows that it is flat, only six or seven inches thick, but three or four feet in length, as if carefully hewn by a stonecutter. Thousands of these stones are lined up vertically along the cliff wall. At their peak grow splendid ancient trees. This is the Tate Ogo, to the right. The left cliff is made of stones of the same size and shape piled up on top of each other, to the same height as the facing cliff. They are so neatly stacked that it looks as if a person had carefully placed them there, one on top of the other, yet this is a miracle of nature. When stones happen to fall from the cliff, the people of Tashiro put them to various uses. It is said, though, that should even the smallest fragment of a stone be used in any other place, divine punishment will result. I have recorded here the fascinating sight I witnessed on my visit to the Seven Kettles that took place on August 7, 1820. There are similar sights in other provinces, where nature is more luxuriant, and a few are described below.

Momoki says: When I was in service as a young man, I heard from the scholar Seki, a retainer of the same daimyo as me, that there was in the lord's private domains at Sasayama in Tamba a cliff made up of natural millstones piled in pillars that ranged next to one another, forming the cliff face. They filled the entire mountain, Seki told me. I have also read, in one of Shunki's writings, that there is a place in the mountains of western Japan where naturally shaped millstones are found, though I can't remember now the name of the place. In the ninth volume of *Tsukushi Journey* by Yoshida Shigefusa, we find, in a description of his journey by boat from Naya Village of Keta County in Tajima Province to Tajima Hot Spring, the following account: "We went by boat. To our right passed Mount Atago, Miyashima Village, Nokami Village, and Ishiyama. I saw some very strange stones as I watched the banks of the river while passing Ishiyama. They

The Seven Kettles of Tashiro.

were like millstones, flat above and below, and cut off neatly on three, four, five, six, seven, or eight sides, as if by a mason. They were bluish black in color, and there were caves, indicating that some of the stones had been dug out. Indeed there are many strange things in the world.'' Since this is another description of strange stones, I have added it here.

BOOK SEVEN

Strange Beasts

The town of Tokamachi lies about eighteen miles from Horinouchi in Uonuma County. Though a number of villages lie scattered between the two, they are separated by a range of mountains, through which leads a lonely path. One summer a certain wholesaler of Tokamachi placed an urgent order with another dealer in Horinouchi for a large bale of white crepe. The dealer who was to send the crepe chose a robust fellow, one Takesuke, whom he sent out at around noon with the load of crepe.

By the time Takesuke had almost half of the way behind him, it was already three o'clock. Taking his load off his shoulders, he settled down on a stone at the wayside and pulled out his lunch of roasted rice balls and began to eat. At that moment, something approached him, pushing through the dense cover of low bamboo that blanketed the valley.

When he looked up to see what it could be, his first impression was that it must be an ape. But then it wasn't, either. The creature had long half-white hair falling down from its head to the middle of its back. It was taller than the average person. And, although its face did resemble that of an ape, it was not red, and its eyes were enormously big and shining.

As Takesuke was a fearless sort, he grasped the mountain axe that he always carried in his belt as a precaution and put himself in a posi-

The strange mountain beast.

tion to defend himself in case the strange creature were to attack him.

However, the queer animal did not show the least sign of aggression. Instead, it only pointed to the rest of the roasted rice balls which lay on the stone beside Takesuke, as if it were begging for some. Takesuke understood what the creature wanted and tossed it some food. With obvious pleasure, the funny beast devoured the treat. Watching this put Takesuke at ease and he gave the beast more, upon which the animal trotted trustingly nearer to him.

"Listen, you, I come from Horinouchi and am on my way to Tokamachi," Takesuke addressed the fellow creature standing nearby. "Tomorrow I'll pass by here again. Then you can have more of my lunch. But since today I have to make a very urgent delivery, I must hurry on."

He arose, intending to load the backpack on his shoulders again, but the animal grasped it instead, lifted it onto its own back as if it were nothing at all, and began to walk ahead. "It's helping me out of gratitude for the rice balls I gave it," Takesuke reflected while following the beast, who proceeded as easily as if there were nothing in the pack at all. Thanks to this unexpected assistance, Takesuke passed over the narrow, winding road in no time and without the least difficulty. After a hike of a good three or four miles, they approached the outskirts of Ikedani Village, where the creature stopped, let down the load, and rushed as quick as the wind back into the mountain underbrush.

Upon his arrival at Tokamachi, Takesuke of course told the people in the crepe-dealer's shop everything that had happened on the way. And although that was forty or fifty years ago, the people still talk about this event. For after that a good number of people working in the mountains spotted the strange creature.

Another meeting with a similar creature was supposed to have occurred at Ikedani Village when I was about fourteen or fifteen years old. The people of Ikedani claim that there was once a young girl in their village known for her extraordinary skill in weaving. Because she was so accomplished, a wholesale merchant had engaged her to do weaving for him on a contractual basis.

As she sat by the window one day, weaving her crepe—the snow in the village had not yet all melted away—she suddenly saw some creature standing outside and peeping in. It looked at first like a monkey, but its face wasn't red and its long hair hung down its back. It was far taller than a man.

As she was all alone, for the other members of her family had all left to work in the mountains, she was both utterly astonished and terribly frightened. She jumped up to run away, but, unfortunately, her sleeve caught in the loom, and while she was desperately trying to free herself the strange creature simply wandered away.

One day not long after, she found the same animal standing by the hearth, pointing to the rice kettle indicating that it wanted something to eat. As the girl had heard about the strange creature in the meantime, she shaped some rice balls and offered it two or three. It took them from her with obvious joy and left.

From that day on, when nobody else was at home it would occasionally appear and beg for food. The young girl lost all her fear, becoming used to its presence. Each time it came she gave it some rice balls.

Now it so happened that just as she was weaving some crepe for a high-ranking customer, her menstruation set in and she could not enter the loom chamber. As the deadline when she was to deliver her full length of crepe drew nearer, she and her parents grew worried.

It was dusk on the third day of her menses. Her parents had not yet returned from their work in the fields. Suddenly the strange creature was there, after quite some absence, at her side. While preparing chestnut rice for the beast, she spoke to it about her distress as if it were human and could understand. The creature seemed to listen to what she said, for this time it did not, as usual, get up and leave at once but stood there for quite a while as if pondering something. Only after having lingered some time did it leave.

That very same evening her menstruation ceased suddenly. And while still wondering how that could have come to pass, she went through the prescribed purification, then entered the weaving room and took up her work where she had left off. She happily finished the full crepe length and took it at once to the wholesale dealer. "Well, I made it after all," she thought when entering his shop.

Barely had she handed over the piece of cloth when her menstruation began again!

"No doubt," she concluded, "that dear thing, hearing my complaints, thought it must find a way to help me," and she told the story to the other villagers. All of them thought it extremely curious.

After that the wondrous animal was seen occasionally, now here, now there, in the mountains. Yet whenever more than one person was walking through the hills, it refused to show itself.

Another story tells of a Takata clansman who went off to cut lumber in the woods of Kurohime Mountain with some fellow woodcutters. They built themselves a hut up there, where they lived for some time. One evening, an apelike animal about six feet tall showed itself. It had red hair, while the body was naked and gray, without fur. From its waist down it wore a kind of apron woven from grasses and it showed itself to be rather tame. It responded to the men's attentions and in a short time it became quite attached to them, according to the account of the Takata clansman.

The "Apes" chapter of *The Illustrated Encyclopedia of China and Japan* states that such animals are found at Mino in Hida as well as the deep mountains of western Japan. They are, no doubt, found in deep mountains everywhere.

Asbestos

During the Horeki era (1751–63) Hiraga Kyukei (also known as Gennai) invented asbestos cloth and composed *A Study of Asbestos*, in which he quotes many ancient Chinese and Japanese sources, taking great pride in his unprecedented discovery. But when he died his art was lost, much to the regret of the amateur scientist.

As a matter of fact, the mineral from which asbestos cloth is woven was previously mined in our province, where it is found at Kinjosan, Makihatayama, Naebasan, Hakkaisan, and other places. The stone itself is soft and can be scratched with a fingernail. It is blue-black. A mineral filament can be obtained by breaking the stones. I acquired some stones myself for examination and found that the mineral filaments were like narrow twisted cotton threads, cut into two- or three-inch fragments. There is a secret method by which filaments can be spun into thread, and it is from this thread that asbestos cloth is woven.

A fellow from our post town, Inariya Kichiemon, pondered long and hard to find the method for spinning the filaments into thread, and at last succeeded in weaving his own asbestos cloth. At the same time, a doctor named Kuroda Genkaku in the nearby village of Osawa also discovered how to weave the cloth. What a marvelous coincidence that two men should, at the same time and in the same place, suddenly discover the means to weave asbestos cloth, especially since neither dared to share his secret technique with any other. This was about 1821 or 1822.

Both men say that if they exert great effort they can weave a piece of cloth more than three yards in length; and both also say that the technique is not an easy one. In *A Study of Asbestos,* Gennai says that he could not weave more than five or six feet of the material. Genkaku's efforts also surpass those of Gennai in that Genkaku has invented inflammable paper and ink, too. You can hold a message written in this ink on this paper in a brightly burning flame and, if you then take the paper gently from the fire and wait for the flames to die, the message and the paper it's written on will be just the same as before. Yet there is little practical use for such things, because they can't really be depended on to survive a fire. They burn when set aflame, and if there is no one to take them out of the fire, they crumble to pieces. Their only virtue is that they aren't reduced to ash. The best use for these inventions will most likely be in playthings.

After the miraculous appearance of these two, who rediscovered the secret of weaving asbestos cloth after it had been lost with Gennai's death, what a terrible shame it would be if they fail to teach the technique to others and it is lost once more. Gennai is renowned for his discovery because he wove his asbestos cloth in glorious Edo; these two are unheard of because they live in far-off Echigo. So it is that I have recorded their accomplishments here, another anecdote for those of scientific interests.

SNOW COUNTRY TALES

The Mummy of Priest Kochi

Priest Kochi was of the Kodama clan from Yamakuwa Village in Shimoosa. He studied esoteric Buddhism at Mount Koya, later returning to his place of birth, where he took up residence at the Rengedera temple at Oura. During his pilgrim's wanderings, he also visited Echigo. He stayed his staff finally at a place called Iwasaka, to the east of the Saishoji temple of Kaiunzan near Nozumi Village ("Nozomi" in the local speech) of Mishima County. There he built a hermit's hut and, on the second day of November, 1371, he entered nirvana. His farewell verse has been handed down through the ages:

> Should people ask
> Who is the master of Iwasaka,
> —The soughing wind through the pines
> Of an ink painting.

His body was not buried, and though 477 years have passed since his death, the mummy today, in 1838, looks as if it were still alive.

Kochi's mummy is counted as one of the twenty-four wonders of Echigo. Though it has been mentioned in various works, none of them provides illustrations—which I have seen fit to do here. My drawing records what I saw myself, when I traveled to Lower Echigo last year. All that is visible is the face. The hands and feet cannot be seen, and a temple regulation prohibits too close an approach. The mummy's eyes are closed, as if in sleep, with wrinkles at the corners. The head covering and robe the mummy now wears cannot be the original ones. Yet this is certainly a wonder of Echigo, unheard of in other provinces.

Momoki remarks: There are, in China, mummies similar to that of Kochi. When the Tang-dynasty monk Yicun died, his corpse was placed in a casket, from which it was lifted each month to have the nails and hair trimmed. The body had not decomposed even after one hundred years. Later, during the rebellions and uprisings at the

BOOK SEVEN

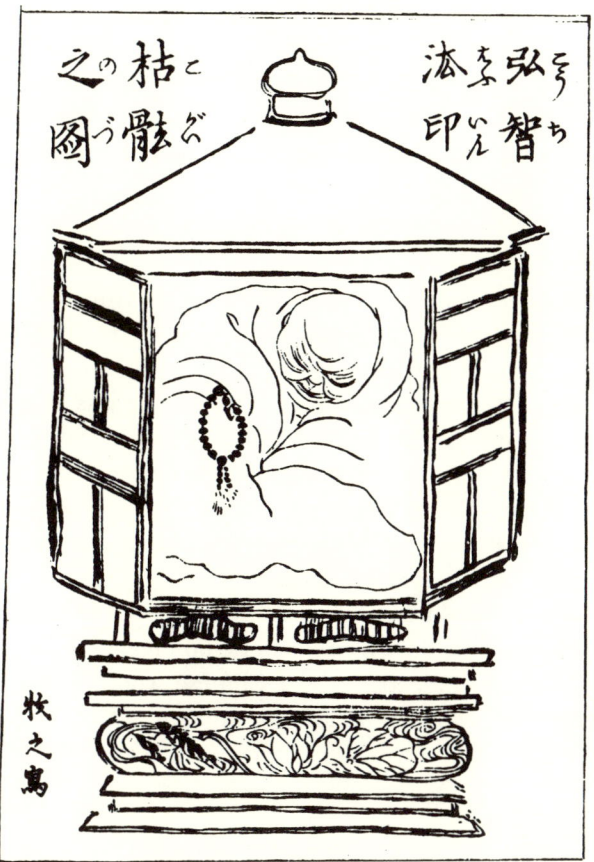

The mummy of Priest Kochi.

end of the dynasty, it was cremated. The Song-dynasty Chinese Peng Cheng records in his collection of poems and tales *Moke Huixi* that the monk Wumeng of Ezhou was not buried, and his nails and hair grew just as did those of Yicun—until the corpse was touched by the hand of a woman.

This phenomenon is mentioned in *The Five Miscellanies,* where many opinions about mummies are offered, but the whole idea is an insult to Shakyamuni's teachings of the impermanence of all compound things, and cannot be praised. (I think I recall that Yicun is mentioned in *Biographies of Illustrious Monks,* but I haven't checked the details.)

The Buried Ship

About two and one-half miles from the town of Goizumi in Kambara County is the village of Shimoshinden. One year when the people of this village were digging in the banks of the Aka River, they unearthed a ship some eighteen feet in length. It was in perfect condition, but of a style quite different from ships of today, and baleen had been used in place of all hardware. There was no metal to be found in the boat. Nor could anyone identify the wood from which the boat was constructed. Finally the conclusion was reached that it must be a ship from a foreign land.

When I was in Lower Echigo, visiting the home of Ono Sagoemon of Sugita Village, I was shown an inkstone box made of the wood from the ship. It seemed, indeed, to be a Chinese wood. Perhaps it was a Chinese ship that was cast ashore in ancient times.

The White Raven

As I wrote earlier, the proper subject for these *Snow Country Tales* is snow, and any other subject is as inappropriate as a poem that belies its title. Yet I will return to the subject of snow in the end, and for a moment wish to allow my brush to follow my wandering thoughts.

It happened in 1820. A tall tree stands before a certain key-maker's shop in the central district of Shiozawa where I live. A crow built its nest in that tree, and when at last the chicks began to poke their heads over the nest's rim, one white head was visible among the rest. The master of the key shop thought this strange, and had a person go and catch the baby bird. It turned out to be a crow indeed, but white all over, with red beak, eyes, and legs. Everyone gathered to see this marvel.

The key-shop master had a cage built posthaste and took great pains to raise his little white charge. When it first began to call, sure enough, it was with the voice of a crow. Since the shop was near my home, I saw the bird every day. So rare it was that many begged its keeper to sell them the bird, and several suggested that it be sent to Edo to appear in sideshows of wonders and marvels there. But the key-shop master would have none of this.

Then winter came, and all was buried in snow. As always happens, the badgers and foxes of the forests and mountains began to prowl around houses in search of food. One of these beasts broke open the crow's cage, and all that was found of it was a heap of white feathers under the eaves.

A Two-headed Snake

On October 27, 1827, the farmer Dazaemon of Yokawa Village in the nearby post town of Muikamachi caught a two-headed snake under the eaves of his house. It was less than one foot in length, and its two heads lay next to each other like a forked tree branch. Otherwise, it was no different in shape or color from a normal snake. Wishing to keep it, he put it in an old box and gave it food, but sometime in the next two or three days it escaped, and though he searched all about for it, it was nowhere to be found.

Floating Islands

The village of Yoshitani is located some two and one-half miles west of Ojiya. Here there is a pond known as the Lord of the County's Pond. It is several hundred yards square, and in it are thirteen floating islands. At daybreak on clear days when there is no wind, the thirteen little islands can be seen to drift apart and float here and there, as if playing on the pond's surface. As the sun sets, they gather together in the center of the pond again and form a single island. There are a great many strange things about this pond, but as my essay would grow too long, I will not mention them. The floating islands of Oshu are often written about and known by many, but very few know of the islands of Yoshitani Village.

The Stone-tossing Deity

There is a small shrine on the land of a certain farmer in Ojiya. It is called the shrine of the Stone-tossing Deity (Ishiuchi Myojin), and has been worshiped from times of old. I have managed to learn of its origins, and will relate them now.

The deity cures warts, and is prayed to by those who want to get rid of them. First they rub their warts with a small stone. Then they toss the stone behind the lattice bars beneath the elevated shrine corridors, and their warts fall off in a few days. Another curiosity of this shrine is that the stones, whatever shape they may have been at the start, gradually grow as round and smooth as if polished, and the area underneath the elevated corridors is filled with round stones, large and small.

Momoki remarks: When I was in Ojiya I saw these stones and heard their story, too. Thinking to take one home with me, I was warned by the local people that the deity treasures these stones, and I quickly returned the one I had picked up to its place. A careful look at the thousands of stones showed that they did seem to have been polished by men. How indeed can we mortal men fathom the wonders of the gods?

A Beauty

Momoki continues: While I was staying at the home of Gankyo

in Ojiya (it was in September of 1836), I one day grew tired of my writing and went on a stroll, thinking to take in some of the autumn scenery. Climbing a hill that looks over the river that runs in front of the town, I decided to sit there and write. I spread a mat beneath an old tree and, puffing away at my tobacco, took in the view. The boats being pulled upstream looked not to be moving at all, while those heading downstream were as if in flight. Geese on the wing overhead seemed to trace graceful calligraphy, and the woodcutters on their way home opened a lovely painting before me. The forest was tinged with frost and glowed scarlet; the mountain peaks were touched with bits of snow, gleaming brilliant white. The autumnscape of the north country made new my weary eyes. I began to compose a Chinese verse as I drank in the view, when I saw three young women of sixteen or seventeen, each carrying a brushwood basket on her back.

They were climbing the hill, for I heard them talking and laughing among themselves, preparing to take a rest. But I lost myself again in the landscape until I heard a voice say, "Please, may I have a light?" A hand extended a pipe bowl toward mine, and when I looked at the face from which the words had come I saw a girl lovely as a jewel, a sensual flower of great natural beauty, her hair tantalizingly astray. This gem of Zhao was wrapped in rags. Astonished, I abandoned my scenic pleasures and looked at the girl. She bowed in thanks and took the pipe bowl, now glowing, back to the tree where she and her companions were sitting. Resting on the grass and stretching out her legs, she sat with them, as all three smoked tobacco.

It was as if the beauty Xishi were speaking with two hags, or rough reed grasses gathered round a strong and lovely tree. Her white teeth shone as she laughed like the white lotus swaying in a soft breeze as it breaks the surface of the pond. "What a terrible waste!" I lamented. "That such a beauty was born in this out-of-the-way place, where she can only become the wife of some boorish bumpkin." The thought of such a wonderful woman sleeping with a country clod, this flower rotting together with the weed, was too sad to contemplate.

"If only she could be taken to Edo, and brought to bloom by being taught the niceties of social intercourse in a fine household, or transplanted to the reed plains of Yoshiwara, and bear the golden fruits that flourish there—she would earn a name as a famous beauty to compare with Ono no Komachi of old, who was born in Dewa, not far away. How could Heaven have made such a gross error as to bring her to life here, in this wasteland?" And so my silent dirge went on. Just as I was about to address her, the girls rose, shouldered their baskets again, and departed. As I watched them go, I thought how deserved was Echigo's reputation as the home of beautiful women.

It is because of the water. For the same reason, there is no cloth more pure than Echigo's white crepe. The area around Ojiya produces especially lovely white crepe, which is proof of the extreme purity of its water. Thinking how true were the words of Xie Zhaozhi, "Because the waters of the Jiang River are pure, beauties abound there," I headed back to my lodgings. When I arrived the first thing I did was to tell Gankyo of my encounter with the beautiful girl, moment by moment.

Gankyo nodded and replied, "Yes, she's known as a beauty hereabouts. She must have recognized you as an outsider and gone to borrow a light from you on purpose. Oh, how wicked of you! And how I envy you!" "Not wicked at all," I replied. "I merely tried to lend a little fire to the beauty, and provoke a little warmth in return." At this Gankyo began to laugh and clap, "No, no, you've made a terrible mistake. For she's the daughter of an outcaste." And I received my second surprise of the day. For the only thing to liken the connection to would be a glorious flower growing out of a dung heap.

Ono no Komachi was the daughter of the governor of Ushu, Ono no Yoshizane. Yang Guifei was the daughter of the governor of Shuchuan, Yuan Yu. In both China and Japan, country girls of the far north have left behind their names as great beauties. The saying that beauties are found in the north country is true because the prevailing yin energy of the north is bound to produce beautiful women. The second Takao (Manji) was born in Noshu, and the first Usugumo was from Shinshu. Both made great names for themselves in the brothels of Yoshiwara. The Echigo beauty that I met was just another lovely product of the north country.

BOOK SEVEN

The Bridge Signpost from Mount Omei

In January of 1825, a certain fisherman from Shiiya in Kariwa County of Echigo (which is under the rule of Lord Hori) was fishing in the sea when he saw a piece of wood floating toward him. Thinking to dry it and use it for firewood, he plucked it from the waters and carried it home. As it was standing beneath the eaves of his house drying, an amateur scientist and collector of curiosities walked by and saw it. He realized that it was no ordinary tree, and upon closer inspection found carved into it the words: Bridge Below Mount Omei. Concluding that it was from China (where Mount Omei is located, of course), he arranged to exchange it with the farmer for some firewood.

Now my old friend the holy Kanrei, a monk at the Pure Land temple Yukoji in Tazawa Village, Shiiya, had a reputation of great learning as well as a strong passion for collecting curiosities. He traced and then carved in woodblocks those letters and sent them to friends of like interests, asking them to compose poems on the theme of the bridge signpost. He planned to have the collection published and distributed, but for various reasons he has not yet accomplished this.

It is said that the signpost later came into the possession of the lord of the region. Though Shiiya is in the same province, it is some distance away, and I did not have a chance to actually see the post, which I now much regret. At any rate, I have included a copy of a picture of it that was supplied to me.

Momoki comments: When I saw the picture that Bokushi sent with the manuscript, I was much struck by it and so I have researched it carefully. The results I garnered are as follows.

First I gained introduction to one of the lord's retainers, a Master Aiba, who happened to be a friend and correspondent (as well as a fellow versifier) of one of my acquaintances, the holy monk Ryoa. Upon meeting Aiba, I asked about the bridge signpost. He told me that it was not, after all, a bridge signpost but a road sign, and pulled out a piece of paper normally used for envelopes and drew me a picture of the object. My friend the painter Chiharu, with this sketch as his model, made a reduced drawing for me, and Aiba copied the characters with great concentration in his own hand. (The illustration is this.) Aiba explained that the head of a man carved at the top of the signpost is turned to the left to indicate that Mount Omei Bridge (the name of which is written on the sign) is ahead to the left. This makes unarguable sense. Nowadays we often see signs with a finger pointing in the direction of the place written below. The customs of China and Japan are much the same, after all.

When I asked how this sign board was actually discovered, I was told the following story. When winter arrives, the winds all along the coast of the northern sea are wild, the waves are rough, and all sorts of things are tossed up on the beaches. There is a scarcity of firewood in Shiiya, and so the poorer people are always picking up things on the beaches to burn as fuel. In January of 1825, there were several people on the beach as always, searching for firewood, when they saw a thing resembling a pillar rocking on the waves. It seemed to have a human head, and they feared it an evil omen, so they ran off terrified. Watching from some distance, they saw the thing finally wash up on the stones. Venturing closer, they discovered writing on it, but—alas—not one of them could read it. While they were offering all sorts of opinions as to what it might be, a young priest from the Saizenin nearby happened to pass and recognized the name Mount Omei, which he knew from a collection of Tang poetry. "This is from China!" he told them, and no sooner did they hear that than they lifted it up and carried it back. But since it was from China they didn't use it as firewood. Eventually its discovery became known all about town, and in the end it came into the hands of the lord of the region.

Mount Omei is a lofty peak in north China, as great as our Mount Fuji. The slopes of the peak stand in a great inverted V, and that is how it got its name, which means "arching eyebrows." Thinking to trace the sea route the road sign from Mount Omei must have taken to reach Japan, I pored over a collection of maps of China, *Historical Maps of the Provinces of China*. The Qing-dynasty map shows that Mount Omei is some one thousand miles to the north of the Qing capital. A great river near the mountain flows to the east. All the smaller rivers and streams of Mount Omei feed into this river. The great river flows through Luzhou and down three valleys until it reaches Jiangnan and enters Jingzhou. Flowing through four great waterways—Lake Dongting, the Red Cliffs, and the upper and lower reaches of the Yangzi River—it arrives in Jiangnan and from there pours into the eastern sea. This waterway is fifteen hundred miles in length.

The road sign in question must have fallen into a river during a flood. It flowed through the four great waterways without sinking and down, down, the more than fifteen hundred miles into the eastern sea. Tossed by huge waves and turned by raging breakers, it remained in one piece. In fine, firm shape it bobbed along in the Japanese sea, approaching the northern shores of our nation, to be picked up by the poor folks of Shiiya and lifted from the water at last. Someone who could read the words written on it happened to pass along just as it was about to become another stick of kindling, saving it from extinction in the flames. Now poems were solicited in its honor, and it earned the favor of the lord of Shiiya, finding a safe haven in his trove of treasures. It will be preserved for eternity. How incomprehensible, how marvelous its fate—surely a rarity among rarities is its story.

The signpost from Mount Omei.

SNOW COUNTRY TALES

Mount Naeba

Mount Nacba ("Seedbed Mountain") is the tallest mountain in Echigo. It is located in Uonuma County, and is said to be a five-mile ascent. At the summit are what appear to be seedbeds, which is why it was named Seedbed Mountain in ancient times. How strange it is to find seedbeds at the top of such a towering peak! I longed to see this marvel with my own eyes, and so decided, in August of 1811, to climb the mountain. Four friends and I set off in the predawn darkness of the fifth of that month, with servants to carry the provisions and other things we brought along.

That night we stayed at Mitsumata Post Town. The next day we walked through the dawn to reach the quarters of the local Shinto official. There each of us purified ourself, and we hired a guide. The guide walked ahead of us, dressed in white and waving a Shinto wand. We crossed Kiyotsu River and at last reached the foot of the mountain. We traced a steep and rugged path as we climbed, shaded from the summer heat by rows of beech trees. The mountain bamboo grass grew so thick that it blocked the road. We climbed over ancient trees that had fallen over the path, as if stepping on the backs of sleeping dragons. After crossing a small stream through a valley, we climbed another mile or so. Then the path began twisting to the right and left as we continued on, climbing ever upward. On every side there were oddly twisted trees and rocks of fantastic shapes, defying description.

Long before we reached our destination, the songs of birds were absent from the air. The road seemed as if to disappear, and east and west were lost to us. But the guide knew the way and continued on, pushing aside the bamboo grass, waving his Shinto wand, and showing us the way. Wild wisteria vines pulled at our hats and bamboo thickets hid us from each other. The rock sides were high and the road narrow; not once did we take two steps on level ground. Sometime after noon we arrived at the halfway point and, discovering somehow a tiny level place, spread our mats under a tree and ate of our provisions.

After our brief rest, we set off climbing again. We reached

Kaguraoka, "Heavenly Music Hill." From this point on there were no trees except larches. A forest of these twisted evergreens, stunted by the wind, their crowns frozen and browned by the snow and frost, spread low about us. Climbing just a bit and then descending again, we came to a place called Ohanabatake (Flower Garden), where mountain cherries bloomed in profusion with golden lilies, blue bellflowers, and pinks, just as if they had been planted by man. There were also many plants whose names I did not know. The guide said they were medicinal herbs.

We continued up, up, as the path became like a suspended bridge. Grasping the roots of bamboo grass growing in the rock face as our handholds, we edged forward with great concentration, calling out with each step, until we were covered with sweat—and had reached, after what seemed a thousand pains and a million trials, a place called Umanose: Horse's Back. To right and left was a valley that dropped several thousand feet; the path was a mere two or three feet wide. One false step and you would find yourself dashed to pieces. Taking each step as if our lives depended on it (and they did), we finally reached the summit.

First all twelve of us rested on the grass. It was already late afternoon. Our guide had warned us in advance that the road was too steep to make the journey of five miles there and back in one day. There is a hut on the peak, and those who climb the mountain always spend the night there. It proved to be the sort of shelter enjoyed by a wandering outcast, the most casual construction of tree branches, bamboo, and dried grasses bound together by vines. The thought that this should be our night's lodging gave us all quite a laugh. The servants gathered sticks and stones to make a cooking fire and set about preparing our dinner for us. It was amusing to see them making tea and warming sake over this makeshift flame.

A look around showed that not only was all of Echigo visible, but we could see the smoke rising from far-off Asama, and the mountain peaks of Shinano ranged before our eyes like great breakers. The silver thread of the Chikuma River unwound below us, and the island of Sado sat like a stone on the shining blue tray of the sea. The cape of Susaki in Noto arched as gracefully as the eyebrows

The view from Mount Naeba.

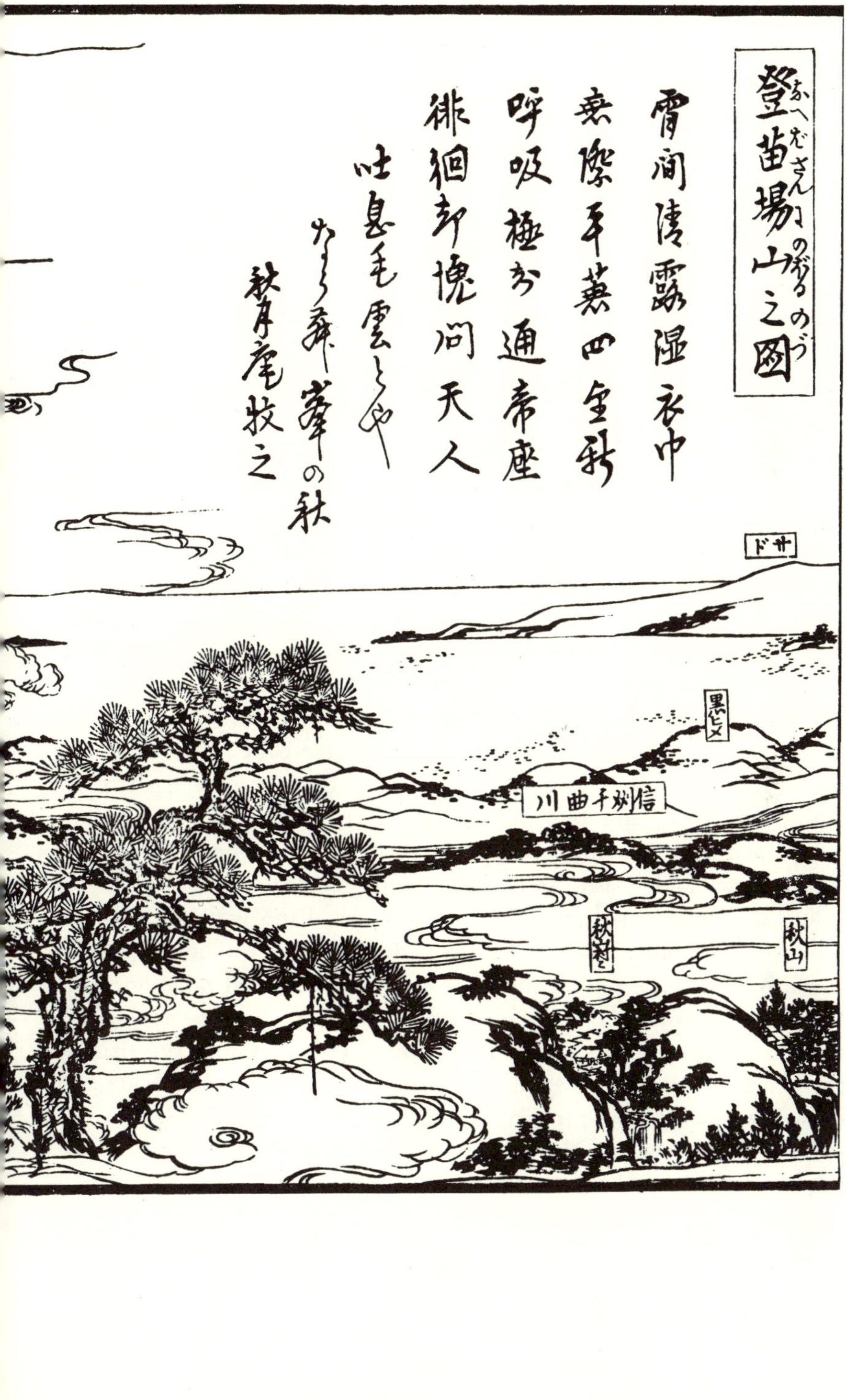

登苗場山之圖 (なへばさんののぼるのづ)

霄間清露濕衣巾
衰際平蕪四望新
呼吸極方通帝座
徘徊却愧問天人

吐息毛雲となり舞峯の秋
　　　　　　秋屋庵牧之

黒ヒメ
信州千曲川
秋山
秋山

of some beauty, and the mountains of far Echizen were their delicate smoke-blue traces.

Adjusting our gazes, someone spotted Mount Fuji, the mountain of mountains. It looked like a gracefully placed cone-shaped handful of snow 'midst the other peaks. Everyone clapped their hands for joy and exclaimed at the wonder and the beauty of it.

But we had little time to gaze at these marvelous sights. Clouds began to gather at our feet, and in the next instant the sun was shining brightly into our eyes. It was as if we were standing above the heavens watching the world below. The peak is said to be two and one-half miles in circumference. It is a flat plain covered with luxuriant growth. No depressions or hills were visible. The "seedbeds" of the mountain's name were to be seen all about. They looked indeed like seedbeds made by men, and in them were growing some wild plant that resembled rice seedlings. Some looked as if they were only half-planted, or a portion of the seedlings had already been taken away, which we thought strange. Frogs and grasshoppers lived in the seedbeds, just as in a real rice paddy. We were told, too, that no matter how fierce the drought, these fields never dry up. Looking out over the several miles of the peak, I was struck by the extreme strangeness of this holy mountain.

Our guide told us that there was another road leading from Ohanabatake, which we had passed earlier, to a place called Dragon Cave, through which a clear stream flowed. Many old coins were scattered about the place, and two gongs hung there, where the gods were worshiped from ancient times, it is said. The path is now overgrown with grasses and brush, and hard to follow.

On the peak is a stone in which are carved the words Naeba Dai Gongen (The Holy Manifestation of Mount Naeba). The guide said these were not carved by human hands, but a natural phenomenon. Certainly this must be a local legend. As we looked about at this and that, the sun began to descend and we entered the hut. We lit lanterns inside and a fire outside, to cook another meal. As we ate and drank, we gazed at the moon, which on the sixth day of September was shining brightly in the sky and looked so close that it seemed we might reach out and break off a branch of the Katsura tree that is said to grow there. We composed Chinese and Japanese poems, and the time passed. Soon the cold had become quite fierce and penetrated even the heavily padded garments we had brought, so we edged close to the campfire, unable to sleep, waiting for the first rays of the dawn to break.

"It's time to worship the rising sun!" cried our guide at last, and we did as he said, bowing down before it. Then we made our preparations and descended from the peak. (I have written of this journey elsewhere in some detail. Here I present only an abbreviated version.)

Momoki adds: When I was in Echigo, heard about this mountain from Bokushi, and viewed some pictures of it, I came to the conclusion that long ago people lived on the mountaintop. After all, it has a plentiful source of water; and how else to account for the flat paddies and the artifacts at Dragon Cave? In ancient times, these people built rice fields on the peak and, relying on the narrow ridge of Umanose as their natural defense, settled and cultivated here. After they perished for some reason, their spirits remained and sustained these miraculous rice paddies of the peak. A search through national histories may turn up some further clues, and I await the opinions of scholars on the subject.

Snows of April and May

In our province, no rain falls in winter of course, and spring, too, is without rain until March. All this while, snow is falling in its stead. By midspring, showers begin to fall occasionally. Only at this time does the snow that has accumulated since last year begin to melt—on sunny days especially, but on windy and rainy days as well.

The northeast corner of the house is the last to thaw, and the mountain snows thaw later than those in the villages and towns. When the snows do begin at last to melt, the rivers all rise greatly, and there are floods year after year. Toward the end of the spring season, people begin to remove the snow from their houses, pushing it off and carrying it away in baskets, without waiting for the natural thaw.

As the snow begins to melt in May.

Some cut away the blocks of snow with saws and pile them up like timbers in a sunny place to melt. All of this is to hasten the departure of the snow. (Shallower patches of snow can be encouraged to melt by tossing earth or ashes on them.)

Since winter, clear, bright days have been rare, even when it did not snow. Buried as the houses are in snow, they are so dark it is hard to see even your hand in front of your face. Though we have been born and raised in this world and dwell here year after year, we still grow depressed and dazed buried under the snow, and it is not by any means pleasant. When, halfway through the spring, we clear away the snow and for the first time in months the sun's rays come flooding brilliantly into our lives, we feel as if we have come out at last into the human world again.

One summer I gave lodging to a poet on a pilgrimage from Edo. He asked me, "The gardens of the better-off families here show every sign that great pains are taken to make them attractive, but why is it that all the fences are so rough and shoddy?" "It's only natural that you should ask that. They are built that way because of the snow. No matter how strongly it is built, no fence can withstand the weight of twenty feet of snow, so they are built lightly and removed when the snow begins to fall. When April comes around, the first thing we do is to build fences again."

Since horses and oxen cannot walk through the snows, they must spend one hundred days out of the year imprisoned in their stalls. (In some parts of Echigo, only oxen are kept.) When the snow begins to melt, the horses sense it; they start to whinny eagerly at the thought of prancing down the roads again. When we lead them from the stables to stretch their cramped legs, they leap in the air in joy, and we ride them bareback, with only a belly strap, to a field where the snow has melted. Depending upon how they were cared for over the winter, some horses are lean and spare and others are fat and glossy. The poor means of their masters are apparent in the skinny horses.

Our children, too, have had little chance to play outside since the snow began to fall. At last, when summer approaches, they can put away their winter clogs and straw snowshoes and wear ordinary straw sandals, as they dash happily about flying kites and playing all sorts of games. The cherries and peaches begin to bloom now, too, and we in Echigo view these heavenly flowers against a fast fading blanket of snow.

The Crane's Gratitude

A crepe merchant from Ojiya by the name of Yoshisawaya Togoro (his pen name was Nimatsu) went on a business trip to the western provinces. While he was staying at a certain castle town, he heard this story from the master of his inn. It seems a certain farmer of that area found a sick crane in his fields. It was at the point of death, but he nursed it back to health with carrots that he had stored away as his winter provisions. In a few days, the crane recovered and flew away.

In November of the next year, two cranes suddenly came circling down near the yard of the same farmer's house, where they dropped two rice stalks, let out a cry in unison, and flew off again. The farmer picked the stalks up and examined them. They were more than six feet in length, and each ear bore four or five hundred grains of rice! The farmer immediately concluded that the crane he had saved the year before had come to show his gratitude by delivering this grain from some foreign land. "Whatever their source, these are marvelous rice ears," he thought, and decided to present them to the local lord.

After examining them, the lord returned them to the farmer and told him to plant and care for the grain. When the time came to start the rice seedlings he took great pains with them, and they grew into plants every bit as remarkable as those brought him by the crane. In the end, they were even offered to the ruler of the province.

Togoro asked the name of the village and the man, and it turned out to be a household that he had sold crepe to, so he went there and inquired about the matter in great detail. He asked for a grain or two of the rice as a token to bring back to his own province. The farmer had heard of Echigo's reputation as a famous rice-growing region and insisted Togoro take back fifty or sixty grains, telling him to plant them. Togoro carried his treasure home and presented it to our lord, relating the story of the fabulous grain. The lord had him plant it in the castle seedbeds, and rewarded Togoro richly— or so say the people of Ojiya when they speak of the incident.

It is only because I was blessed to be born in this time of peace that I, a humble farmer, am able to live a life of comfort and take up my brush as I have. With prayers, then, for another thousand years of peace, I put my brush to rest with this tale of the crane. Many are the strange stories of life in the snow, odd tales of all sorts of things, that I still could tell. And when I have time, in the bustle of life, I shall write another volume, someday.

Glossary

This glossary is meant to explain and identify persons, places, texts, and miscellaneous phenomena that crop up in the text of *Snow Country Tales*. The criteria for selecting the entries vary a bit from category to category. All texts mentioned by Bokushi and Momoki have been included, for example. Authors are identified, Japanese (and, when appropriate, Chinese) titles are supplied, and the content of the text is briefly described.

Place and personal names have been more rigorously winnowed. The rule for place names has been to include primarily those which: (1) have been renamed or have ceased to exist; (2) have undergone a change in pronunciation since Bokushi's day and therefore might not be recognized or may be thought to be mistaken; and (3) are of intrinsic interest because of the role they play in the *Tales*. Many of the places in the last category are in a different administrative category than they were in Bokushi's day. For example, villages have become sections of larger towns and towns have become sections of cities. The modern locations (unless otherwise specified, all are in Niigata Prefecture) are given to help the reader who wishes to trace the locales into the present, along with the suffixes *-gun* (county), *-shi* (city), *-mura* (village), *-machi* (or *-cho,* town), and *-oaza* or *-aza* (large section or section of a village), hyphenated as in the accepted system for romanizing Japanese addresses.

The criterion for personal names has been to include those of figures about whom more is known than Bokushi provides in the text. The reader who wants to know more about the farmer Souemon ("A Two-headed Snake"), for example, will be disappointed: we know nothing; and though we know a considerable amount about Priest Kochi, Bokushi tells it all in the tale of his mummy, so Kochi isn't listed here either. Some Japanese

GLOSSARY

names have variant readings. All names appear in the form given by Bokushi in his text: Fujiwara Karyu, for example, rather than Fujiwara Ietaka—though alternative readings are given when appropriate. Bokushi is inconsistent in his use of the particle *no* in the names of ancient figures, and I have followed his usage. Figures to whom Bokushi refers by their pen names appear under the pen names, and the surname and personal names are given when known. People referred to by a title, such as Abbot Hokko or Lord Teika, are found under that title, not the name. The dates of birth and death of all figures are given when they are known.

Miscellaneous information has been included whenever it was thought that information would increase understanding and appreciation of the text. The glossary entry appears in the form found in the text, or one very similar.

Besides the standard reference materials, I am indebted to the authors of the Nojima Shuppan annotated edition of *Hokuetsu Seppu,* in particular Keiryu Inoue and Minoru Takahashi, who worked on the notes to that edition. I have relied heavily on their impressive efforts, especially with regard to local history.

Abbot Hokko (1506–86). Born in Ushu (another name for the combined area of the provinces of Ugo and Uzen, modern Akita and Yamagata prefectures), Hokko traveled throughout Japan before settling at the Undoan. He gained the patronage of the famous warlord Takeda Shingen (1521–73), ruler of Shinano (modern Nagano Prefecture), and established the Ryuunji temple in that province.

Abbot Shitchu. Zentei (d. 1824). The fourteenth head priest of Tenshoji temple in Omoigawa. He was Bokushi's maternal uncle. "Shitchu" also refers to quarters near the main hall of the temple; priests were frequently known by the name of the quarters they occupied.

Abbot Tsuten. Reputed to have been the grandfather of Uesugi Kenshin (1530–78), the medieval daimyo who ruled the Echigo region. He was given his religious name and the purple robes of the clergy by Emperor Ogimachi (r. 1557–86).

Abe Uemon no Jo. Abe Masakichi (d. 1582). A general who served under Uesugi Kenshin (1530–78) and died in battle.

Agatsuma County. Modern Yame-gun, Fukuoka Prefecture.

Agon Kyo. The Chinese recension of a group of texts of early Buddhism known as the Agamas in Mahayana Buddhism and the Nikayas in Theravada Buddhism. They were once thought to record the original teachings

GLOSSARY

of the Buddha, but in fact date from a considerably later period, when the Buddhist religion had already split into various sects. Still, they present the core teachings of the religion.

Aiba, Master. *See* Master Aiba.

Aka River. Now called the Aganogawa, or Agano River.

Akazuka Village. Now Akazuka in Niigata-shi.

Akiyama. The villages of Akiyama that Bokushi identifies as located in Echigo—Shimizukawara, Mikura, Nakanotaira, Oakasawa, Amasake, Shimoketto, Sakamaki (an error for Sakasamaki), Kamiketto, and Maekura—are all found in Tsunan-machi, Naka Uonuma-gun, with the exception of Amasake, which is actually in Nagano Prefecture. The Shinano (Nagano) villages—Koakasawa, Uenohara, Wayama, Oakiyama, Yashiki, Yumoto, and Amasake (mentioned above)—are located in Sakaemura, Shimominochi-gun, Nagano Prefecture.

Almanac. Saiji Ki. A catalogue of annual events and ceremonies, ancient historical anecdotes, animals, birds, fish, and plants divided into the months they occur in or are associated with, by the Confucian scholar Kaibara Ekiken (1630–1714). *See also* Master Kaibara.

Almanac of Poetry, The. Haikai Saijiki. A collection of over 2,600 poetic phrases associated with the various seasons of the year, published by Takizawa Bakin (1767–1848) in 1803. Bokushi's reference is somewhat ambiguous. He may be referring to the genre of poetry almanacs in general, but given his correspondence with Bakin, it is also possible that he chose to mention the latter's work specifically.

Amasake Village. *See* Akiyama.

Amida Buddha (Skt., Amitabha, Amitayus). The Buddha who presides over the Pure Land of the West, which he created by perfecting the vows he made as a bodhisattva. One of those vows was to enlighten all beings who heard his name, thought of him, and wished to achieve enlightenment. This is the basis of the practice of nembutsu, or thinking of the Buddha. *See also* nembutsu; Pure Land.

Anju, Princess. *See* Princess Anju and Prince Zuiomaru.

Annals of Nintoku, The. Nintoku Ki. A portion of *The Chronicles of Japan* (*Nihon Shoki*) recording the events of Emperor Nintoku's reign (313–99). There is a mention of ice from an ice chamber presented by an imperial prince to Emperor Nintoku in the sixty-first year of his reign. *See also Chronicles of Japan, The.*

annals of the Ise clan. The Ise clan served the shogunate in a ceremonial capacity during the Muromachi (1392–1568) and Edo (1600–1868) periods, and in the writings on etiquette by several high-ranking Ise officials, mention can be found of Echigo cloth as the proper summer dress for samurai.

Another Hundred Verses. Soto Hyaku Ban, a sequel to *One Hundred Verses (Uchi Hyaku Ban)*, a seventeenth-century collection of lyrics. Anonymous.

Arakawa Village. Now Arakawa, Shibata-shi.

Bando Hikasaburo (IV; 1800–73). A Kabuki actor active in the 1830s and 1840s in Edo.

Basho. Matsuo Basho (1644–94). The great haiku poet, essayist, and travel diarist who contributed enormously to the perfection of the haiku and *haibun* genres. He passed through Echigo on his famous journey through northern Japan recorded in *Narrow Road to the Deep North (Oku no Hosomichi)*. There is no poem about Kiso by Basho (or any other poet) with the lines Bokushi quotes in "Ancient Ways of Akiyama." A similar poem about Sarubashi in Yamanashi Prefecture contains the lines about the teetering butterflies, but it was not composed by Basho. On the section concerning Sarutobi Bridge in his *Record of a Journey to Akiyama (Akiyama Kiko)*, Bokushi cites a different poem, this time by Basho and set in Kiso: "On the log bridge / My life entwined / By twisting wisteria vines." The poems mentioned by Bokushi in "Poems in Basho's Hand" are Basho's, though the poem Bokushi claims was composed at Teradomari was actually written after Basho had passed through that town.

Bien He (J., Hen Ka). A man of the kingdom of Chu during the Spring and Autumn Annals period (722–481 B.C.). His story is told in *Han Fei Zi* and is often quoted in Japanese works such as *Tales of Now and Then (Konjaku Monogatari)*, *The Record of Great Peace (Taiheiki)*, and *The Illustrated Encyclopedia of China and Japan (Wakan San Sai Zue)*. He found an unpolished gem in the mountains and presented it to the king, who refused to recognize its worth and ordered Bien He's left leg cut off. When the king's successor ascended the throne, Bien He once more presented the gem, and the new king ordered his right leg cut off. Finally, Bien He presented the stone to the second king's successor. This monarch polished the stone and found it to be the gem Bien He claimed it was from the start. This same stone later came into the possession of the King of Zhao and became known as the gem of Zhao.

Biographies of Illustrious Monks. Gao Seng Chuan (J., *Ko So Den*). This collection of biographies of the eminent monks of China in fourteen volumes was composed by the monk Hui Jiao (497–554). It spans 453 years, from

GLOSSARY

67 to 519, and is a widely quoted source in Chinese and Japanese literature.

Bishamon. Bishamonten (Skt., Vaisravana). One of the four guardian kings, in particular the guardian of the northern direction. Though Bishamon was, along with the other guardian kings, a fierce, martial deity, he was also regarded as a bestower of wealth, which may explain the role he plays in the ceremony of the hall-pushing at Urasa.

Bokusai. Miya Jihei, an otherwise unidentified friend of Bokushi who lived in Horinouchi.

Book of Changes, The. Yi Jing (J., *Shu Eki*). The ancient Chinese classic of yin-yang divination, thought to date from the Zhou dynasty (1122–255 B.C.).

Book of Songs, The. Shi Jing (J., *Shi Kyo*). One of the Five Confucian Classics, this compilation of 305 ancient poems and lyrics dates from the tenth to the seventh century B.C.

Bosai. Kameda Bosai (1752–1826). Born in Kozuke (modern Gumma Prefecture), he became a renowned Confucian scholar and calligrapher of Edo. At the invitation of his disciples, he spent two years in the Echigo region, from 1823 to 1825.

Bright Moon Diary. Meigetsu Ki. The diary of Fujiwara Teika (also, Sadaie; 1162–1241), one of Japan's greatest classical poets. The text in its extant form begins in 1180 and continues until 1235. Bokushi seems to be in error regarding the year in which the event he quotes took place: according to the *Diary*, it occurred in 1202, not 1204. *See also* Lord Teika.

Broken Mirror Picture Scroll, The. Kagamiwari no Emaki. An illustrated scroll of the Muromachi (1392–1568) period, also known as *Kagamiwari no Okina Ekotoba* and *Kagami Otoko no Emaki*. In fact, the story told in this picture scroll is not set in Echigo but in Omi (modern Shiga Prefecture), and Bokushi seems to be confusing this work with another, later recension of the story, *The Gift of a Mirror* (*Miyage no Kagami*).

Chain of Stories from a North Window, A. Hokuso Sadan. A two-part, eight-volume collection of miscellaneous essays about things past and present published by Tachibana Shunki (1753–1805) in 1829. *See also* Shunki.

Chiharu. Takashima Chiharu (1777–1859). A painter of the Tosa school. Born in Osaka, he resided in both Kyoto and Edo and was known for his interest in paintings in ancient and classical styles.

Chikuma River. An archaic name for the Shinano River.

Chotokuji. A local legend of Echigo tells of a monk of great strength who

GLOSSARY

resided at the Chotokuji temple in Yokotomura (now Yokodo, Katahigashimura, Nishi Kambara-gun) during the 1760s and 1770s. Head monks were often known by the name of their temple.

Chronicles of Japan, The. Nihongi or *Nihon Shoki*. The first of the official "histories" (it also contains much mythology) of ancient Japan, it was completed in 720. In thirty volumes, it relates the history of Japan from its earliest beginnings up to 697, the end of the reign of Emperor Jito.

Chujo Village. Now Chujo-machi, Kita Kambara-gun.

Classic of the Way, The. Dao De Jing; also known as *Laozi* and *Laozi Jing* (J., *Do Toku Kyo; Roshi; Roshi Kyo*). This famous work by the ancient Chinese philosopher Laozi, traditionally considered the founder of the Taoist religion and philosophy, has been translated into English countless times under a variety of titles. The date of composition is problematic, but most agree it is a very early work. The earliest sections may date from the fourth century B.C., though the text in its present form is thought to be from the second century B.C. *See also* Laozi.

Cloud-Essence Annals, The. Unkon Shi. The gem collector Kiuchi Sekitei (1724–1808) composed this fifteen-volume encyclopedia of minerals and gems from 1773 through 1801. The reference to fox jewels appears in the first volume of part two of the work, where they are described as beautiful white gems that shine in the dark. *See also* Sekitei.

Codes of the Engi Era, The. Engi Shiki. A fifty-volume work whose compilation began in 905 of the Engi era (901–23) and continued until 927. It includes law codes, details of court ceremonies, and Shinto observances and prayers.

Collection of Chinese Characters, The. Zi Hui (J., *Ji I*). A twelve-volume dictionary by Mei Yingzuo of the Ming dynasty (1368–1644), the first Chinese dictionary to order characters by stroke count.

Collection of Curiosities, A. Kotto Shu. Published in 1813 by Santo Kyoden (1761–1816), this collection of essays in three volumes discusses ancient customs, dress, utensils, and foods. *See also* Hermit Santo.

Collection of Everyday Expressions, A. Kagaku Shu. Composed in 1444 by Toroku Hano, who may have been the head monk of the Kenninji in Kyoto. Organized under eighteen different headings by content, it is thought to be an antecedent to *A Collection of Handy Phrases*.

Collection of Foolish Scribblings. Shui Gu So. A four-volume collection of the poetry of Fujiwara Teika (1162–1241). Of the 3,829 poems included, the first was composed when he was twenty and the last when he was seventy-two. *See also* Lord Teika.

Collection of Handy Phrases, A. Setsuyo Shu. This remarkable dictionary remained in use (though it went through many editions and revisions) for nearly four hundred years, from its creation in the late fifteenth century to the late nineteenth century. It was so widely used because it was one of the few dictionaries of colloquial Japanese and because of its "alphabetic" *iroha* arrangement—in fact, it is thought to be the first dictionary to adopt that organizing principle. Bokushi identifies Hayashi Soji (1498–1581) as its author, but this is impossible, since Hayashi was born two years after the dated preface to the work was composed. Some suggest that either a Hayashi Soji of an earlier generation composed the work or that Hayashi revised someone else's composition. *See also* Hayashi Soji.

Collection of Ten Thousand Leaves, A. Manyoshu. The earliest extant collection of Japanese poetry. It contains over 4,500 poems in twenty volumes. The earliest poems are thought to date from the fourth century and the most recent one is from 759.

cormorant fisher's song. A reference to the Noh play *Ukai (The Cormorant Fisher)*, which relates the story of a cormorant fisherman who is condemned to hell because he earned his livelihood by taking life. He is saved by an itinerant priest who heeds the plea of his spirit to pray for his repose.

Crevice Mountain. J., Waremekiyama, also Warimekiyama. Though the exact identification of this rocky peak is uncertain, Bokushi may be describing Tengu Rock northeast of modern Shimizu, Shiozawa-machi, Minami Uonuma-gun.

Customs of Japan, The. Ripen Fengto Ji (J., *Nihon Fudo Ki*). This five-volume work was completed around 1592 by the Ming-dynasty (1368–1644) Chinese Hou Jigao and describes Japanese geography, customs, and culture.

Daikoku. Daikokuten (Skt., Mahakala). One of the seven gods of good luck in Japan, in India, where he originated, Daikoku was a god of darkness and, later, a martial guardian deity of the Buddhist religion. Traces of his warlike nature remained in China, but by the time he entered popular faith in Japan he had come to be thought of as a god of wealth, particularly rich harvests. He is usually depicted standing on two bales of rice with a sack over his shoulder and a magic, wish-granting mallet in his hand. A rat sits by his side. He was associated with Ebisu, another god of plenty, and like Ebisu was worshiped in farming households as a kitchen god, which is no doubt why the children of Echigo built shrines to him in their snow houses. *See also* Ebisu.

Daiten, Reverend. *See* Reverend Daiten.

GLOSSARY

Date Masamune (1567–1636). Date became the daimyo of Sendai toward the end of his illustrious career as a warrior, during which he served both Toyotomi Hideyoshi (1536–98) and Tokugawa Ieyasu (1542–1616). He was also known for his interest in the tea ceremony, painting, and poetry.

Deep Blue Memory Jewel of All Things, The. Shiwu Ganzhu (J. *Jibutsu Kanshu*). A forty-six volume (Bokushi's claim of twenty-four volumes is mistaken) encyclopedia compiled by Huang Yizheng of the Ming dynasty (1368–1644).

Dewa Province. Modern Yamagata and Akita prefectures.

dharma-lineage certificate. A sort of Buddhist "family tree" showing the transmission of the teachings of a certain sect of the religion from master to disciple over the generations.

Diary of Ben no Naishi, The. Ben no Naishi no Nikki. In two volumes, this diary by a court lady of the Kamakura period (1185–1333) begins in 1246 and continues until 1252. It includes many poems as well as descriptions of court ritual.

Dictionary. Gaku Go Hen. A two-volume dictionary by Reverend Daiten, the monk Kenjo (1719–1801), published in 1772. See also Reverend Daiten.

Dictionary of Japanese Readings, The. Wa Kun Kan, according to Bokushi; also *Wa Kun no Shiori.* A ninety-three-volume dictionary of Chinese characters that provides their Japanese readings, literary examples, and colloquial expressions, arranged in Japanese alphabetic order. Compiled by Tanigawa Kotosuga (1709–76), it was published after his death in 1776. See also Tanigawa Kotosuga.

Doctor Rai. Rai Sanyo (1781–1832). A Confucian scholar, historian, and poet. Born into a commoner's family, he eventually made a life for himself as an independent (that is, not affiliated with any fief) scholar, writer, and teacher based in Kyoto. He is known as one of Japan's finest poets in the Chinese language and as the author of an important history of Japan, *Nihon Gaishi*.

Ebisu. One of the seven gods of good luck, Ebisu can be traced back to the "leech child" of the ancestral couple, Izanami and Izanagi, who was cast afloat on the sea. In turn, Ebisu (the origin of the name is problematic) became the god of the sea and its riches. He is usually depicted carrying a fishing pole in one hand and a sea bream in the other. The first catch of the season was traditionally presented to Ebisu. He became by extension a god of prosperity and success in business. In farming communities he was worshiped as a god of the kitchen, and in the latter two roles he was frequently paired with Daikoku. It is his association with the house and

GLOSSARY

the kitchen that led him to be venerated in the snow houses Echigo children built. *See also* Daikoku.

Edo. Modern Tokyo. Edo was the capital of Japan throughout the Tokugawa period (1600–1868).

Eikokuji temple. An error for the Yokokuji temple, founded in 1504 and located in Mitono, Muramatsu-machi, Naka Kambara-gun.

Etchu Province. Modern Toyama Prefecture.

exorcists (*yakuharai*). It was the custom for beggars and itinerant entertainers to make the rounds of houses on certain days—the New Year and the holiday called Setsubun, in particular—and chant felicitous phrases such as "*Yakuharai, yakuharai*" ("Shake off impurities, shake off impurities") in exchange for donations.

Ezo. The ancient name for Hokkaido.

Five Miscellanies, The. Wu Zazu (J., *Go Zasso*). Xie Zhaozhi of the Ming dynasty (1368–1644) composed this sixteen-volume work which is divided into five sections, one each on heaven, earth, man, things, and events. *See also* Xie Zhaozhi.

Food Classic, The. Both the work and its author are unknown. The reference may be to a Chinese work, in which case the title would be *Shi Jing* and the author's name Cui Yuxi. Sai Useki is the Japanese reading of the author's name, and I have used it in the text as the most reliable information we have.

Forty-Seven Loyal Retainers, The. Kanadehon Chushingura. One of the classics of the Japanese traditional stage, both in the puppet theater and Kabuki. Based on historical fact, but transposed into the past to bypass government censorship, it relates the story of the revenge of forty-seven samurai against the villain who unjustly caused the death of the daimyo they served. The play remains popular today and is as central to Japanese culture as *Hamlet* is to the English-speaking world.

Fujiwara Karyu (1158–1237). Usually Fujiwara Ietaka. One of the compilers of the eighth imperial poetry anthology, *The New Collection of Poetry Ancient and Modern* (*Shin Kokin Waka Shu*), in which forty-three of his own poems were included. He was a pupil of Fujiwara Toshinari (also Shunzei; 1114–1204) and Fujiwara Teika (also Sadaie; 1162–1241) and one of the outstanding poets of the age.

Fujiwara Tamekane. Kyogyoku Toshinari (1254–1332). The great-grandson of Fujiwara Teika (also Sadaie; 1162–1241), he is more commonly known by the name Kyogyoku than Fujiwara. Implicated in a conspiracy plot, he was banished to the island of Sado off the coast of Echigo in 1298.

GLOSSARY

Later he was pardoned and returned to Kyoto to compile *The Jewel Leaf Collection* (*Gyoku Yo Shu*). His authorship of the poem Bokushi cites, however, is doubtful. It doesn't appear in any collections of Kyogyoku's poetry. See also *Jewel Leaf Collection, The.*

Fujiwara Teika. *See* Lord Teika.

Fujiwara Tokihira (871–909). Also Shihei. As minister of the left at the Heian court, he was locked in a power struggle with Sugawara Michizane (845–903), who was banished to Dazaifu in Kyushu at Tokihira's urging. In popular literature, particularly the puppet and Kabuki theaters, Tokihira is depicted as a villain who received his just deserts when Michizane, transformed into a god after his death in exile, struck Tokihira dead with a bolt of lightning.

Fujiwara Toshinari (1114–1204). Also Shunzei. One of the major poets and poetry critics of the twelfth century and the father of Fujiwara Teika (also Sadaie; 1162–1241). He compiled the seventh imperial poetry anthology, *The Poetry Collection of a Thousand Years* (*Senzai Waka Shu*). See also *Poetry (Collection) of a Thousand Years, The.*

Fusekishi. Kuraishi Kenzan (1799–1869). From Takata, he excelled at poetry and painting.

Futai Peak. Now Futai, Mikuni-aza, Yuzawa-machi, Minami Uonuma-gun.

Gankyo. *See* Iwabuchi Gankyo.

Genji clan. Also known as the Minamoto, this was one of the two warrior clans that came to power in the twelfth century. Like their rivals the Heike (also, Taira) clan, they were descended from the imperial line. Genji forces led by Minamoto Yoritomo (1147–99) defeated the Heike in the Gempei War (1180–85) and founded the Kamakura Bakufu (1185–1333) in the city of that name in eastern Japan, the traditional power base of the Genji. The Genji was a large clan with several distinct branches, and leaders of later Japanese military governments, including the Ashikaga, Muromachi, and Tokugawa shogunates, all claimed Genji descent.

Gennai. *See* Hiraga Kyukei.

Geno, High Priest. *See* High Priest Geno.

Gochi Nyorai temple. The Gochi Kokubunji temple in Joetsu-shi.

God of Straw Sandals. The passage from *The Five Miscellanies* reports that the amusing tale of the God of Straw Sandals began when someone happened to hang a pair of old straw sandals on the limb of a tree. Others imitated his action and the tree was eventually covered with thousands of pairs of sandals. A certain fellow then laughingly called the shoe-laden

GLOSSARY

tree the God of Straw Sandals, after which a shrine was built beneath the tree and the whole was regarded as a great supernatural wonder.

god of the year. The god who represents the lucky direction of the New Year. A shrine shelf is hung in that corner of the house and offerings set on it.

gorinsho. According to *The Chronicles of Japan (Nihon Shoki),* the Sun Goddess Amaterasu ordered her grandson Ninigi no Mikoto to descend to earth carrying grains of rice from the heavenly rice fields. He descended to Mount Takachiho in Hyuga, usually identified as being in Kyushu. Thus he bestowed rice on the world, bringing fertility to the earth just as the shrine's messenger bestows the blossom-water on the married couple, bringing fertility to their union. The male and female deities Sarutahiko and Ame no Uzume no Mikoto (Usume) played an important part in Ninigi no Mikoto's descent, and they are included in the Blossom-Water Festival as well. *See also* Sarutahiko; Usume.

Go Shummei. Igarashi Shummei (1700–81). Born into the Sano family of Niigata, he was orphaned in childhood and adopted by the Igarashi family. He went to Kyoto as a youth and studied Chinese poetry. Later he journeyed to Edo and studied Kano-school painting. He worked primarily in the Chinese manner and he was honored with a request to present his work to the shogunate.

Goya Village. Probably an error for Yago Village, now Yago, Tsuchitaru-aza, Yuzawa-machi, Minami Uonuma-gun.

Gozan. Koshigaya Gozan (1717–87). Born into a wealthy farming family in Musashino (modern Saitama Prefecture), Gozan became a poet in Edo. He is known for compiling the first dictionary of regional Japanese, published in 1775.

Grains of Sand from the Sea of Words. Wen Hai Pi Sha (J., *Bun Kai Hi Sha*). By Xie Zhaozhi of the Ming dynasty (1368–1644), this eight-volume work records stories of oddities and strange occurrences.

Grass Hut Collection. Soan Shu. A compilation of the work of the poet-monk Tona (1289–1372), published in ten volumes in 1359. *See also* Tona.

Great Learning, The. Da Xue (J., *Dai Gaku*). One of the Confucian classics, included in the Four Books, the core of the Confucian canon. The date of its compilation is uncertain but has been estimated as between 500 and 200 B.C. Only in the ninth century A.D. did it come to have importance as an independent Confucian text, but from that time it was very popular in both China and Japan.

Great Record of the Taiping Era, The. Taiping Guang Ji (J., *Taihei Ko Ki*). A five-hundred-volume collection of traditional anecdotes, tales, and

GLOSSARY

historical accounts compiled during the Song dynasty (960–1126) by Li Fangdeng. *See also* Li Fangdeng.

Great Shrine. *See* Ise Shrine.

Gyokoji. Local legend has it that during the 1660s and 1670s there was a head monk of the Gyokoji temple in Tanne Village (now Tanne, Kashiwazaki-shi) who was so strong that he once separated two battling oxen. The same monk was said to have been able to walk eighty-five miles easily in a single day. Head monks were often referred to by the name of their temple.

Gyokuzan. Okada Gyokuzan (1737–1812). A painter from Osaka, he corresponded with Bokushi and encouraged him to have *Snow Country Tales* published. His artistic name Gyokuzan means jewel mountain, which is the inspiration for Bokushi's pun, "a flaw in the jewel of Gyokuzan's reputation." Gyokuzan was said to be particularly skilled at the detailed underpaintings for woodblocks, and he was a prolific illustrator. His masterpiece, an illustrated version of the tale and drama *Taikoki (Account of the Great Uprising)* was published in installments from 1797 to 1802 and banned by the shogunate in 1804 for violating the proscriptions against depicting certain historical figures.

Hachiman. A martial deity whose origins are unclear. As early as the Nara period (646–794) he was regarded as a protector of Buddhism. From the Heian period (794–1180) he was identified as the deification of the legendary emperor Ojin (r. 270–310 B.C.). He was later adopted by the Minamoto (Genji) clan as their clan god. The main shrine dedicated to Hachiman in eastern Japan is the Tsurugaoka Hachiman Shrine in Kamakura.

Hair Mound of Sekiyama Village. A grave mound in a cemetery in Sekiyama, Shiozawa-machi, Minami Uonuma-gun.

Hangaku. A woman of the Jo clan based at Torisakayama Castle in Kaji. The aunt of Jo no Sukemori, she is said to have helped to defend the castle against the forces sent by Minamoto Yoriie (1182–1204) and led by Sasaki Moritsuna that attacked the Jo clan in 1201. She adopted the dress of a young boy and fought fiercely from the lookout tower, for she was an excellent archer. Hangaku was captured and taken to Kamakura, but she refused to ask for pardon. Her bravery provoked the loyal warrior Asari Gien to ask permission to take her as his wife (her husband had died in the battle). When Yoriie inquired why Asari should want a traitress for his wife, Asari replied that she would bear brave, martial sons to defend Yoriie's reign. In *The Mirror of the East* (*Azuma Kagami*), Hangaku is iden-

GLOSSARY

tified as Jo no Sukemori's married aunt. No other source gives her birthplace as Koshi. *See also* Torisakayama Castle.

Han Yu (768–824; J., Kan Yu). A scholar, philosopher, writer, poet, and official of the Tang dynasty (618–907). He is most renowned for his advocacy of the use of free-style prose writing *(san wen)* to replace the restrictive, formulaic, rhymed verse *(pian wen)* that had been in use since the Six Dynasties period (420–589), and it was largely through his considerable influence that it became the standard form of written Chinese and remained so until the Cultural Revolution. He was also a staunch Confucian and a sharp critic of Buddhism and Taoism.

Harumatsu the tofu vendor. According to local records, Harumatsu was awarded three pieces of silver in 1805 for his filial service to his father and his devotion to his children after the death of his wife. There is no Tsukahara in Echigo; other sources point to Katsurazuka in Kita Kambara-gun as the place Harumatsu lived.

Hatsugimi. The courtesan is mentioned in the preface to the poem attributed to her in *The Jewel Leaf Collection*. *See also* Fujiwara Tamekane; *Jewel Leaf Collection, The*.

Hayashi Soji (1498–1581). Born into a long-established merchant family that sold *manju* (bean-paste filled buns), he studied poetry with the Muromachi-period (1392–1568) *renga* (linked verse) poet Shohaku (1443–1527) and was an accomplished poet himself. He could not have written *A Collection of Handy Phrases,* since its preface is dated two years prior to his birth. Some suggest that either it was composed by the Hayashi Soji of the previous generation (it was a common practice to pass names along from father to son) or that this Hayashi Soji edited or supplemented an earlier work by an unidentified author.

Heike clan. Also known as the Taira, this was one of the two great warrior clans that came to the fore in the twelfth century. The Heike were an offshoot of the imperial line. They came to be based in eastern Japan, and first acted as constables for the Fujiwara family. Gradually they usurped more and more control of the government until Taira Kiyomori (1118–1181) became prime minister and effective ruler of Japan. In 1180, however, the rival Genji clan rose in revolt and triumphed in the Gempei War (1180–85) that followed. All the major figures of the Heike clan were killed, including Kiyomori's grandson, the infant Emperor Antoku (r. 1180–83). There are many legends akin to that of Akiyama telling of Heike survivors tucked away here and there in inaccessible parts of Japan, but the facts are less romantic. Provincial Heike families continued to play important roles locally and the Hojo family, who led the Kamakura

GLOSSARY

shogunate (1185–1333) founded by the Genji rival Minamoto Yoritomo (1147–99) after his death, claimed Heike descent. *The Tale of the Heike* (*Heike Monogatari*) is a classic of Japanese literature that relates the story of the declining years of the clan.

Hell Valley. Now Jigokudani, Sakuramachi-aza, Ojiya-shi. Natural gas deposits are still plentiful here.

hellwagon (*kasha*). In Buddhist mythology, a hellwagon driven by demons comes to the sinner's deathbed to cart him or her to hell. At an early period, however, a cat-demon came to be associated with the occasion and name of the hellwagon, replacing the original image in popular belief. The *kasha* demon was thought to descend on the coffin during the funeral procession, tear it open, and make off with the corpse.

Herbal Encyclopedia, The. Bencao Gangmu (J., *Honzo Komoku*). Li Shizhen completed this fifty-two volume work in 1578. It is mainly a herbal, but also includes sections on mankind, animals, and nonorganic materials. In Japan it became the central text of the disciplines of herbal medicine and natural science.

Hermit Konron. Tachibana Shigetsugu. Little is known of him except that he was the author of *Strange Tales of North Etsu*. See also *Strange Tales of North Etsu*.

Hermit of Komagai. Makinoshima Terutake. A scholar of the classics active from the late seventeenth to the mid-eighteenth century. He composed stories relating events at court and military annals. See also *Reference of Works, Words, and Characters, A*.

Hermit Santo. Santo Kyoden; also Iwase Samuru, Iwase Denzo (1761–1816). The son of an Edo pawnbroker, his family moved from Fukagawa to Ginza when he was very young. While running a tobacco shop there he also pursued a career as a writer of comic and satirical fiction, popular stories, and as a woodblock-print artist (the latter under the name Kitao Masanobu). His writings earned him great popularity, but also drew the censure of the shogunate, and he was fined and otherwise punished on several occasions for violating censorship regulations. So devoted was he to literature that, it is said, his death was brought on by an attack of apoplexy after a vigorous debate with acquaintances on that subject. It was to him that Bokushi first brought his writings on Echigo, and Kyoden's younger brother Kyozan (1767–1858) became Bokushi's editor after Kyoden's death. *See also* Kyozan.

Hida Province. Now the northern portion of Gifu Prefecture.

High Priest Geno. Geno Shinsho (1326–96). A high-ranking Zen monk of the Soto sect. He entered Buddhist orders at eighteen. In his subsequent

316

travels around Japan he received the patronage of local rulers and the people and founded many temples, eventually gaining the support of the shogun Ashikaga Yoshimitsu (1358–1408). He is widely known for destroying "the killer stone of Nasuno." This stone was thought to harm any living creature that came near it. Geno smashed it with his Buddhist staff while reciting a verse.

Hiraga Kyukei. Hiraga Gennai (1728?–80). A multitalented figure who not only invented asbestos cloth but was also a doctor, a specialist in herbal medicine and natural science, a scholar of the classics, a playwright, and a comic writer. Born in Sanuki (modern Kagawa Prefecture), he came to Edo at the age of twenty-six. Of samurai birth, he left his official employment to pursue his many interests. Initially he met with great success, but eventually he grew greatly frustrated with the strictures of his feudal society. He died in prison, where he was being held after killing one of his disciples with a sword in a fit of madness.

Historical Maps of the Provinces of China. Morokoshi Rekidai Shugun Enkaku Chizu. A 1789 Japanese edition of twelve historical maps of China.

Hitachi Province. Modern Ibaraki Prefecture.

Hokko, Abbot. *See* Abbot Hokko.

Hokuyo, Master. *See* Master Hokuyo.

Honen (1133–1212). The founder of the Pure Land (Jodo) sect in Japan. Honen spent most of his life in the vicinity of Kyoto, except for a ten-month period of exile in Shikoku that began in March 1207. There is no evidence that he ever traveled to Echigo. *See also* Shinran, who was one of his leading disciples.

Horinouchi District. An area including twenty-nine villages centered around Horinouchi, now Horinouchi-machi, Kita Uonuma-gun.

Hosoi Shoan. Actually, Hosokawa Shoan (fl. eighteenth century). Bokushi has mistaken both his surname and his literary name, which was Tosetsu, not Toun. According to one account of his life, he was the son of a fief doctor and became one himself, in the employ of the Matsudaira clan. He was also a devoted student of the classics and enjoyed literary pursuits, particularly poetry. He is said to have treated Basho for an illness that afflicted the latter on his journey through northern Japan. This provided an occasion for the exchange of poems recorded by Bokushi. A conflicting account claims that he was in fact a town doctor by the name of Kumakura.

Hui, King. *See* King Hui of Zhao.

Hundred Verses of Emperor Horikawa's Reign, A. Horikawa Hyakushu. The poem cited by Bokushi is not found there but in *One Hundred Verses of 1116*

GLOSSARY

(*Eikyu Yonen Hyakushu*), compiled by retainers of Emperor Horikawa (r. 1086–1107). The verse in question refers not to Echigo but to Echizen (modern Fukui Prefecture), where Arachiyama (Mount Arachi) is located.

Hyuga Province. Modern Miyazaki Prefecture.

Ichiemon. Fukuhara Ichiemon (d. 1837). Nothing more is known of him except that he was Bokushi's host when he visited Koakasawa in Akiyama and that he owned the largest house there.

Ichifuri Village. Now in Omi-machi, Nishi Kubiki-gun.

Ichikawa Danjuro V (1741–1806). Active in the 1790s, he was a talented player of women's roles and a gifted playwright.

Ichinomiya Village. Now Ichinomiya, Sakuramachi-aza, Ojiya-shi.

Igarashi Village. Now Sekiyama, Shiozawa-machi, Minami Uonuma-gun.

Iizuka Tomoyoshi (1764–1840). A wealthy farmer of Shindo Village who was fond of poetry.

Ikedani Village. Now Ikedani, Tokamachi-shi.

Illustrated Encyclopedia of China and Japan, The. Wakan San Sai Zue. The preface of the 105-volume work is dated 1712. It was compiled by Terashima Ryoan (fl. early eighteenth century) in imitation of the illustrated Chinese encyclopedia *San Cai Tuhui.* See also *Illustrated Three Levels, The.*

Illustrated Three Levels, The. San Cai Tuhui (J., *San Sai Zue*). An encyclopedia-like work in 106 volumes consisting of illustrations gathered from a variety of sources. There are three main divisions, or "levels," heaven, earth, and man, and fourteen subcategories. Compiled by Wang Qi of the Ming dynasty (1368–1644) the work has a preface dated 1607.

Illustrations of Snowflakes. Sekka Zusetsu. By Doi Toshitsura (Lord Kyoroku; 1789–1848) and his retainer Takami Tadatsuna, compiled after twenty years of observing the shapes of snowflakes and finally published in 1832. Some ninety-eight illustrations of snowflakes are included in the work. *See also* Lord Kyoroku.

Imamachi Village. Now Imamachi, Mitsuke-shi.

Inakura Village. Now divided into Kami Inakura and Shimo Inakura, Horinouchi-machi, Kita Uonuma-gun.

Iosan Beisanji temple. This was the inclusive name for all the temples on the mountain. Once there was a flourishing complex at the foot of the mountain as well, near Kakizaki, but it exists no longer. The Yakushi Hall is administered by a temple of the Shingon sect in Kakizaki.

Ise Shrine. The ancient shrine dedicated to Amaterasu, the Sun Goddess. It is located at Ise in Mie Prefecture.

GLOSSARY

Ishiuchi Myojin Shrine. Now known by the name Zuitama Shrine, it is located in Chiyagawa, Ojiya-shi.

Itoikawa Castle Town. Now Itoigawa-shi.

Iwabuchi Gankyo. Identified by Kyozan as the eldest son of Iwabuchi Iinosuke of Ojiya. Kyozan says that Gankyo is twenty-four or twenty-five, the same age as Kyozan's son Kyosui, but the family register of the Iwabuchi family lists no male of that age. Iinosuke's oldest son, Ugoro, was thirty-eight at the time of Kyozan's visit.

Iwai Tamanojo. Perhaps a punning reference to Iwai Hanshiro, the hereditary name of ten generations of Kabuki actors. From the fourth Iwai Hanshiro (1747–1800), the actors of this name were known for their excellence in women's roles. This passage probably refers to Iwai Hanshiro V, who was extremely popular at this time.

Iyahiko no Yashiro shrine. Located in Yahiko-mura, Nishi Kambara-gun, it is one of the most ancient and revered Shinto shrines in Niigata.

Jewel Leaf Collection, The. Gyoku Yo Shu; also *Gyoku Yo Waka Shu.* The fourteenth of twenty-one imperial poetry anthologies, compiled by Kyogyoku (also Fujiwara) Tamekane at the request of Retired Emperor Fushimi (r. 1288–98) in 1312. *See also* Fujiwara Tamekane.

jewel of Sui. The duke of the state of Sui during the Spring and Autumn Annals period (722–481 B.C.) is said in *Zuo's Commentary* on *The Spring and Autumn Annals* to have possessed a marvelous gem.

Jikoji temple. A Zen temple of the Soto sect located in Muramatsu-machi, Naka Kambara-gun. It was founded in 1404.

Jizo Bodhisattva (Skt., Ksitigarbha). One of the most popular bodhisattvas in Japan, Jizo is depicted wearing a monk's robes and holding a staff; often he is in a child's form, for he is regarded as the special patron of children and is also believed to intercede for sinners in hell.

Jo no Taro Sukenaga. A local ruler who lived in Shirakawa Gokan, present-day Kita Kambara-gun. He was struck by illness in 1181 while trying to raise troops to defeat the Genji warrior Kiso Yoshinaka (1154–84), who was then campaigning in Echigo.

Joshu. Another name for Kozuke Province, modern Gumma Prefecture.

Juntoku, Emperor (1197–1242, r. 1210–21). The third son of Emperor Gotoba (r. 1183–98), he mobilized troops to overthrow the military government in Kamakura, and when the plot was exposed he was exiled to the island of Sado, off the coast of Echigo. He died there twenty-one years later. Neither of the poems Bokushi attributes to him appear in any collections of his work, and neither are thought to be of his hand. Their true authorship remains in dispute.

Kagekatsu. Uesugi Kagekatsu (1555–1623). Adopted by Uesugi Kenshin (1530–78). Later he allied himself with Toyotomi Hideyoshi (1536–98) and became the ruler of the Aizu fief. After Hideyoshi's loss at the Battle of Sekigahara in 1600 he was reduced to ruling the smaller Yonezawa fief.

Kagekiyo. Taira Kagekiyo (d. 1196?). This famous Taira warrior is a frequent figure in drama and song. He is said to have been captured and blinded. Later he is supposed to have become a wandering minstrel.

Kaibara, Master. *See* Master Kaibara.

Kaji Manor. Now Hayamichiba and Kamitate in Shibata-shi.

Kajimaya Gentabei. This was the name of the head of the Kajimaya family, one of the great merchant houses of Osaka in the Edo period (1600–1868).

Kaji Myojinzan castle. There is no record of a mountain of the name Myojinzan in Echigo. The castle of the Jo family was located in old Kaji Manor, now Hayamichiba and Kamitate in Shibata-shi.

Kakizaki Post Town. Now Kakizaki-machi, Naka Kubiki-gun.

Kamakura, Lord of. Minamoto Yoritomo (1147–99). The leader of the Genji clan, after successfully defeating the rival Heike forces, established a military government and made Kamakura, in eastern Japan, his capital. Thus began the first of several military governments in Japanese history and the period known as the Kamakura period (1183–1333).

Kamiketto Village. *See* Akiyama.

Kannon Bodhisattva (Skt., Avalokitesvara). This bodhisattva was male in India but was gradually transformed into a beautiful and merciful female figure in China and Japan. Kannon is widely worshiped for her expansive compassion and is regarded as the special protector of women, who pray to her for children and safe childbirth.

Kano Tsunenobu (1636–1713). A painter of the Kano school, he studied under his grandfather Tanyu (1602–74).

Kanrei (1795–1860). Born in Niitsu City, he succeeded to the post of head monk at the Yukoji temple in Tazawa. He corresponded with the literatus Bosai (1752–1826) and the famous Zen monk and poet of northern Japan, Ryokan (1758–1831). *See also* Bosai.

Kashiwazaki Post Town. Now Kashiwazaki-shi.

Kashu. Another name for Kaga Province, modern Ishikawa Prefecture.

Kawaguchi. Now Kawaguchi-machi, Kita Uonuma-gun.

Kikaku. Takarai Kikaku, also Enomoto Kikaku (1661–1707). Born in Edo, the son of a physician, Kikaku became a disciple of Basho in 1673 and

GLOSSARY

showed great promise as a poet. After the master's death he composed a memoir of Basho's last years and, in 1683, compiled the first collection of the haiku of Basho and his disciples.

King Hui of Zhao (J., Jo no Kei O). Hui Wen, King of Zhao, one of the kingdoms of the Spring and Autumn Annals period (722–481 B.C.). The incident regarding his famous jewel is related in *The Book of History (Shi Jing)*.

King of Chu. The ruler of the Chu kingdom during the Spring and Autumn Annals period (722–481 B.C.) is known for having realized the value of the unpolished gem presented to him by Bien He. His story appears in *Han Fei Tzu* and is widely quoted in Japanese literature as well. *See also* Bien He.

King Zhao of Qin (J., Shin no Jo O). The ruler of the state of Qin during the Spring and Autumn Annals period (722–481 B.C.). The story of his offer to purchase the gem of the King of Zhao is related in *The Book of History (Shi Jing)*.

Ki no Tsurayuki (872?–945). A leading poet of the Heian period (794–1185) and the compiler of *The Collection of Poems Ancient and Modern (Kokin Waka Shu)*. His critical writings helped to establish the direction of *waka* poetry in successive generations. This poem, however, does not appear in any published collection of his work and is of doubtful authorship.

Kinouchi Kohan. *See* Sekitei.

Kitei. Hinata Yoshikata. From Kamo in south Kambara County, he traveled to Edo in his youth and opened a school for the local people upon his return to Echigo. He was a close friend of Bokushi.

Koakasawa Village. *See* Akiyama.

Koidejima District. An area including thirty-nine villages centered around Koidejima, now Koidejima, Koide-machi, Kita Uonuma-gun.

Kokujoji temple. An ancient temple of the Shingon sect in Kokugami, Bunsui-machi, Nishi Kambara-gun.

Komagai, Hermit of. *See* Hermit of Komagai.

Konron, Hermit. *See* Hermit Konron.

Koshin Mound. A mound built in connection with the Taoist-derived religious observance called Koshin because it falls on the day of the conjunction of the *ko* and *shin* signs of the Chinese astrological cycle. On the night of Koshin, it was believed, the "three worms" that dwell in all human beings left the body to report on each individual's conduct to the Lord of Heaven, who would then shorten one's life according to one's deeds. To prevent the worms from escaping, Koshin practitioners stayed

GLOSSARY

awake all night engaging in a variety of practices. Koshin mounds are stone images or earthen mounds used in the ceremonies. Because the *ko* sign is the sign of the monkey, Koshin celebrations came to be associated with the monkeylike Sarutahiko and, through him, the Way Gods as well. Some Koshin mounds or stones have images of the three monkeys—See No Evil, Hear No Evil, Speak No Evil—carved on them and others have Way God, or Dosojin, figures. *See also* Sarutahiko; Way Gods.

Koshinoumi (fl. 1750s and 1760s). A sumo wrestler, he is said to have been from Imamachi in modern Mitsuke-shi.

Kounji temple. A Zen temple of the Soto sect located in Murakami-shi. It was founded in 1394.

Kozuke Province. Modern Gumma Prefecture. Also, Joshu.

Kumonryu. It isn't clear which of several sumo wrestlers by the name Kumonryu Bokushi refers to. One was born in Arai, Kubiki-gun. Over six feet eight inches tall, he went to Edo where he reached the rank of *ozeki* before retiring from the sport, returning to Arai, and dying in the 1790s. Another Kumonryu (1765–1808) was born into a farmer's family in Sone, Takashimura-oaza, Naka Kubiki-gun. He was large and strong from childhood and is said to have carried his grandmother and brother into the house—tub and all—when a sudden rain began to fall during their outdoor bath. He attracted the attention of the first Kumonryu, became his disciple, and eventually went to Edo, where he too achieved the rank of *ozeki* and found employment with the Harima fief. After a period as one of the sumo stars of Edo in the 1790s, he retired, became an elder in the sumo guild, and eventually returned to his native Echigo. Because the Kumonryu Bokushi mentions is said to be from Imamachi (in modern Mitsuke-shi), he may be a third Kumonryu, about which nothing else is known.

Kunikami, Mount. The actual name of this mountain is Kugamiyama, or Mount Kugami, written with the same characters used by Bokushi but pronounced differently.

Kuroda Genkaku (1779–1835). After studying medicine in Edo, he returned to begin a practice in Echigo. He also was active as a teacher, writer, and inventor.

Kurohime Mountain. There are several mountains of this name in Niigata, but based on a similar account in *Strange Tales of North Etsu* (*Hokuetsu Kidan*), Bokushi probably refers to the mountain of that name to the south of Mount Myoko, which would place it in Kamiminouchi-gun, Nagano Prefecture.

GLOSSARY

Kurokawa Castle Town. Now Kurokawa-mura, Kita Kambara-gun.
Kyoden. *See* Hermit Santo.
Kyoroku, Lord. *See* Lord Kyoroku.
Kyosui. Santo Umesaku. The second son of Santo Kyozan (1767–1858). He illustrated many of his father's works and traveled with him to Echigo from June through September of 1836. He is said to have committed suicide at an early age.
Kyozan. Iwase Momoki (1767–1858). The younger brother of Santo Kyoden, he was born after the family moved to the Ginza district of Edo. After service with the Aoyama clan in Tokyo as a young man, he began to take part in his brother's literary circles. He wrote while pursuing a profession as a seal carver and, later, a cosmetics and medicine dealer. He was also a tea-ceremony master and he generally prospered, much improving his family's finances. His second son Umesaku illustrated many of Kyozan's works under the artistic name Kyosui. Kyozan entered the Buddhist order in 1840 and devoted his later years entirely to literature. He was reputed to be sociable and pleasant, but he felt a fierce antagonism for Takizawa Bakin, his brother's ex-student, and their rivalry contributed to the long delay in the publication of Bokushi's work. Kyozan made a trip to Echigo in the summer and fall of 1836, and as Bokushi's editor, he saw fit to include many of his experiences in the work.

Lake Suwa. The legend of Lake Suwa, located in Nagano Prefecture, has it that the fox god Suwa Myojin indicates when the ice is firm enough to cross the lake's frozen surface. The story was well known and is featured in popular dramas of the Edo period (1600–1868).
Laozi (J., Roshi). The semihistorical founder of the Taoist religion and philosophy, also reputed to be the author of *The Classic of the Way* (*Dao De Jing*). There is much dispute as to his dates, some holding that he lived in the fifth century B.C. and others centuries later, but there can be no dispute about his contribution to Chinese and Japanese culture, in which the "natural philosophy" of Taoism has served as a balance to the social philosophy of Confucianism over the ages. See also *Classic of the Way, The.*
Li Fangdeng. Li Fang (J., Li Ho). Active during the reign of Emperor Dazong (r. 976–98) of the Song dynasty (960–1126), he composed *The Great Record of the Taiping Era* at imperial request. See also *Great Record of the Taiping Era, The.*
Long, Long Time Ago, A. Mukashi Mukashi Monogatari. A one-volume work

dating from the early eighteenth century, it discusses customs in the early years of the Edo period (1600–1868). Composed by Shimmi Masatomo (d. 1717), a chief clerk of the archives of the shogunate.

Lord Kyoroku (1789–1848). Doi Toshitsura. He ruled from Kokawa Castle in Shimoosa (modern Chiba Prefecture) and composed *Illustrations of Snowflakes* after twenty years of observing them and recording their shapes.

Lord of the County's Pond. The source of the Sago River, which flows through Yoshidani.

Lord Sotai. Uesugi Kenshin (1530–78). Actually born into the Nagao family, hereditary provincial governors of Echigo. He was adopted by Uesugi Harukage, who was his older brother, to settle a succession dispute. In 1561 he became head of the Uesugi family. Kenshin governed the province of Echigo from 1549 until his death, ruling from Kasugayama Castle in Takata. He is known as one of the most powerful daimyo of the Warring States (1467–1568) and Momoyama (1568–1600) periods and for his prolonged rivalry with Takeda Shingen (1521–73) of neighboring Shinano Province (modern Nagano Prefecture).

Lord Tamekane. *See* Fujiwara Tamekane.

Lord Teika. Fujiwara Teika (also Sadaie; 1162–1241). The last son of Fujiwara Toshinari (also Shunzei; 1114–1204), Teika became a leader in the world of poetry of his age and one of the main figures of Japanese literature of all ages. He assisted in the compilation of the eighth imperial poetry anthology, *The New Collection of Poetry Ancient and Modern* (*Shin Kokin Waka Shu*) and compiled the ninth anthology, *The New Imperial Poetry Anthology* (*Shin Choku Sen Waka Shu*), on his own. He is renowned for his critical writings as well, which helped to shape the aesthetic aims and poetic vocabulary of generations of poets.

Lotus Sutra, The. Saddharmapundarika Sutra (J., *Hoke Kyo*). One of the most important sutras of East Asian Buddhism. It teaches the eternity and unity of the Buddhist truth, universal salvation, and the bodhisattva practice of wisdom and compassion. One of the common practices based on the *Lotus Sutra* in Japan is to copy the scripture as an act of religious merit.

Lower Echigo. The portion of Echigo occupied by Kambara and Iwafune counties.

Lu of China. Lu Bao (J., Ro Ho). A man of great learning who lived in the Nanyang region during the Jin dynasty (265–419).

Maekura Village. *See* Akiyama.
Makinoshima Terutake. *See* Hermit of Komagai.

GLOSSARY

Mangen. Hirohashi Mangen (1659–1718). From the Nara area, he traveled to Echigo where he took up residence in a hermit's hut on Mount Kokujo and devoted himself to restoring the Kokujoji temple. See also Kokujoji temple.

mani jewel. A jewel in Buddhist mythology that was believed to save its possessor from all harm and fulfill his every wish. It was taken from the brain of the Dragon King.

Maruyama family. Both Bokushi's host and the host's grandfather were named Motosumi. The exact dates of Bokushi's host are unknown, but his grandfather, author of *Names of Echigo,* was born in 1687 and died in 1758. The elder Maruyama studied medicine in Kyoto and returned to Echigo to open his practice in Teradomari.

Masaki. See Miya Masaki.

Master Aiba. An official appraiser of the Shiiya fief.

Master Hokuyo. Shibuya Hokuyo, also Denroku (fl. mid 1800s). A poet from Mitsuke-shi.

Master Kaibara. Kaibara Ekiken (1630–1714). A humanist scholar of the Confucian classics, medicine, and *The Herbal Encyclopedia.* See also *Almanac.*

Matsumae. An old name for Hokkaido in general and specifically for the fief of Matsumae, which was located in the Hakodate area.

Matsunaga Danjo (1510?–77). Also Hisahide. A warrior of the Muromachi period (1392–1568). He was finally defeated by the forces of Oda Nobunaga (1534–82) and committed suicide.

Matsunoyama District. The area including modern Matsunoyama-machi and Matsudai-machi, Higashi Kubiki-gun, was known earlier as Matsuyama Village or simply the territory of the Matsuyama Clan, as well as Ashiya Manor. There is no evidence that it was ever known as Matsunoyama Manor.

May Rain Mountain. See Samidareyama.

Mikkaichi Castle Town. Now Mikkaichi, Shibata-shi.

Mikuni Highway. The Mikuni Highway split from the national Naka Sendo Highway at Takasaki in Gumma Prefecture, threaded over Mikuni Pass, crossed Uonuma County and the Nagaoka fief, and finally reached Izumozaki on the coast.

Mikuni Peak (also Mikuni Pass). A pass at the border of Niigata and Gumma prefectures.

Mikura Village. See Akiyama.

million-nembutsu rosary. A large rosary used for a group chanting of a million nembutsu. This is a Pure Land sect practice in which a number of believers sit in a circle grasping the rosary. As each utters a nembutsu he passes the bead he holds to the person next to him, and the rosary thus rotates round the circle until one million nembutsu have been recited.

Minamoto clan. *See* Genji clan.

Minamoto Kanemaki. Born into the Uda branch of the Genji (Minamoto) clan.

Minamoto Nakamasa. This late-Heian-period poet served under Retired Emperor Shirakawa (r. 1072–86).

Minamoto no Shitago (912–83). One of the Thirty-six Great Poets. Though frustrated in his attempts to rise to a high position in the aristocratic bureaucracy, he was renowned as a poet, and his works were included in several imperial anthologies. He was one of the five officers to be appointed to the Imperial Poetry Bureau when it was established in 951. *The Thesaurus of Japanese Names* was a work of his youth. See also *Thesaurus of Japanese Names, The*.

Minamoto Toshiyori (?–1129). The compiler of *Golden Leaves of Verse* (*Kin Yo Waka Shu*). This poem appears in slightly different forms in several major poetry collections. "Traces" (*omokage*) seems to be a copyist's error for "bridge" (*hashikake*), and the poem should actually begin, "The bridge in the valley. . ."

Mirror of the East, The. Azuma Kagami. A historical record composed by anonymous scribes and archivists in diary form, it describes the military government in Kamakura from 1180 to 1266. Several versions exist, the longest in fifty-two volumes.

Misashima. Now Misashima, Muikamachi, Minami Uonuma-gun.

Mishima County. During Bokushi's lifetime there was no Mishima County. In the eighth through tenth centuries there was a Mishima County in Echigo. It may have been in the vicinity of modern Kashiwazaki-shi. Later the area came to be known as Kariwa, after a private manor of that name in the region. In the Edo period (1600–1868) it was officially called Kariwa County. Another portion of Echigo, called Koshi in the eighth century, came to be called Santo County in the Edo period. The characters for Santo ("east of the mountains") were sometimes mistakenly replaced with homophones reading "three islands." Mishima is another way of reading the latter compound, and this is what Bokushi has done. Kyozan has not corrected him, and perhaps the two were aiming at evoking an old-fashioned elegance with this archaic reading of Santo County.

Mitama Village. Now Mitama, Tsunan-machi, Naka Uonuma-gun.

GLOSSARY

Mitsumata Post Town. Now Mitsumata, Yuzawa-machi.

Miya Jihei. *See* Bokusai.

Miya Masaki (1796–1847). The *kannushi,* or head, of the Hachiman shrine in Horinouchi. He was also a classical scholar and a writer.

Moke Huixi (J., *Bokukaku Kisai*). A ten-volume collection of poems and anecdotes from the Song dynasty (960–1126) by Peng Cheng.

Momoki. *See* Kyozan.

Monzaemon, son of farmer Tatsunosuke. Local records tell us that Monzaemon of Arakawa Village (modern Arakawa, Shibata-shi), who never married, was awarded seven pieces of silver in 1803 for his filial service to his parents.

Mountain Hermitage Collection. Sanka Shu. A collection of poems by the poet-monk Saigyo (1128–90), who is counted as one of Japan's Six Great Poets. *See also* Saigyo.

Mountains and Seas Classic, The. Shan Hai Jing (J., *San Kai Kyo*). An eighteen-volume work describing the natural and supernatural flora and fauna of "mountains and seas." Traditionally regarded as composed during the age of the legendary emperor Shun (r. 2255–2205 B.C.), it is actually no earlier than the Qin dynasty (255–206 B.C.). Snow insects are not mentioned in any extant version; Bokushi seems to have been misled by a mistaken reference to the *Classic* in another work.

Muikamachi District. An area including sixty-six villages centered around Muikamachi, now Muikamachi, Minami Uonuma-gun.

Murakami Castle Town. Now Murakami-shi.

Murata Harumi (1746–1811). A poet and scholar of Nativist, or National, Learning (*Kokugaku*). Born into a wealthy merchant family in Edo, he inherited the family business at eighteen and was bankrupt by thirty-five. His discovery and introduction of *The New Mirror of Collected Characters* to Edo-period intellectual circles was one of his most important contributions, but he composed many of his own works as well. *See also New Mirror of Collected Characters, The.*

Murata Village. Now Murata, Wajima-mura, Santo-gun.

Murayama Fujizaemon. An error for Murayama Fujiuemon, the elder brother of Bokushi's son-in-law.

Muso Kokushi. Muso Soseki (1275–1351). A high-ranking Zen monk of the Rinzai sect who served Emperor Godaigo (r. 1318–39) and later founded the Tenryuji temple. He is thought to have resided at a temple in Teradomari for three years during a period of seclusion in northern Japan in the early part of his career. He served as the head priest of the Nanzenji

GLOSSARY

temple in Kyoto, is known for designing the garden of the Saihoji temple in Kyoto, and is regarded as instrumental in spreading the influence of Zen Buddhism in medieval Japan.

Mutsu Province. Modern Fukushima, Miyagi, Iwate, and Aomori prefectures. Also called Oshu.

Naba Doen (1595–1648). A Confucian scholar who served Tokugawa Yorinobu (1602–71).

Nadachi. Now Nadachi-machi, Nishi Kubiki-gun.

Nagahama. Now Nagahama, Joetsu-shi.

Nagao Iga. A general under the daimyo of Echigo, Uesugi Kenshin (1530–78). He defended Shimizu Castle against troops led by Hojo Ujimasa (1538–90).

Nagaoka Castle Town. Now Nagaoka-shi.

Nakanotaira Village. See Akiyama.

Naka Village. Now Naka, Shiozawa-machi, Minami Uonuma-gun.

Names of Echigo. Echigo Na Yose. An encyclopedia of Echigo completed in 1756 by Maruyama Motosumi. In addition to names of geographical features, it includes names of temples and shrines, towns, local products, and medicinal herbs. Bokushi is mistaken in his statement that it contains three hundred volumes. There are only thirty-one. Neither is there any mention of the strange thing about Mount Hishiyama in the work. *See also* Maruyama family.

Nankei. Tachibana Nankei. See Shunki.

Naoenotsu. Later Naoetsu, finally absorbed into modern Joetsu-shi.

Naoe Sanjo (1560–1619). Also Naoe Kanetsugu, later Shigemitsu. Born in Echigo, he served under the famous warrior Uesugi Kenshin (1530–78). In addition to his military and political adventures, he wrote manuals of military strategy and farming technique and was an accomplished poet.

nembutsu. Originally the practice of meditating on Amida Buddha, later the practice of reciting the phrase *Namu Amida Buddha* ("Praise to Amida Buddha"). *See also* Amida Buddha; Pure Land.

New Mirror of Collected Characters, The. Shinsen Ji Kyo. Composed ca. 900 by the monk Shoju (dates of birth and death unknown), this twelve-volume work gives definitions and pronunciations and is the first Japanese dictionary to provide native Japanese readings for Chinese characters. It is organized by radicals.

Nezumigaseki Village. Bokushi is mistaken in placing it in Iwafune County. Actually located in Atsumi-machi, Nishitagawa, Yamagata Prefecture.

Nichiren (1222–82). The founder of the school of Japanese Buddhism that

GLOSSARY

bears his name, he was a devout monk who insisted on exclusive faith in *The Lotus Sutra,* and his condemnation of other Buddhist sects resulted in his exile to Sado, where he lived for several years. He passed through Echigo on his way to the island, sailing from Teradomari.

Nigihayai no Mikoto. This deity is said to have descended from the heavens to earth in a stone boat to assist the legendary Emperor Jimmu (660–585 B.C.) in his conquest of Yamato. Later he was revered as the ancestral deity of the powerful Mononobe clan.

Nigoro Village. Now Nigoro, Yoshitani-aza, Ojiya-shi.

Niimatsu. *See* Yoshisawaya Togoro.

Nine Heavens. There are several different accounts of the Nine Heavens. According to *The Illustrated Three Levels,* which Bokushi often relies on, they are (in order of proximity to the earth): the Moon Heaven, Mercury Heaven, Venus Heaven, Sun Heaven, Mars Heaven, Jupiter Heaven, Saturn Heaven, Star Heaven, and the Milky Way Heaven.

Nosho Post Town. Now No-machi, Nishi Kubiki-gun. Bokushi's reading is mistaken. It has always been known as No, not Nosho.

Notes on Things Ancient and Modern. Gu Jin Zhu (J., *Ko Kon Chu*). A three-volume work by Cui Bao of the Jin dynasty (265–420) that discusses famous treasures of past and present.

Nozumi Village. Now Nozumi, Teradomari-machi, Santo-gun.

Nyohoji Village. Bokushi consistently errs, calling the place Myohoji (or Myoho) Village. It is located in modern Sanjo-shi.

Oakasawa Village. *See* Akiyama.

Oakiyama Village. *See* Akiyama.

Oi County. Though the source quoted by Bokushi identifies Oi as a county of Echigo, it was actually located in what is now Fukui Prefecture.

Ojiya District. An area including thirty-eight villages centered around Ojiya, now Ojiya-shi.

Oka Village. Now Okanomachi, Takayanagi-machi, Kariwa-gun.

Okura Village. Now Okura, Yamato-machi, Minami Uonuma-gun.

Okuyama Taro. Also, Nagaie. A fourth-generation descendant of Taira no Koremochi, he governed Okuyama Manor, present-day Kita Kambara-gun.

Old Man Abe. The head of the Abe clan. The hereditary post of village head (*shoya*) belonged to the head of the Abe family.

Omoigawa Village. Now Omoigawa, Shiozawa-machi, Minami Uonuma-gun.

onna taiyu. During the Edo period (1600–1868), entertainers were outcasts, lumped together with criminals and the *eta* class. During festivals

GLOSSARY

the *onna taiyu* went from house to house singing celebratory songs and accompanying themselves on the three-stringed shamisen.

Ono estate. Now Ono-shi, Fukui Prefecture.

Ono no Komachi (fl. mid-ninth century). The most famous beauty of Japan and one of the Six Great Poets of the Heian period (794–1185). She served as a lady-in-waiting at the imperial court between 850 and 869. There are many legends concerning her life and loves, themes which have been treated frequently in all genres of the Japanese visual and performing arts. Her poetry is passionate, and her reputation as a beauty was so great that her name became a generic prefix for beautiful women of the Edo period: "The Komachi of Edo," for example.

Ono no Yoshizane. Ono no Komachi's father and the governor of Dewa Province (modern Akita and Yamagata prefectures). *See also* Ono no Komachi.

Osanotaro Sukemori. "Sukemori" is written with different characters than those of Jo no Sukemori, and this seems to be an error on Bokushi's part, as does his claim that Hangaku was Sukemori's wife rather than aunt. *See also* Hangaku.

Osawa Village. Now Osawa, Shiozawa-machi, Minami Uonuma-gun.

Oshu. *See* Mutsu Province.

Oyu Village. Now Oyu, Yunotani-mura, Kita Uonuma-gun.

Peach Valley. A Taoist Shangri-La of sorts, a hidden paradise of immortal sages and fairies living in transcendental simplicity. Advanced Taoist practice forbids eating meat, which is the point of Bokushi's remark that the inhabitants of Akiyama are like Taoist sages except that they eat meat.

Penetrating Darkness. Dong Ming Ji (J., *To Mei Ki*). This four-volume work is said to have been composed in the Later Han dynasty (25–220) by Guo Xian. It contains mostly fabulous stories and accounts of supernatural happenings. Though there are stories concerning magical gems, there is no mention of luminous stones.

Pillow Book, The. Makura no Soshi. The early eleventh-century collection of occasional pieces by Sei Shonagon (dates unknown), who served Empress Sadako (r. 976–1001) in the 990s.

Poetry (Collection) of a Thousand Years, The. Senzai Waka Shu. An official imperial poetry anthology in twenty volumes compiled by Fujiwara Toshinari (also Shunzei; 1114–1204) at the order of Retired Emperor Goshirakawa (r. 1155–58) in 1187. *See also* Fujiwara Toshinari.

Prince Shotoku on a Black Steed. This painting still exists and is in the possession not of the Yamada family but of the Abe family, a clan that was also based in Akiyama, contrary to Bokushi's assertion that the only two families in the region were the Yamada and the Fukuhara clans.

Princess Anju and Prince Zuiomaru. A legendary princess and prince. They were kidnapped while on their way to their father, who had been unjustly exiled to Kyushu, and sold as slaves to the evil Sansho the Bailiff. He treated them cruelly and they planned to escape. Zuiomaru found his way to safety but Anju was caught and died in torture. Zuiomaru returned to court, cleared his father's name, and avenged himself on Sansho. He was reunited with his mother and they built a shrine to Anju. The tale was spread throughout Japan in the form of minstrels' narratives and puppet plays. It appeared in Edo-period (1600–1868) popular fiction and on the Kabuki stage, and was picked up by the writer Mori Ogai (1862–1922) in the Meiji period (1868–1912) as well.

Prince Zuiomaru. See Princess Anju and Prince Zuiomaru.

Pure Land. A realm of enlightenment, popularly envisioned as a paradise. The most widely known pure land was said to be ruled by Amida Buddha and located in the west. Believers sought birth there through many religious practices, including the nembutsu. See also Amida Buddha; nembutsu.

Qianque Anthology, The. Also, *The Qianque Pavilion Anthology. Qianque Lei Ju Shu* or (J., *Senkaku Rui Kyo Sho*). A Ming-dynasty (1368–1644) anthology of information culled from a variety of works and gathered into a 120-volume encyclopedia format by Chen Renxi.

Rai, Doctor. See Doctor Rai.

Raiko Village. An error for Raikoji Village, now Raikoji-mura, Kawauchi, Muramatsu-machi, Naka Kambara-gun.

Record of a Journey to Akiyama. Akiyama Kiko. This illustrated work in two volumes, completed by Bokushi in 1828, is a more complete version of the description of Akiyama included in *Snow Country Tales.*

Record of Supernatural Events, A. Shen Yi Ji (J., *Shin I Ki*). Bokushi probably refers to *Shen Yi Jing, The Classsic of Supernatural Events* (J., *Shin I Kyo*). That work, in one volume, is traditionally attributed to Dong Fangshuo of the Han dynasty (206 B.C.–A.D. 220) but was actually a post-Jin (after 420) pseudepigraph. It contains no specific mention of shining stones.

Reference of Works, Words, and Characters, A. Sho Gen Ji Ko. An expanded version of *A Collection of Handy Phrases,* in ten volumes, by Makinoshima Terutake. Also called *The Supplemented Collection of Handy Phrases. See also* Hermit of Komagai.

GLOSSARY

Reports of Weird Occurrences. Guang Yi Ji (J., *Ko I Ki*). A one-volume work by Dai Fu of the Tang dynasty (618–907).

Reverend Daiten. Kenjo (1719–1801). Born in Omi, this illustrious Zen monk became in later years the head of the Sokokuji and the Nanzenji temples in Kyoto. He had close ties with the shogunate and was sometimes called upon to assist in diplomatic affairs.

Rites of Zhou, The. Zhou Li. (J., *Shu Rai*). This semifictional account of the rituals of the ancient Chinese state of Zhou (122–255 B.C.) is one of the Thirteen Confucian Classics.

Ryoa. Murata Ryoa (1772–1843). Born in a pipemaker's household in Asakusa, Edo, he studied Japanese and Chinese literature and Buddhism, became a monk, and eventually entered retirement at the Asakusadera temple in Edo. He excelled at poetry, comic verse, painting, calligraphy, and was also the author of a thesaurus.

Saburomaru Village. Now Saburomaru, Shiozawa-machi.

Sagami Province. Modern Kanagawa Prefecture.

Sagoromo. The Tale of Sagoromo (*Sagoromo Monogatari*). A four-volume romance by a court lady variously identified as Senji, Seshi, and Seji (d. 1092) who was an attendant of Princess Baishi (1039–96). Probably composed in the late 1070s. Sagoromo, "Narrow Cloak," is the nickname of the handsome hero of the story.

Saigyo (1128–90). A poet-monk of the Shingon school. Born into a samurai family, he entered the priesthood at twenty-two and embarked on the life of a wandering ascetic, traveling around Japan. He is revered as one of the greatest of Japanese poets and is especially known for his sensitivity to nature and his expression of the sentiment of *sabi,* or quiet loneliness. See also *Mountain Hermitage Collection.*

Saijozan Kangoji temple. A Zen temple of the Rinzai sect located in Shiozawa-machi, Minami Uonuma-gun. It was founded in 1410.

Sai Useki. See *Food Classic, The.*

Saizenin. A Shingon-sect temple known as Saizenji and located in Shiiya-shi.

Sakamaki Village. An error for Sakasamaki Village. *See* Akiyama.

Samidareyama. Now known as Gozusan.

Sand and Stones Anthology, The. Shaseki Shu. A collection of Buddhist tales and sermons in ten volumes composed by the monk Muju Ichien (1226–1312) from 1279 to 1283. It contains no story similar to that of Kiku.

Sanjo Town. Now Sanjo-shi. It has always been in Kambara County and was never a part of Koshi.

GLOSSARY

Sansho the Bailiff. *See* Princess Anju and Prince Zuiomaru.

Santo Kyoden. *See* Hermit Santo.

Sarutahiko. Also Sarudahiko. Sarutahiko is described in the ancient semi-mythical annals of Japan as having a nose "seven hands" in length, a wide grin, and bright red eyes as shiny and round as mirrors. According to myth, when Ninigi no Mikoto, the descendant of the Sun Goddess, was preparing to descend to earth at her command, one of his messengers was blinded by the great light shining from the mouth and buttocks of Sarutahiko. Ninigi no Mikoto sent the goddess Ame no Uzume no Mikoto to inquire. She bared her breasts and approached Sarutahiko in a smiling and provocative fashion, and he informed her that he was merely waiting to escort Ninigi no Mikoto to Mount Takachiho. Ninigi no Mikoto descended and in gratitude gave Ame on Uzume no Mikoto to Sarutahiko as his wife. Finally Sarutahiko leapt into the sea, making it fruitful by his death. Sarutahiko seems to have derived from a monkey figure, a fact which has linked him to the Koshin rites. He is also a strongly sexual figure, and with his consort has been incorporated into the worship of the Way Gods as well. It is only natural that the two deities should be represented as sexual talismans in the Blossom-Water Festival described by Bokushi. *See also* Koshin Mound; Usume; Way Gods.

Sasaki Saburobei Nyudo Seinen. Sasaki Moritsuna (1151?–?) The son of Sasaki Hideyoshi of the Uda branch of the Genji clan and a follower of Minamoto Yoritomo, who awarded him the stewardship of Kaji Manor (present-day Kita Kambara-gun).

Seiro. Kita Seiro (1766–1848). Also Yaneya Miuemon. Born into a restaurateur's family in Shimbashi, Edo, he was adopted by the Kita family, who were roofers by profession (hence Yaneya, "roofer"). An adept writer of comic verse and a learned classical scholar, his writings were censored on at least three occasions, and he gained quite a reputation because of his refusal to amend them.

Sekinoto (d. ca. 1790). This sumo wrestler first went to Edo in the 1770s and rose to the rank of *sekiwake,* changing his name from Araiumi to Sekinoto. His birthplace is identified in one source as Araigahama, Chujo-machi, Kita Kambara-gun.

Seki Post Town. Now Seki, Shiozawa-machi, Minami Uonuma-gun.

Seki Sanjuro. Probably Seki Sanjuro II (1786–1839). His career began in Osaka when he was adopted by the first Seki Sanjuro (1747–1808). Later he began to perform in Edo and became one of the four great stars of the Kabuki stage in that city.

GLOSSARY

Sekitei. Kiuchi Sekitei (1724–1808). Born in Omi (modern Shiga Prefecture), he was an enthusiastic mineralogist and collector of stones and gems. See also his work, *Cloud-Essence Annals, The*.

Seki the scholar. The Seki family served the Aoyama fief in Tokyo for generations. Kyozan may be referring to Seki Nanka (1759–1819).

Sekiyama Village. Now Sekiyama, Shiozawa-machi, Minami Uonuma-gun.

Senju. Bokushi refers to Kotsukappara, one of the execution grounds of Edo, located at Minami Senju, Arakawa-ku, Tokyo.

Sequel to the Guixin Collection of Miscellaneous Facts, The. *Guixin Zashi Xu Ji* (J., *Kishin Zasshiki Zoku Shu*). An eleven-volume sequel to the earlier miscellany, both composed by Zhou Mi of the Song dynasty (960–1126).

Seven Kettles (of Tashiro). Located on the Kama River, a branch of the Kiyotsu River, this remains a favorite beauty spot even today.

Shakatsuka Village. Now Shakatsuka-machi, Mitsuke-shi.

Shibata Castle Town. Now Shibata-shi and written with different characters than those used by Bokushi.

Shibumi River. Bokushi seems to be mistaken in his description of the Shibumi River as a fast-flowing current. It is a slow, shallow river.

Shidaihama. Now Shidaihama, Seiro-mura, Kita Kambara-gun.

Shigetsuji temple. An error for the Shugetsuji temple, a Zen temple of the Soto sect in Iwamuro-mura, Nishi Kambara-gun.

Shiiya Castle Town. Now Shiiya, Kashiwazaki-shi.

shimenawa. These sacred straw ropes are used in the Shinto religion to mark off holy precincts or to suspend offerings to the deities. They are frequently decorated with the folded paper streamers called *gohei*.

Shimizukawara Village. See Akiyama.

Shimizu Village. Now Shimizu, Shiozawa-machi, Minami Uonuma-gun.

Shimoketto Village. See Akiyama.

Shimoshinden Village. Now Shimoshin, Niitsu-shi.

Shimotsuke Province. Modern Tochigi Prefecture.

Shinano Province. Modern Nagano Prefecture.

Shindo Village. Now Shindo, Kakizaki-shi.

Shinho Village. Now Shippo, Sakuramachi-aza, Ojiya-shi.

Shinran (1173–1262). The founder of the True Pure Land (Jodo Shinshu) sect of Buddhism. A disciple of Honen, he was banished from Kyoto in 1207 with his master and fellow disciples. Wandering through rural Japan, first in Echigo and then the Kanto region, he faced hardships as a layman that shaped his religious philosophy of profound and relentless introspection and gratitude to Amida Buddha, the symbol of enlightenment.

He taught the utterance of the nembutsu as an act of thanks to the Buddha. *See also* Honen.

Shinroku. According to local legend, Shinroku of Shakatsuka Village (now Shakatsuka-machi, Mitsuke-shi) did not marry but devoted his life to caring for his blind mother.

Shiozawa District. An area including fifty-eight villages centered around Shiozawa, now Shiozawa-machi, Minami Uonuma-gun.

Shitchu, Abbot. *See* Abbot Shitchu.

Shobu Village. Now Shobu, Oshima-mura, Higashi Kubiki-gun.

Shoju. *See New Mirror of Collected Characters, The.*

Shunki. Tachibana Nankei (1753–1805). Born in Ise (modern Mie Prefecture), he traveled to Kyoto to study medicine, grew interested in poetry, and made several extended journeys about Japan, writing travel accounts. *See also Travels to the East* and *Travels to the West.*

Shunkin. Uragami Shunkin (1779–1846). A literati-style painter born in Bizen (the southeast portion of modern Okayama Prefecture), he studied the art from his father, traveling with him to Edo and elsewhere around Japan. Eventually he settled in Kyoto.

Shuten Doji. A notorious bandit of legend. He began as a temple acolyte but was driven away for his misdeeds and fled to the outskirts of Kyoto, where he became a bandit chief.

So Waterfall. Located at the confluence of the Shinano and the Nakatsu rivers in Niigata Prefecture.

Spring and Autumn Annals, The. Chun Qiu (J., *Shun Ju*). A brief chronological sketch of the events that occurred at the court of the state of Lu from 722 to 481 B.C. One of the Five Confucian Classics.

Stones of Clouds and Forests. Yun Lin Shi Pu (J., *Un Rin Seki Fu*). A three-volume work by Du Wan of the Song dynasty (960–1126). It lists more than one hundred stones, describing their shape and provenance.

Strange Tales of North Etsu. Hokuetsu Kidan. A collection of tales of weird happenings and wonders, set in Echigo. Composed by Tachibana Shigetsugu (Hermit Konron; dates unknown). Though Bokushi is correct in that there are no descriptions of snow in the work, the word does appear incidentally in three places. *See also* Hermit Konron.

Study of Asbestos, A. Kakan Fu Setsu (Bokushi has *Ko* instead of *Setsu*). Published in 1764 by Hiraga Gennai (1728?–80). *See also* Hiraga Kyukei.

Study of the Development of Foods, A. Shokumotsu Enkaku Ko. In spite of Kyozan's claim to authorship, there is no evidence that such a work was ever published.

GLOSSARY

Sugawara Michizane (845–903). A revered scholar and statesman, he served as minister of the right under Emperor Daigo (r. 897–930). He was charged with treason by Fujiwara Tokihira in 901 and banished to Dazaifu in Kyushu, where he died. After his death, several of his enemies met with unexpected disasters and unprecedented catastrophes struck Kyoto. The court strove to placate his angry spirit by deifying him as the god Tenjin and a shrine was erected in his honor at Kitano in Kyoto in 947. Also known as Temmangu (the name of his shrine), he is worshiped even today as the god of learning.

Sui, jewel of. See jewel of Sui.

Sukawa Village. Now Sukawa, Yasuzaka-machi, Higashi Kubiki-gun.

Sunagotsuka Village. Now Sunagotsuka, Bunsui-machi, Nishi Kambara-gun.

Supplemented Collection of Handy Phrases, The. Gorui Setsuyo Shu. See Reference of Works, Words, and Characters, A.

Suzugamori. One of the execution grounds of Edo, located in Minami Oi, Shinagawa-ku, Tokyo.

Tagami Valley. A valley at the foothills of Mount Tanakami in southern Shiga Prefecture.

Taira clan. See Heike clan.

Taira no Koremochi. Though the exact dates of his birth and death are unknown, he was a late-Heian-period (866–1160) general of the Heike clan sent by the imperial court to battle with the Fujiwara clan of Mutsu and Dewa.

Tajima Hot Spring. Now known as Kinosaki Hot Spring, Kinosaki-cho, Yushima, Hyogo Prefecture.

Takachiho Peak. Variously identified with the peaks of that name in Miyazaki and Oita prefectures and Mount Kirishima in Kagoshima Prefecture.

Takahashi Mitsunori (1761–1824). The head of Yahiko Shrine, in present-day Niigata Prefecture, during much of Bokushi's lifetime.

Takao (Manji). A celebrated courtesan of the Yoshiwara pleasure district of Edo (modern Asakusa, Tokyo). Takao was a hereditary name of famous geisha of the Edo period (1600–1868). This Takao was said to have been from a farmer's family in what is now Tochigi Prefecture.

Takata Castle. The castle was constructed in 1614 by the Matsudaira clan. During Bokushi's lifetime, the Sakakibara clan was in residence there.

Takata Castle Town. Now pronounced Takada, this important castle town of the Edo period has now been incorporated into Joetsu-shi.

Takayanagi Village. Now Takayanagi-machi, Kariwa-gun. Bokushi mistakenly asserts that it is located in Uonuma County, but this has never been the case.

Tale of Genji, The. Genji Monogatari. Murasaki Shikibu's (fl. eleventh century) massive novel—the first work in world literary history to fit that description, according to many. The author was lady-in-waiting at court, the daughter of a provincial governor. Composed in the eleventh century, the Tale has been translated into English twice. There are many scenes describing illness caused by spirit possession, and priests and mountain ascetics were regularly called upon to cure such illnesses with exorcisms, esoteric rites, and prayers.

Tales from the Imperial Chamber. Xuanshi Zhi (J., Senshitsu Shi). A ten-volume collection of supernatural tales by Zhang Du of the Tang dynasty (618–907).

Tambajima. Now Aokijima-machi, Nagano-shi, Nagano Prefecture.

Tamekane, Lord. See Fujiwara Tamekane.

Tanabata Festival. One of the five annual Japanese festivals, Tanabata originated in China, where it was celebrated to commemorate the meeting of the Weaver Star (Vega) and the Cowherd Star (Altair). These associations remained with the festival in Japan. Tanabata is celebrated on July 7 in most of Japan nowadays; originally it was observed nearer to August 8. The most common Tanabata practice seen today is the display of bamboo branches, often hung with paper slips on which wishes are written.

Tanaka Village. Now Minami Tanaka, Shiozawa-machi, Minami Uonuma-gun.

Tango Province. Now the northern part of Kyoto-fu.

Tanigawa Kotosuga (1709–76). From a family of doctors in Ise (modern Mie Prefecture), his profession, too, was medicine but he also studied the classics and was interested in the Nativist (Kokugaku) movement. He was particularly devoted to the study of The Annals of Japan (Nihon Shoki). His dictionary was published posthumously. See also Dictionary of Japanese Readings, The.

Tanine Village. Now Tanne, Kashiwazaki-shi.

Tashiro Village. Now Tashiro, Nakasato-mura, Naka Uonuma-gun.

Tateishi Village. Now Tateishi, Izumozaki-machi, Santo-gun.

Tazawa Village. Now Tazawa, Nishiyama-machi, Kariwa-gun.

Temmangu. Temmangu actually refers to a shrine dedicated to Temman Tenjin, or Tenjinsama, the deification of Sugawara Michizane (845–903) as the god of learning.

GLOSSARY

Tenjinsama. *See* Temmangu.

Tenkichi (1780–1855). The head priest of the Tennozan Kisshoin temple in Muikamachi and an active figure in local poetry circles.

Tenshoji temple. A Zen temple of the Soto sect and a branch temple of the Undoan. It was founded in 1490.

Teradomari Town. Now Teradomari-machi and Izumozaki-machi, Santo-gun.

Thesaurus of Japanese Names, The. Wa Myo Ruiju Sho. Composed by Minamoto no Shitago (912–83) circa 934. A ten-volume and a twenty-volume version exist, but the former is thought to be the original form. The *Thesaurus* is divided into subjects such as "Cosmology" and "Morals," and these topics are subdivided into categories containing related Chinese characters and compounds. *See also* Minamoto no Shitago.

Tochio Village. Actually Tochimata, Oritate-aza, Yunotani-mura, Kita Uonuma-gun.

Tokakushi. A fictional character invented by Bokushi for this story.

Tokamachi District. An area including nineteen villages centered around Tokamachi, now Tokamachi-shi.

Toko Abyss. Now called Tokoin Abyss, it is located approximately one-half mile upstream (Bokushi is mistaken in placing it downstream) of the Yokokuji temple, Mitono, Muramatsu-machi, Naka Kambara-gun.

Tona (1289–1372). A poet-monk of the Tendai school who is known for reviving the fortunes of the Nijo school of Japanese poetry. He was a major figure in poetry circles of his day, assisting in the compilation of several imperial anthologies (in which his poems were well represented) and counting leading figures of the court and the arts as his students.

Torisakayama Castle. Bokushi seems to have regarded Tosakayama (written with the same characters that Bokushi glosses as Torisakayama) in Arai-shi in southwestern Echigo as the site of the castle of the Jo clan, but it was probably built by the Uesugi clan at a later period. The Jo clan was based in Kita Kambara-gun (then called the Okuyama and Shirakawa manors), and the attack on Torisakayama Castle was led by the lord of Kaji Manor (also in Kita Kambara-gun), Sasaki Moritsuna. Thus Torisakayama was probably also located in Kita Kambara-gun. Tossakayama (another reading of the same characters) in Chujo-machi, Kita Kambara-gun is a likely candidate.

Toshinamigusa. Kajitsu Toshinamigusa. A collection of *kigo,* words used in Japanese poetry that have seasonal associations, it was published in twelve volumes in 1783 by Ugawa Sobun. The passage by Koshigaya Gozan that Bokushi claims can be found in the work is not in fact there.

GLOSSARY

Toun. *See* Hosoi Shoan.

Travels to the East. Toyu Ki. The travel diary of Tachibana Nankei (also Shunki; 1753–1805), recording his journeys during the Temmei era (1781–89) to the Kanto, Ou, and Hokuriku regions. The description of a petrifying valley mentioned by Bokushi appears in the fifth volume of the work, where it is said to be located in Uchiname Valley near the city of Ono in modern Fukui Prefecture. *See also* Shunki.

Travels to the West. Saiyu Ki. The travel diary of the journey of Tachibana Nankei (also Shunki; 1753–1805) to western Japan. He does record seeing mysterious lights from a mountain in the Amakusa Islands. *See also* Shunki.

Tsubakizawa Village. The exact location of this village is uncertain. It may refer to a small mountain settlement in the hills behind the Fukoji temple. There is also a section of Mitsuke-shi in central Niigata by that name.

Tsukahara Village. There is no Tsukahara in Echigo. Probably an error for Katsuratsuka Village, now Katsuratsuka-machi, Kita Kambara-gun.

Tsukanoyama Peak. Now Tsukanoyama, Koshiji-machi, Santo-gun.

Tsukushi Journey. Tsukushi Kiko, by Yoshida Shigefusa, a record of Yoshida's travels through western Japan, published in 1806. *See also* Yoshida Shigefusa.

Tsumari Manor. Bokushi writes both Tsumari and Tsumaari. The former is correct for this place name that derives from an ancient manorial domain located in the region of Tokamachi, Naka Uonuma-gun.

Tsuten, Abbot. *See* Abbot Tsuten.

Ueda Manor. An archaic place name deriving from the ancient manor of that name in Minami Uonuma-gun.

Uenohara Village. *See* Akiyama.

Ugachi Shrine. There is no other record of the Hachimangu shrine of Horinouchi having been referred to by this name.

Ugachi Village. A village in the old Yabukami Manor, by Bokushi's time already a part of Horinouchi.

Undoan temple. Located in Shiozawa-machi, Minami Uonuma-gun.

Undo Village. Now Undo, Shiozawa-machi, Minami Uonuma-gun.

Upper Echigo. The portion of Echigo occupied by Kubiki and, in some accounts, Uonuma counties.

Urasa District. An area including fifty-four villages centered around Urasa Village (also, post town), now Urasa, Yamato-machi, Minami Uonuma-gun.

Urasa Post Town. Now Urasa, Yamato-machi, Minami Uonuma-gun.

GLOSSARY

Usami Suruga (d. 1564). A retainer of Uesugi Kenshin (1530–78), the great warlord who ruled the Echigo region in the sixteenth century. Though the dates of his birth and death are disputed, in Bokushi's day it was believed that he died in 1564. According to the account given in a local military history, *Hokuetsu Gunki*, Kenshin ordered Usami to assassinate the rival general Nagao Masakage, and Usami carried out the order by inviting Nagao to a boating party on Nojiri Pond, then capsizing the boat and sinking with Nagao to the pond's bottom in a death embrace. It is uncertain whether Nojiri Pond is the same as the pond in the garden of the Undoan.

Usugumo. A celebrated courtesan of the Yoshiwara pleasure district of Edo (modern Asakusa, Tokyo). She is said to have been from modern Nagano Prefecture.

Usume. Ame no Uzume no Mikoto. The goddess is best known for her dance before the cave into which the Sun Goddess, Amaterasu, had shut herself away. With bawdy and humorous gestures she caused the watching deities to laugh and aroused Amaterasu's curiosity, so that she peeped out of the cave to see what was happening and light returned to the world. Ame no Uzume no Mikoto was also sent by Ninigi no Mikoto, who was preparing to make his descent to earth, to ask the god Sarutahiko why he was blocking the way. She bared her breasts and approached Sarutahiko in a smiling and provocative fashion, and he informed her that he was merely waiting to escort Ninigi no Mikoto to Mount Takachiho. Ninigi no Mikoto descended and in gratitude to Sarutahiko ordered Ame no Uzume no Mikoto to become his wife. The goddess has strong sexual associations, and she is also sometimes associated with the Way Gods. *See also* Sarutahiko; Way Gods.

Warino Village. Now Warino, Shimofunato-aza, Tsunan-machi, Naka Uonuma-gun.

Washigahama (d. ca. 1790). A sumo wrestler from Niigata, he gained employment with the Kurume fief and reached the rank of *ozeki*.

Wayama Village. *See* Akiyama.

Way Gods. Variously known as Sae no Kami, Sai no Kami, and Dosojin, the precise origins of these ancient folk deities are uncertain. They were regarded as road or way gods and thought to prevent harm from entering the villages whose crossroads they guarded. They were often depicted as a couple in embrace, and more specifically sexual representations of the reproductive organs are also found, for the Way Gods were also gods of marriage, fertility, and procreation. Festivals for the Way Gods were held

GLOSSARY

throughout Japan around the fifteenth of the first month of the New Year, and children played a major role in these rites, as they do in Bokushi's description. The Way Gods are also sometimes associated with the deities Sarutahiko and Ame no Uzume no Mikoto. *See also* Sarutahiko; Usume.

Wu, land of. Modern Shandong Province in China.

Xie Zhaozhi (J., Sha Chosetsu). A Ming-dynasty (1368–1644) scholar and bureaucrat born in Fuzhou who served as the governor of several different provinces and was renowned for his just government. *See also Five Miscellanies, The* and *Grains of Sand from the Sea of Words.*

Xishi (J., Seishi). A famous beauty of the Spring and Autumn Annals period (722–481 B.C.). It is said that the King of Zhao brought ruin to his state because of his infatuation with Xishi, who had been sent to him by the King of Wu.

Yabukami Manor. An archaic place name deriving from the ancient manor of that name in Kita Uonuma-gun.

Yabukawa Shinden Village. Now Yabukawa Shinden, Ojiya-shi.

Yahagi Village. Now Yahagi, Yahiko-mura, Nishi Kambara-gun.

Yahiko no Yashiro shrine. *See* Iyahiko no Yashiro shrine.

Yakamochi. Otomo Yakamochi (d. 785). Son of Otomo no Tabibito (665–731) and a representative poet of *A Collection of Ten Thousand Leaves* (*Manyoshu*). The first poem credited to him by Bokushi is listed as anonymous in that work. The second and third poems are not to be found in either *Ten Thousand Leaves* or Yakamochi's collected poems, nor do they show stylistic signs of belonging to his oeuvre.

Yakushi Bodhisattva (Skt., Bhaisajyaguru). The buddha of healing, who reigns over a lapis lazuli pure land in the east.

yamabushi. Ascetics who retreat to the mountains and practice austerities such as fasting and standing under waterfalls to gain magic powers. The *yamabushi* are associated with the syncretic Shugendo sect of Japanese religion which combines mountain worship with the practices of esoteric Buddhism. They wear a distinctive costume consisting of baggy pants, a vest, and a surplice with tassels and pompoms, and they carry a Buddhist rosary and a conch shell. *Yamabushi* were frequently called on to exorcise evil spirits and cure illness.

Yamanaka Tansaku (1755–1807). A scholar from a merchant family in Ise (modern Mie Prefecture).

Yang Guifei (719–56; J., Yo Kihi). The great Chinese beauty who was said

GLOSSARY

to have been the downfall of Emperor Xuanzong (r. 713–56) of the Tang dynasty (618–907).

yasha (Skt., *yaksha*). Originally a nature spirit in ancient India, the *yasha* were followers of Vaisravana (J., Bishamonten), the guardian king of the north. They were regarded ambivalently from the start, recognized for their destructive powers and later, in Buddhism, as guardians of the Buddha's teachings, protecting believers but chastising the unfaithful. As they traveled with that religion to China and Japan, they became increasingly demonic figures. Female *yasha*, in particular, were popularly depicted as flesh-eating monsters. Though depicted as half-human, half-demon figures, they were not the cat demon described in the story of Abbot Hokko.

Yashiki Village. *See* Akiyama.

Yicun (J., Gison). A monk from Quanzhou, he founded a temple on Mount Hsianggu and was awarded an honorary title by Emperor Xizong (r. 874–89) of the Tang dynasty (618–907).

Yoita Castle Town. Now Yoita-machi, Santo-gun. Yoita was once ruled by Uesugi Kenshin's (1530–78) retainer Naoe Kanetsugu (1560–1619) and later by the Makino and Ii clans.

Yokawa Village. Now Yokawa, Muikamachi, Minami Uonuma-gun.

Yokoi Onsenji temple. A Zen temple of the Soto sect founded in the 1560s by Takeda Shingen (1521–73), located in Shibu, Yamanouchi-machi, Takai-gun, Nagano Prefecture.

Yonezawa. An old castle town in southeast Yamagata Prefecture.

Yoroigata. Located east of Maki-machi, Nishi Kambara-gun, the natural lagoon was reduced by half due to the land reclamation efforts of the Nagaoka fief.

Yoshida Shigefusa. A merchant from Nagoya, he left the family business to his son and traveled around Japan. The *Tsukushi Journey* (*Tsukushi Kiko*) is the record of his travels through western Japan.

Yoshida Village. Bokushi is wrong in locating it in Mishima (that is, Santo) County. Now Yoshida-machi, Nishi Kambara-gun.

Yoshisawaya Togoro. The Yoshisawa family (*-ya* is a professional suffix) are an old Ojiya household, and Togoro and Tojiro are the traditional names for the head of the family. It is uncertain precisely which Togoro Bokushi is referring to.

Yoshitani Village. Now Nishi Yoshidani and Higashi Yoshidani, Ojiya-shi.

Yoshitsune. Minamoto Yoshitsune (1159–89). Half-brother of Yoritomo (1147–99), the founder of the Kamakura shogunate. Yoshitsune joined Yoritomo in his campaign against the rival Taira (Heike) clan in 1180 and led the Minamoto (Genji) forces to many brilliant victories, but eventually he fell victim to his brother's suspicious nature. Persecuted by Yoritomo, Yoshitsune was forced to flee to the north, and on that journey to the headquarters of the Fujiwara clan in Oshu, he is said to have passed through Echigo, stopping at Teradomari or perhaps Naoetsu (both in modern Joetsu-shi). He committed suicide at thirty, with his wife and daughter, and is one of the great tragic heroes of Japanese legend and literature.

Yoshiwara. One of the pleasure districts of Edo, where brothels were located. During Bokushi's time it was located in what is now Asakusa, Taito-ku, Tokyo.

Youyang Miscellany, The. Youyang Zazu (J., *Yuyo Zasso*). A twenty-volume collection of weird stories and strange accounts (with a ten-volume sequel) by Duan Chengshi of the Tang dynasty (618–907).

Yuan Yu (J., Gen Kyoku). Bokushi's mistake for Yuan Yan, Yang Guifei's father. *See also* Yang Guifei.

Yukoji temple. Founded in the late 1500s, it is affiliated not with the Pure Land sect (founded by Honen) but the True Pure Land sect (founded by his disciple Shinran).

Yumoto Village. *See* Akiyama.

Yurime, daughter of farmer Ihei. Local records show that the daughter of the farmer Ihei of Murata Village (modern Murata, Wajima-mura, Santo-gun) was awarded twenty pieces of silver by Lord Makino of Nagaoka in 1742 for her filial service to her mother-in-law.

Yu Wang (r. 2205–2197 B.C.; J., U O). A legendary sage-ruler of ancient China, he is regarded as the founder of the Xia dynasty (2205–1766 B.C.).

Zenkoji temple. Located in Nagano Prefecture, the temple is thought to have been founded in 642. It is affiliated with both the Tendai and Pure Land sects of Buddhism and remains a center of popular faith today.

Zhao. *See* King Hui of Zhao.

Zhao, King. *See* King Zhao of Qin.

Zuiomaru, Prince. *See* Princess Anju and Prince Zuiomaru.

Zuo's Commentary. Zuo Chuan (J., *Sa Den*). Counted as one of the Thirteen Confucian Classics, this independent work dated from sometime between the late fourth and early second centuries B.C. is traditionally treated as a commentary on *The Spring and Autumn Annals*.

Biographical Note

JEFFREY HUNTER is a professional translator and editor concentrating in Buddhist studies and Japanese literature and culture.

ROSE LESSER, active educator and folklorist, is a teacher of English and German at Hosei and Nihon universities, Tokyo.

ANNE WALTHALL, associate professor in the Department of History, University of Utah, is a specialist in Tokugawa peasant history.

The "weathermark" identifies this book as a production of John Weatherhill, Inc., publishers of fine books on Asia and the Pacific. Supervising editor: Michael Ashby. Book design and typography: Miriam F. Yamaguchi. Production supervision: Mitsuo Okado. Composition: Samhwa Printing Co., Seoul. Printing of the text, engraving and printing of the illustrations: Kinmei Printing Co., Tokyo. Binding: Makoto Binderies, Tokyo. The typeface used is Monotype Perpetua.